Rule of the Elite

Second Book of the Promissa Trilogy
E.R. Phoenix

E.R. Phoenix

Contents

Trigger Warning

The dystopian romance Rule of the Elite takes part in a society where injustice, persecution, and brutality are rampant. Some of the incidents described may be disturbing to some readers. A few scenes depict torture. There are also instances of gore, alcohol consumption, weapon use, and explicit sexual content.

To soulmates and lovers.
When things get hard, keep fighting.
When you feel there's no hope, embrace one another fiercely.
For love can overcome any obstacles and darkness,
and will always prevail.

They put Us far apart—
As separate as Sea
And Her unsown Peninsula—
We signified "These see"—
They took away our Eyes—
They thwarted Us with Guns—
"I see Thee" each responded straight
Through Telegraphic Signs—
With Dungeons—They devised—
But through their thickest skill—
And their opaquest Adamant—
Our Souls saw—just as well—
They summoned Us to die—
With sweet alacrity
We stood upon our stapled feet—
Condemned—but just—to see—

Permission to recant—
Permission to forget—
We turned our backs upon the Sun
For perjury of that—
Not Either—noticed Death—
Of Paradise—aware—
Each other's Face—was all the Disc
Each other's setting—saw—

—Emily Dickinson, "They put Us far apart"

Chapter 1

Davon

November 10, 2213

T he forest seemed to go on forever. The afternoon sun shone through the trees, and the chilly wind made a soothing sound as branches swayed against each other. Leaves crunched beneath my feet, and the earthy scent of fall surrounded me. What should've been a beautiful autumn day became an endless void as I recalled the devastation in Abi's eyes.

Our mission was to reach checkpoint four, where my father's soldiers waited to take us into Electi. Once inside, I'd work on Deb's rescue mission while Abi made her way into the elite society. Our goal—to free Deb and discover who the spy was planted inside Janus Peak. The one responsible for countless deaths in my name.

I was sure we'd make it, just before everything went to shit.

Our captain of the runners, Jimmy Thompson, blamed me for his sister's death. He always doubted me because of my father, the minister of human control and chairman of the New World Government council. The most powerful man in the system.

Jordan Niles took control of the eastern coast of this continent decades ago after the wars ended. He implemented the regime that has oppressed Promissa citizens since 2203. But I was not my father.

At nineteen, I created the People's Revolutionary Front with Connor and Deb. I'd dedicated the last decade of my life to their fight, and I wasn't about to give up. They were my family.

Jimmy followed us into the forest, but he was a changed man. He wouldn't listen to Abi or me, and he shot my shoulder. He was about to finish the job when Abi put herself between us, her lover and her best friend. The moment she pulled the trigger and shot Jimmy, our fate changed.

Accepting that we had to part ways was the most difficult decision I'd ever made. But she'd never forgive herself if Jimmy died. She loved him.

I'd accepted it even though it stung to know she might feel that way about another man. However, it was the type of affection one had for family. That's why leaving him behind wasn't an option. He'd bleed out before reaching the peak. Even I wouldn't forgive myself for such an action.

That last goodbye ripped my soul in two, but I vowed to see her again. I closed my eyes, hoping she made it back and was safe inside the bunker, surrounded by our family. That's all that mattered.

I stumbled and hit a tree branch. A wave of pain pierced my shoulder. "Fuck!"

Abi's tourniquet had loosened over time, and my shirt was soaked with blood.

I failed to fix it, so I went on, spurred by my promise to her. I jogged for what felt like hours, but now, with my vision blurred and the intense dizziness that had overtaken me, I could barely walk. Sweat trickled down my face at the effort.

I tripped and fell. A cry escaped me as I attempted to break the fall, instead collapsing from the anguish that shot through my shoulder at the impact. I was almost there. The clearing was right ahead. I crawled forward, almost seeing it, but everything turned dark.

A persistent beep woke me, and I cringed at the brightness of the room. A sharp pain shot through me as I tried to sit up. Hooked to my side, a machine monitored my pulse and blood pressure. The acrid smell of disinfectant assaulted me as I glanced outside to find the magnificent Lake Egregie and my father's mansion on the horizon. Its marble walls and balustrades were a symbol of power and perfection.

I was alive.

Soldiers must have heard my cry and brought me here.

Around my wrist, a hospital wristband read, "Davon Niles, 10-28-85. Admitted 11-11-13."

I was in the Electi Medical Center for Advanced Care, EMCAC for short. It offered the most innovative and sophisticated medical care in the city. All this just for a few, while most were denied access. The injustice of it all made me sick.

Back in Promissa, the medical staff worked mostly on research. The common citizens received only essential medical services, nothing compared to what elites had here.

I pulled down my hospital gown to find sutures on my left shoulder. There was no inflammation, which could only mean I'd been asleep for days.

I needed to know what day it was and to find a way to let Janus Peak know I'd made it.

My backpack rested on a table to my right. I examined it since Abi had told me she'd hidden confidential information in it. I moved my stuff to the side and found stitches at the bottom. I broke the seam and discovered a packet and a small black journal with an envelope.

My heart skipped a beat at Abi's handwriting, and I couldn't stop myself from opening it. I did so inside the backpack in case cameras were hidden in the room.

Davon,

If you're reading this letter, it means something happened on our way to the city. I leave you this journal, which was my sole companion during my time out there.

I entrust you with my memoir. Here lies the piece of my soul you saved the day you came into my life. If I could survive all that time out there, I'm sure you'll overcome anything waiting for you inside the city.

I love you with all my heart, and I won't rest until we're together and free.

Yours,

Abi

Tears streamed down my face. I clutched the letter, then put it back inside the seam with the journal. I'd trust in her strength and focus on my mission.

The doorknob rattled, and I quickly closed the bag.

A thin nurse with a black bob entered the room. Her eyes opened wide. "Welcome back, Mr. Niles. I'm glad to see you finally awake, sir. How are you feeling?" Her voice was a bit too sweet. Making a good first impression must be high on her agenda.

"I'm doing okay, miss..." I paused to look at her nametag and clenched my fists against my sheets.

"I'm Annie. Annie Davis, at your service." Her fake smile and bubbly attitude only added to my disdain.

Abi's aunt. The one who had made Sarah's life a living hell. Having Annie Davis as my nurse took me by surprise and a bad one at that. This meant she was admitted inside Electi as payment for giving up her niece to the government, for becoming an informant. I clamped my teeth shut and took a deep breath.

How could someone turn in their own family to step up in society? How vain could you be?

I put on my best face. "Nice to meet you, Miss Davis. How long was I out?"

"You were unconscious for three days, Mr. Niles. I'll let Dr. Johnson know you're awake so she can further explain." She checked my vitals and walked out.

I loosened my grip on the sheets. It figured Matt's mother would be the one to attend me, knowing our close relationship.

Five minutes later, Lisa came in. She adjusted her high ponytail. Her long golden strands framed her face. Her grin was as sincere as her son's, brimming with compassion and concern.

She rushed to me. "Davon! Thank God you're awake! How are you feeling, dear?"

"I'm good. Hurts like hell, but I'm alive."

Lisa was a true hero, a rebel within Electi, giving her all for her patients' well-being. A devoted advocate for equal access to medical care for all Promissa residents.

It was no question that her influence drove Matt and me to join the People's Revolutionary Front.

Matt's father, on the other hand, took Jordan's side. As minister of health, he used Promissa as his laboratory and its people as a means to an end. Nausea churned in my gut at the thought of what he might be working on now.

Lisa pressed her palms into her eyes.

"Lisa?" I seized her hand.

"I'm sorry. I'm just glad you're okay." Tears peeked out of her honey-brown eyes. "Your shoulder was…" She shook her head. "It was a long surgery. We repaired the damage caused to an artery and did a wound debridement to take all the bullet fragments out of the soft tissue. An emergency arthroplasty was done to replace your shoulder joint, which was shattered, and we had to reconnect your humerus, which was fractured as well. The nerve damage was not grave. I'm sure with continued therapy you should be as good as new in two to three months."

God. Jimmy really messed me up.

With what she said, I wasn't sure how I made it out of the forest alive.

She squeezed my hand. "I was scared you wouldn't make it. When you came in, you'd already lost a lot of blood. Your father matched you and donated so we could operate. Your mother was desperate. They never left your side. I just sent them home an hour ago to rest."

My thoughts froze. Father saved me? I never thought him capable of such a selfless act. Or was it really?

My chest tightened. Knowing him, he'd expect something in return.

"How's Matt?" Lisa widened her eyes. "Was he out there with you?"

I shook my head. "He should be okay. Last time we spoke it was at his clinic. I'm sure he'll come by soon. You know he's a workaholic."

Her eyes gleamed. "I'm glad he's doing fine."

We fell silent for a moment.

"Rebecca and Jordan are worried sick. What happened to you out there?"

I lifted my chin. "I'm helping Father take out rebel factions. I was out there when a rebel attacked me. We need to stop them and protect what's ours by right."

Lisa grimaced and let go of me. "What the hell, Davon? After all I've taught you?" Her eyes misted.

"I just see the truth now, as should you and Matt. Your ideas are dangerous. What Matt does out there..." I exhaled hard. "You both need to stop. I can't believe I let myself be brainwashed by your beliefs. Father was always right."

She took a shaky breath. "You'd never..." Her lips trembled.

Is this how it feels to have true power?

I shivered at the thought.

"You know I'd never hurt Matt. He's still my best friend. I already talked to him about it. He needs to stop this nonsense, or I'll be forced to talk to Father about closing his clinic for good. An elite working for the common citizens... It's disgusting."

Her face turned ashen, and she stepped away.

A heaviness settled in my heart. That was the final blow of my deceit.

My body ached, not just physically but emotionally, at the pain I was inflicting on this woman. I'd known her since I was a child. She was like a second mother to me.

She wiped away the tears that trickled down her cheeks, then wrote something in my file.

I controlled the urge to call her name and comfort her as she walked to the door.

She glanced back with a flat look. Lost was the tenderness behind her gaze. "I'll let your father know you're awake. The release documents are ready. Physical therapy and further treatment will be provided in the comfort of your own home. Hope you recover soon, Mr. Niles." She rolled her shoulders back and left.

An hour later, the door squeaked. My lovely mother entered the room, followed by the imposing figure of my father.

My father's personal bodyguards waited by the door. Both were ruthless and trained to kill whoever endangered my family. Neither looked at me.

It figured my father wouldn't come without his usual entourage. The attack against me must have rattled him. That made him even more dangerous.

Mom rushed to my side and took my hands. "Davon! Are you okay? I'm sorry I wasn't here when you awoke." She brushed my hair back.

I smiled. "It's okay, Mom. I'm good." I loved her with all my being. More than a year had passed since our last goodbye.

Dad wore his usual black suit, all elegance and prestige. Our resemblance was undeniable. Only the signs of aging and his peppered short hair distinguished us from each other.

He gave a small smile, opened his jacket, then sat beside me and sighed deeply. "Good to see you finally awake, son. You had us worried."

Both had dark circles under their eyes. Had they even slept?

I darted my gaze between them. "I'm fine. Still hurts, but I'm glad to be back."

And I was happy to see them, especially Mom.

"What the hell happened out there?" Father's voice was sharp, menacing. Not for me but for whoever did this to me.

Even though I hated the man my father was today, some corner inside me guarded the memories of who he was before everything changed.

I distanced myself from those thoughts and refocused on the mission at hand.

"About eight miles in, while searching for more rebels, I heard footsteps. A second later, a bullet hit me. I shot back, and someone grunted. I think I hit whoever attacked me. I crawled my way to cover, unsure if there were others. After I stopped the bleeding, I ran until I passed out."

Father appeared calm, but his jaw was set. He fisted his hands over his knees.

He cracked his neck from side to side. "I don't like surprises. We need to crush these rebels before they turn into a real problem."

He was in for a surprise.

"Can we please not talk about this right now?" Mom's voice pierced through the tense atmosphere in the room.

She usually stopped us when we talked politics in front of her, but it wasn't always like this.

When Matt and I were younger, Lisa came over frequently. She always tried to sway Mom to see the truth.

That was until Father walked in on us one afternoon.

We were all in the garden conservatory when it happened. With a tight smile, Father told Lisa to leave.

Mom fought him on this, but Lisa stopped her and left. That was the last time she came over.

"She's filling your mind with lies," he said afterward. "Do you really believe me capable of such things?"

Mom chose to believe him.

Defying my father had consequences, and after that day, he destroyed Frank and Lisa's marriage.

I pulled away from those memories.

My mom's compliance angered me, but I couldn't blame her. Not really. I knew how it was.

The brainwashing, the constant reminder of how society needed to be this way to function. It came to a point when you started believing it yourself, when you stopped thinking about it and just accepted it.

It was an easy choice. A safe one.

My father's gaze turned soft toward Mom, and he took her hand. "I'm sorry, dear. It's just...he could've died." His voice cracked. A single tear slid down his cheek.

My father? Crying?

My heart pressed against my ribcage, and I moved my hand to his on instinct.

He jerked toward me. His eyes wide, a gentle smile covered his face. He took my hand in both of his. "Thank God we found you."

We stayed there, Mom on one side, Father on the other. In that moment, we were a family again. No wars. No conspiracies. Just us.

Mom clasped my hand. "What about the girl? Jordan said you were bringing someone over."

I'd mentioned Abi—I mean, Gabrielle. I couldn't just waltz in with her and expect them to accept her, so in my last communication with Father, I told him about my informant and hinted at our relationship and the need I had to protect her after she helped me get the intel.

As Mom waited for my answer, I couldn't help glancing at my father.

His eyebrows furrowed.

I looked down, remembering Abi. My vision blurred, and I turned to my mother. "Gaby found a group and befriended them to see if they had any info on the location of the base. She was undercover when I left. I hope she's safe."

Mom leaned over me. "You love her." It was a statement, not a question. Her eyes sparkled. "I'm sure she's okay. I'm so sorry she couldn't come. I was hoping to meet her."

Father cocked his head and narrowed his eyes. "You didn't mention anything about a mission in your last communication."

Fuck.

Father crossed his arms. "I'll send a team in to get her."

A shiver ran up my spine. "Please don't. She's already in. Any suspicious activity could blow her cover."

No matter how many soldiers he sent in, they'd never find her.

Dad watched me for a moment and nodded. "Okay. I'll let her be for now. But I'll tell the soldiers to keep an eye out for her. At the first sign, they'll bring her in."

Mom left after a while to get something to eat.

Dad leaned back and crossed his legs as his other persona took over. All business. "Thanks for the intel, son."

"Always."

The air around him thickened. "We've made a lot of progress in the last couple of months thanks to you. Still, I need to know exactly what happened out there and where."

He bent forward, resting his elbows on his knees. "I need you to start working on my council as soon as possible. There's much to do."

With that, he patted my good shoulder. "Lisa told me your release papers are signed. You're not to stay here a minute longer. Two physical therapists and a nurse will continue treatment at home. I'll go get everything ready."

Without wasting another minute, he left. His bodyguards followed like lapdogs waiting for a treat.

Once I was alone, two questions kept bugging me. What would my job be on the council? Would Abi really be safe here?

I scowled. Without a doubt, my life would be monitored up to the very last detail. If there was anything my dad valued, it was control.

I inhaled. As soon as I was out of this hospital, my true mission would start.

I couldn't let them down.

Chapter 2

Abi

November 10, 2213

Light peeked through the trees as we hiked up Janus Peak. My entire body ached from the exertion, especially my thigh. It hadn't hurt much lately, but today it was throbbing.

I remembered that rainy night as if it happened yesterday. My pounding heartbeat as Davon and I ran hand in hand. The sound of the bullets behind us. The blazing pain when one hit my thigh. That was the day we escaped Promissa.

Today we were supposed to go back in. But that was lost now, our mission sabotaged by Jimmy's hatred and resentment.

I raised my gaze. The sun was directly over me. Noon. We would've made it into Promissa by now.

Hours had passed since Davon walked away from us. I bit my lip as tears threatened to fall, then a tug on my side reminded me of my current goal—to get Jimmy back before I lost him too.

I lifted him. Today he was the one who got shot in the thigh, and I was the one who did it.

Flashes from the fight sliced through my mind. Jimmy's unsettling eyes. His demanding voice. The hatred behind his words as he shot Davon.

He hadn't uttered a word since it all happened, heeding my command, and as hours passed, the heaviness in my chest started to ease.

He groaned in pain. "I can't…"

I could hardly hear his voice as he slumped and we fell to the ground. I crouched beside him. His blue eyes were empty of their usual luster.

A tear escaped him. "I don't think I'll make it." He reached for my cheek. "I'm sorry."

"Don't give up, Jimmy. Come on. We're almost there." I tried to help him up but failed.

"I...love you." His fingers dropped from my face, and his eyes closed.

No! This can't be happening.

"Jimmy! Wake up! Jimmy!" I shook him.

His wound was bleeding again.

Shit.

I checked his pulse. It was faint but there.

I can't lose him. Not like this.

I laid him down. "I'll get help. You'll be all right." I didn't know if he could hear me, but I held on to hope.

I ran toward the bunker. We were so close.

Soldiers surrounded me. They cocked their guns when I entered the perimeter. Many faces I knew well. People I'd trained with.

I put my hands up. "Please help us. He's hurt."

Connor stepped out of the foliage. He halted when our eyes met and blinked, his gaze shifting around and behind me.

"What are you doing out here?" Connor's face was stern.

"Jimmy needs help. He's close by."

He walked to me and grabbed my shoulders. "Jimmy? Where?"

I pointed back to where I left him. "About five minutes downhill. Please go get him. He lost consciousness. I don't know how much time he has left." My voice lodged in my throat.

Connor widened his eyes and tilted his head toward the soldiers. "Find Captain Thompson, and get him back to the bunker. The rest of you, keep searching the area. I'll take Miss Davis back for interrogation."

Two soldiers ran in the direction I pointed, and the others spread toward the forest.

My legs failed me.

Connor caught me before I hit the ground. "Abi!"

I grabbed onto him and regained my balance.

He cupped my cheek, his calloused hand gentle on my skin. He scanned my face. "What happened out there?"

I focused on his brown irises and his soft gaze. This was the man who helped me get through my parents' death. I covered his hand with mine.

"Come here." He pulled me into a hug, and I was young again.

The warmth of his embrace eased my turbulent thoughts. In that instant, I was home. I'd find a way to be whole again. With my family.

He caressed my hair. "It's okay. I'm here now."

All my pent-up emotions burst free. I held on to the man who was like a father to me and let it all out. All the anger and the sadness. All the frustration and the heartbreak.

Another sentiment surged inside me. I clenched my fists until my fingernails dug deep into my skin, almost tearing it.

I needed to get back to Davon.

I stepped away from Connor. "I'm going in no matter what. I'll do whatever is needed to get into Electi and complete our mission."

Connor narrowed his eyes and nodded. "I'll ensure you make it, whatever it takes."

Command was chaotic when we stepped inside.

Armed soldiers rushed in and out of the bunker. More people than usual filled the desks as Nina shouted orders.

A commotion drew my attention as Connor and I were about to reach Nina's desk.

Two soldiers carried Jimmy between them. Red stained the floor behind them as his feet dragged. He was still unconscious.

I swallowed hard. Was he alive? Was I too late?

Dr. Lewis hurried in with a gurney, Matt by his side. Even with one arm in a sling, Matt managed to help the soldiers place Jimmy on it.

Something inside me broke at the sight. There was too much blood.

I ran to him. "Jimmy!"

Connor grabbed my shoulders. "Calm down. Let them take care of him."

My chest tightened painfully. I did this to him. What if he didn't make it?

Matt checked Jimmy's pulse, then looked at Dr. Lewis. "His pulse is weak, but he's still alive. Get everything ready. I'll be right behind you."

Dr. Lewis wheeled the gurney into the corridor. Rachel waited outside.

Matt turned, and our gazes caught.

Surprise. Sadness. Love. All that transpired between us.

He held my arm. "Are you okay?"

I nodded, then looked to the hall. "Save him. Please."

He squished his eyebrows together and glanced around the room. "Are you sure you're all right?"

"I am."

"I'll do all I can for Jimmy." He squeezed my arm. "We'll talk later." He dashed out of the room.

I breathed out.

Jimmy was in good hands.

Connor pulled me away, one arm around my back. "Let me speak to Nina, and then we'll talk."

I nodded.

We reached Nina's desk. One of her monitors showed video feeds while she worked on another full of codes.

"Anything yet?" Connor asked.

"A short blackout occurred at about 3:00 a.m., causing damage to the surveillance system. For an hour, nothing was recorded. The cells were open for a few minutes. Davon must have used that moment to escape."

"Son of a bitch!" Connor punched her desk.

"Abi?" Maria ran to my side. "What happened? Matt just took Jimmy into the infirmary. What were you doing out there?"

Connor crossed his arms. "Lieutenant Diaz, get as many soldiers as possible out there, and secure the perimeter."

"Yes, sir." She brushed my arm. "We'll talk later."

Connor's office was disheveled. He sat behind his desk. Paperwork and maps were scattered all over it.

I was about to sit when Sarah entered.

"Abi!" She hugged me, and I almost fell back. She examined me. "What the hell happened out there? Did he hurt you? What are you doing here?"

I shook her off and stepped away.

Just like Jimmy, she held Davon's parentage over him as something that immediately made him a villain. She suffered, trapped inside her own hell for the past decade after the New World Government killed my parents in front of her and stole her child. Three years ago, when Deb helped me get away before they took me into the facilities, the NWG imprisoned Sarah once Aunt Annie accused her of being a rebel.

Four months ago, Deb helped her escape. Now Deb was in their grip.

After ten years of being apart, Sarah found her partner again inside the People's Revolutionary Front main base, Janus Peak, where I stood at this moment. She lost Carlos in one of the checkpoint executions and blamed Davon for it.

"I don't need this right now," I said.

"I'm your sister. I have every right to know what happened out there."

"You don't. Right now, Davon's out there, hurt. He's fighting for his life so he can get in and rescue our sister. And you still blame him?"

Connor raised his eyebrows. "What do you mean he's hurt? What happened?"

Shuddering, I sat. "We were sure we'd made it, then Jimmy showed up. He threatened to kill Davon to avenge Christina, and no matter how much we tried to explain, he wouldn't listen." I touched the sapphire pendant Davon had given me and took a calming breath. "Davon was defenseless when Jimmy shot him. When I rushed to help him, Jimmy aimed his gun at Davon's head, and I had to decide, so I shot Jimmy."

My eyes glazed over. Despite everything, he was still my best friend. "I shot him to save Davon. He would've murdered him. It was in his eyes. The intent to kill."

Tears streamed down my face for both Davon and Jimmy. For the cruel fate that fell upon us just a few hours ago.

Connor reached for my hand. "I'll ask our people in the city if anyone has been taken into Electi. But if he's already inside, we're in the dark. We need to be patient and wait for him to contact us."

"But..." Sarah said.

Connor put up his hand. "Think hard about what you're going to say next, Sarah. This is not the moment for your petty beliefs and clouded judgment. Our general just saved his captain and is risking his life for all of us. If you have nothing of importance to say, please leave."

I was speechless as I stared at our general of the army. His words were absolute, leaving no space for a rebuttal.

Sarah stood motionless next to me. "Yes, General Harris. What about the people? As I'm the contact between command and the citizens, they'll ask me about what happened."

"We'll have a compulsory assembly in a couple of hours. Until then, what happened here remains confidential. I'll explain everything then and discuss what our response to this threat will be."

"As you wish." After glancing at me, she ducked her chin and left.

As the door closed, countless questions bombarded me at once. Did Davon make it? How long would we be in the dark? Would he still be able to get Deb back safe and catch the spy? Would Jimmy survive?

I looked up. "Do you think Jimmy will make it?"

God, if he died, I'd never forgive myself.

Connor straightened. "I'm sure he will. He's in good hands. Dr. Lewis and Matt should be operating already."

He rested his elbows on the desk and intertwined his fingers. "Where was Davon shot?"

"His shoulder. It looked bad. I fixed it as best I could and planned to go with him, but he told me to stay." I closed my eyes, trying to envision his face at that moment. "He sacrificed himself. Jimmy was in bad shape, and Davon made a decision as a general to save his captain. Even in that moment, he gave it all up to save the man who shot him. I followed his orders and said goodbye." I opened my eyes. "Connor, what will happen to me now? Will I be arrested?"

He rubbed his brow. "No. We'll claim Jimmy took you out on patrol. You're a cadet now, so it's not out of the question. After a couple of hours scouting, there was a noise, and you followed it. When you discovered the source, Jimmy drew his gun and called out, only to discover it was Davon. You attempted to stop him, but Jimmy fired. Davon shot back, striking Jimmy. You'll still plead his innocence, saying Davon promised before running away that he'd prove it."

We had to keep our story straight. Since Davon's arrest three days ago, the bunker believed him to be a spy, a traitor, and a murderer. His escape was needed to move the mission forward and to bait the real spy into using the opportunity to get inside command. Everything was monitored, and surveillance around the peak improved. It was a dangerous plan, but we were out of options. We needed to find the spy before they found our location.

Connor rounded his desk and approached me.

I stood.

He clutched my hand. "I need to go back out there. Stay here. I'll call Aoki over. I'm sorry about everything. We'll make this right."

Silence. A deep void settled within me as I turned to the empty office. The place where Davon told me who he truly was. Where a few days ago we decided to leave together.

I touched Mom's silver bracelet, brushing the golden heart with my thumb. Everything came crashing down on me, and I slumped to the floor, my sobs drowning out the sound of the door as it opened. Two warm arms enveloped me.

"I'm here." Aoki's soft, caring voice was the trigger as I let it all out.

And right then and there, I knew I hadn't lost everything. I still had them, and I would fight, not only for Davon but for my family.

I woke to the woodsy scent of Davon's room. Earlier, after I cried my eyes out, Aoki gave me a letter with Davon's key.

I clutched his letter to my chest, hoping he found the one I hid in his pack. It seemed we both thought of the possibility of everything going wrong.

I read it again, and tears spilled onto the pillow.

Love,

I leave you this letter, as my hope falters and I dread something may happen. I don't know how to put everything I feel into words because it's so much deeper. You've made my life better. From the moment I saw you, I knew everything had changed. I'm whole again, and now I see there is so much more to fight for. I was consumed by hatred and rage, but you brought happiness to my life. A sense of peace.

We need to trust that we'll be all right and that we'll find each other again.

I want you to be strong and continue with your training.

You know what this mission entails and the atrocities I'll have to commit. I ask your forgiveness beforehand. Please don't think less of me.

I'll never abandon my pledge to the community or to you.

Don't let yourself fall back into the dark place you once were in. YOU ARE NOT ALONE.

I love you always.

—D

P.S. My room is yours. Please be safe.

A knock sounded on the door. "Abi, it's Matt."

I opened it.

Matt hugged me tight. "Are you all right? I'm sorry I couldn't come earlier."

I clung to him. "How's Jimmy?"

It was the first thing that came to mind because even though it would be hard to forgive him, he was still my friend.

Matt stepped back. "The bullet nicked an artery and shattered his femur. The surgery went well, and after three to four months of therapy, he should be back to normal. He lost a lot of blood, but we found a couple of donors in the community, so he'll regain his strength soon."

Months in therapy. I didn't think of it when I shot him. It was a spur-of-the-moment decision. I had to stop him. There was no other way.

"Thank you for saving him." I cast my gaze down.

Matt tipped my chin up. His eyes searched mine. "What happened out there?"

"He told me to stay." My voice broke. "He was wounded, and he told me to go back. To save Jimmy. Then he walked away."

Matt took my hand. "Come on. Let's sit." He led me to Davon's settee.

I collapsed onto it. "Jimmy went crazy. He wouldn't hear me and shot Davon in the shoulder, then aimed for his head. I had to do something, so I shot Jimmy." My ears pounded, and I gritted my teeth. "We were so close, Matt. So freaking close."

His eyes glazed for a moment, but he blinked the tears back. "He'll be all right. They'll take care of him in Electi. I'm sure he made it." He clasped my hands. "How are you holding up?"

I took a deep breath. "When you're ready to go out there, I'm going with you."

"But, Abi..."

"Matt, I was supposed to go with him. Niles was expecting me. I have to go, and since we have time, I want you to teach me everything I need to know about Electi and Davon's family. We'll go out there with a plan. Will you help me?" My words were sharp. No hesitation. No doubts.

Eyes fixed on me, Matt nodded. "I'm with you."

A couple of hours later, I sat in the dining hall, waiting for the assembly to begin.

Aoki sat next to me and glanced up.

I tilted my head up. Standing next to me was an average-height man with straight black hair that dropped down his brow. His tanned skin contrasted with his white button-down shirt.

Aoki stood. "David! When did you get back?"

David shook Aoki's hand firmly. "Hey, man! I just got here this morning. We were at risk out there, so we received orders to abandon our post." His hazel eyes, the same color as mine, settled on me. They were gentle, and a hint of curiosity flashed through them. "And you are?"

"Abi. Nice to meet you."

He raised an eyebrow at Aoki.

"She's Deb's sister," Aoki said.

David's eyes widened and darted back to mine. "No lo puedo creer." He shook his head. "Did you get here alone? You were lost for so long. I went out there once in one of the first missions to get you. We searched for weeks."

"I came back with Matt and Davon."

He furrowed his brow and took a seat next to me. "I didn't know you were part of their mission."

Aoki sat and leaned forward. "She wasn't. They were out there under-cover, and she found them."

It was true, then. Matt and Davon went after me on their own. In secret. On Deb's orders.

David nodded and tipped his head toward me. "Well, I'm happy you're safe now. You don't believe Davon is guilty, right? I mean, I just got here, and I don't know the details, but it doesn't make sense."

There was truth in his eyes, and I smiled. "It doesn't."

He turned his attention forward.

"A penny for your thoughts," Aoki muttered near my ear.

I scooted closer to him. "I'm worried. I can't stop thinking about Davon."

"I'm sure he made it. He's not a man to give up easily, more so since he met you."

I twisted toward him.

His eyes gleamed. "It's true. I've told you. He's a different man, and knowing him, he'll do everything in his power to be safe so he can be with you again." He brushed one of my golden tresses away from my face. "Are you going to leave your hair highlighted? Don't get me wrong. It looks great."

"I am. All part of the plan. Didn't Matt tell you?"

"He did. And I get you. I'd do the same for him."

Matt entered, his gaze resting on Aoki, his lips curving in a hint of a smile.

Everyone went silent when Connor came in behind him, followed by Maria.

"I called this assembly to inform you of the latest developments to the community," Connor said.

The tension grew. Some whispered about Davon. My name rolled through some conversations.

Aoki took my hand.

Connor cleared his throat. "Due to the latest developments, there are some changes I wanted to pass by you before making them official."

Maria stepped forward.

"All in favor of Lieutenant General Diaz being promoted to general," Connor said.

People stomped their feet. The sound reverberated across the dining hall.

Connor nodded. "Good."

Maria stepped back, and Matt moved forward.

"All in favor of Colonel Anderson being promoted to lieutenant general of the PRF."

"Colonel?" I turned to Aoki.

He tilted his head toward me. "He never uses his rank. Hates it, actually."

"I knew he had to be high up but a colonel? Why didn't anyone tell me?"

"Does it make a difference?"

I shook my head.

"Then it's of no importance. He's the same Matt you know."

I returned my attention to the assembly. Some hands shot up.

Connor gestured to the back of the room. "You in the back."

"How can we trust the colonel? He was General Niles's right hand."

Others erupted around the room.

"True!" someone yelled close to me.

A woman in the front pointed at Matt. "He's with him!"

A soldier shook his head. "There's no way Colonel Anderson is a traitor."

Matt dipped his head as people passed their judgment.

Aoki fisted his hands together, and his jaw muscles twitched.

"Silence!" Connor's command echoed around the room. "Did you forget General Niles was my right hand also? He was my friend and my brother. If I deem Matt an accomplice simply for being his partner, this room would be filled with traitors. We all trusted him, and that was our mistake."

His words drilled a hole in my heart, and even though I knew they were lies, they cut deep.

People sat and stomped their feet until the room vibrated.

Matt stepped back.

"Now that it's settled, we move on to the next point in our agenda." Connor gulped down some water. "Davon Niles escaped last night."

The place transformed into mayhem. Some people stood in protest, their chairs falling. Others stayed in their seats but commented to their neighbors.

"How could this be?" a man yelled.

A mother stood, carrying her child. "Are we in danger?"

"Should we get ready?" a cadet to my right asked.

"We're not safe," a guy said from the other side of the room.

Pedro punched a table, then glared at me. "Son of a bitch! Someone had to have helped him."

Connor waited until the room slipped into an uneasy truce. "I understand how you all feel, but we have trained for this."

A soldier stood. "But how did it happen?"

Connor motioned for him to sit. "We're not sure. There was a short blackout that caused the surveillance system and the locks in the prison to malfunction. We believe he used that moment to escape. Captain Thompson and Cadet Davis were outside scouting and saw him about ten miles out. They tried to stop him but failed. Nevertheless, the captain did wound him, but Niles shot back and ran away. Captain Thompson is recovering as we speak."

"Wait. Cadet Davis? Isn't she with him?" a young woman said to my left. She was one of Maria's trainees. "I bet she helped him escape."

People's attention locked on me. Some held cold stares, others frowned, and a few shifted their gazes to the ground.

"Everyone, quiet!" Connor bellowed.

The whispers stopped, and Aoki squeezed my hand under the table.

"This is no time to point fingers. We have no evidence that anyone helped him. We're investigating what caused the blackout, but we all know they do happen. Davon Niles knew everything about this place, and everything points to him working alone. We need to stand together for what's coming. Now I leave you with General Díaz." Connor stepped to the side.

Maria stood tall. "Janus Peak is on high alert. All children will be taken north to the farming and engineering bunker. At this moment, that's the safest place, being the farthest from the city. One parent will be allowed to go with each child. Councilmembers Walters and Abrams have already agreed to shelter all and to secure a wing of their bunker for any others who wish to leave. Vehicles will be here tomorrow morning to get the children out. As of this moment, all soldiers and cadets are on duty, and all able citizens will aid in the protection of the bunker. If you decide to stay, your children will be taken care of."

Sobs erupted. Mark hugged Carol, a confused Diane at their feet. The same picture was all around the room.

Everyone lost in war.

Flashes from my time out there invaded my mind. I covered my face as I recalled the escapees who were abused and the youngsters who stayed with us in the tunnels before being taken away. This was the right call. We needed to protect them.

Aoki rubbed my back. "Are you okay?" His face was solemn.

"It's nothing. I just had some flashbacks."

"We can talk about it later if you want."

I gave him a soft smile. "Sure. Thanks."

Aoki kept me grounded. His calm attitude always pulled me back from my dark thoughts.

Maria cleared her throat, drawing my focus back to the assembly. "The perimeter will be secured, and soldiers will be sent across our bunkers to aid in their protection. All who choose to stay will be trained, and those who are not soldiers can help the community in a way they see fit. War is coming."

Chapter 3

Abi

November 17, 2213

The bunker was on high alert, and the children were moved out.

The troops relocated throughout the bunker system, and everyone worked around the clock to keep it safe.

I trained with Maria daily to keep my mind busy.

As for Jimmy, we still hadn't talked. That last conversation with him replayed in my mind: *"I love you."*

I suspected as much, but to hear it from him made it all too real. He was heartbroken, and like a hurt beast, he acted on instinct to protect me. I believed he wasn't in his right mind but still... How could I face him after everything?

Yesterday we held a memorial for Richard and the seven soldiers who were executed at the checkpoints.

As I surveyed the room and the candles lit for each soul, I thought about what awaited us in the near future.

War was inevitable, and many would die.

My chest tightened, and my throat burned at the thought. We'd all lost so much.

Jimmy was there, as was everyone else. He said some words for Richard but couldn't finish. I hadn't seen him this affected since Christina's death.

I wanted to go to him, but I couldn't move. The wound he'd inflicted on me remained too close to the surface.

Maria took Jimmy away, and Matt finished for him. He'd found Richard a couple of months ago, living in his own filth and about to die of malnourishment. He was brought into the People's Revolutionary Front, and Jimmy trained him as a runner. A couple of months later, he was murdered by the spy who lived among us right here in Janus Peak.

I'd never forget that night, but what would haunt me forever was the image of Richard's lifeless body on the generator room's floor. He was only sixteen.

Following the memorial, I locked myself in Davon's room, seeking solace in the middle of the maelstrom that had engulfed my spirit. I hadn't been able to get out of bed. Not knowing if Davon was dead or alive had overtaken my mind, and an empty void swallowed me. I tried to be strong, but with every passing day, light seemed to fade until all that remained was darkness.

Even though we were so far away from each other, while I lay cocooned in his bed here, he seemed closer.

A hard knock echoed around the room.

"Honey, we haven't seen you since yesterday. Please let us in." Matt's voice was urgent.

"Abi, Davon wouldn't want this." Aoki's melodic voice filtered in, and I sat up. "We don't have to talk if you don't want to. Let's just have breakfast together."

I opened the door.

Aoki had his dark hair braided to the side, reaching his waist.

Matt was radiant as always, his emerald eyes shining with love.

At their smiles, I couldn't help but throw myself at them.

Aoki hugged me. "Oh, Abi."

Matt embraced us both.

The pressure in my chest eased, and I thanked the heavens for these two men who had become my brothers. My family.

We sat to have breakfast. Aoki brought toast and coffee.

I scrunched my eyes. Last night, I stifled my screams. The snapping sound as the shot struck Davon. His bloody form slumped in front of me. Jimmy's agony after I shot him. It always ended the same way. I called for Davon, and he vanished into the forest.

A lone tear escaped my eye.

Aoki took my hand. "You're not alone."

I nodded. "I..." I cleared my throat, my voice hoarse. "I'm sorry. I just..." I shook my head. "What if...?"

"Don't you dare finish that thought," Matt said. "We need to trust he's all right."

I took a deep breath and repeated Davon's words in my mind: *"Be strong and prepare."* He'd keep his promise, and I'd keep mine.

I looked at them. "You're right."

Matt smiled, and Aoki nodded.

After breakfast, I bathed and donned my training gear to join Matt at the training center. He wanted me to meet someone.

I'd find Connor afterward to check if he'd heard anything from Davon. He said he'd keep me posted but still nothing.

The training room was full of life, with Maria's cadets practicing with blades.

"Keep sparring against each other!" Maria's booming voice filled the room.

She came to me. "How are you? I didn't see you at dinner." She greeted me with a kindness that contrasted with her commanding attitude.

"I'm okay. Just anxious to get news. Have you seen Matt?"

She pointed toward the back. "He's waiting for you in the sniper room. He came in a while ago."

When I was halfway across, she called back, "Hey, Abi! Remember our training later."

"Of course." I winked. "Hope you're ready to get pummeled."

"You wish." She gave me a wicked smile and went back to her cadets.

I passed the shooting room on my way. Davon's image passed through my mind. My breath caught, and I couldn't stop the memories from coming back. Of our fight and the first time I blurted that I loved him and heard the same words from him.

The pressure in my chest was suffocating, so I leaned against a wall to get a few breaths. After a short pause, I shook my head and continued.

Matt stood inside the sniper room, and David set up a rifle close to the floor.

Matt offered me a warm smile. "Hello again. This is David. He's taking over your sniper training."

I peered down. "We met in the assembly last week."

David glanced at me and raised his chin slightly. "Hey. Good to see you again." He stood and motioned for me to get down. "It's ready."

I took my position and searched the forest with the scope. The targets were farther away than the last time I practiced with Davon.

Breathe, Abi.

The tug on my chest faded. "So what are we going to do today?"

Matt moved closer. "We'll work on honing your sniper skills. Davon wanted me to train you, but since I'm still recovering, David will lend a hand."

Matt worked hard to recover from the shot he took in his right arm and chest during their last mission. He'd been practicing and was improving, but he needed more time.

Matt stared at the rifle and shifted in place, brushing his fingers across each other. "I'm sorry I can't train you, but we need to move forward. This is a vital part in our plan to retake Promissa."

Matt, Maria, Connor, and I met two days ago to discuss potential tactics for retaking the city. To strike, we needed the support of our undercover agents, the rebel factions spread within the city, and our full military force. Yet the odds were not favorable. That's why snipers would be strategically placed throughout the city to attack when the moment came.

We covered a lot of groundwork, but we wanted additional people to offer more input and different perspectives.

Since Connor demoted Jimmy to first lieutenant for his actions, Jimmy was not invited. The explanation for this change was that he resigned his post after Davon attacked him. The community thought Jimmy a hero.

Mark was promoted to captain of the runners, and he already confirmed he'd join us.

If David did too, he'd help with the strategy, being the best sniper in the system.

"Are you ready?" Matt asked.

Both men locked their eyes on me, resolve in their gazes.

I sneered. "Let's crush those bastards!"

"That's my girl!" Matt smirked.

David winked. "I think we'll get along just fine."

David was a great teacher, patient and clear in his instructions. He prepared his own sniper rifle next to mine and told me to mirror him. I followed his instructions to the letter and, by the end of the session, hit most of my targets.

The training flowed naturally, both of us falling into a certain routine. Take position, align the scope, breathe in and out, squeeze the trigger gently, and shoot. Keep your eye on the target, and adjust your aim after the recoil, then start again.

"We're done for today." David put away the sniper rifles. "Next time we'll meet outside. A sniper needs to adjust for wind, elevation, and other factors as well as distance."

I massaged my shoulders.

David swung the duffel bag across his back. "How do you feel?"

"A little sore." My shoulders burned, my neck was stiff, and my back was killing me.

He smiled ruefully and patted my shoulder. "With time, the soreness will ease, but you'll always feel it."

I huffed. "Thanks for the heads-up."

He shrugged. "Just being honest."

Maria was still drilling the cadets when we walked back through the training center. One group did burpees with 180-degree jumps, while another crawled under an area of ropes that Maria placed just a foot and a half off the floor. She was brutal.

As we stepped into the hallway, David stopped in front of the armory. "See you later. I'll put these babies away."

He was a kind and funny guy, twenty-one years old, same as me. He came in years ago, brought in by Davon and trained under Connor.

I chuckled. "Thanks for everything. I'm glad you came back."

His demeanor shifted, and his eyes lost their natural gleam. After a heavy sigh, he raked his hair back, failing to control it from falling back into his face. "I wish I could've done something to save the others."

His words hit hard. Jacob and Bonnie's loss still burned within me. I could still hear Paul's pleas as they took him away. There was no way around it. The guilt would never leave me.

"There was nothing you could do about it," I said.

He pocketed his hands. "I ask myself why I was spared when the other checkpoint soldiers died. It's unfair. Many of them had families. And I survived?" He palmed his chest. "No one would've suffered if I died."

A shiver ran down my spine at his words. "How can you say that?"

His eyes glazed over. "It's the truth."

"No, it isn't. I'm sure you have people who care for you."

He shifted his feet, eyes downcast.

I grabbed his arm. "David, I know how hard it can be. I've been in your shoes. But Matt told me once not to question why I survived, why I'm here while others aren't. He believes there's a purpose for everything, and the same goes for you. Don't dwell on the past. Focus on what you can do for our future."

The words came out hollow at first. How could I help David when I was just as wounded as him? Then I realized that everything I'd done recently was to ensure the safety of everyone I cared about. When I met Davon and Matt, I blamed myself for not doing anything about Bonnie's rape and Jacob's execution. But I'd grown and moved forward. If I could help David do the same, I would.

He raised his head. "I hope you're right." Then he entered the armory and closed the door behind him.

I made my way through the throng of people that filled the common area toward hall A.

Matt and Aoki agreed we'd eat in their apartment until I was comfortable dealing with others.

The dining hall was always the same: "Do you know where he is?" "Did you ever suspect him?" "Poor thing." If they didn't ask, they'd stare relentlessly and murmur around me. It was suffocating.

Aoki cooked burgers. The wafting aroma swamped my senses, and I couldn't help but moan. I was starving.

"How did the training go?" Aoki asked.

"It went well, much better than last time."

"I'm glad. He's the best. You're in good hands," Matt said. "Are you better with a sniper than with guns?"

"Much better. Guns don't go with me." I shrugged.

Matt frowned. "Still, you need to learn how to master them."

I rolled my eyes.

Aoki offered a half smile. "And about this morning. Are you feeling better?"

He got me, really got me.

I put my hamburger down and rubbed the back of my neck. Ever since I got back, everything weighed on me. The tension in my neck and back was sometimes unbearable. "It's hard. Sometimes when I wake in the middle of the night, I forget Davon's away and keep expecting to see him by my side. Then when it all comes back, I wonder if he really made it. I think about Deb all alone in that prison and can't help but question if Davon will be able to get her out safely. Being in the dark is driving me crazy."

These thoughts gutted me from the inside out. But I had to concentrate on what I knew and believe it would all work out.

Aoki patted my thigh. "Trust him. Everything will be all right."

After lunch, I went straight to Connor's place.

He was having his morning coffee.

I sat beside him on his taupe leather sofa.

He set his mug on the round table in front of us and turned toward me, his arm resting on the backrest. "I'm glad to see you up and about. Maria says your training is going well, and David just told me he's training you as a sniper."

"I've been working hard, but I know I can do better. I need to for Deb and for Davon. I worry about them, Connor. Jimmy fucked up the mission, and now Davon will need time to recover while God knows what Deb's going through inside that prison."

Connor placed his elbows against his knees. He stared ahead, his gaze lost. "I think about her all the time. Sometimes I look around, expecting to find her sitting here or resting in bed. Everything reminds me of her. Being apart and unable to protect her makes every moment a living hell, but I know she'd want me to focus on the task at hand and protect our people." He grabbed my hand. "If you ever need to talk or just sit in silence with someone who understands you, I'm always here for you. No matter what."

I squeezed his hand. "Thank you. I'm sorry about all this. I know it's hard for you too."

He nodded and let go of my hand, then picked up his mug and sipped his coffee.

"I'm determined to get back out there. Davon will need all the help he can get. Matt's teaching me about Electi, Davon's father, and how the government works. I'm hoping Davon contacts us soon. We need to get the upper hand, and having us inside gives us a huge advantage."

My body vibrated at the prospect of getting into Electi. I was dead set on giving my all to Deb and the community.

Davon was alone out there, and he hadn't even started with the hard part. What would become of him once he started torturing Deb? And what would happen to Deb, knowing what Davon told me? His father made him into a monster and expected that kind of treatment toward my sister.

Would I ever be able to deal with what he'd do to her? Would I see him the same way as before, or would everything change?

I didn't want to lose him and my sister in the process, and for that, I needed to be there and make sure everything worked as planned.

Once inside, we'd be able to find allies and get the intel we needed.

Connor watched me. "You're just like Deb, you know. There's nothing I can say to stop you, so I may as well help you." He grinned knowingly. "Now for the good news."

I shifted toward him and gripped his arm. "Did you hear about him?" My heart pumped wildly.

Connor put his hand on top of mine. "He's alive and well. We just received the news. Not directly from him but from an informant at the hospital. Davon was there for a couple of days, then moved to his father's house."

I smiled and sagged against the sofa.

He's alive.

I clasped Connor's hand. "How did he look? Do you know anything else?"

He shook his head. "He was moved on a wheelchair with a sling and bandages on his shoulder, conscious and in good condition. That's all we know."

I closed my eyes. "That's more than enough. So he's already with his father."

"Yes, but Niles's house is impenetrable. A fort. We've never been able to get anyone inside. Until he's out, we're in the dark. I'm sure he'll take his position on the council as soon as possible, but because of his injury, it may take a couple of weeks."

The mission would hold even if it took some extra time, but we still had a spy to catch.

"Have you found out anything about the spy?" I asked.

"We've been investigating Richard's case. I'm certain he was innocent. We found no evidence against him. As to why he was killed, I'm sure he found something he shouldn't have. I suspect the spy isn't working alone.

We may be dealing with something far bigger than we thought. I only hope we can catch them before more damage is done."

"What's the plan?"

"We're checking all runners and controlling their routes. The spy won't be able to use that strategy anymore. Nina opened positions in the command and computer center. I'm confident they'll take advantage of this and apply if they haven't already."

"I hope it works." The spy had already killed, and I hoped it was the first and last time they did so.

"Me too. As soon as I receive word from Davon, I'll let him know you'll both be joining him."

I nodded. "You know we'll do everything in our power to get her back."

He smiled. "I know you will."

Chapter 4
Davon

November 15, 2213

"*October 1, 2211: I can still hear her screams, the echoes of the gun-shots, the blood... I'm alone, filthy, and hungry as hell. Patrols keep circling the empty storage space I've been staying in for the last couple of weeks. I need to find a way out soon.*" (Abigail's memoirs)

Two days trapped under my father's roof. I could only hope news of my arrival reached the peak. This place was surveilled continuously, and it was impossible to get intel in or out.

Did Abi make it back? Did she get Jimmy back in time?

Those two questions troubled me constantly, but I had to trust all was well.

The harsh sound of the Velcro being pulled open to remove my blood pressure cuff interrupted my musings.

"Everything is stable. If you need anything, remember to ring. I'm just a floor away." Abi's aunt was always around, like a guard dog.

"Sure, have a good night."

Most of my time I spent reading in our family library, and in the after-noons, I'd sit with Mom to talk.

She asked me about Gabrielle daily.

I told her everything I could and all there was to love about her.

"I'll make it back to you. I promise." The last words Abi spoke echoed in my mind. We'd see each other soon.

I visited our gym daily to do my therapy exercises and some cardio with the spinning bike. The sooner I got better, the sooner I could start my mission.

My shoulder was more mobile by the day, and the therapists expected me to be fully recovered within a month with my cryotherapy chamber sessions. The fucking injustice of it all made me nauseous.

Matt's arm would take months to recover, while I stayed in a mansion with the latest medical advancements, a personal gym, and my own therapists, just to get me up and running for the government's benefit.

I sat at my bay window and faced north toward the forest.

Home. When would I get to glimpse those honey-green eyes and kiss her soft skin again? I could almost smell her sweet fragrance as I shifted my gaze toward the mountains in the distance. Was she doing okay? Were her nightmares back?

I walked to my bookshelf and took Abi's journal out of its hiding spot. I could almost hear her voice. Her perseverance and will to survive made me rethink all the moments I implied she couldn't protect herself.

She was a force to be reckoned with, and when the moment came, my father would fear her.

I drifted to sleep while thinking about her, hoping she was safe.

November 17, 2213

I swallowed hard and wiped the sweat from my brow.

"Just one more time, Mr. Niles. Move your fingers up the wall until you reach the highest point, then go back down."

I clenched my jaw and followed the therapist's instructions. The pressure inside my shoulder and across my upper arm increased. Who would have thought something so simple could cause so much pain?

"Perfect. Done for the day. Remember to do your stretching exercises as many times as you can. It will help you recover faster."

I gulped some water. When I was about to start stretching, my father entered our home gym.

This place had state-of-the-art machines and all the equipment needed to train.

My parents even bought a cryotherapy chamber so I wouldn't have to go out for my sessions.

Father loved this place as much as I did, but I liked it more without him in it.

"Hey," he said.

This was my opportunity to find out what my role in the council would be. We still hadn't talked about it.

I put on a big smile. "Are you going to do some cardio or just lift?"

My father was very strict with his exercise regimen. At fifty-two, he was as chiseled as me. I learned from him about discipline and consistency.

"Power and control over your own body are equally as important as over the country. Never forget that," Father used to say.

He rolled his shoulders back, then opened and closed his arms. "Upper body. Want to spot me?"

I lifted an eyebrow and tilted my head toward my shoulder. "I don't think I can be of much help."

Father chuckled. "Just stay with me. We never talk."

Yes!

"Okay."

I followed him to the cable machine. He started doing upright rows.

I stayed close and did some mobility exercises the therapists taught me.

"How are the therapies going?" Father asked.

"Good. The shoulder hurts like hell but is much better. Today I started lifting light weights. Baby steps, right?"

He nodded and set the cables for straight arm lat pulldowns. "And the cryotherapy sessions?"

"They helped with the inflammation. Now I use them mostly for the pain."

"That's good. I talked to your doctor, and he says you'll be able to start working very soon. Are you ready for it?"

I slowly rolled my shoulder. "I am. I'm not sure what your plans are for me, but I'm anxious to work with the council."

Father paused mid-repetition. "Me too. I've always wanted to work hand in hand with you. For so long I thought you weren't going to rise to your potential. But at last, I see you understand the need for our actions. With your intel, you helped us move forward toward taking out those bastards."

My insides knotted at the thought of all the people we'd lost. "I'm glad I could help."

Father started his second set. "How exactly did you get that intel?"

I scoffed quietly. He never missed a thing.

Connor and I expected as much and prepared for it.

I continued stretching. "It all started shortly after Gabrielle came to work with us. We had already started going out, and one evening, I walked her home. There were suspicious people moving along the alleyways. We hid and watched them go out of the city and into the forest. I told her she needed to be careful, that those people were dangerous. I don't know why, but I trusted her, so I explained we worked for the NWG and that we needed to stop these rebel activities to protect Promissa's citizens. Sometime later, she told me she wanted to help, so she started befriending people at the clinic. She talked about the need to free the people from the government's regime and take back the city. A couple of weeks later, she got an invitation. They were rebels. I followed her intel. After finding the first checkpoint, I sent you the letter, and kept looking for more."

Father completed his set and watched me. "Why didn't you engage them? You could have taken the group down."

I stared back at him. "It was a tough call, but having Gabrielle go to their meetings was a better plan. It got us the rest of the checkpoints."

He studied me. "You told us in the hospital that she was undercover, but in your last communication, you said she was coming. What changed?"

The hairs on the back of my neck rose. I had to make something up. But what?

I kept my eyes on him. "The night before they shot me, Gabrielle got a letter from one of the rebels. Another meeting." I shifted in place. "She never came home that night."

Father lifted one eyebrow. "And you just left her?"

I suppressed a shudder. "She had a bad feeling, and after we said goodbye that night, she made me swear I'd go back to Electi with or without her. She promised she'd get back to me."

My eyes misted at the memory of the promise she made. Of her face when I told her to stay. "It hurt to leave Gaby behind, but I trust her. She'll get back to me."

He grabbed my good arm. His gaze was warm. "I'm so sorry this happened. Are you sure you don't want my agents to look for her?"

I relaxed at his comforting touch, and without giving it a second thought, I covered his hand with mine. "Thanks, but Matt said he'd look for her and bring her back. I trust him."

He smiled and nodded. "I'm sure he'll get her back for you."

I continued stretching.

My father got his mat and was about to start his second round of exercises.

"Father?"

He sat on the floor. "Yes?"

"Can you give me a hint about what I'll be doing on the council?"

He curled one corner of his mouth up. "I'll let you know on your first council meeting, but I assure you, you'll like what I have in mind."

My gut tightened at his words. What was he planning?

November 21, 2213

Dawn's first rays of light streamed into my room as I sat on the windowsill. Today I'd talk to my father. I needed to be free of this place.

Nothing around the room said it was mine, only a picture that sat on the bedside table—one Matt took more than ten years ago.

My father's arm was around me, and Mom kissed my cheek. A huge blue birthday cake lit with fifteen candles sat on a picnic bench.

My smile was genuine. It had been a perfect day at Lake Egregie.

Matt spent the whole birthday weekend with us. We swung from tree vines and splashed around all day, not a worry in the world.

I ran my finger along the edge of the picture frame and smiled wistfully. Could things ever be the same?

My father's voice drifted from outside. "Son, can I come in?"

"Sure." I put the picture back on the table and straightened. A response ingrained in me after twenty-eight years of upbringing by Jordan Niles.

Presence. Control. Authority. That's what was expected of me as his son, and it couldn't be helped. It came naturally.

My father had control over most of the eastern territory.

We had a president, Ulysses Orville, a puppet under my father's command. He was put there for all he'd donated during the wars. A symbol of the power the elites had over the New World Government.

But the real mastermind, the most powerful man in the NWG and the one who made all the decisions, was at this moment entering my room.

"Why not just take over?" I asked him once.

"As chairman of the council, I can do as I please. Better that than being in the spotlight."

Nevertheless, he loved basking in his power.

"How are you?" He leaned against the doorway, wearing his usual suit, ready to take over the world.

"Much better. I'm glad you came. We need to talk."

Stepping away from the door, he put his hands in his pockets and walked toward me. "Sure, what is it?"

"I'm moving back to my penthouse." I never asked permission. There was no place for weakness in front of him.

He sat by the bed and focused his dark gaze on me. "I don't see why you wish to leave, but I expected this. You've never liked it here. Are you leaving today?"

I nodded.

"Okay. I'll make the arrangements. I came to tell you there's a council meeting in three days. I'll assign two bodyguards for you. They'll shadow you and take you anywhere you need to go." It was not a request but an order.

"Do you think it necessary?" With someone always on my tail, the mission would be complicated.

"It is. You'll be working from Promissa, and your mother and I want you to be safe."

Good. Soon I'd know what my assignment would be. Then my true mission would begin. From now on, I was to become whatever Father wanted. My every action would be committed to the cause of the New World Government.

"I'll be there. These insurgents will pay for what they've done." I covered my shoulder and looked straight at him. "I won't stop till I crush them all."

I knew how he operated, and cruelty appealed to him. That's how tyranny worked: no mercy toward insubordination.

There was a gleam in his eyes. "I'm glad you see it my way. We're close to removing this threat, and I want you with me when we do it." As he was about to leave, he paused. "I'll tell Rebecca to come by so you can tell her about this yourself. I'm sure she'll understand."

He turned to leave. "Someone will help you get ready. I'll send a car to pick you up in an hour."

Three hours later, I was settled in my apartment overlooking the Central Train Station and the Electi Entertainment District to the northwest. Eden Gardens, where the homes of the government higher-ups were located, surrounded Lake Egregie to the northeast.

My loft took up the thirtieth floor of an opulent apartment building that lay in the center of Electi. An equivalent to my father's authority. I moved here when I turned twenty-one, tired of living under my parents' roof.

My rock playlist played in the background as I served myself a glass of whiskey, then sank onto my black leather sectional sofa.

This was my haven in the city, a place where I could be myself.

I missed Matt. The last time we were in the city we stayed for two years in our search for Abi. His apartment stood empty one floor down, smaller than mine but just as luxurious.

According to our original mission plan, he'd be here in a month. But with what happened, I wasn't sure anymore. I just hoped he'd come soon and bring Abi with him. Father was not a patient man.

"How are you, Abi?" I murmured.

I missed her remarks when she wouldn't take my bullshit and her laughter when she teased me. Her warm skin as I caressed her. Her willing body as she gave herself to me.

How long until I could be with her? Chat about our plans, our dreams...

I needed to find a way to let her know I was okay. That everything was going according to plan.

A knock on the door took me away from my thoughts.

I checked the camera feed on my phone. Grace waited by the door.

Fuck. Who the hell let her in?

Grace was President Orville's daughter. My father had always pushed me to marry her and get into a position of power, but I never agreed.

Nevertheless, the pretentious woman was always following me around if I was in the city.

She was gorgeous—there was no denying it. Her long, silky red hair and dark-green eyes were visible through the video.

To say I was ashamed to have slept with her only touched the surface of my problems, as after that, she'd grown attached to me.

It happened five years ago after Elaine died. My first love.

Her death destroyed me, and I wasn't myself. I started questioning everyone and became violent. Connor told me to take some time off, and I moved to my apartment in Electi to be alone.

Grace started to visit.

I was drunk most of the time, drowning my pain. One night, one thing led to another, and we had sex. It continued for about a month until she started demanding a commitment. She followed me everywhere and started moving her stuff to my place till I snapped and told her to leave. I ended everything.

At the time, she was just an outlet, a way to move on. It was wrong, and I led her on. Now karma was back to bite my ass.

I put my drink down and walked barefoot to the door.

Grace tried to step in, but I blocked her path. She gave me a sultry look, no longer the twenty-one-year-old who used to cower in my presence.

"Hi, Davon. Long time no see. Aren't you going to invite me in?" Her voice promised something more.

"Grace, what are you doing here?" I asked in my most detached voice.

"I wanted to see you, of course. Dad told me you were injured. I came as soon as I heard."

She put her finger through the loop of my pants and dragged me in. "Now that you're back, maybe we can pick up where we left off."

I clenched my teeth and fisted one hand on the doorframe, then pulled her off me. "Where we left off? As I remember, I ended things last time we met. There's nothing here for you, so you may as well leave."

She pressed herself against me. "But I've changed. I'm no longer that girl you met. We can make of this what you want. Nothing serious. No commitment."

She brushed her hand over my lower abs.

I flinched and stepped back with a stern stare. "Go. Don't waste your time on me."

She opened the top two buttons of her black satin shirt, giving me a view of her cleavage. "I want you, and I know you want me. It doesn't have to mean anything."

I averted my eyes.

She wanted to trap me, but that would never happen, for as enticing as she was, the idea of sleeping with her repulsed me.

I was in love with Abi, and that was it. There was no one else but her.

"Have a good night. And please don't come back." I was done with Grace.

She widened her eyes, her mouth slightly open, and I closed the door.

I leaned on it, wishing I was back at the peak with my family.

Chapter 5

Davon

November 24, 2213

"*November 14, 2211: Another nightmare... As the patrols became more aggressive in their search for us runaways, sleep eluded me, and hunger struck me hard. How long can I take this? Will Deb ever come back for me? (Abigail's memoirs)*

A golden hue entered my room as the first hints of sunrise filled the horizon.

What are you doing right now? Training? Having breakfast? Planning a mission?

The comfort of my penthouse fell short, as its four walls confined me in an unending loop. Father even moved the cryotherapy chamber into my apartment so I could focus on my recovery. Between the therapies and Nurse Davis checking in on me, my every step was controlled.

Yesterday I was fed up with all of it and told Father to call off the nurse and the therapists. My shoulder had much more mobility than a week ago. I would continue on my own. No one was setting foot in my penthouse. Not anymore.

I hadn't seen Lisa since the hospital. At least I knew my act had worked. Nevertheless, she'd texted me, telling me if I needed anything, she was there for me. She was family, and she wouldn't back away even when I was being an asshole.

Grace, on the other hand, hadn't stopped texting. I talked to the bodyguards my father assigned to protect me right after she texted that she was coming over. I watched the security cameras through my cell phone. They stopped her before she reached the elevator. She was no longer welcome.

I grimaced when she looked straight at the camera and smiled. She took out her phone and started typing something.

A moment later, my phone beeped.

"Take all the time you need. I'm a patient woman. I know what happened out there has you on edge. You think rekindling our affair is off the table, but it may be just what you need. Call me if you change your mind. See you soon."

I threw my phone on the coffee table and slumped back into my sofa, rubbing my neck. I'd have to keep an eye out for Grace.

After taking a moment to calm down and to make sure Grace left the building, I hid the cyphered note I wrote inside my navy-blue blazer and took the elevator down. Today I'd be joining my father's council.

My personal bodyguards waited for me the moment I stepped out. Getting rid of them to get word out would be a total pain in the ass, but I'd handle it.

Aiyla Bayat and Patrick O'Hare were quite a pair.

Bayat's short dark-brown hair accentuated her light-brown almond-shaped eyes. She was the serious type, always following orders. A strong soldier.

O'Hare was more of a fun guy, continuously trying to piss her off. It was obvious he liked her. His red hair and blue eyes countered both Bayat's and my complexion. He was always smiling and giving each conversation a certain hint of humor.

"Morning, Bayat, O'Hare."

"Mr. Niles," Bayat said. "The train is ready to take you to the government center in Promissa. If you would follow us, please."

"I know the way. You can take the day off." I threw my dice, knowing it wouldn't work, but I had to start somewhere.

O'Hare smiled. "That wouldn't be a bad idea. We've been stuck here for weeks. I think my feet are growing roots. Some time off sounds perfect."

Bayat frowned. "We have orders to get Mr. Niles all the way to the conference room, and we will not ignore them."

O'Hare smirked. "How about once we get him there, we get some breakfast." He winked. "They'll be locked in that room for hours."

She rolled her eyes, but there was a hint of a smile as she did so. Was she softening toward him?

I had to give it to him—he wouldn't give up. This banter happened daily. He always tried to get her to lighten up, and I served as his wingman.

Today I'd make sure he got his wish. "I know you follow my father's orders, but as you are my bodyguards for the time being, my order today is for you two to go eat something and relax while I'm at the meeting. I'll contact you when it's done."

Bayat's shoulders sank. "Understood, but O'Hare and I will be back in no time."

"Thank you, Commander Bayat."

Putting a hand in my pocket, I walked toward the train station, our sole mode of transportation to and from Promissa. In Electi, we had cars, but over there, citizens believed resources to be scarce and depended only on the solar-powered train system.

The station stood one block west of my apartment building, south of the Electi Entertainment District. The latter was already bustling with activity, with people having breakfast and enjoying a morning out.

All eyes were on me as I entered the central station. Being a Niles was close to being a celebrity, and it was my first appearance in over a year.

To maintain the face in front of the common citizens, the outside of this car was plain, same as the rest. Inside it was the opposite.

Mahogany walls surrounded the opulent setting as Chesterfield-style furniture was set around a lounge area with a bar and a private bathroom. Only councilmembers were allowed inside this car.

I sat at the bar and asked the attendant for a glass of whiskey on the rocks.

Today Councilmember Niles from the New World Government would start his mission. My primary goal was to get into a position of power that would allow me to gain access to the government's inner workings to learn about its spies, plans, and high-security facilities. I needed to get inside the prison where Deb was confined and find out how much they knew about the People's Revolutionary Front.

Connor wouldn't risk any offensive action until Deb was safe inside Janus Peak, so her rescue was my priority because as things were, we didn't have enough time.

My skin crawled at the notion of what I'd have to do to earn my father's trust, knowing he'd expect me to prove myself to him in brutal ways.

Would Abi forgive the things I'd do to her sister? Would it tarnish my friendship with Deb and Connor?

The screech of the brakes halted my thoughts as the train arrived at the government center station. I gulped down the rest of my drink and exited the car.

The NWG's approach to this structure could be summarized in one word: lavishness. White marble floors, walls, and Tuscan columns.

Gods. That's how they portrayed themselves and thus managed to create a space to make people see them as such. No other place in the city carried as much power as this building.

I looked down at everyone and continued on my way, letting the same arrogance of my father gush through my pores. No one dared approach me as I entered the elevator.

Bayat took out the key to the top floor and turned it in the elevator's panel.

O'Hare whistled as he gazed down at the city through the glass.

Promissa. The modern architecture of the buildings surrounding the government center stood proof of its past magnificence.

When we reached the fifteenth floor, the war-affected regions of Promissa began to show through. Behind it, the majestic mountains rose against the blue sky. It was breathtaking. I'd read wartime accounts and journals that my father had preserved. The attacks claimed many lives, and the NWG's bombings destroyed the area.

Some fled into the forest, and many of them were now part of the People's Revolutionary Front. I still recalled entering the farming bunker for the first time. The residents fled in fright, believing the NWG had finally discovered them.

I leaned against the side of the elevator, clasped my hands around the rail, and closed my eyes. In a few minutes, I'd be seated among the same individuals who ruined this city. I had to pull my act together in front of them.

Once on the twentieth floor, I took a deep breath and stepped out, holding my arm out to stop O'Hare and Bayat from following. "Go out and enjoy your morning. That's an order. I expect you back by lunch."

Bayat tried to talk back just as the elevator door closed.

Now to get word out to Connor. He activated three sleeper agents inside the government center and a couple of time drops, and one was on this floor.

At the end of the hallway, two NWG soldiers stood guard. They both donned white uniforms and were armed with electric batons and firearms.

I winked at them. "Need to take care of some business first."

Following Connor's instructions, I went into the second stall of the restroom and hid my coded letter in a pocket hidden between the floor and the toilet.

I scrubbed my face, gripped the wash basin, and took a few deep breaths. I stared at my reflection and straightened my man bun, attempting to make it look as refined as possible. After double-checking my navy suit and adjusting my obsidian cufflinks, I put my hands in my pockets. A Niles through and through.

You can do this.

I stepped into the hall and approached the conference room. Both soldiers saluted before opening the door.

A long, oval-shaped meeting table took up most of the space, with a glass panel behind it that offered an amazing view of Promissa. To the left was a bar with an assortment of sweets and tea or coffee to suit everyone's tastes.

When I walked in, all talks halted. The leaders of each government agency stood before me. My father, the minister of human control and chairman of the council, led the group, with the ministers of labor, health, housing, resources, transportation, and military surrounding him.

Aristotle used the term oligarchia to designate the rule of the few when it was exerted unjustly by bad people rather than the best. What was in front of me now was the most accurate representation of what he meant.

In Promissa, governing elites were set apart from the rest of society by prestige and favors served to the country during the war. These elites only exercised power in the interests of their own class.

As to where I fit in this room, I had no idea. My father hadn't divulged my position yet.

"Son, we were waiting for you. There's a lot to discuss. Please take a seat."

I nodded and sat in the last empty space next to him.

All councilmembers sat after me.

My father cleared his throat. "We've gathered here today to welcome my son, Davon Niles, as the new minister of security and sedition control, a new department formed in response to recent events. He's been a valuable contributor for many years, and his intelligence has provided us with a significant win."

Dad patted my shoulder and smiled. "Five insurgent checkpoints were destroyed. Unfortunately, no rebels could be taken in for questioning, as all nine militants were killed in the struggle to take control of the sites."

I swallowed hard and pressed my lips together. Struggle? It was a slaughter.

He motioned to me. "Nonetheless, this is a huge step forward. Let us welcome Davon into our council and recognize him for the tremendous victory he's given us."

The whole council stood and applauded. My insides recoiled at the display, one only meant to please my father.

The Department of Security and Sedition Control.

I wanted to run at my father's satisfied smile.

My mind went back to the night they killed Leon. On our last operation together, Matt and I were sent to inspect the attacked checkpoints and inform command of their status. When we reached checkpoint six, we had to fight. Leon was killed in front of us, and we barely saved Rachel. That was the day Matt was shot.

A bitter taste filled my mouth at the complete disregard for human lives inside this room. All those dead soldiers were just numbers, pieces of a game that were no longer in play. How I kept my countenance escaped me.

Everyone sat.

My father faced the minister of the military. "General Lavigne, do you have a report on the efforts in finding the rebel base?"

Minister Peter Lavigne was a seasoned general in his late forties. He was an elegant man with a strong complexion that portrayed incredible authority and strength. Almost my height, he had features that resembled mine except for his porcelain skin and blue eyes.

He not only trained me during my teenage years and the beginning of my adulthood, but he also became like a father to me. I never blamed him for anything, knowing the cruelty behind it all came from my own father.

I once caught them arguing at home. I was eighteen at the time. Their screams filtered outside my father's study.

It was the day after one of the most painful beatings I'd taken.

My father insisted on my fighting three seasoned soldiers at the same time.

Lavigne stopped the fight.

"There's no need for the training to be so harsh. They almost beat him to death yesterday," Lavigne said.

"Davon needs to be strong, and this is the only way. When we're done with him, he'll be fearless and a formidable opponent." My father's commanding tone was followed by a hard thump.

"You're going to fucking kill him if you keep this up. He's your son, for God's sake! I can train him without hurting him."

"Stop this nonsense, Peter, and do as I say. That's an order!"

Following that day, Lavigne stayed with me after every training session. He taught me to be strong and to never show weakness in front of others. It was my only means of survival in my father's world. Here the weak were trampled upon, and only the strong moved forward.

We talked a lot, and he always listened. He knew about my hatred toward my father and never divulged my secret.

To see him shuffle through his papers, his hands shaking, was unsettling. I learned to study body language early in my life since elites sometimes hid their true feelings and intentions. I sighed silently, knowing before he spoke that the government had no leads on our location, one of our greatest concerns in terms of the mission.

"Minister Lavigne, we're waiting." My father's tone turned serious.

Finally, Lavigne raked his black hair back and rose. "Chairman Niles. Members of the council. We've been sweeping the forest area near the captured checkpoints. We've gone about ten miles in and still haven't found any trace of rebel activity or any base. The search will continue until we find them. Rest assured that we will emerge victorious in this endeavor and squash once and for all this threat to our way of life."

My father rested his elbows on the table and regarded Lavigne with a murderous glare. He was a man of little tolerance and expected fast and positive results always.

"We've been through this, and you still show no results. Either you step up and find this group, or I will terminate your position within this council and assign a more capable person to take on your post."

This wasn't a meager threat. My father could destroy his reputation and status with a flick of his fingers. He wouldn't only remove him from his post but would probably expel him from Electi, stripping him of all his rights and privileges in a matter of days.

"Understood, Chairman Niles. We won't rest until we find and destroy them." Lavigne organized his papers and sat back down.

The other councilmembers watched in silence, no reaction evident unless you paid attention. A nervous tick, a movement below the table, and an averted gaze were the only indications of the intense tension overtaking the room.

Father looked at Minister Frank Anderson, Matt's dad.

The last time I met him was over a year ago at one of my father's events. He was a good father to Matt and always treated me well.

As head of the health department, he oversaw the Genetic Enhancement and Population Control Program (GEPCP) approved ten years ago. He took on all the responsibility of the program and made sure it ran without a hitch.

"Minister Anderson." Dad dipped his chin.

Frank grinned back. The resemblance between him and Matt was uncanny. Similar expressions, features that resembled those marble statues in museums, and the same emerald eyes. Their only difference was the hair color. Frank's hair was deep brown and long, held back by a ponytail. He appeared young for his age, and his fine looks drew a lot of attention from the general population.

"How is the Elysium Genome Project coming along?" Father asked.

Frank stood, both palms resting on the table. "Everything's good. Our scientists are constantly genotyping DNA from our egg and sperm storage and creating superior combinations daily. These will aid in producing a supreme workforce."

My body went numb, and all my thoughts halted at once.

Genetically modified embryos? What the hell?

Two years ago, during my mission to get information on Sarah and Abi, I found out about a project to use rebellious Promissa citizens as surrogate mothers. I thought it ended there, but to use them as guinea pigs to create enhanced humans was beyond twisted.

Frank glanced at his papers. "Many of the subjects will be made into enhanced soldiers. In less than a decade, we should have enough numbers both to defend our territories and to invade more regions. And this is without counting our enhanced army in Halcyon."

I clenched my jaw and tried to digest what I just heard. This far surpassed what I thought my father was capable of.

An army at Halcyon?

I suppressed a shudder.

Frank handed me a file. "Minister Niles, here's a complete run-through of the projects we're running. As you will be working hand in hand with my department in handling most of our test subjects, I need you to study the project and let me know if you have any questions."

I opened the file—approved 2193. My breath faltered.

This had been their plan since they created the New World Government even before they had control over Promissa. It had begun in Halcyon, our second largest city. Signed by Minister Anderson, Chairman Niles, and General Steele.

My heart pumped wildly as I went over the signatures for a second time. I was not mistaken. General Thorne Steele was part of this.

I held on to the file, trying to control my trembling hands.

The general of the army, the second most feared man in the NWG, was behind this project. He'd given a shoot-to-kill order when he took over Halcyon. Thousands died. Witnesses said he executed most citizens personally even after they surrendered. Men, women, and children alike.

We were dealing with something far worse than we thought.

I closed the file. "Thanks. I'll go over it as soon as possible. Please continue."

Frank nodded. "Over two hundred women are currently pregnant, all from our prison system and secure facilities. We move them to the obstetrics facility during their second trimester so we can monitor them better. Once they have their babies, they continue their current sentence in their original prison facilities to be used again for the program as needed."

Bile shot up my throat as he offered me a map.

I placed it on the table.

"The facilities to care for these children are marked. Loyal citizens from Promissa live in these state-of-the-art facilities where they take care of them and teach them our way of life from preschool age."

He indicated some facilities east of the prison system, bordering Electi to the west. "These are the ones where the children and teenagers receive military training until they're ready to join our ranks. Children age five and up are educated. They begin drills and military training at a young age to build the unstoppable combat force we're striving for."

Deb and Connor learned about these facilities during their three years of education, but we hadn't heard any more of it and thought the project had died.

I looked around the table. Not even a slither of guilt passed across their faces.

How could they accept this? They were only children.

Frank pointed west. "New facilities are being constructed over here."

I studied the map.

Once finished, these last facilities would be immense, built in the same area where Abi had found us.

I kept my gaze and expression detached. "Thank you. I'll be sure to study this."

"Good." Frank looked at my father. "Getting to the rebel base is essential to move this project forward at a higher rate. We don't know the numbers, but if they have over five hundred able bodies, the benefits to our project would be enormous. With them and all the other rebels being held, we could create an endless superior workforce that would labor and fight without our having to deal with disobedience."

We were to be their lab rats. The fate of our people would be tied to this project if we were ever discovered.

Frank turned toward Lavigne before sitting. A look passed between them.

Lavigne nodded slightly.

I darted my gaze between them. What was that about?

My father smirked. "Thank you, Minister Anderson. As always, you never disappoint."

Twenty years of abuse going on right beneath our noses.

I needed to alert Connor.

The war had already started.

November 24, 2213

"*December 30, 2211: The patrols pushed me north into an abandoned area. Solitude would suffice, as I wouldn't put myself in that situation again. Not ever. Every couple of days I braved into a community or apartment building to get some food and return to my hiding spot. For now, it would have to do.*" (Abigail's memoirs)

An hour later, the minister of transportation's briefing was about to end. She talked about train security and the status of new routes.

The train already went all the way east into Halcyon, but Father wanted it to cover more areas until it reached our frontiers to the north. Why the NWG needed this escaped me, but I'd dig into it. Something must have happened.

"Taking up these new routes is much needed. Do you think they can be ready for use within the next couple of months?" Father asked.

Ms. Fernandez fixed a rebellious strand that had escaped her coifed hair, then checked her paperwork. She shook her head slightly before settling her gaze on my father. "I don't think it can be ready by then. We need to make sure the new train works, but it's still under construction. Once it's ready, we must complete a series of test runs to make sure everything runs smoothly."

Father tapped his pen on the table.

She blinked and scratched her neck.

"That's disappointing." He tightened his jaw and blew out an exaggerated breath. "We need this done. If you can't do it, tell me now, and don't waste my time or that of the council."

Something was up with my father. He rarely lost his shit. And this had him on edge.

Ms. Fernandez's chin trembled. She squeezed her file tightly.

Father leaned toward me and whispered loud enough so the others could hear. "You see what I have to deal with. We need to excel, but they just don't get it."

She looked at me.

I could use this in our favor, but it was a dangerous game.

I slumped back in my seat and crossed my arms. "I see what you're saying," I said to Father, then looked at the minister of transportation. "What do you need? More workers?"

She nodded. "That would help."

"How many?" I asked.

Her eyes appeared glassy, and she averted her gaze. "Maybe a hundred."

"Do we have enough people in the facilities inside Electi?" I asked Father, referring to the hundreds of citizens who were kept as a workforce under inhumane conditions.

"We do, but most are assigned to other areas. We could spare some but not too many."

I stroked my stubble, leaning sideways with my elbow resting on the chair arm. "If we need more workers, why not send more troops into Promissa? We could take rebellious citizens and put them to work."

Lavigne put his hand on the table. He clenched his fist, knuckles white. "With all due respect, they've been complying these past years. Do you want my troops to just barge in there and take them?"

I shrugged. "Just make something up. It's always good to remind them who's in charge. And there's no better way than spreading fear. We kill two birds with one stone and suffocate their little rebellion at the root."

Father sneered, then eyed Lavigne. "Send more troops in. Get the number of people needed. I don't care what age or gender. What Davon says is true. We're in charge here, and they need to know."

I nodded and gazed back at Lavigne.

He searched my eyes, a stony expression on his face. "It will be done."

What Father thought would work in the NWG's favor could end up helping the PRF in the long run. The unjustified arrests might trigger something more. It would ignite a spark that would otherwise stay dwindled.

This would give the citizens a reason to fight. To step out of the comfort zone they'd accepted and reach for something more.

Gaining my father's trust was crucial even though my chest ached from the consequences that would result from my decision, especially for the innocent people of Promissa.

A chill ran down my spine at what I'd done. Was I becoming as ruthless as my father?

How many would suffer from this initiative? Would we be able to stop it before they were harmed?

I was putting innocent lives in danger to move our cause and without Connor's permission.

Did I really need this to gain my father's trust and secure my place in the NWG?

I sighed. It needed to be done. I couldn't back out now.

Father patted my shoulder. "Thank you, son."

I dipped my chin.

He studied the councilmembers. "I guess you're all curious about Davon's deeds during the last couple of months and how he found these rebel checkpoints." He watched me. "Can you explain what you found and if you have any intel on the location of their base?"

Even though I was convinced Father didn't know about Janus Peak, I hid my relief at hearing his words.

The councilmembers gave me their attention as I stood.

"First of all, it's an honor to fulfill my duty to the NWG. Being part of this council far surpasses my expectations. As you're all aware, I've been living in Promissa for the past year, conducting investigations within its perimeter as an undercover agent."

I looked at Frank Anderson. "Matt's clinic has proven to be quite effective in discovering what's going on deep within Promissa's society. Conversations, insurgent groups, threads connecting to the rebels. Everything was a piece of cake once we gained their trust. We didn't need them to tell us, just to loosen their tongues in the office. Surveillance did the rest." I organized my papers and sighed, all part of the acting. "That and the assistance of a loyal citizen."

I cleared my throat and recited the speech I'd practiced for the last couple of weeks. "Our informant joined an insurgent cell that directed us toward that first checkpoint. I followed her intel and pursued a couple of rebels as they exited the city through an unguarded area with a young woman in tow. Once in the forest, they met with a couple of guards. These were heavily armed and radioed in their arrival. The two men returned to the city, and after an hour, another team came to lead the blindfolded woman away."

"Why didn't you follow?" Frank asked.

"I didn't want to risk not getting this new information back. I was alone out there. If they found me or an ambush awaited farther in, my capture or death would have been imminent, and the intel would've never reached this council."

He nodded.

Father gestured for me to continue.

"My informant heard about rebel nets set up around the city, and after thorough investigation, we found a whole network of checkpoints."

My father's eyes gleamed, and he relaxed back in his chair.

Frank leaned forward. "What's the name of your informant?"

I took a deep, shuddering breath but kept my composure. I'd keep her safe. "Gabrielle. Her name's Gabrielle Jones."

Frank smiled. "I'm anxious to meet her."

Father nodded. "Me too. I already sent agents in to keep an eye out for her."

My heart skipped a beat. "But you could endanger her cover."

Get a grip, Davon.

Father shook his head. "You underestimate my spies. I sent in some of the best, and they're hidden among the population. Nothing will happen."

I held my chin up and nodded, keeping the creeping sensation dredging through my soul in check.

Father crossed his arms. "Your information opened a new chapter in our control over the region. Concerning the recent events, please share with the rest of the council what happened the day you arrived."

I clasped my hands behind my back, stifling a flinch as a stab of pain shot through my shoulder. "I was about eight miles out in search of the location of the rebel base when someone approached from the west. I aimed my gun toward the sound but was hit in the shoulder by a bullet. I took my shot. A pained cry followed, and I knew I'd struck my mark. I didn't risk chasing after this rebel, unsure if he was acting alone, so I turned back until

I reached the perimeter of the city. That's the last thing I remember before waking up in the hospital a couple of days later."

"We're glad you made it back safely," Frank said.

I bowed and sat.

"We all are," Father said. "From now on, as minister of security and sedition control, your new office will be at the Niles High-Security Prison. After lunch, I'll take you there. I'll show you the ropes for a couple of weeks and leave you to it when you're ready."

My heart hammered. If I gained control over the prison, it would make everything so much easier.

Father passed me a file.

I opened it and furrowed my brow as I stared at a picture of Deb. Her dark curls reached her shoulders, and her hazel eyes were devoid of emotion as she stared into the camera.

I narrowed my eyes. "Deborah Davis?"

"She's an insurgent who aided in an escape about four months ago. A tough one to crack. I'm sure you'll be able to get more information out of her."

I browsed through the file. "What kind of information are we trying to obtain?"

"Based on her family history, I believe she's key in finding the rebel group."

I glanced up. "Her family history?"

"Ten years ago, her parents tried to leave the city with the eldest of their three daughters. We eliminated them and left the three daughters under the care of kin who were loyal to us. Three years ago, her younger sister escaped the night before her advancement. Deborah vanished that same day, leaving behind their oldest sibling. We imprisoned Sarah Davis but were never able to get any good intel from her. Our experts believed she didn't have that information but that she was hiding something, so we kept pushing for more. That's where Deborah came in. We captured her after she aided Sarah in her escape. You are to get the information we need—the location of their base."

My whole skin rose in goosebumps as he verified all the information we had on Deb. She was alive, and now it was my job to get her to talk. I'd have to make my role believable, and with my father watching, it would be difficult not to harm her. The methods I employed were brutal. I only hoped she could endure them.

Father would leave me when he was certain I could complete the task. I only needed to be diligent, learn quickly, and demonstrate that I could handle things on my own. Once alone, I'd get Deb out before I damaged her permanently.

I closed the file, giving it everything I had to maintain a calm and authoritative demeanor. "Ready when you are."

After we had an uneventful lunch in the conference room, Bayat drove an NWG van toward the north district of Promissa. O'Hare took the passenger seat. He glanced sideways a couple of times, but Bayat kept her eyes on the road.

"You know, I still had my doubts about you, son. About your loyalty to us," Father said.

I frowned. "I don't understand."

He dusted off his slacks and gazed outside. "In truth, when we got your first note, I doubted it would bear fruit. For so many years, you'd given us intel that never moved us forward. I was beginning to think you weren't on our side. When I got the call that the first checkpoint was real, I couldn't believe it."

Fuck. He already suspected me. Was I that close to being discovered?

"But..." I tried to talk, but he put his hand up, and I stopped.

He shook his head. "Even after we got your other letters, the same doubts kept bugging me for some time, but when they found you almost dead, I..."

I touched his knee. "Father, we may have had our differences in the past, but I'd never betray you."

He watched me silently. "I know that now. I hadn't planned on giving you control of the prison so soon. I had an office prepared next to mine in the government center, but after what just happened at the council meeting, I decided to trust my instincts. As I said, I'll be with you until I see you're ready to take the reins, then I'll leave it to you. As for Miss Jones, I still need more time."

Abi... What would make him trust her? Maybe our plan of her getting close to Mom could work. If Father had his doubts, Mom could sway him to trust her.

"More time? But she's done nothing but help," I said, my tone firm. She was my girlfriend after all.

Father raised an eyebrow. "I know what you've told me, and I believe you. But you're in love, Davon, and love can blind men. When I meet her, I'll decide whether to trust her or not."

I nodded and looked out my window. I had no doubt he'd interrogate her. I hoped Abi was a good actress.

"We're here," Father said as we approached a security gate half an hour later.

The guard on duty glanced inside and opened the gate.

My brain kicked into high gear, and I scanned my surroundings.

I followed my father through a security checkpoint until we reached a three-story building with ivory walls and no windows. I examined the forested area to the west. This was the exact spot Matt and I found the night we searched for a plausible escape route for Deb.

My father scanned a key card on a gate pad, entered a security code, and put his finger on a digital fingerprint sensor while a biometric face scanner authenticated his identity.

He opened the door to let me in. "Your credentials will be ready soon so you can come and go whenever you please."

Two soldiers were stationed at the end of a long, bright hallway lined with doors.

Halfway through, my father opened a door to his left.

The scent of antiseptic hit me as I entered the cold room. A couple of stainless-steel gurneys sat next to an autopsy table in the middle of the space.

My stomach roiled at the realization of where I stood. A morgue.

Drains were distributed around the area. Dark smears encircled each. Ivory tiles covered the rest of the floor. I grimaced as I spied a red stain under a gurney.

"Chairman Niles, to what do I owe the honor of your visit?" a man in a white coat said from an office at a corner of the morgue.

"Doctor Singh." My father shook hands. "This is my son, Davon."

Singh cleaned his glasses with his coat, then clasped my hand. "Great to finally meet you. Are you here to see the bodies?"

I found myself unable to breathe.

"We are," Father said.

"Please follow me." Dr. Singh walked in front. "These two were the first to come in. As instructed, we kept them in our negative temperature refrigerators to preserve them."

He opened the coolers and slid out two metal slabs.

A sour taste rose to my mouth when he unzipped the bags. Carlos and Christina. Nausea struck, and my hands shook, so I tucked them into my pockets.

My father smiled at me. "I wanted to show you firsthand the results of your intel. These two were the first we executed. The numbers went up exponentially thanks to you. Finding the rebel base is of utmost importance. You'll be leaving on a mission with General Lavigne's units soon. I'll fill you in on it later."

I approached the coolers with a smirk, suppressing the knot that had formed in my throat. "Thank you for this, Father. Knowing we got them puts me at ease. We have a similar mindset, you and I."

I zipped the bags, turned away from Father, and closed my eyes briefly to pay my respects to my two friends. I pushed both metal beds into their respective refrigerated units.

My father placed his hand on my shoulder. "We'll get them all. I have no doubt we will. Now to see the prisoner I told you about."

I focused my thoughts on the mission. I was going to see her at last.

We went through another gate down the hall, and the whole ambience changed. A large dark room with gray cement walls surrounded us. A damp smell mixed with the stench of urine and excrement filled my nostrils, and I tried not to retch.

Metal doors were all around the room, each with a small window at eye level and another near the floor. Soft moans echoed around us.

This must be where solitary confinement prisoners were kept.

We moved up to another floor, and an oppressive force hit me in the chest as I realized the entire jail system was identical. Solitary confinement units built for despair. To break the minds within. It was a living nightmare.

We continued toward the right-hand corner of the room and stopped in front of a cell.

My father opened the window. "Hello, dear. It's been a long time since I've personally come to visit. How are you doing? Do the arrangements satisfy you?"

A deafening bang came from inside.

He chuckled. "Always so eager to see me! I brought someone for you to meet. He'll be spending a lot of his time with you."

He gestured for me to come closer.

I swallowed dryly and approached the door to peek inside.

A pang hit me as a set of hazel eyes I knew very well stared back at me. They widened.

I exhaled, and my vision blurred for a moment. She was alive.

Knowing my father was watching, I put all the hate into my fevered stare. "Hello, Miss Davis. Father tells me you've been a difficult guest."

Her eyebrows squished together, and her eyes became glassy.

I blinked slowly.

She nodded.

I turned to my father. "When do we start?"

Father grinned. "Whenever you want. She's yours to do with as you wish."

I glimpsed her eyes. "It will be my pleasure. She'll learn who the boss is and will sing in no time." I closed the window.

He patted my back. "Exactly what I wanted to hear."

We walked back the way we came, and a loud bang reverberated throughout the room.

"You'll never get anything from me!"

Her voice wrecked me, but I knew my ploy had worked. She was with us.

December 1, 2213

Cheers boosted my adrenaline as I got up after getting knocked down for the second time. My muscles strained, but I reached deep for strength and squatted, dodging a punch. My roundhouse kick struck Maria, and she went down but not before grabbing me and taking me with her. Hands around my waist, she flipped me over and sat on my back, her sweat dripping onto me.

"Do you yield?" Maria rasped.

I smirked, used my core to push me up, and flipped us over. Holding one elbow to her chest, I shifted all my weight onto her.

"General, do *you* yield?"

Warmth trickled down the right side of my face.

Maria was an amazing fighter, but Davon's moves had given me an advantage as well as my size. She was almost a foot taller than me, and it allowed me to dodge some of her attacks. Nevertheless, she had hit my temple, and I was bleeding a lot. I'd responded by striking her right cheek with a solid punch, causing blood to spurt from her mouth.

We fought as if we were on the battlefield.

My ribs still hurt from our fight two days ago when she knocked me down with a side kick, but as my body strengthened, so did my resilience.

Maria panted and hit the floor with her palm, which let everyone know she conceded victory.

This was the first time I had won against her. I smiled and stood, lending a hand to my friend.

Once up, she leaned close to my ear. "Good job. Today you beat me in every way. Davon would be proud."

Tears threatened, but I smiled as she raised my hand.

Cheers erupted all around the training center. From a corner, Aoki whooped, and Matt watched me with a huge smile.

Everyone scattered.

Maria hugged me. "I'm proud of you, Abi."

I grinned. "Thanks. That means a lot."

She took a step back and examined my temple. She winced. "Sorry about that. Better take care of it."

"I will. And you?"

Her mouth had smears of blood around it, and her jaw was swollen.

She shook her head, then touched her jaw. "This?" She waved dismissively. "Don't worry about it. I'll take care of it."

Maria high-fived Matt and Aoki as she walked by them on her way out. They exchanged a few words.

Matt's eyes gleamed as he approached. "That was amazing. Maria says you're a fast learner."

I patted his arm. "I have the best teachers."

He held a palm to his chest. "I knew this day would come. When you at last accepted that I was the best."

I hit his good shoulder playfully, and he chuckled.

He leaned toward Aoki, who threw his arm around him.

Heat radiated through my chest. Now that we were spending more time together, we'd become closer. They gave me the strength to move forward.

Matt brushed his hand over my temple, and I flinched. It burned.

"We need to stitch this up. I don't think Davon would approve of Maria's training methods." Matt winked at me. "He'll kill me if I don't deal with your wounds."

Back at the infirmary, as Matt fixed me up, I watched Rachel organize a medical cabinet. After last month's checkpoint attack, she had taken the role of lead nurse here at the base. I didn't think she'd go out there again. Not after losing Leon and being brutally beaten by two government soldiers.

"She's doing better, right?" I whispered as Matt threw away a bloody piece of gauze.

He shrugged. "I think so. At least she's trying to." His green eyes seemed devoid of their usual shine as he peered sideways at her. "We all have a lot to deal with."

I grabbed his hand. "Are you good?"

He sighed and shook his head. "Too much stuff going on and..."

I squeezed his hand. "Tell me."

"I'm worried about Davon." He put his hand on top of mine. "We need to get inside as soon as possible. Jordan gets angsty when things don't go as anticipated, and he was expecting you. He may be searching for Gabrielle Jones as we speak, and we don't want him to get suspicious. I'll talk to Connor."

I dulled my senses during training to ignore the emptiness that grew in my soul. Only three weeks had passed, but time moved so slowly that it seemed like months. We hadn't heard from him yet, and even though we knew he was alive, much of the mission depended on me. "I'll go with you."

He nodded and continued working on my wound. "Later, in the strategy meeting, we'll let Maria, Mark, and David know the details. Before we go, we need to lay the groundwork for our strategy to defend the bunkers and regain the city. We could be gone for a long time. They must be prepared."

I cringed as he sutured the wound even though I'd grown accustomed to the procedure.

Once finished, he grazed my right cheek, right over my scar.

I jerked my head back. "Sorry. I..." I rubbed my temple and flinched at the recently stitched wound. I didn't want him to think I was shallow, but I hated my scar. There was no way of hiding it, so it was a constant reminder of what happened out there. Of when we were attacked.

"Honey, it's only a scar. You're beautiful no matter what. And if it helps, it looks badass." He winked.

"It's not that. It reminds me of when I almost lost you."

That night we were caught by two NWG soldiers, and while the man holding me cut my skin, the other soldier held Matt at gunpoint, and I was almost sure I'd lose him. If it weren't for Davon coming in at the last moment, he wouldn't be here.

Matt's face flushed. "I...I didn't know you felt that way. That night I only saw red. I only thought of saving you. My life was of little importance at that point."

I swatted his left arm. "Your life is as important as mine. What about Aoki? What about your family?" I cupped his cheek. "She almost killed you that night, Matt."

"I never saw it that way. You shouldn't dwell on that memory. We're here. Alive. That's all that matters."

I nodded. "I try to move on. Believe me, I do. But the memories keep coming back, one after the other. It's like my mind can't move forward and make peace with them."

He touched the cut he just sutured. "We all have scars, Abi, and some are not just physical but are much deeper. To move forward, we need to accept them and how they've made us grow. Own them."

He clasped my shoulder. "You'll be all right."

Matt took a step back and put his hands on his hips. "Well, good as new! Next time please take it easier."

I smirked. "Feel free to tell Maria about it."

"Will do. I'll go check on her now."

Maria was too proud to come to the infirmary, so Matt always checked on her after.

I chuckled and rose from the gurney. "Okay, I'll wait here so we can go see Connor together. I'll help Rachel in the meantime."

I stood next to her and started unloading another box from the science and technology bunker. They supplied the communities with medicine and equipment.

"Hey!" Rachel glanced at my temple and lifted an eyebrow. "Another exciting training lesson?"

I shrugged. "You could say that."

Rachel grabbed a box of medications I passed her. "How's Maria?"

"Matt just went to treat her. You know how she is."

Rachel closed the cabinet she'd been organizing. "She's a tough one. Matt tells me you've improved. Will you be going out there soon?"

I leaned against the counter. "That's the plan. We need to have as many soldiers as possible ready to fight."

She looked down at her hands for a second. "Please be careful." Her eyes shone with unshed tears.

I brushed her arm. "Everything will be okay."

These past weeks, she'd been there to help me through my anxiety and loneliness. She confided that Leon was her partner not only in work, but that they'd been together for a couple of months when the attack happened.

After Davon left, she helped me get through the pain of losing him, putting aside her own. Today, as I hugged her, the roles were reversed. She trembled and sobbed.

"I'm sorry, Abi." She shook her head. "When will it end? I don't want to lose anyone else."

I squeezed her hands. "We *will* win this, Rachel. There's no doubt in my mind."

We both turned as the door opened.

Matt's eyes were huge. "We've just been summoned to command."

My heart stopped for a moment. It had to be Davon.

We ran through the halls to get to Connor's office.

Nina, with the help of some engineers, had installed more security features, including a biometric and fingerprint scanner for Connor. No one could enter his space without his say-so.

We waited by the door until he beeped us inside.

I reached his desk, taking a moment to catch my breath.

Connor held a letter. Sarah stood beside him.

I frowned. What was she doing here?

I ignored her and faced Connor. "What happened?"

Matt closed the door behind him, still panting from our run.

Connor handed me the letter. It was coded.

I turned toward Matt. He was teaching me to decrypt codes.

He came up beside me. "Go ahead. Let's see if you're ready."

A jumble of symbols and letters met my eyes, and as Matt had taught me, I started decoding. It was clear as day. The training over the last two weeks had worked.

Connor,

My infiltration into the city went as planned. My shoulder was reconstructed, and I'm well into full recovery. I moved to my place a week ago, and today is my first council meeting.

Father is anxious to meet Abi, so she needs to be sent in as soon as possible.

Please let me know if she made it okay and if Jimmy's alive.

I'll continue my mission as agreed.

—Davon

The pounding of my heart reached my throat, and I sagged against Matt. He held me.

I folded the letter, and my eyes flooded with tears.

He's safe.

All the anxiety from the last couple of weeks, all the fear and worry that had taken root deep inside me, eased.

Matt took my hands in his. "He made it."

Connor cleared his throat. "Please sit. We have much to discuss."

We did as asked.

"Now that the mission is underway, we need to be ready for what comes next. Last night we received news from our mole inside the prison. Davon has been visiting the Niles High-Security Prison daily and stays throughout the day, so my guess is that his position rests inside the facility. If this is true, we may be able to retrieve Deb sooner than expected, but we must give him time. I'll send him a reply to the prison and wait for him to make contact again."

Matt rested his palm on Connor's mahogany desk. "With all due respect, I think Abi and I need to move in. Jordan will get suspicious if he doesn't meet Gabrielle soon. Davon's covering for now, but knowing Jordan, he may be searching for her."

Sarah approached the desk. "But it's too early to—"

Connor lifted his hand.

She lowered her head.

Connor leaned forward, his face stern, capturing our full attention. A leader through and through. "I understand, but we need to secure the perimeter first. Government soldiers have been sighted eight miles in, still far from here, but we can't let them get any closer."

I shifted. "But..."

He sighed. "We need to make sure you can make it into the city."

I slumped back into my chair.

Connor placed a map on the desk and pushed it toward Matt. "Maria will take Abi as close to this area as possible. Since you're still recovering, your task is to help them set the strategy for this mission so they can lead the troops away by leaving false evidence of recent activity. It can be a note, a knife, the remnants of a fire, anything that will make them think they're getting closer. Southwest is our best option, as far as you can get them from here, being careful not to put the import, construction, and storage bunker in danger. Katherine and Seth already know of our plans and have a team guarding the perimeter."

Connor shifted his attention to me. "You'll leave tomorrow morning. I already briefed Maria. Go out armed, wear bulletproof vests, and do not engage unless attacked."

My nerves were on edge. It was the first time I'd be out there without Matt or Davon, but I trusted Maria. I had no doubt we'd succeed.

I nodded.

Matt and Connor stood and shook hands.

I followed suit.

"We'll get it done," Matt said.

"We'll meet in the afternoon again to make sure everything's in order and to go over the last details." Connor clasped my hand. "Consider this your first official assignment." His features softened. "Trust me, please. I'll send you in soon. I just want to make sure you can make it out and secure the area. Once that's done, you have the go to enter Electi."

I looked at Sarah.

She was silent, eyes fixed on me. She parted her lips, but no words came out.

I knew she was command's voice for the citizens, but this was a private issue.

My pulse thrummed beneath my skin. "Why is she here?"

Her attitude and beliefs toward Davon were dangerous, and she could threaten the mission if she spilled the intel we were sharing inside this room.

Connor closed his eyes. "She asked to be part of the mission."

"I don't trust her."

Sarah shifted in place. I doubted my sister could remain objective on this mission.

"Remember when Davon wanted to keep you out of the loop?" Connor asked.

My breath caught for a moment. I did recall the betrayal and despair of being pushed away.

"But this is different," I said, knowing deep inside it wasn't true.

"How is it different, Abi? Sarah is Deb's sister too. She has the same right as you to know how the rescue mission is going. She's family."

I touched my forehead, sensing the start of a headache. "I don't like it, but you're right." I crossed my arms and looked at her. "As long as you keep your opinions to yourself."

Sarah nodded, then averted her gaze.

I sighed and turned to Connor. "What about the spy?"

Connor pocketed his hands. "We recruited about a dozen citizens to work in the command center. The spy may be already inside as we speak.

All data coming in and out is being monitored as well as the browsing history and files on each computer, but until Davon accesses the files from the city database, we can only do so much."

An image of Richard's bruised neck and his lifeless body splayed on the floor flashed before my eyes. As long as that spy was with us, we were in grave danger.

With a nod, I followed Matt out.

Many new faces filled the command room, and one of them was probably the spy. I shivered at the thought that an assassin was here at this moment, planning their next assault.

"Abi!" Maria stood between Tammy and a man in his forties.

He rubbed his freshly groomed goatee as he studied the computer before him. He had dark skin, deep-brown eyes, and a sharp jawline. Very handsome.

There was something about him, some kind of familiarity. Like I had met him before.

"Hey, girls!" I glanced at Tammy. "I didn't know they moved you here."

Tammy smiled. "I decided to stay behind, and since the children are no longer here, I needed a new job."

Maria brushed Tammy's shoulder and smiled down at her. "She's in charge of scheduling the interviews for the citizens." She gestured to the man on her left. "This is Mr. Jackson. He's in charge of keeping track of anybody who enters or leaves the bunker."

Mr. Jackson... Oh. The nighttime professor.

He put his glasses on the desk and stood. He straightened his dark-blue suit, then extended his hand toward me.

I took it in a firm grip. "Mr. Jackson, I'm Abi. I've heard a lot about you. I'm glad to finally meet you."

He gave me a soft smile that pulled at my heart, but I couldn't put my finger on why.

"I hope all was good. And please call me Abraham." He winked at me.

A heavy weight crushed my heart, causing it to falter for a beat.

Abraham Jackson?

Hot tears threatened to leave my eyes. Abraham's dark eyes were the same as his. And his smile was as gentle as his son's.

My hands trembled.

Could this really be his father?

His other hand enveloped mine. "Are you all right?"

I swallowed and grinned back. "All good. Are you still teaching the night classes to adults?"

He shook his head. "I sometimes do my lectures, but since everyone's dealing with the emergency, I decided to help in any way I could." He sat and put on his glasses. "Protecting the bunker against any attack or government plot is our priority now. We all knew it would come to this someday."

I nodded and glanced at Maria and Tammy. "I'll see you later."

"See you." Maria waved goodbye.

I needed some air. "Sure."

Mr. Jackson, Abraham, waved goodbye and continued his work.

I walked over to Matt, who waited for me by the door.

"Everything okay?" he asked as we exited the room.

"Yeah, it's just... Do you know anything about Mr. Jackson?"

"Not much. Just that they found him lost in the forest about a year ago, looking for a family member. I think it was his son who ran away, but I'm not sure. The guy's a genius. I've been to some of his classes. He was a history teacher in Promissa."

Lightheadedness assaulted me. My feet faltered, and Matt caught me just before I slumped down.

"Are you okay?"

"I need to sit." I couldn't breathe.

Matt helped me to the infirmary, and we sat on a bench.

He stroked my back. "Just breathe."

I gripped my chest.

His green eyes were creased and centered on me. "What happened just now?"

I took a long, deep breath, settling my heart. "Mr. Jackson is Jacob's father."

Matt widened his eyes.

I couldn't hold back the tears anymore. "How do I tell him?" I gripped Matt's hands. "How do I tell him Jacob was murdered? That I left him there in that tunnel? Alone."

Matt took me in his arms, holding my head against his shoulder, and I crumbled.

All the memories from two years ago flooded back, and I was drowning.

Matt held me close. "I'm so sorry."

His shirt was wet by the time I stopped crying.

He wiped away my tears and cupped my cheek. "Are you sure it's him?"

I nodded. "He needs to know. Otherwise, he'll wait for him forever."

Matt took my hands. "When you're ready to talk to him, I can go with you so you're not alone."

I shook my head. "I need to do this alone, but I need time."

He gave me a comforting smile. "If you change your mind and need a helping hand, let me know. You're my sister, and that's what family is for."

I'd talk to Jacob's father before I left for Electi. He had a right to know, to make peace with his son's death.

We stayed there for a long time until I had my control back.

I squeezed Matt's hand. "Thank you."

Davon was the only one who knew all the shit I'd been through, the one I talked to when despair took control of my mind. And now, without him, I was lost.

A month ago, Matt told me I suffered from anxiety. He had medications to help me, but I didn't want them. I needed to find a way to work through it, or I'd never be able to go out there. He told me I should get therapy, but every time I decided to go, I froze by the door, too terrified to talk to anyone about it. After everything Sarah went through, I didn't trust therapists. They wouldn't understand all the shit I dealt with.

Aoki and I meditated almost daily and did breathing exercises for when I was on the verge of an attack. He was a huge help.

Matt and Aoki could maybe help even more, but I didn't want to burden them.

Matt and I walked in silence toward hall A, and he opened his apartment.

Aoki rested on the sofa with his feet up and a washcloth on his head.

Shirokuro, their black-and-white cat, cuddled beside him.

Matt gave Aoki a swift kiss. "Feeling better?"

Aoki shook his head.

"I'll get you more meds." Matt went into the kitchen.

I put my problems aside and focused on my friend. "Hey, what's wrong?" I sat on the coffee table.

"It's one of my migraines." His eyes were red rimmed, but he smiled, nonetheless.

Matt sat next to him, and Shirokuro moved to my lap, purring.

Aoki took his meds.

"Come here." Matt pulled him onto his lap and massaged his temples.

Aoki closed his eyes. "Any news?"

"Davon reached out. He's all right!" I said.

Aoki sat up in surprise. "Really?"

I grinned.

"I'm so glad." He let out a long exhale. "We should celebrate but this headache."

"Having you both here to share this moment with me is all I need. Now rest and let your husband take care of you."

He smiled warmly and slumped back into Matt's lap as I detailed the contents of the letter and Matt explained about tomorrow's mission.

Aoki just listened, taking it all in.

Once Matt finished, Aoki regarded me with a pained look. "Please be careful out there."

I nodded. "I will."

God. I'd miss him terribly once we left for Electi.

Matt combed Aoki's long dark hair gently with his fingers.

It wrenched my heart to know they would be separated so soon after their reunion. "Matt, can't Aoki come with us when we leave for Electi?"

Matt widened his eyes, and his hand stilled.

They looked at each other, sharing unsaid words.

Aoki squeezed Matt's hand.

Matt threaded his fingers through Aoki's. "We've talked about it, but Aoki prefers to stay here."

Aoki turned his head slightly to look at me. "I don't want to leave Mark, and what about the community? There's no better cook than me." He winked.

I bit my lip. "But what will you do when we leave for Electi?"

He gazed at Matt. "Trust that he'll come back to me safe."

Matt smiled and kissed him. "No force can keep me away from you."

I couldn't help but miss Davon, but I also wondered how long it would be until I saw the others again once we left—that is, if I ever made it back.

Chapter 8

Abi

December 1, 2213

The room was empty, a ruffled bed and a discarded duffel bag the only sign that anyone resided in it. David arrived about a month ago, but you would expect at least a picture or something.

I'd been training with him for the past few weeks, and we talked about random stuff, but I still hadn't been able to break through the awkwardness from that conversation weeks ago.

He peered out after I entered. "Where are the others?"

"They're coming soon. We were with Connor, discussing our mission tomorrow. They stayed since they had to discuss some stuff about the security of the bunkers."

The meeting had been long and tedious. My eyes hurt from the lack of sleep, but with everything going on, I couldn't rest.

I gestured to his black sofa. "Can I?"

"Sure, go ahead." He went to his counter, where a small metal cask rested. He served himself some hazy yellowish liquid, then gulped it down and sighed.

My mouth watered. "What's that?"

He wiped the froth from his mouth. "This? It's beer. Haven't you had any before?"

I shook my head. I'd heard about it but never tried it.

He widened his eyes. "You haven't? This is my own brew. A hazy IPA. I prepare it right here, hence this." He opened a cabinet beneath his counter to show me some buckets and tubes. "Michael from science and Steven from farming helped me get everything I needed for a reasonable price." He winked at me. "A keg a month for each. I always have some at home. Do you want one?"

I shrugged. "I guess." It would be a good reprieve from all the pressure I'd been feeling lately.

"Sure." His smile reached his eyes.

I hadn't seen him like this before, so relaxed. He grabbed a steel mug and poured some for me.

"Salud. For moments like this." He clinked his mug against mine and sat beside me.

The bitter liquid refreshed my throat. It was a different kind of taste but one I could get used to.

"David?"

"Yeah?"

"Can we talk?" My voice was but a murmur.

He gave me a quizzical look. "Sure. About?"

I bent forward, holding the mug between my knees. "It's something that's been bothering me since our first training together. Something I can't just ignore."

He furrowed his brow.

"I can't stop thinking about what you said a couple of weeks ago. That no one cared. That you should have died."

He raised his hand and shook his head. "I don't want to talk about it." He put his mug on the table. "I get that you want to help me, but you don't understand."

"I do!"

"How can you?" he yelled, his face inches from mine.

I jumped back.

He widened his eyes. "Fuck!" He stood and raked his hair back. "I'm sorry. It's just...you don't know me."

He started pacing, and I was at a loss for words.

He put his palms on the table, his back to me. "I lost everyone I cared for." He turned, leaning back on the table. His hazel eyes appeared haunted.

"What happened?" I asked.

He closed his eyes. "When Davon found me six years ago, I was almost dead, clutching to my parents' rotting bodies."

Bile rose to my mouth at the image. "How old were you?"

He opened his eyes. They were filled with tears. "I was fifteen."

I wanted to reach for him, to ease some of his suffering.

I stood, leaving my beer mug next to his. He was at least a foot taller than me, but at that moment, he appeared small. Broken.

I touched his arm.

His eyes clouded, as if he were lost in a different time and place. "Dad injured his back while working on the construction of the train tracks, and Mom had dementia. Because they were incapacitated, the government moved us to the northern slums. We received the bare minimum, and they gave their food to me. I wanted to deny them, but I was so hungry."

He hung his head, and his tears finally reached the floor. "My father slowly disappeared until one day, he didn't wake up. He hadn't eaten for weeks, same as Mom. I didn't have the strength to move him, so I left him on the bed, 'sleeping' next to Mom. I tried to get help, but the patrols beat me up and told me to stop bothering them. A few days passed, and my mother followed him. My limbs wouldn't sustain me anymore, so I stayed on the floor, holding Mom's hand. Waiting to follow them both."

He collapsed into me and cried, holding me tight. His weight crushed me as he trembled in my arms, but I held on.

"I have no one. I'm all alone." He wept like a child and clutched me until his tears dried.

To suffer so much loss and survive was unimaginable. The anguish of knowing there was no one left for you in the world, that you'd lost all your family, must have been unbearable.

Even though I'd lost hope many times, I always envisioned myself finding Deb or Sarah. Knowing they were out there. Somewhere.

But he was wrong about one thing, I did understand feeling lost. I knew what it was to be alone. To lose all hope after watching your loved ones die. It was true—what he went through was different, but we'd both suffered.

"I'm so sorry, David."

He took a step back and wiped away his tears. "I've never told anyone about it. Not even Davon."

"Can we sit?" I asked.

He nodded and followed me to the sofa.

I took a deep breath. "I understand what it's like to lose hope. To see everything around you turn dark. I just want you to know that I'm here for you."

He sighed. "Thank you. Those last months out there have plagued me for years. To finally say it out loud somehow eased some of the pain."

I took his hands. "You're not alone anymore."

He nodded. "I know. It's just...sometimes I wish I died during the attacks instead of the others. Just to forget all that happened. To erase those dark memories."

"But you have people who care for you here."

He glanced at me. The depths of his eyes carried so much pain.

Did my eyes look the same when Davon found me? Was David troubled by nightmares like I was?

"I shouldn't have burdened you with my memories." His voice was but a whisper.

"We all have a story of loss. One of terror and agony. Never apologize for it. We need to use it to become stronger so others don't suffer like we did."

My mouth turned sour at the memory of that man. Of his body pressed against mine and the metallic taste of his blood.

I shivered.

"I'm also here for you if you need to talk," he said.

His warmth pulled at me.

Could I talk to him? Only Davon knew of that horrible day.

I looked at him. His gaze was soft and steady. It gave me a sense of comfort, like Deb's.

I squeezed his hands. "Out there, many people were taken away, but I held on to hope and met two souls who welcomed me into their family. I lost them both."

He moved his thumb over my hand languidly. "Tell me more."

"After that, I lost myself. It was like watching a movie play in front of my eyes. I went on but was trapped in an unending loop of sorrow. I didn't want to suffer anymore, so I stayed alone."

I gripped his hands as the vivid memory of my attack came back as clear as the day it happened. "One day, I was very weak, rummaging around, when a government officer found me."

David went still. There was a shift in the room. A tension that wasn't there before. His arm muscles twitched.

"Out there, power and intimidation are weapons. Many officers abuse their rank and do the unthinkable." I glanced toward the coffee table, unable to confront his stare. "I killed him." I pressed my eyes closed.

"Abi, what did he do to you?" His voice was terse.

Why I decided to trust David escaped me. Maybe it was because I knew he'd understand. That he'd suffered as I did.

I opened my eyes. "He raped me."

David dropped his gaze. He clenched his jaw and breathed deep and hard. After a few long minutes, he closed the space between us.

Even though I pushed through the trauma and Davon helped me move on, reliving the events ravaged my soul.

When my parents died, I was in denial for a long time, and Connor was the one who helped me through it.

Today, as David embraced me, the pressure inside me eased. Maybe I should have shared it with someone else a long time ago. Someone I could talk to without feeling ashamed. Someone who could understand me.

He cradled the back of my neck. "You're safe now. You killed him, and he'll never harm you again."

We stayed like that until we both calmed.

I shook my head. "I'm sorry. You were talking about your past, and I just blurted out mine."

"Don't say that." He brushed my arm. "You can always talk to me, you know. Whenever you need."

"Thank you."

David studied me and raised an eyebrow, tipping his head slightly to the side. "Are you better now?"

I nodded. "You're the only person I've talked to about it besides Davon."

"I'm glad you did." He passed me my beer and gripped his mug. "We have to do something. We can't let them keep pushing us down."

I raised my beer. "So that no one else suffers by their hand. For us destroying their regime once and for all."

He clinked his mug against mine. "We'll crush them."

We drank and talked for about half an hour. We were already on our second beer when someone opened the door.

Matt entered, followed by Maria and Mark.

Matt opened his mouth in protest. "Hey. That's not fair. You started the meeting without us."

David stood and grasped Matt's hand in a strong hold, then Mark's. He gave Maria a hug. "Welcome to my humble abode. Would you like some of Dave's Rebel Brew?"

Maria nudged his shoulder. "As if you need to ask."

David chuckled.

Matt went with Mark to the kitchen to help.

After each took a mug, Maria sat beside me, and the three guys sat at the table.

"As much as I'd like to just sit here and drink beer with you guys, we need to start." Matt took out a notebook and a pencil. "First and only point on the agenda, how can we take our city back from these assholes?"

David massaged his brow. "It's going to be hell out there. We don't have the numbers."

Matt rested his elbows on his knees. "That's exactly why I asked you to join us. As you said, we don't have the numbers, but with your sniper skills, if we build a team and train them, we may have an advantage."

David exhaled. "It'll take time to get a team ready."

"But can it be done?" Matt asked.

David eyed Mark. "Maybe you can help me. You have mad skills."

Mark chuckled. "How can I refuse when you say it like that?"

Maria sat forward. "Perfect. Anything else?"

"I want Abi on the team," David said, his eyes set on me.

Matt frowned. "Really? Abi?"

I put my beer down and crossed my arms. "What do you mean? I know you're busy with all that's happening, but I've gotten better."

Matt widened his eyes. "I didn't mean it like that. It's just...you're no good with guns, and I thought..."

"Okay. I understand, but with the sniper rifle, it's different."

David was an exceptional teacher. I wanted to be part of his team.

David took a gulp of his beer. "She's ready, Matt. You should come see her. I like her spirit. I think having her on the team will be beneficial to all. She survived out there a long time and knows the city well. Also, she's strong."

Matt relaxed back. "Okay. I'll trust you on it."

Maria finished her beer and set the mug down. "The plan is to hide the team around the city. Once every sniper is in place, our main forces will approach from different areas. We're working on finding a way to enter. We need to coordinate our attack so the NWG army will think our numbers are higher than they truly are. This confusion will make them disperse throughout the city. If they're disorganized, we may have a chance."

David interlaced his fingers. "Sounds great when you say it, but will it be enough?" He looked up. "Our best bet would be to find those rebel factions that have been acting around the city. With them, we can create a good offense. They know the city better than us."

"True," Matt said. "That's why our spies are already searching for them both in the city and inside the facilities. If we get them to help us, it could turn the tide in our favor."

David nodded. "It might give us a fighting chance. But what about the NWG main force, the one inside Electi? Once we enter the city, I'm sure General Lavigne will deploy them, and then we'll be fucked."

"That will depend on what we achieve once we're inside," Matt said.

David furrowed his brow. "I don't understand."

"We're not sure when we're leaving, but Abi and I will go into Electi undercover. Our main purpose is to get powerful allies inside."

David clenched his hands. "What? You're letting Abi go inside again? And into Electi? I get you going in. You're an elite after all. But why her?"

I scowled. What the hell did he mean by letting me go?

Matt held up a hand. "She was ready to go in with Davon on his mission. It just didn't go as planned."

My mouth dropped open as Matt revealed Davon's mission.

David bent forward. "What are you talking about?"

Matt cleared his throat. "What I'm about to tell you is strictly confidential. Davon's arrest and his escape were all part of a plan. There's a spy inside the bunker. A murderer. They used Davon's position to get the intel out of the bunker and into the city. Davon took the blame so he could infiltrate Electi and search for answers. Abi was going with him."

David glanced at Maria. "Did you know about this?"

"I was informed after I became general."

He looked at Mark. "And you?"

Mark nodded.

"So it was all planned?" David asked. "Is the spy still inside?"

"Yes," Matt said.

David darted his eyes from Matt to me, his gaze pleading. "You're sure about going out there?"

I clasped my hands together. "I am. There's no other way. We need to gather forces from inside."

"But aren't you afraid? I get that you want to fight, but going undercover is on another level. If you're found out, God knows what they'll do to you."

I remembered the night I met Jacob and his words when I asked him about being scared. "I'm terrified, but it won't keep me from fighting back. We can't continue living like this."

David looked me straight in the eyes and nodded. His eyes gleamed for a second before he set them on Matt. "What's the plan?"

The meeting continued, and about thirty minutes later, someone knocked.

"I'll get it." I took my beer and opened the door.

My mug clanked against the floor, and beer splashed over my boots.

I took a step back as his light-blue eyes met mine.

So many contradicting emotions hit me at once.

He looked well if you ignored the crutch and his pale skin.

This was my first love, my best friend, and the man who almost killed Davon.

Jimmy tucked his dirty-blond hair behind his ear. "Abi?"

I clenched my teeth and fisted my hands to my sides. "What are you doing here?"

His hand brushed mine, and I jerked away.

"Who is it?" Matt yelled.

Jimmy's gaze was pleading. "Please hear me out."

Matt came to my side. "What the hell are you doing here, Jimmy?"

Jimmy lowered his head. "Connor sent me."

Mark approached and clutched Jimmy's shoulder. "I'm sorry. I forgot to tell you about this, but Connor wants him in our meetings. He says since he knows the runners and the area, his presence is essential."

Matt humphed. "I'm not convinced about having him here, but if it's an order from Connor, I'll accept it."

Mark and Jimmy passed by us.

I faced Matt. "This is wrong."

Matt nodded. "I think so too, but Connor is our general. If he says he's needed, we must listen. We're going to have to learn to work together."

"I'm not sure I can do that." With one last glance inside, I turned my back on Matt and left.

Chapter 9

Abi

December 2, 2213

Sleep escaped me for half the night. Images of Jacob's lifeless body lingered in my dreams. Maybe after I talked to Mr. Jackson, I'd feel better. But when?

A thump on the door stopped my wandering thoughts. "Come in!" I yelled as I put my combat boots on.

"Hey." David came in. "Wow, I never once entered Davon's apartment." He glanced at the weapons and books. "He has quite a collection."

After the meeting, I went with David to the dining hall and told him about Davon and me. He'd heard about it but still couldn't believe I'd softened the man. Those were his exact words.

"Hey, what are you doing here?" I finished tying my boots and went to the chest at the end of the bed.

He put a bag on the table. "Can't a guy bring a friend some breakfast?" He watched as I opened the chest. "Ready for the mission?"

"Just finishing up." I put Paul's hunting knife in the rucksack and closed it, then secured my pocket khukuri and my trench knife on Jacob's leather belt. I closed my eyes and exhaled. I glanced up.

David took out two cups of coffee and two croissants from the bag.

My mouth watered.

I sat with him. "Thanks. I thought you were Matt when you knocked. He's usually the one who brings breakfast over."

"He was at the mess hall. I asked about the mission, and he told me you and Maria were leaving soon. I told him I was coming to wish you luck, and he said to bring you breakfast. He appeared a bit flustered and said he had to take care of something. So here I am." He opened his hands in a comical gesture.

I furrowed my brow. "Do you know what he was talking about?"

He shrugged. "No idea."

I scowled.

David eyed my untouched croissant. "Aren't you going to eat that?"

I pushed it toward him. "You can have it."

He stopped it midway. "Have you been eating? Or is sleeping the problem?"

I withdrew my hand. "I don't know what you're talking about."

Was it that obvious?

"You look tired. Your eyes..." He lowered his voice. "I know how it is, Abi. Do you have nightmares? Insomnia?"

I touched the golden heart on my wrist and closed my eyes. "Everything's fucked up."

David just sat there quietly.

I opened my eyes. "I'm not sleeping." There, I said it. As much as I dared to hope everything would be all right, it wasn't.

He reached over to me but stopped before our hands touched. "How can I help?"

"I can deal with it. Been dealing with it for three years."

David crossed his arms and rested back in his chair. "You know, I'm stubborn as hell just like you, and I know exactly what you're doing."

"Yeah?" I raised my eyebrows. "What is it that I'm doing?"

"You're keeping everything to yourself because you don't want to trouble anyone with your problems, and you prefer to keep it all inside rather than to share it. But in the end, it will backfire. Someone told me yesterday that everyone needs a helping hand."

"I don't need help. All right?" I bit into my croissant, ignoring him. I could feel his eyes sinking into me.

"Abi?"

I swallowed hard and returned my gaze to him.

"Tell me what's happening."

I exhaled. "If you promise to take back what you said about me being stubborn."

"But you are!" He snickered. "Okay, I'll think about it. But only if you tell me."

After yesterday, telling David about my nightmares shouldn't have scared me this much, but I couldn't stop my belly from knotting over itself.

I rubbed my eyes hard. *Here goes.*

"You know I've been through a lot, and I keep reliving the memories since Davon left. His presence somehow soothed me, but now that he's gone, I don't know how to handle it."

David leaned forward. "Are they nightmares?"

"Why is that of importance?"

He exhaled hard and raised an eyebrow. "Just tell me." His voice was deep.

I sighed. "Every night I wake up drenched in sweat after watching my loved ones die again and again. Sometimes it's my parents, sometimes my friends, other times Davon and my family here. Training helps get my mind off it, but they won't stop."

He held his chin. "Have you tried music?"

I glanced down at my coffee. "I've tried meditation. Aoki showed me some techniques."

David chuckled. "The master of all Zen and tranquility. Has it helped?"

"A little." I shrugged. "Not much."

David sat back. "Try music. Some soft jazz or mellow instrumental."

Would that really work?

"Have you tried it?"

He nodded. "It helps soothe my mind." He brushed my hand lightly. "Promise me you'll try it."

I could program my MP3 so my speaker would play soothing jazz all night. "Sure." I took a bite of my croissant.

He cleared his throat. "Are you sure you're ready to go out there?"

I stared at him. "I am."

His gaze was dead set on me. "Out there, it's life or death. You need to be present."

"I am. Trust me." I didn't look away. I was ready, and I would deal with my issues one way or another.

He nodded and went back to eating. "I wish I could go with you."

I was sure he was a hell of a fighter. He'd trained with Connor and was a force to be reckoned with, according to Matt. "You need to get the team ready. I'll be all right. Don't worry."

We ate in silence until the doorknob rattled.

Matt entered. "Ready?" His voice was giddy.

I narrowed my eyes. Something was up.

Matt wore his camouflage clothes like me, his two guns secured by his sides.

He walked toward David and patted his back. "Hey, man. Thanks for covering."

I stood. "Covering? Why are you dressed like that?"

David left his chair. "I have somewhere to be."

I put my hands on my hips. "What the hell is happening?"

Matt grinned.

David pointed his thumb at him. "He told me to do it, and he's our lieutenant general, so I couldn't deny him."

"That's bullshit."

David chuckled and hugged me. "Don't be too hard on him. And please be careful out there."

I hugged him back. "Thanks."

David took his coffee and left.

"Explain," I said.

Matt put his rucksack on the floor and sat at the table. "I'm coming with you."

My heart raced. "But your arm!"

He waved dismissively. "I'm going directly to import and will wait for you there. On the way, I'll check if the coast is clear for you two."

"You don't have to go. What if something happens out there?" I couldn't bear it if anything happened to Matt.

What if he encountered soldiers out there and was all alone? What if they shot him like last time?

He tilted his head. "I'll be okay. I talked to Connor about it. I've been training and can shoot with my good arm. If I stay stuck here for another day, I'll go crazy." He ate the piece of croissant that David left.

I sat opposite him. "Promise me you'll be careful."

"I will." He checked his rucksack and took out a gun. He pushed it across the table with its leather holster.

I inspected the pistol. It was a semiautomatic Glock 19, the same I'd practiced with during my training with Matt and Davon when we were out there.

"It's yours," Matt said.

I wrinkled my brow. "Are you sure?"

"Yes, you need protection, and you already proved yourself when you saved Davon out there. I know you prefer blades, but guns are better when it's a life-or-death situation."

"Take this." He passed me two magazines.

I loaded the gun and hooked it to my belt, then put the extra magazine in my pocket. "Thank you."

I sipped my coffee, letting its warmth soothe me. "How does Aoki feel about this?"

"He understands I need to help." He fiddled with his silver wedding band. "I can't just sit here and do nothing. Every minute that passes, they could be getting closer."

I bit my lip. *Please let him be safe.* "Did Connor brief you?"

"He did." He finished the croissant.

Connor found a good spot southwest of Janus Peak to lead the government soldiers away. Once there, we'd get the evidence planted. Burnt wood from a campfire, a cache with weapons and medications, and footprints in a snowy area leading to the west.

Once that was done, we'd go five miles southeast and shoot a couple of rounds. For the plan to work, the NWG soldiers had to follow us toward the area we'd prepared and lose us.

Seth and Katherine were informed of our mission, being the bunker farthest to the west from our main base. Seth oversaw defense and had soldiers stationed around the area with sufficient firearms for a counterattack if needed. As for Katherine, she'd stay in the bunker in case an evacuation was needed.

I hoped she finally realized that her relationship with Davon was over. She treated me as if I were nothing and was all over him the last time we met. He made it clear that he was with me, but she didn't take it well.

Having to see her again had me on edge, but as Matt said, we had to work together, and that was it.

"About yesterday." Matt interrupted my thoughts.

I shifted in my seat. I didn't think I'd be able to work with Jimmy. How could I work with someone I didn't trust?

"I talked to Connor. He wants us to move on. He said Jimmy will be working with us whether we want it or not."

I exhaled hard. "What reason did he give you?"

Matt slumped back. "Something about him knowing much more about the routes than we do. He says we need his knowledge and that runners listen to him."

I stiffened. "But isn't Mark supposed to be doing that?"

Matt shook his head. "Mark's doing the best he can, but he just started."

I tapped my foot violently. "I need more time."

Matt left his seat and crouched beside me. "Me too, but we don't have that advantage. We need to trust Connor's judgment. Please. Work with us."

I closed my eyes. "Okay."

Maria, Matt, and I were out by seven. It was cold, and snow began to fall in the forest. Nevertheless, visibility was good, so we were more than halfway through by ten in the morning.

Our boots crunched across the white bed that had started to cover the ground. The dark green of the pine trees speckled in white and the deep crimson and orange of the dogwood leaves made the forest look like a beautiful art palette. The maple trees had begun to lose their leaves, starting their long journey toward spring.

By one in the afternoon, our fire was built, and meat and potatoes were cooked. Based on the runners' intel, the government soldiers were more than ten miles away.

"These potatoes are heaven right now. Fifteen miles is not a walk in the park." My traitorous nerves were getting to me as time closed in on us. We didn't know what to expect or how many soldiers were in the group.

Matt chuckled as he munched on some meat. "For you, all food is good, honey. You're always hungry. That's how I know when to worry." He offered me some meat, and I took it.

We ate in silence and had our fill, uncertain of how long the rest of the day would be. We left some food as evidence, then prepared the cache.

Matt stood, ready to continue his journey toward import. "I'll leave footprints to the west in different areas and break some branches on the way for the trackers. You two, put out the fire, and start going east to meet the patrol."

He squeezed my arm. "Be careful out there. I'll see you soon." He turned to Maria. "We don't know how many are out there. Try not to engage, and run once they sense your presence."

Maria nodded and glanced at me. "Ready for showtime?"

I touched my khukuri. "Ready."

In a couple of hours, we'd be running for our lives.

It was midafternoon when we heard movement. I followed Maria behind a tree.

My breath hitched. More than a dozen armed soldiers stood about fifty feet away.

This is it.

Maria aimed her gun toward the sky and shot twice.

A second of silence passed before chaos erupted. We ran as fast as possible as they started their hunt. The ringing of gunshots and shouts seemed too close, and I glanced back.

It can't be.

I stumbled and fell. A sharp pain sliced across my shoulder as I hit a boulder on the ground. Still, I had to look again.

My entire world stopped.

He was here.

Davon took a step forward. He widened his eyes. The soldier at his side aimed his gun at me.

"Run," he mouthed, then fired a wide shot that split the man's focus.

The soldier's bullet narrowly missed us as it wheezed to the left.

I froze, taking Davon in.

Unspoken words filled the space between us as Davon's eyes centered on me.

He mouthed, "Go."

Someone grabbed my arm and pulled me up. Coming out of my haze, I followed Maria.

Tears slipped down my face. My lungs burned, and my chest hurt as the distance grew between us.

The mission was to lead them as far as possible and into the false cache, so we ran for more than an hour.

The soldiers kept their pursuit. Shots kept ringing through the forest as we put more distance between us.

We hid behind a boulder about fifty feet north of the burnt firewood we'd left behind.

Soldiers spread throughout the area, their footsteps coming closer.

"Lavigne!"

My heart pounded in response to Davon's voice and the name he called out.

Maria held my hand.

"There are some footprints and broken branches this way!" Davon shouted.

The soldiers started moving toward him.

I scanned the area. Davon stood about twenty feet west of us next to a tall, imposing man. As opposed to the white uniform the rest of their militia wore, his black double-breasted leather jacket stood above the rest. Its black epaulets carried the symbol of the New World Government, a coiled silver snake with a crown above its head. Silver chains draped down his sleeves.

His voice boomed. "Search west. Be ready to shoot at first sight. Do not aim to kill. We need them alive."

Soldiers stood at attention. "Yes, sir," they said in unison.

Davon glanced our way as if sensing my presence. Our eyes met. His lips parted.

I rubbed my palm against my heart, and a wistful smile spread across his face. We'd be together soon, but this wasn't the time.

He turned around.

Maria tugged at me. "We should go."

I nodded.

We walked north and reached Seth's scouts by nightfall. They guided us to the bunker. Matt waited for us.

I let all the emotion from the encounter flow out and threw myself into his arms.

He cradled my head. "Are you okay?"

"I saw him." Seeing Davon gave me solace, but having to turn away from him broke my heart into pieces again.

"Davon was out there." Maria's voice was no more than a whisper.

Matt laid his good arm across my back. "Come on."

Maria went ahead of us. As we walked toward the bunker's entrance, the silence of the forest engulfed me. I closed my eyes briefly and saw his face. He was alive and well.

I looked up and thanked the heavens.

My legs moved automatically, almost as if I was just a spectator, but Matt's warmth brought me back to the present.

I'd see him again soon. Matt and I would go into Electi, and we'd be together again.

Chapter 10

Abi

December 2, 2213

J ust as the entrance to import came into view, Seth was there to welcome us. He smiled, but when our eyes met, he creased his brow.

He said something to the soldiers guarding the entrance and jogged toward us. "Are you okay?"

Matt squeezed my shoulder. "We need privacy. Where can we go?"

"Follow me." Seth led us inside and through a hallway that looked just like the ones in the peak.

My vision blurred as I entered the room and crouched on the floor. My chest hurt like a ton of lead pressed down on me. I closed my eyes and breathed like Aoki had taught me.

Matt squatted in front of me. "Are you better now?"

I opened my eyes. "Yes."

Seth moved to his side. "What happened out there?"

Matt glanced at him. "Please don't tell anyone about this. Can you give us a minute?"

Seth nodded. "This is my room. You're safe here. Please let me know as soon as you're ready for the briefing."

Maria sat in a chair in the opposite corner. Elbows on knees, hands interlaced and covering half her face, she watched us.

When Seth left, Matt pulled me into a tight hug. "Oh, hon. I'm so sorry."

He turned to Maria. "What happened out there?"

"After I fired a few rounds, I realized we weren't as far out as we had thought. We ran, but Abi stumbled and fell. When I was about to help her up, I noticed a soldier had her in his sights. I spotted Davon at that point. He fired near the soldier, breaking his focus and causing the bullet to miss us."

Matt cocked his head and peered at me before returning his attention to Maria. "Anything else?"

Maria relaxed, her back against the chair. "We managed to flee. He led them west. General Lavigne was by his side."

"Fuck. That's not good." Matt cupped my cheek. "We'll get to him soon."

"I know. I'm okay now." I stood.

Matt followed. He, like Davon, was one of my anchors and always managed to get me back no matter how far gone I was.

He eyed Maria. "As for our safety, I'm not sure we'll survive his wrath once he confronts us for being out there. For which I will quickly direct him to Connor and protect my existence."

I chuckled softly.

"That's my girl. You have us now. Out on the outskirts, we almost lost you. We can't go through it all over again. You're stronger than you think."

"I know. Thank you," I muttered with my head down.

He lifted my chin. "Trust me. Trust him."

I nodded. "I'm sorry I lost it."

"Don't be. Now, are you ready to get out there and see your favorite person in the whole wide world?" He grinned.

Matt knew about Katherine. He claimed he'd never understood how Davon had been with her for such a long time. He couldn't stand her either.

I needed to brief her and Seth about what happened.

Was I ready to talk to her? No.

Was I going to do so, nevertheless? Yes.

I would do nothing less for Davon. We needed their help, so I would swallow my pride and work with her.

"I'm ready when you are," I said.

"Excellent. Now let's get this over with so we can get back home as soon as possible. I'm relieved Davon is out there. He'll keep them off our tail so we can focus on our mission."

When we entered the office, Katherine was doubled over her desk, studying a map with Seth.

She leaned back and curled her lips. "Matt, Maria, Abigail. Welcome. We were discussing the safest way back to Janus Peak but needed you to confirm if the mission was a success." Her eyes were cold, but she smiled, her tone soft and welcoming.

She looked at Maria. Her eyes never met mine.

I gripped Maria's arm and stepped forward. I'd be the one to explain. "The mission was a success. A dozen guards were moving north when we intercepted them. They hunted us for about an hour, but we made it to the rendezvous and escaped in time."

Katherine tensed and cast a questioning look at me. "Did you see them follow the false trail?"

"They followed it. They had a tracker with them who guided them west. They must be about five miles off by now."

It would be counterproductive to announce Davon's presence at this point. Maintaining the belief that he was a traitor was a safer course of action. Connor had no idea if the spy was connected to other councilmembers. Therefore, we had to proceed cautiously.

Seth stepped away from the desk. "I'll get a team ready to continue throwing them off the trail. If what the news says about Davon is true, he's already recovered from Jimmy's shot. They could already know our location." He furrowed his brow. "What I don't get is why the forest isn't swarming with soldiers already. There should be more."

The thrumming inside my veins eased at this. I wanted the community to see the truth for themselves.

"I still don't believe Davon is a traitor. There's something off," Katherine said.

I moved toward her. "I know he's innocent. He'd never betray the rebellion. But until we know what's going on, we need to keep our guard up."

She smiled subtly and offered me a slight nod.

"Whatever the situation is, we follow Connor's orders, no questions asked," Matt said.

"Understood," Katherine said. "Stay the night. You must be tired. Tomorrow, before the sun rises, go back to Connor. A group of soldiers is monitoring the area to keep it safe. Seth and his troops will create outposts in the west to monitor the government's soldiers."

"Thank you," Matt said.

Seth urged us to follow him out.

We walked in silence.

Matt and Maria entered our room before me.

As I was about to enter, Seth touched my arm. "Are you better? What happened out there?"

I covered his hand with mine. "I'm fine. Just the nerves and the drop of adrenaline. Thank you for what you did for us."

"Anything for you, my friend. I'm sorry about Davon. It must be hard for you, but I'll be keeping to the facts. We need to protect our people and be cautious. I hope you understand."

I clutched his hand. "I do. Don't worry about it."

"Have a good night. I'll be back before the sun rises."

December 3, 2213

By 6:00 a.m., the morning mist covered the forest. It was simple to forget about yesterday's struggles with the soothing sounds of songbirds and the invigorating, sweet scent of the pine trees. We tried to be as quiet as possible, but the crunch of our feet on the snow was enough to give away our position.

I nudged Matt as we walked side by side. "Can you tell me about General Lavigne?"

Last night, I kept replaying yesterday's events, and I wanted to learn more about him. For a moment there, it appeared that Davon and he were close.

"General Peter Lavigne, the minister of the military forces." He looked at the horizon and then back at me. "He's like a father to Davon. They were inseparable during his teenage years. Everything good in Davon he got from Lavigne. A very honorable man but a dangerous one too. It's sad to think he's our enemy now." Pain entered his gaze.

An uncomfortable silence followed. It was clear the conversation was over.

How difficult this must be for both of them. Even though they were against the government, these were people they grew up with. People they cared about.

By noon, we were back in Connor's office, explaining everything that happened.

"So he was out there with Lavigne?" Connor asked.

Maria nodded. She sat in the chair next to mine.

"Everything seems to be going according to plan." Connor closed his journal. He always had it with him during our meetings and kept it in a safe inside his desk. "I'm glad Davon was there to help, but it was a close call. We need to keep our guard up. He's just one man, and Lavigne might send more troops back when he notices there's nothing west. In a matter of weeks, they could be on our doorstep. We may have to give up the import bunker if they go north. Let's hope it doesn't come to that."

I gasped. He'd give up a bunker?

Connor intertwined his hands. "Look, I know this may seem rash, but we can relocate everyone. The militia can move here, and civilians can move north with a skeleton crew of cadets for protection. I'm sure the other bunkers can accommodate them. There are also the caves to the north, which can serve as a haven. We've talked about this."

My thoughts froze for a moment. "Caves?"

I was so lost. What was he talking about?

Connor nodded. "There's a system of caves to the north of the farming and engineering bunker. They stretch for kilometers, and a water system runs through them. Jimmy found them a few years back. We've monitored them ever since."

Matt crossed his arms as he rested against a wall behind Maria. "People won't be happy about it, but if it's for the good of the rebellion, they'll understand."

"It would give us time," Maria said.

For me, giving away part of our community was a terrible idea, but this was war. Connor had experience with the NWG army. He knew what needed to be done, so I'd trust him. The important thing was keeping the community safe even if a bunker had to be surrendered.

Connor straightened. "Even if they find the bunker empty, we'll leave enough evidence so they know it was fully functional. That way they'll take time to investigate, giving us a reprieve to prepare our offense. We should be ready to launch our first attack in a couple of months."

Matt moved away from the wall and put his palms on the desk. "We need more people, Connor. How are the spies doing with the search?"

"Last I heard, they were tracking some citizens in the northern slums. Hopefully, they're part of the insurgent cells." Connor tapped his fingers on the desk and looked down. "But you're right. Even with these cells on our side, I fear it won't be enough."

Maria leaned forward. "Our strategy will work, but we need to send Abi and Matt into Electi as soon as possible. If we can move elites to our cause and activate our dormant agents inside the government, we might have a chance."

Connor humphed. "Okay." He rubbed his stubble for a moment before regarding Matt. "I'll let you go in as soon as I get another letter from Davon. I need to be sure how things are moving inside before risking you. We have people coming in from other bunkers. Use the time to train and get more cadets ready."

"Perfect," Matt said.

I was almost out of my seat. At last, Connor gave us the go. Davon would find a way to reach us soon, more so after yesterday's encounter.

Connor stood. "If any communication reaches command, you'll be summoned."

We left after saying our goodbyes.

Matt and I stopped between our apartments.

"I'm sorry about what happened yesterday. We hardly had time to talk," he said.

I took Davon's key out. "No worries. Soon we'll be with him." I brushed his arm. "I worry about you, though. I know leaving Aoki behind is hard for you, but you never show it."

"I knew what I was getting into when I signed up for this shit. Aoki understands, but it's still hard as hell. More so knowing we're on the verge of war." He paused, his eyes downcast. "I worry about him. He's not a fighter."

My throat burned. If anything happened to Aoki...

I grabbed his hand. "We're together in this, and we'll win this thing." I smiled. "Go to your husband. Tomorrow is another day to keep fighting. Today we rest."

He grinned back. "You always keep me grounded, Miss Abigail Davis. I'm so glad we found you." He kissed my cheek. "Have a good night, sis."

My heart swelled at his endearment.

My brother.

I strolled into Davon's apartment and closed the door, inhaling its musky, warm aroma. So much could go wrong. I shook my head and walked to the bar. I skimmed my fingertips over the rim of the glass Davon used to drink from. I poured myself some whiskey and collapsed onto the sofa.

The smoky flavor slid down my throat, and a sensation of calm washed over me.

I'd put my trust in Connor and pray that everything would work out.

Chapter 11

Davon

December 2, 2213

"2212: I don't know the exact date, but I think soon I'll be twenty if I'm not already. It's getting chillier lately. I've been moving from place to place, but recently, I had to move closer to the apartment buildings near the northern outskirts. The government is working on some new projects, and the number of troops in the area has increased in the last couple of weeks. Still, I'm in a safe area for now. I hope to stay here for some time." (Abigail's memoirs)

General Lavigne surveyed our surroundings. "The trail ends here. We lost them."

Maybe today's endeavors could buy Lavigne some time, but he needed results and soon.

I led the patrol as far west as I could, following Matt's trail. I recognized his handiwork. But where was he?

Abi... Her shocked face flashed through my mind, and I shook my head. I needed to focus on getting them away from the import bunker.

We found a cache and the traces of a campfire. We took everything with us and continued our search.

I peered at my watch. They must have made it back by now.

"Soldiers, look around for more clues. They can't just disappear," Lavigne said.

Everyone scattered.

Once alone with me, he straightened his jacket. "Where do you think they are?"

"They must know these woods better than we do." I shrugged. "Who knows? They may be using the trees to climb up, caves... This mountain system is immense. They could be anywhere."

Lavigne stared at the horizon. It was close to nighttime.

"We'll stop for the night and continue tomorrow." He exhaled. "I'm going for a walk." Hands in pockets, he walked about twenty feet away. His head hung low as he leaned against a tree.

The soldiers started coming back. Just as expected, they had nothing to report.

"Get the tents ready. We're staying for the night," I said.

All followed the order. They were organized, but still, we had the advantage.

One PRF soldier had more will to fight than all these soldiers put together. I guess that's why the government wanted to create a new army because this one was based on fear, not loyalty. They needed strong and willing soldiers, ones who would die for the NWG without thinking twice.

I went as far as I could without raising suspicion, then knelt on the ground to process all that had happened.

Abi...

Seeing her again rocked me to the core. When I saw her standing there, a gun aimed straight at her, I wanted to kill the soldier on the spot. To run to her and get her away from danger.

As our eyes met, I witnessed her love. Her longing. She was fighting for me as I was for her. I hoped my smile showed her how relieved I was to see her alive and well. How she gave me the strength to move forward. I wouldn't fail her.

The storm of emotions that ran through me was unbearable.

She was a soldier now and as capable as any other. But the urge to protect her ran deep within me. If only there was a way to keep her safe from all this.

I picked up a rock and threw it. As the sun set, I remembered all those times we used to train out here. She was ready. She'd be okay.

"Davon?"

I turned. Lavigne was standing behind me.

I stood. "Yes?"

His look was lost to the horizon as I gazed at him.

I didn't feel pity for any of the assholes working for my father, but Peter Lavigne was different. Ever since my childhood, I looked up to him. He taught me everything about strategy and war, but he also took the time to talk to me, especially after my father started training me to be his weapon. I learned from him that it was okay to question my father. He disliked most of his policies.

As he was an elite military officer, it didn't add up that he couldn't find our people. Sometimes it seemed like he was purposely failing.

"I just wanted to thank you for today," Lavigne said.

My chest tightened. "It's my duty."

He mumbled something.

"Excuse me?" I asked.

"I..." He rolled his shoulders back. "There was a girl. She reminded me of someone."

I clenched my jaw.

"Davon, I've known you since you were a kid, and even at a young age, you never let him shake you. I hope this conversation stays here."

He turned his head downward, guarding his expression. "Soon after the war ended, I was assigned my position. We adopted a baby boy, and our life was happy. When he was just two, he got sick. Some kind of flu. He had asthma, and his lungs couldn't handle it."

He sighed. "My daughter was fourteen when he died, and she suffered terribly. After that, my wife lost it and started overprotecting her. She wouldn't even let my daughter go to school and scolded her constantly." He rubbed the back of his neck and closed his eyes.

Why was he sharing this? I never knew his daughter, and if I remembered correctly, she died years ago. He was very secretive about his personal life, even with me.

I glanced around to make sure we were still alone. "Peter, what we share here will never leave this place. You can trust me."

He took a deep breath. "Soon after her brother died, she found some files in my study. You see, my baby was taken from someone in Promissa and offered to me as an incentive for taking the position. Suzanne couldn't have any more children, and we'd always wanted to give my daughter a brother or a sister. I knew it was wrong, but I couldn't refuse. After my daughter found those files, she started talking about how people should demand fair treatment and stand up to the NWG."

He kicked the ground. "My daughter ran away when she was sixteen. She couldn't handle the situation at home and hated what the government was doing. No one knows she's alive, as we gave her a funeral to protect her. We said she couldn't handle her brother's death and killed herself, then bribed a cremator to say he'd done the deed. He gave us an empty urn, which we buried. No one dared ask, not even Jordan."

He shifted his feet. "I think she made it out and is part of the rebellion. It's the only thing that makes sense. I need to find her before they do. Her name's Carol."

My heart stopped. Carol? Her image flashed through my mind. Her black hair and strong features. Her blue eyes. The resemblance was unparalleled. I remembered when we found her. She was lost in the forest and wouldn't tell us her last name. Mark rapidly grew close to her and convinced everyone to let her stay.

Did he know?

All these years Peter had guarded the secret. Was he purposely failing so he could protect Carol?

If this was real, he'd be an incredible ally to our cause.

I needed to make sure and confirm he could be on our side. Then I would let him know about his family, about Little D. I had to think this through. It could all be a trap.

"Your secret's safe with me. But if she's one of them, I can't help you."

Peter pinched his brow and gave me a stern look. "Why do you lie to me, Davon? I know you hate him. Why did you come back?"

I didn't respond and stood there as the night grew colder.

"In time you'll tell me. Think about it, son, and come to me when you're ready. We don't have much time." He stared at me. "You recognized her. You protected that girl."

I tensed, and my breathing became labored before I could control it.

Then he just walked away.

Leaving me speechless.

December 3, 2213

After a restless night, I woke to the shuffling of soldiers. I grabbed a jerky from my bag and walked toward a lone spot to watch the forest.

The valley stretched far to the west. No sign of the city. Out here nothing pointed to our true reality. To the impending fury of battle.

Lavigne's orders echoed in the distance. "Go out in pairs, and search the whole area. Create a five-mile perimeter. Inform Minister Niles or myself of any findings. If by 14:00 nothing is found, we will reconvene."

I approached Lavigne. I would have to face him one way or another.

"Morning, Davon. I just sent the soldiers away on a chase we both know is useless. Let's sit and talk."

He sat on a rock next to the campfire and passed me a metal cup full of coffee. "How about you tell me the truth, son? Why are you *really* here?" He took a sip of his coffee, as if this was just another simple conversation, not a confession.

In my teenage years, after long hours of training with this man, we'd sit and talk for hours. Countless times he was my outlet to complain to about my father's dealings. He didn't treat me like any other soldier but like family. Stern but never cruel. I could never hide anything from him, and it seemed this still carried on today.

I held my mug as I rested my elbows on my knees. "I could never hide anything from you, could I, Peter?"

He chuckled.

I straightened. "The real question is, are you here to inform my father about me? Or are you really searching for your daughter?" I waited as he put his mug down and clasped his hands together.

He shrugged. "Why would I lie about something like that? Do you think I'm capable? You know me. I'm taking a huge risk by talking to you about this. For all I know, you may be working with your father to find out why the hell I haven't found the rebel group in all these years. My instincts tell me you're not here for the reasons you say you are. And I hope I'm right because otherwise, I've lost everything."

There was truth in his words. He did not have much time until my father decided to end his career and his life as an elite.

The silence of the forest enveloped us. The crackling of the fire was our only witness.

I closed my eyes.

God, let him be true.

I gazed at the flames. "Do you understand how many lives would be at risk if the information I'm about to tell you leaves this place?"

"Please. I need to know. Is my daughter alive?" His anguished gaze shattered my last remaining doubts.

"We found Carol lost in the forest. She was scared shitless, and the only information she gave us was her first name and age. Sixteen. Her black hair reached her waist, and her eye color resembled yours."

He grabbed my arm, his eyes dead set on me. "Is she alive?"

I nodded. "She still styles her hair the same way she did six years ago and loves to cook."

His eyes glazed. "Thank God."

Peter Lavigne was a guarded man. I'd never seen him this vulnerable.

He covered his face for a moment before dropping his hands. "I hoped she'd made it out safe and prayed every day she was still alive. At last, I have peace knowing I haven't lost her."

His features grew solemn. "I don't understand a lot of what's happening. I only have an idea of the number of people who have disappeared in the last decade."

I needed to grasp this opportunity. He'd be an incredible ally. "Will you protect us if I let you in? Or will you run back to my father to secure your position?"

He pressed his lips together and narrowed his eyes at me. "I know he's your father, but I hate Jordan. He's unscrupulous, cruel, and what he's built turns my stomach inside out. Promissa was free before we got here. A prosperous city that he destroyed among the many others under his rule.

He's wrong, and if I have stayed by his side, it's to ensure he doesn't win. I've done terrible things to gain his trust. Things for which I'll never be able to atone. I'm sure you understand."

Oh, I did. My stomach turned as I recalled all the things I'd done to keep his trust.

Peter watched the fire as a piece of wood cracked, creating a spark. "I've suspected you since you turned twenty-one and started going on your so-called missions. All those times you gave information and nothing substantial turned out. Careful to leave a hint behind, something to keep your father interested."

He glanced my way. "You have many allies inside. Of that I can assure you. Some are waiting for the right moment to act. Others are just too scared to do so."

I put into practice all I had learned as a spy. I listened to his tone, studied his body language.

There was no lie. He was telling the truth, and I'd do the same.

"I am the general of the People's Revolutionary Front, sent here on a mission to rescue our leader and find the identity of a spy who has infiltrated our community. I never gave my father the intel he thinks I did. The spy did. As to why they didn't blow my cover, we still don't know. I'm walking on a tightrope, hoping to have enough time before it all goes to shit."

Peter widened his eyes, mouth slightly open. "You're a general?"

I nodded.

"Who's your leader?"

"The prisoner he wants me to torture." I stood and paced till I was opposite him, the fire between us. "I need to get her out."

He stared at me. "I understand. And who's the woman you protected yesterday?"

I pocketed my hands. "She's important to me. That's all you need to know."

"Okay." He put the mug down, then fumbled with a tree branch he found on the ground. "Is Carol safe?"

"She should be. As well as Little D."

Lavigne furrowed his brow. "Little D?"

I smiled. "Your granddaughter. Carol married a good man, and they have a child. Her name is Diane."

He covered his mouth. "I have a granddaughter. How old is she? Does she live where you do?"

"She's six. I'm her godfather." I smiled as I remembered her smiling face and expressive eyes. She was precious. "We used to live at the same base, but they may have already moved to a safe location as we prepare for war."

He stood. "Wait. War?"

"As we speak, our general of the army is getting our soldiers ready for an imminent attack. Many of my people believe I was the one who got the checkpoint soldiers killed. We found the letters with my cypher and planted the evidence to make it seem like I was the traitor. They arrested me, and I escaped. After that, the system went on high alert. They probably transferred the civilians to a safe place since I know where our base is. Our location is unknown to most of our people, a failsafe we have for these types of situations. The spy needs to get inside command if they want to get the intel for my father, and we're hoping to catch them before they get it."

Here was the moment of truth. What would this man be willing to do to protect his daughter?

"We're taking measures to find who this person is, but I need the names of the spies sent out by my father," I said.

"Is there anything I can do to help? I've accepted the fact that your father will throw me out of Electi in a matter of time. I secured a place for my wife in Promissa in hopes that he'll let me continue my profession as a captain of the guard outside. I really don't care what happens to me as long as my family is safe."

"I need those files, Peter. I need to find the spy." If the head of the NWG military joined our cause, we could really have a chance.

He gripped my forearm. "You can count on it, son. I'll help you find this person."

Chapter 12

Davon

December 27, 2213

"*2212: I stopped counting. Every day is the same. Hungry. Filthy. Alone... I miss my family. I'll have to move soon. They're getting closer.*" *(Abigail's memoirs)*

We spent almost a month going back and forth between Electi and the forest. Lavigne followed my directions to the point, knowing we wouldn't find the base. He was true to his word and kept the secret we shared.

At home, I followed the same daily routine: an hour of therapy exercises, a bodyweight workout, and a cryotherapy chamber session. My shoulder was healing fast. Sometimes I even forgot it was injured.

The intel we disclosed to Father gained us some time, but he called us back into Electi a few days ago for a meeting. He wasn't pleased with our failure, but I assured him we'd find what he wanted in no time.

Today I was back at work. I hadn't seen Deb since that first day. A ton of paperwork lay on my desk, but I couldn't focus. During the meeting, Father ordered Lavigne to investigate the dead drop area northwest of the prison system. The same one where Abi and I were attacked.

The problem wasn't the dead drop—it was the energy bunker, which was only seven miles west of that point. It was the closest to the city perimeter.

The clock was ticking.

This was why yesterday, before the council meeting, I left a coded message for Connor in the timed drop at the government center. I advised him to evacuate the bunker and leave nothing behind. It was only a matter of time till we lost it. I hoped he'd get it before it was too late.

As for myself, I was anxiously awaiting news from the peak. The mole assigned to the prison must have already contacted Connor about my new position. Hopefully, Connor's response to my letter was already waiting for me inside the dead drop at the prison's kitchen area.

Four white walls with only a door to the outside comprised my assigned office. I pressed my hands to my brow and tried to control my shaking. I'd confront Deb today. I'd reach into the darkest pit of my soul and welcome the monster I kept hidden inside. The one my father created.

The door creaked, and I tensed.

The room was overtaken by an eerie presence.

With an elegant gait and his tailored suit, Jordan Niles carried himself above all others. There was something about him, some kind of aura that warned the world of the danger that lay within. A gallant and charismatic man who carried shadows inside.

"Morning, son. Are you excited for today?" His evil smirk showed his true self, a sadistic man with a taste for torture. He didn't care to hide it from me.

"Ready as I can be. I'll try to do it without violence, but at the first sign of insolence, I'll strike. She'll learn who the boss is inside this prison. Will you be there today?" I suspected he'd be attending today's session to satisfy his wicked desires.

"I'll keep watch behind the two-way mirror. You have the freedom to use any type of torture, but keep her alive. She's important."

I briefly closed my eyes. At least he didn't want her dead, but something didn't add up.

A dropping sensation swept through me. "What do you mean?"

Dad chuckled and pocketed his hands, then walked toward my bureau. I stood and came closer to him.

I got the bureau before I left with Lavigne. Like similar vintage items, it came with a concealed compartment. I touched the key in my pocket.

Father rummaged through some files I'd left on top. Maps of the new facilities that would be built as part of the Elysium Genome Project.

"Amazing project, isn't it?" He flipped through the pages.

"Sure, but what does it have to do with Miss Davis?"

The hairs at my nape stood on end as he directed a disturbing smile at me.

"You haven't read the file Frank gave you?"

"I..." In truth, I hadn't had time. My skin prickled at the thought of what this project entailed.

Father waved his hands. "Don't worry. You've been away with Lavigne. But as soon as you can, take a moment and read through it. You see, son, we're not only using the Promissa citizens' DNA. The Apex Genome Project is modifying gametes to bring forth traits that will set elite progeny apart and make it rise above the rest. There's more, but that's classified. Just know she's part of something far bigger than you could ever imagine."

A chill ran down my spine to my toes. Apex Genome Project? What the hell did he mean by this?

My heart pumped hard as he walked toward me, then grabbed my shoulder.

"Deborah Davis is carrying your baby brother."

Fucking shit!

It took everything in me not to grab his collar and demand an explanation.

I took a step back. "What?"

I held on to the desk behind me to cover my shaking limbs.

Father gazed down. His thumb brushed across the back of his wedding band. "You know Rebecca can't bear another child. I won't risk her."

My mother suffered from preeclampsia and almost died when she gave birth to me.

"But..."

He rubbed the back of his neck, then rolled his shoulders back. "What kind of ruler would I be if I'm not willing to try this project for myself? I donated my seed and your mother her eggs. They manipulated our genes to create a baby that would be far superior to what we could offer naturally. Your mother always wanted another son. The house is too empty without you." He shrugged. "So I convinced her."

It wasn't enough to torment me for years and turn me into this, but now he wanted another son. One he could make into whatever he wanted. One who'd far surpass me in every way.

What kind of person would my brother be? What sort of monster would my father create?

"Does she know how the project works?" I couldn't imagine Mom accepting this.

"God no! She wouldn't have done it if she knew. I told her we compensate the mothers and that they choose this freely. You know how weak she is in terms of the Promissa citizens. I prefer she stays ignorant."

I snatched a pen from the desk and held it behind me. One stab to the side of his neck would do.

An image of Father on the floor flashed before my eyes. His body lay in a puddle of blood.

At the thought of him dying, my chest hurt as if someone had stabbed me. What was wrong with me?

I thought of Abi and all the people I'd never see again if I murdered him today. To do so now would result in imprisonment. Even death.

To reclaim Promissa, we needed to proceed carefully. Killing him now wouldn't give us that. We had to destroy everything he built first.

I dropped the pen. "Why did you pick Miss Davis?"

"She's strong. For the pregnancy to succeed, we need a healthy subject. And..." He sneered. "I like her spunk. She's one of a kind."

I rounded the desk and sat. "Does she know?"

"Maybe. I don't really care. But soon she'll be moved to the obstetrics facility. Once inside, she'll be under constant surveillance and won't be able to harm the child. I can't wait to see the look on her face when I tell her it's mine. The bitch hates my guts."

He sat in a chair in front of my desk. "So what do you think?"

I think you're a fucking devil. A virus that must be contained.

My insides twisted into knots. I smirked. "I'm thinking I can't wait to meet my baby brother."

He smiled. "I knew you'd understand."

Twisted son of a bitch.

"My methods could put her at risk. How do you intend we do this?" I couldn't understand my father's logic. He was asking me to torture the mother of his child.

Or had he lost it at last?

"She'll be okay. Just don't damage anything vital. The medics will take care of the rest. We need to know what she's hiding. I want to see her break and spill all her secrets. And then destroy her spirit when she finds out the truth."

"And if she loses the baby? You know stress and pain can cause an abortion."

Was this just a game to him?

"You know what you're doing. I've seen your work. You'll shatter her spirit in no time. Everyone has a limit." He rested back and crossed his legs. "Do whatever you want, but keep in mind her condition. We'll give her breaks between each session to make sure she can go on with it. It would be sad if she loses the baby, but in the event she does, we can always do it again. That's the great thing about this project."

My hands itched to choke my father right then and there. To see the light leave his eyes as his own son killed him.

How could I love this man? Why did my resolve falter whenever I considered taking his life? He had no hope. There was no way Father could vindicate himself after this.

Eighteen—that was my age the first time I tortured a rebellious guard. There was nothing to be done, just follow the procedure. I'd never forget his screams as I pulled a molar out. The agony as I cut multiple fingers off his hand. His grunts as I beat him with a bat to the brink of death.

At the end, he was working alone, and my father made me continue beating him until he died. His body was unrecognizable when he took his last breath. I controlled my urge to throw up at seeing the atrocity I'd committed. And my father couldn't have been prouder. He said to be strong I needed to experience firsthand what it was to kill a man. That they all deserved it for going against us.

I walked across the office and opened the door. "Are you coming?"

His footsteps drew near, and he patted my back. "I'm proud of you, son. Working side by side with you has always been my dream. I can't ask for a better partner. We'll achieve great things together."

I suppressed a shudder and carried on. If he wanted a ruthless son, he'd get him, and in the end, he'd be on the losing side.

The interrogation room was in a corner of the first floor.

I watched from the adjacent room as Deb was forced inside. Her hands were shackled in front, and she struggled against the guards.

My father pressed the intercom button. "Rise and shine, my love. I hope you built up your strength in these past few weeks. From now on, you will start cooperating with us whether you like it or not."

She hit a guard with her head, causing blood to spurt from his nose.

A deep chuckle escaped my father. "I'll be right back."

The guards uncuffed her hands and restrained her to the metal chair.

My father entered the room. "Oh, sweetie, you know you can't win. Now, if you behave and give us what we want, I might even let you get a decent bath, not the weekly five-minute hose bath our soldiers love to give you as you squirm."

She fought against her restraints and countered him with a menacing voice. "I'll never fall to your threats. You'll never get what you're looking for, you prick." Her spit landed on my father's face.

My lips twitched. I'd missed that fire.

Father wiped his face with his handkerchief and stepped into her space, then gripped her neck. "That's where you're mistaken, my dear. For that's exactly what you'll do once my son gets his hands on you. You'll be begging for mercy." His tone was controlled, flat.

He stepped away and headed for the door. "You'll soon understand what it means to be on the losing side. You haven't seen anything yet."

His menacing chuckle made my skin crawl.

He came to my side. "Time to get this show started."

I loosened my tie and put it in my pocket.

The interrogation room reeked of disinfectant, and its white walls seemed to press toward me. The chair was centralized and had metal restraints for the hands and feet of the person who was to be questioned or tortured. A metal table stood in front of the two-way mirror—a sick petition probably made by my father. I removed the blanket that covered my tools and skimmed my fingers over them.

When was the last time I used them?

Ugh. Now I remember.

Three years ago when I arrived in Electi to search for Abi.

I would never forget the plump cheeks and easy smile of my victim when I told her to follow me. Maybe she hoped for a higher position or maybe praise for her good job. Everyone knew about the "special" room my father had in the basement of the government center. When we got there, she froze and backed away, but it was too late.

She wasn't at fault but paid the price for being a friend of a found insurgent inside the system.

Esteban, a PRF spy, after years of service to our cause, got careless and didn't hide his work correctly. A slip was all the government needed to uncover him.

My father didn't leave loose ends, so I had to handle her.

She was a shell of herself after I finished.

Father ordered me to keep her alive, but what kind of life could you live after so much trauma? She still worked for him, a silent and obedient worker. If I tried, I could still hear her screams as I cut her tongue out.

I faced the mirror and gave my father a calculating smile, then turned to her.

I cringed.

She looked haggard, clothed in a dark-gray uniform that reeked of urine and sweat. Her once beautiful curly hair was now matted and dirty. Her skeletal features tugged at my heart. Her cheeks were hollow, and her eyes looked devoid of life.

My sister and best friend.

Deb would never say anything. Even if she lied to satisfy my father's demands, she'd be caught in a never-ending loop. Now that she was a part of his horrific scheme, he'd never give her up. I needed to free her before things got worse.

How could he keep her like this when she carried his child? What kind of monster would do this?

She darted her hazel eyes around the room and stopped when she saw the table behind me. After a short gasp, she focused on me, eyes clouded and lost.

Was she still unsure of my allegiance? She knew I had all the information I needed with me. There was no reason for me to extract the intel from a prisoner.

I needed to make sure she understood I was on her side even though I'd have to hurt her.

Connor trusted me with the woman he loved, counting on me to bring her back. I'd rescue her no matter what.

I took a deep breath. The real horror of my mission was about to start.

I removed my jacket and put it next to my instruments. "Hello, Miss Davis. We already met, but let's make it official. I'm Davon Niles. Nice to meet you." I unfastened my cufflinks and rolled up my sleeves.

She avoided my eyes, focusing entirely on the mirror behind me.

The air in the room was thick, and I struggled to maintain an icy demeanor. "Miss Davis? Please answer when spoken to."

She kept ignoring me.

I'm sorry, Deb. I'm sorry, Abi.

I seized her chin and forced her to look at me.

She attempted to wrench her face free from my grip.

Could she think I was as depraved as my father? That I'd torture her just because I could?

Her tears threatened to break me. "Why are you doing this to me? Was any of it...?"

The smacking sound of my hand connecting with her cheek was solid. If not for the metal shackles securing her to the chair, her body would have plummeted to the ground. My heart broke as I grabbed her hair and drew her closer to me, aware of the security camera behind me. I slightly shook my head when we locked eyes, silently asking her not to blow my cover.

She widened her eyes.

"I'm sorry," I mouthed.

Her eyes cleared, and she blinked once. Her left eye began to swell.

This was how it all would start as she accepted her fate and I, my condemnation. I would never forgive myself for what I was about to do.

"Do you think you're special? You're nothing to me. Don't ever talk back to me again, or you'll regret it." I relaxed my grip and let her go, then pulled my shoulders back and readjusted my shirt. "Now, let's try this again, Miss Davis. My name is Davon Niles. Nice to meet you."

She bared her teeth at me and spit into my shirt. "I have nothing to say to you."

"So that's how it's going to be." I chuckled and approached the table, deciding what tool I would use first. I distanced myself from reality, assuming the role of the tormentor. I took a small knife and smirked so my father could see my deranged face through the mirror. He needed to believe I was enjoying every moment.

I ran my fingertips over the knife.

I approached her. "This is how it's going to work, Miss Davis. If you cooperate, measures will be taken to make your stay in our facility a bit more enjoyable. If not, well, I think you already know how it will be."

Her nostrils flared, and she tugged against her restraints. "I'll never say anything to you fucking assholes. You took everything from us, and we'll take it all back. My life can go to shit as far as I'm concerned. Do whatever you want."

In a swift move, I slashed across her left cheek. The gash bled down her face, dripping onto her uniform. Holding the knife to the side of her neck, I pushed against her skin until a trickle of blood stained the blade. Her chin trembled, and her pulse was visible beneath her skin. She was scared.

My stomach hurt. "It won't be that easy, sweetheart. I'll take my time with you. Oh, the things I'll do to you..." I licked the blood off the knife. "Hmm, I can already taste your fear. You will sing, little bird. Sooner or later, everyone will hear your song."

I turned and left the knife on the table, then took my jacket. I was done for the day.

My father knew I took my time and played a lot of mental games.

Let the victim go and think about what was coming next. The uncertainty and fear that this kind of torture created was even more terrifying than the actual physical abuse.

An officer opened the door as I turned sideways to my friend and directed a ravishing smile toward her. "A pleasure to meet you, Miss Davis. We'll see each other soon."

An hour later, I sat at my desk with the letter I'd found in the kitchen timed drop. I was finally able to get it after my father left.

Davon,

We received intel that you're based in the prison and left this message in hopes that it will reach you.

Our comms are operational. Muñoz can access them daily. He was just assigned the night shift on your floor. Tell him via the timed drop whether there's a secure location where he may obtain your intelligence more directly so communication is easier.

A second dead drop is set up at checkpoint one. If our comms fail or you've been discovered, this will be your safety net.

Abi is all right. She and Matt created a strategy team that is working nonstop on building a plan.

Jimmy's recovering. Your decision out there saved his life.

As for command, we recruited many, but everything is moving as usual. We'll keep our eyes open and our security tight. Have you found out anything about the spy yet?

Matt and Abi will join you soon. We're still working on the details.

When you're ready for Deb's extraction, let us know. It's imperative that we resolve this soon so we can move forward with the plan.

We're ready to go at your command.

Connor

My muscles twitched. Abi was coming soon but nothing concrete. I closed my eyes, praying they'd be safe on their way in.

I wrote a letter to Muñoz and included a spare key for the secret drawer in my bureau. I tucked it inside my pocket, then visited the kitchen to drop it before leaving.

As I made it out, I prayed Connor got my letter about the energy bunker before Lavigne was sent out. If not, it would be too late.

Chapter 13

Abi

December 30, 2213

"How did I do?" I gazed up at David from the floor.

He put the binoculars down and cocked an eyebrow. "You hit 80 percent of the targets. That's huge!"

Mark watched from the threshold. "I still don't understand how you can be this good with a sniper and so bad with a gun."

I rolled my eyes. "Thanks. Your words lift my spirit."

Mark chuckled. "I think if you relax your grip when you hold a gun, your aim will improve significantly. You're too tense."

He'd taken over gun training while Matt focused on recovering.

Matt's ribs were mostly healed, but his arm was another matter. Holding a gun with his right hand had proved very painful, yet he trained every day and was already shooting. He was a fighter.

Mark and I could only meet once, maybe twice a week since he was now in charge of the runners. We'd just practiced in the shooting room, and while I struck more targets than before, I missed more than half of them. I kept going back to the night I shot that soldier who tried to kill Davon. In three shots, he was dead. Why couldn't I hit my targets here? I needed to get my mind into it.

I stood. "I have training with Maria." I smoothed my hands over my gray PRF uniform and brushed my fingers over our emblem. Every outfit now had it, a symbol of our fight. A horizontal key with a staff crossed over it vertically. It symbolized transitions, the progress from one vision to another. From past to future.

Tammy created it two weeks ago. Now it was part of every soldier's uniform.

I gave David the sniper rifle. "Thanks. How are the rest of the trainees doing?"

"Good. We have about twenty privates who are proving to have talent. I just talked to Matt about it. We're hopeful."

I put a hand on his shoulder. "I'm sure we'll be ready."

A corner of his mouth lifted. "We will."

We'd become very good friends and drank beer with the strategy team every Thursday.

For an instant, everything blurred, and I remembered last week. I was sitting on David's couch, laughing at one of Matt's antiques, while Maria drew on a whiteboard whatever she read on the cards David and Matt had prepared for today's game. For the moment, we made out a hat, a cape, and a katana. We were interrupted by a knock on the door.

David went to get it.

"A superhero?" I said.

"Cheater! Pause the game while I get the door," David yelled as he opened it.

I looked outside.

Jimmy stood there, cane in hand. His soft blue eyes settled on me, and he gave me a tentative smile.

All conversation stopped the moment I stood.

David glanced at Jimmy, then back at me.

I dashed into the bathroom. I couldn't handle Jimmy.

When I came out, David passed me a beer.

"I told him to leave," he said.

A sense of heaviness had settled within me since that day. Jimmy was trying to reach me, and I kept pushing him away. I was empty inside. That place Jimmy occupied was barren, and I missed him so much.

I jerked my head, coming back to the present.

David had closed the space between us and watched me with a questioning gaze. "I lost you for a minute. Are you okay?"

"Yes. It's just..." I rubbed my brow. "I have a lot on my mind."

"You know you can come to me anytime. Whatever you need."

I nodded and helped him put the sniper rifle away.

He picked up the duffel bag, and the three of us exited the sniper room.

"When are you leaving?" Mark asked.

"We still don't know. Davon hasn't written."

No communication had reached command since I last saw Davon a month ago.

Mark paused and ran a hand over his long brown hair. "It's been a month already. Do you think something happened?"

David gave us some space to talk.

"Our people inside say he's okay. He's been working with General Lavigne and hasn't been around much, but from what they hear, he should be back in Electi soon, if not already." I shifted my feet. "As for Deb, no news yet, but I'm sure she'll be back soon."

Keeping my hopes up became more difficult by the day.

The truth was, day in and day out, I watched the hours go by without news, and no matter how hard I tried, negative thoughts kept creeping in.

Of Deb suffering from Davon's torture. Of her spirit breaking apart because of it. Of us losing her before Davon could get her out.

I thought about Davon. Even though he showed a tough front, he was very fragile when it came to his past. Would he be the same person after all this?

I loved him and trusted him, but Jordan Niles was vile, and having to be with him and appear calm could mess up Davon. I didn't want to lose him. I didn't want him to break apart.

The situation had given us more time to prepare the strategy and the soldiers, but the uncertainty of it all had even Connor on edge.

He tried to hide it, but it was clear. He had bags under his eyes, and unkempt stubble covered his face. He worked all the time.

Yesterday morning I went to his apartment early to invite him for breakfast. When there was no response, I went to command and found him hunched over his desk, sleeping. He said it was because of the situation at the bunker, but he was clutching their wedding picture, and his eyes were red rimmed.

It was fucking hard.

Mark adjusted his glasses. His brown eyes weren't as vibrant as usual.

"Mark, he knows what he's doing. We need to trust he's okay," I said.

Mark nodded. "I know."

We went to David and continued on.

Maria was on the padded floor, resting against a wall with her head between her knees.

Something was up.

"See you guys," I said.

They waved goodbye.

I went to her. "What's going on?"

She lifted her head a bit and sighed. "It's Tammy."

I cocked my head. "What happened?"

They were usually all over each other and seemed happy.

She shook her head. "Forget I said anything. Come on." She left the floor and walked toward the center of the room.

I grabbed her arm. "I'm a good listener."

Maria always acted tough and never talked about her problems.

Her shoulders slumped. "She's changed. She's been working nonstop, even more than me. We hardly see each other anymore. She comes home late and leaves very early. I miss her, so this morning I confronted her."

Her eyes were teary. I'd never seen her cry before.

She took a deep breath. "She was pissed. Told me she couldn't believe I was throwing it in her face when I was always the one absent before all this. That she was focused on helping the bunker and I shouldn't be selfish. Then she slammed the door and left."

God! What was Tammy's problem?

I understood how things were, but to treat the person you love like that...

Why would Tammy change so drastically?

What if...?

I shook my head. Maybe the stress was finally getting to her.

I threw my arm around Maria, holding her close as she cried.

"I've never seen her so mad. It was like she was a different person." Maria sobbed.

"Maybe she's stressed by all that's happening. Hell, we all are. She'll come to her senses. You'll see. After all, she has the best girlfriend in the world." I hugged Maria. "Everything will be okay. Now, how about some sparring to get the blood flowing and the bad thoughts out?"

She patted my shoulder. "That sounds perfect."

We sparred for an hour and were exhausted by the end. We'd been practicing with blades for a couple of weeks, and she was a beast as an adversary. I betted she and Davon would be quite a pair in a fight, both relentless and savage. Her moves were more fluid than Davon's, the difference being his strength, but her agility surpassed his.

I walked to my room. A shower and a nap sounded amazing at this moment. My room gave me a sense of self, one I needed to embrace.

I still slept at Davon's. The nights were more bearable within his space. I'd tried music as David suggested, and it helped somewhat, but some nights the nightmares still came. Waking up at Davon's gave me solace.

I stopped midstride once I entered hall A. Jimmy stood by my door and turned toward me.

I stepped back.

"Stop. Please, Abi. We need to talk." His pleading voice rooted me to the spot.

I took a deep breath and inched forward, making my feet move again and again until I reached my door. I didn't look at Jimmy as I opened it.

My heart beat painfully against my chest. It was thrumming. Screaming inside my ears.

The thump of his cane followed me in.

I entered the bathroom and rinsed my face. I looked in the mirror.

You can do this.

Three breaths later, I exited and served two glasses of water, then sat at the table.

I slid the glass toward Jimmy, who stood opposite me. "Sit."

The chair screeched, and he sat, holding on to the table for balance. I glanced up in time to see him flinch from the effort.

My stomach plummeted. This was my friend, my family, and he was hurting.

But then I remembered his cruel face. The boom of the gun as Davon fell. The drenched shirt as blood oozed from Davon's shoulder. Our good-bye as my world collapsed and I stayed behind to save Jimmy.

I clenched my fists on top of the table and counted to ten.

I could do this. I needed to do this.

"Abi?"

His voice was a stab in my heart.

"Why?" My voice sounded hoarse. My hands trembled. "Why couldn't you just let us go?"

"Abi, I..." He looked down at his hands. "I was mad with rage."

I furrowed my brow.

He interlaced his fingers. "I'm not making excuses. I know what I did was unforgivable. I thought I was doing the right thing, and then I knew. The moment he asked you to save me, I knew I was wrong. That I had destroyed us."

A lump threatened my throat, and he grabbed my hands.

I shook and focused on his blue eyes, ones that overflowed with unshed tears.

"I will do all I can so you get back to him. I'll never forgive myself for breaking your heart. I love you, and I know you'll never feel the same way about me, but I want you to be happy. Please...let me help you. Let me make amends."

I took my hands back. I wanted to hear him out, to fix everything and have my best friend back, but still...

"Can you give me some time?"

"Whatever you need." He stood and walked to the door.

"Jimmy?"

His gaze barely met mine. "Yes?"

"Come to David's for beers."

It was as good a start as I could give him. Maybe with other people we could start talking. But it would take some time.

He bowed his head. "I'll be there. Thank you."

It was after lunch when I left my apartment. I wanted to ask Connor if he had any news.

Command was full of activity, and I caught a glimpse of Mr. Jackson. I hadn't talked to him even though I attended some of his lectures to get to know more about him. His mannerisms, ideals, and sense of justice reminded me so much of Jacob that it hurt.

I was a fucking coward. The right thing to do was to tell him, but I didn't have the guts. Maybe I could ask Matt for help. He said he'd come with me if I needed it, and I think I did.

Looking down, I made it to Connor's office. He was drowning in paperwork when he let me in. The circles beneath his eyes were evidence of another sleepless night.

"Sit. Give me a moment." He rummaged through some files, then rubbed his neck and stretched his back.

Being in his spot had to be hard.

His gaze angled toward me. "I'm sorry, Abi. How can I help you?"

I shrugged. "Same as every day. Any news about Deb or Davon?"

With a shake of his head, my hope shattered.

He put away his paperwork. "What about Sarah? Have you talked to her?"

I shook my head.

"You need to move past everything that happened. She's your sister."

"I know. But it's as if there's a wall between us. I don't know what to say."

I saw her every day, but we both kept our distance. Sometimes we even sat at the same table but stayed silent. We were like strangers.

What Connor said was true. I couldn't leave things as they were and move to Electi. If something happened, I'd never forgive myself.

"I know she hurt you, but she's suffering as much as we are. We're family, and the uncertainty of Deb's rescue is difficult for all of us. She's been coming daily just as you are, desperate for news about Deb. She's asked about Davon also and about you. I asked her, and she gave me the same answer you just did. She doesn't know what to say."

Sarah suffered so much, and I didn't stop to think how all this affected her. How selfish could I be? I sank into my seat, unable to meet Connor's eyes.

"Make your peace with her before you leave, Abi."

I nodded.

"How about some coffee at my place?" He approached me and held out his hand. "Come on."

Walking at Connor's side was never boring. Everyone greeted him, and he somehow knew about what every citizen was going through. He was a beloved leader and a respected one.

We reached our hall and entered his room. I dropped onto his sofa and put my feet on his coffee table. I was exhausted.

He smiled and went to his coffee machine. Same as me, he was a caffeine addict.

Two weeks ago, I finally asked how they had coffee out here. He told me they did it the same way as in the city. The labs in the science and technology bunker used cellular agriculture to grow and brew coffee. It was a complex process, but with the right equipment, it took roughly two weeks and could supply the whole system. It was amazing.

A few minutes later, he handed me a mug of coffee and sat beside me.

Its scent alone heightened my senses. It made me feel alive.

Connor sipped his coffee. "God. Afternoon coffee is the best. I'm so glad you share my love for it. I mostly drank alone before you came."

I scrunched my eyebrows. "Really? Deb used to love it."

He smiled. "She did, but she forced herself to quit it because she was too addicted. I couldn't do it." He glanced at a solitary teacup that rested on top of a shelf. "She started drinking tea. The ones without caffeine."

I imagined her sitting at the table, drinking her tea. Connor laughing as she explained coffee was bad for him.

The atmosphere suddenly became infused with an overwhelming sense of sorrow. Connor leaned forward, staring blankly ahead. "I miss her so much."

A tear trailed down his cheek.

I took my feet off the table and moved closer to him. "I miss her too."

He scrubbed a hand over his face. "I wish things could've been different. She wanted you to be happy, and everything went wrong."

I finished my coffee and put it on the small table. "You couldn't have known. Things just...happened."

When he finished his coffee, he stretched back and put his arm around me, then hugged me to his side.

I was home.

His soft scent of sandalwood always gave me peace. The warmth of his embrace reminded me of my father's.

"I know you're suffering too, but I'm sure Davon and you will soon be together, and you will bring her home." He squeezed my shoulder.

"Thank you, Connor."

He brushed my hair back. "For what?"

I snuggled into him. "For being my father when I lost my parents. For being there for everyone even though you're hurting so much."

His heart raced beneath my ear, and his chest trembled. He was crying.

"I should have done more." His voice was raspy, filled with pain.

"You've done enough."

I jumped at an urgent knock on the door.

We were still sitting on the sofa.

I shook Connor awake. "Connor, someone's at the door."

He rubbed his eyes. "What time is it?"

I looked at my watch. "Nine. We must have dozed off."

He chuckled.

"What?"

"Only a coffee addict falls asleep right after drinking coffee."

I smiled. "I don't see anything wrong with that."

He put his hands over his knees and stood. "I taught you well."

I took our mugs and went to the sink to wash them when whoever was at the door knocked again furiously.

Connor opened it.

Someone rushed inside. "Sir! This just came in!"

It was Nina.

A surge of adrenaline ran through me. I left the mugs and darted over to them.

Connor was reading a letter.

I tried to make out the writing, but he was much taller than me, and I couldn't see. I looked at the discarded envelope on the table. My breath hitched as I recognized the code. A letter from Davon.

His eyes darted frantically through the letter, and he frowned.

Something's wrong.

Connor folded it. "Nina, call Maria, Matt, Mark, and Jimmy in. Emergency meeting at my office in twenty. If you see Sarah, tell her to come also."

Nina hurried out.

"What happened?" I asked.

"Give me a moment, please." He entered the bathroom and closed the door.

I paced outside.

What if something happened to Davon? Or was it Deb? My heart was about to come out of my chest when he opened the door.

I grabbed his arm. "Please, Connor, don't keep me in the dark."

"Let's sit."

He served two glasses of water, and we sat at the table.

My legs bounced uncontrollably. I held on to the chair's armrests for my life. The trembling wouldn't stop.

I closed my eyes as Aoki taught me and took three even, long breaths. I couldn't fall into panic right now.

He covered my hand. "Davon's okay. He's back from his assignment with Lavigne. He met Deb."

I jerked forward. "He saw her? How is she?"

"She's all right, and he believes she already understands he's there to help her."

He opened the letter again. His hand fisted around it, wrinkling it. "He's apologizing for what he'll have to do but promised that on his next contact, he'll give us the details for her retrieval."

Oh God.

"We knew this would happen, but still..." I was out of words.

Connor nodded. "It hurts, but I know she'll make it. She's strong."

Thinking about the things Davon would do to her gave me the chills. But I was sure he'd be careful. She'd make it.

"Do you think he read our letter?" I asked.

Connor sent a letter in response immediately after the forest events a month ago.

"I don't know, but I'm sure he'll get it if he hasn't yet."

I calmed down, but then I recalled his order to Nina. "Connor, why did you call for an emergency meeting?"

He stood. "Come with me to command. It's better if we're all together."

We entered his office.

As we both sat, Matt came in. "What happened?" He stood behind me.

"Let's wait for the others," Connor said.

Matt bent toward me. "Is everything all right?"

I nodded. "Davon is okay as well as Deb. But something happened. He didn't say more."

Connor stared at us. "*He* is sitting right here, so stop muttering stuff as if I can't hear you."

Matt came to my side. "Scoot over."

I looked up. "There's another chair."

He put his hands on his hips. "I came across Jimmy and Mark on my way here. Jimmy needs it more than I do."

He started sitting, shifting me to the right.

"Matt!" Sometimes he was such a child.

"Come on. Move. I'm exhausted."

I moved to the back of the chair.

He sat at the edge, squeezing me behind him and to the right.

"I'm starting to understand Davon."

He winked at me with a devilish smile. "I can't help being irresistible. You two simply can't handle all this." He gestured to himself.

I rolled my eyes but couldn't hide my smile.

"Sometimes I'm surprised you're two grown adults," Connor said.

We both chuckled.

A moment later, Maria walked in, followed by Nina and Sarah. They all stood next to the desk.

Sarah and I shared a look for a second. We really needed to talk.

Jimmy entered last with Mark by his side, then took the seat next to me.

Connor stood. "There's a new development. We just received a letter from Davon. There's good news and bad news. The good news is Davon saw Deb. She's okay, and he'll let us know as soon as he has a plan to extract her. There's another piece of good news. Lavigne is with us. He's an ally."

Time stood still. Lavigne, the general of the NWG army, was on our side? How did Davon manage that?

Maria broke the silence that engulfed the office. "For real? Can we trust him? It seems too good to be true."

Matt looked at her. "I think we can. He was like a father to Davon. If the letter says he's with us, we can trust it to be true. I always wondered how in seven years they haven't found us. Maybe he's always been on our side."

"I met Lavigne briefly during my time teaching. He's an honorable man. I trust Davon." Connor moved his gaze around the room. "This is a huge step forward for the rebellion, but Lavigne needs to maintain his position, so on paper, he's still our enemy. Davon said he'll be helping with the spy situation, trying to get into the system."

"So what's the bad news?" Matt asked.

"Lavigne's troops are coming into the forest again. This time they'll investigate the compromised dead drop area. Jordan Niles ordered them to sweep the place and search deeper. Davon fears they might find the energy bunker and that we should consider an evacuation."

Again, silence filled the office.

This was a nightmare. What if they were already on their way? So many could die.

Maria stepped forward. "Ready when you are. Since the import bunker is safe, we have space to accommodate the people from energy among the other bunkers. Maybe we should consider readying the caves in case they decide to move deeper into the forest."

Jimmy slid to the edge of his chair. "The runners know the caves." He glanced back at Mark. "They can help you get them ready." He turned his attention to Connor. "It'll take some time, but in a month or so, we can have them up and running. DeLuca or Faez can aid us in developing some kind of emergency energy system. There's room enough for everyone. They stretch for kilometers underground."

He gripped his thigh, slightly wincing as he switched positions in the chair.

Sarah moved beside Jimmy. "The children are already settled in the farming and engineering bunker. We can move the people from energy to the science and technology bunker until the caves are ready, leaving a skeleton crew behind until they can move the technology and machinery up there."

Connor nodded. "We'll get the caves ready, then, but there's no need to worry about the energy. The system is already autonomous. The generators can be moved. What worries me most is the data."

"I can take care of that," Nina said.

We all turned to her.

"We already moved all the files from the import bunker to our database. I can do the same for the energy bunker. I developed a defense system in case we lose command, and all the information will be deleted automatically. I copied everything to the databases in the science and technology bunker, which is the farthest away."

"Thank you, Nina," Connor said. "Everyone, go and rest. That's an order. Tomorrow you'll each work on your respective assignments. Let's do this."

Everyone nodded and left except for Connor, Matt, and me.

Matt stood and stretched, then helped me up.

I grunted. I couldn't feel my ass.

"What are you doing now, Abi? I don't think I'll be able to sleep. Want to come by? We can hang for a bit," Matt said as we made our way to the door.

"Sure. I just slept a couple of hours, so I'm not tired anyway." I wanted to see Aoki and Shirokuro.

"You have the go," Connor said.

I jerked my head back to him. "What did you say?"

"You're leaving for Electi. I'll give you the details later. Now go. Relax."

As if I could. We were leaving at last.

Tears welled up in my eyes. "Thank you."

Matt grabbed my hand. He smiled, but it didn't reach his eyes.

My body was heavy as I followed him, knowing we'd be leaving people we cared about behind. I prayed they'd be safe and that we'd see them again.

Chapter 14

Davon

December 31, 2213

"*2212: I can't write anymore. Nothing matters. I want to die.*" *(Abigail's memoirs)*

A tightness in my chest took over me after that last entry in Abi's journal. It must have been written after the rape. My blood boiled as I remembered her words that morning in the forest. She'd suffered things that not many could endure, but she kept going. Just thinking about how close she was to giving up when we found her drove me nuts. It could've been too late.

Grace's laughter dragged me back to the present.

Champagne flute in hand, I smiled as another of my father's supporters came to greet me.

She stood beside me as Dad chatted with President Orville.

The president smiled and greeted, as was expected given his role in the government. His appeal was as strong as his daughter's. His short auburn hair faded in comparison to Grace's flaming tone, but he shared her same dark-green eyes. Everyone wanted to be near them simply to get a peek at their power.

Lavigne stood a couple of meters away with his wife and raised his flute toward me. I tilted my head, returning the gesture.

The 2214 New Year's Eve celebration of the New World Government promised to be unforgettable. A pompous affair done to impress elites and gain more support for the regime.

The venue in the entertainment district was huge, its dome filled with sparkling lights to emulate the night sky. Round tables filled the indoor garden. Some people sat, while others stood, drinking and talking.

A cello, violin, and double bass formed a harmonic trio that enthralled the room. A gorgeous middle-aged woman in a long red dress with a halter neckline stood in front. Her arms were wrapped in black gloves as she held the microphone to her lips. She mesmerized the audience with one of the most exquisite voices I'd ever heard.

Couples swayed to the music on the dance floor.

Mom knew how to throw a memorable party.

Grace leaned toward me. "A penny for your thoughts."

I stepped away.

She closed the distance. "Why are you like this?" The words rolled off her tongue like honey.

Her strapless forest-green dress reached the floor, its small train falling behind her. No one could deny she looked beautiful. The gown hugged her, calling attention to her curvy body and ample breasts. A design to make any man quaver, except for me.

"See something you like?"

Her deep-green eyes were glassy, a hunger I knew too well swimming behind them. Her smile, though charming, sent ripples of unease through my veins. She wanted something from me, and Father, even knowing about my feelings for "Gabrielle," kept trying to push us together.

I tilted my head toward her. "I've told you before, and I'm telling you again. Whatever happened between us is over. You have enough ogling eyes set on you to take your pick."

"But I don't want anyone else." She stroked my arm. "You know we're a good match." Her lips grazed my ear. "In more than one way."

I grunted.

She was a skilled lover—no one could deny that.

I recoiled at the memories that flashed through my mind. She was a choice made from desperation. I used her to satisfy my needs and forget about Elaine. That was the moment I turned into a cold bastard. A man without feelings.

Until I met Abi.

The bitter aftertaste of regret filled my mouth, and its burden dragged me down. Now I had to deal with my past mistakes.

Matt warned me repeatedly that this game I played would bite me in the ass one day.

It seemed my time was up.

I needed to make it clear to her that this would not work, no matter what my father, or hers, had promised. I already made my choice.

With so many eyes on us, I couldn't just take her away to chat. The paparazzi watched our every move. There was only one option, and even though it posed a threat and headlines would swarm tomorrow's tabloids, it was safer than disappearing with her behind closed doors to let the reporters make their own story.

I put my flute down. "Let's dance."

The music played as the singer's voice filled the room. Her soft baritone wrapped around me like a gentle breeze, reminding me of Abi's touch. The warm resonance of the cello cradled my sorrows.

All that crumbled when Grace locked her arms around my neck, dragging me down about half a foot to reach my ear. "I see you've changed your mind. I've missed you."

She kissed my neck. There were no goosebumps. No current running down my body. Her voice and touch only made me more certain of what I needed to do.

My hands barely touched her hips as we swung to the music. "Grace, I only asked you to dance to protect your pride. This ends now. There's nothing between us, and there never will be. We're done."

She stood on her tiptoes. Her mouth trailed up my neck, brushing my ear. Her nails bit into my nape, and I suppressed a flinch. "You will regret this, Davon Niles." Her voice slid down like venom.

When the song finished, she kissed my neck again. Her tongue languidly tasted my skin.

She caught my earlobe between her teeth. "I will destroy you and everything you hold dear. No one denies me." She stepped away and left the dance floor.

The rest of the night was uneventful.

Grace ignored me as she paraded across the venue, charming all the people of power. I was glad about that, but her words lingered. Unlike her father's passive countenance, she was a dangerous woman I had to watch out for.

I needed to break my dad's trust in her so he'd forget about bringing the two families together. Because if I was forced to be with her, she'd make my life a living hell.

After the fireworks, people went home.

The night was calm as I stood by the glass wall, looking out from my penthouse. Now all that was left was to miss Abi and wonder what she was doing right now. I pressed my palm against the glass, wishing I could reach out and touch her.

A hollow feeling filled my chest as I thought about home. I missed the peak and my family. Did they get my warning? Would they be okay?

Being so far away drove me crazy.

What if everything we planned failed and I got stuck here? What if I couldn't protect them?

I walked to the bedroom, discarding my suit and tie as I went.

I gulped what was left of my drink and put it on the nightstand. Then I kicked off my shoes and sat on my empty bed.

When will I see you again, Abi?

Not bothering to change clothes, I lay down and fell into nothingness.

January 3, 2214

"In your report, you state you found a trail that led to nothing. They're playing with us. Go deeper on this next mission. Don't leave any leaf unturned. They're out there. I'm sure of it." Father closed the file and waited for Lavigne's answer.

We sat in the government center's conference room, going through our report on last month's mission. We were the last ones to brief Father on what happened out there, and everyone waited for Lavigne's take on it.

"My soldiers will cover the area. I'm confident we'll find them." Lavigne rested back in his seat.

I had to give it to him. He was a great actor because I was sure he was dying on the inside. Just last night we met in his study. He'd checked the space for hidden microphones and cameras and assured me it was safe.

During the week we'd been back, he'd found some files that could aid us in discovering the spy, but gaining access to them was becoming a challenging task.

Nevertheless, our meeting was not to talk about the spy. Peter was worried about Carol and my people. Their mission to search the forest had him on edge.

I hadn't disclosed the exact location, hoping they wouldn't find the bunker. The bloodbath that could result would be comparable to the loss of the import base three years ago. I just hoped Connor got my communication in time to evacuate the area.

The attack on the energy bunker was imminent, and I feared the worst.

January 4, 2214

Mom asked me to stay at home last night, and I couldn't deny her.

Silence enveloped me as I lounged in a chair, reading a book on war strategies. We had half the number of soldiers compared to the NWG armed forces. Our only choice was to create a strategy that took out the patrols one by one because to face their whole army at once would be suicide. Many wars were won with small numbers. We just needed to plan it thoroughly. I didn't doubt the strategy team at the peak had already accounted for this, but I wanted to lend a hand.

Mom's echoing footsteps broke the silence. When she opened the door to the library, I was already smiling. I'd missed our conversations and valued these stolen moments.

Her short turquoise sundress and sandals made her look refreshed. Her hair was swept back in a ponytail. Her black tresses reached her waist. She looked so young.

"Good morning. How are you doing?" She kissed my cheek and sat beside me, coffee in hand.

"Good. And you?"

She sighed. "I'm happy. The party was a success. If we're to measure the year by how it started, it promises to be exciting."

My stomach clenched at her words.

War was coming. It was inevitable. And I didn't know how to protect her.

For ten years, we talked about it, but nothing could prepare me for this. Many good people resided in Electi. Many lives would be lost.

War was unforgiving. It didn't recognize friend from foe, threatening everyone equally. The thought of losing Mother burned through me, the pain almost physical.

"Something's bothering you. Is it Gabrielle? Have you heard from her?" Her words brought me back from my wandering thoughts.

I shook my head and closed the book. "No. Still nothing."

She covered my hand. "I'm sure she'll be home soon. Your dad sent soldiers in to search for her."

A shiver ran down my body. "I hope his actions don't blow her cover. She's playing a dangerous game, and Dad might be making it worse."

She patted my hand. "Jordan knows what he's doing. He'd never endanger the woman you love."

I cocked my head. "Mom, you know Dad doesn't approve. He's still trying to strengthen our ties with the Orvilles."

She sighed and withdrew her hand. "I know. I talked to him about it. He just wants what he believes is best for you, but I think I'm swaying him toward our cause. We married for love after all, and he understands you need to be happy to work better. After the party, even though the tabloids were packed with pictures of Grace and you dancing, he understood. He saw a sad man, one who was missing something essential. He witnessed your sorrow and told me he'd find her for you and bring her home."

The headache that threatened to set in calmed at that moment. Could he truly give up on his dream of uniting the families? Did he care that much?

"I can't wait to meet her. She must be lovely and strong as hell to capture your heart," Mom said.

I gave her a genuine smile as Abi's image took over my thoughts. "She's the strongest woman I know."

Her eyes sparkled. "Your eyes light up when you talk about her. I'm so happy for you."

"Thanks, Mom."

For a moment, I pictured the four of us sitting in this library. The warm light of the room and the rich aroma of books and wood wrapped around us as we talked about trivial stuff.

A world where we broke down the barriers that divided us and lived with each other as equals.

Could we achieve that peace one day? Could we ever be a family again?

The image broke into pieces as the door opened and my father's dark aura entered the room. The lightheartedness that he tried to convey didn't hide his true colors from me.

Today was Sunday, and he wore long gray sweatpants and a black V-neck. His skin glistened from sweat.

Mom stood. "Morning, honey."

"Hi, love. Sorry I'm all sweaty. I needed to blow off some steam, so I hit the gym early."

She eyed him seductively and put a hand on his chest. "Do you see me complaining?"

My dad chuckled, brought her to him, and kissed her.

I rolled my eyes.

"I was just talking to Davon about Gabrielle. Do you have any news?"

"Not yet, but I'm confident we'll find her." His eyes moved to mine, then back to her. "Love, could you give us a moment?"

"Sure thing. I'll wait for you in the dining room. Breakfast should be ready in a few." Mom kissed his cheek and looked back at me. "See you later."

When she left, Dad took her chair.

I opened the book and continued reading, ignoring the dropping sensation in my stomach as my father fixed his attention on me.

"Son, we need to talk." His voice was bitter.

I closed the book and twisted toward him.

His stare lacked the warmth that met my mother's eyes just a few minutes ago.

"President Orville just called me. He said Grace was disheartened after the party. He thought it was nothing, but three days have passed, and she's still not her usual self. What happened?"

An unnatural silence settled between us.

"Son?" His tone was hard.

"What happened that night is our business and ours alone."

He grabbed the armrest of his chair and leaned toward me. "What you do to the president's daughter is my business as much as yours. You know how important this is for me. Maybe you should forget about this woman you're infatuated with. It's the New World Government's future we're talking about, and you need to put those trivial thoughts aside and take on your responsibility as our future leader."

My jaw hurt from my clenched teeth as I controlled my urge to beat him senseless. I quickly organized my thoughts. "Father, I will not sacrifice my happiness for the NWG. I can lead without binding my life to the Orvilles. I don't trust Grace, and neither should you. She's dangerous, and she may well be trying to take over all we've built."

Father's face tightened as his eyebrows drew closer. He was attempting to read me, just like he did with everyone else.

I kept a straight face and breathed steadily. My body relaxed.

He'd taught me everything about strength and being in control of my emotions. I learned to lie to him as a child, and he couldn't see through me unless I wanted him to.

His eyes widened. "You're being serious. You truly believe she's planning to overthrow us after all I've done for them?"

I kept a stony expression as excitement burst through my veins. It worked!

"If I marry her, she'll fight for control. And I don't believe the president knows. He'd never oppose you. He's the richest man in the NWG thanks to you, and he doesn't do a thing. He just smiles, reads the speeches, and maintains a face for the elites. But Grace is different. I've seen it in her eyes. Her thirst for power. You know she tried to move in with me without even asking me about it. And she was always curious about government stuff. Trying to get intel from me. That's why I broke up with her."

"We can't have that." Father slumped back. "Now that you say it, everything makes sense. My spies told me she was fucking General Steele. I didn't believe it, but now..."

My thoughts swirled so fast I couldn't follow them. She was sleeping with General Thorne Steele? And to think I'd made up her hunger for power to get Father on my side, but it was real. And if she had General Steele in her grasp, she was a danger not only to me but to everyone.

We fought for Promissa, but there were other oppressed cities throughout the system. Steele governed over Halcyon. He was loyal to my father, but a woman could easily break loyalty apart. This was way more complicated than I imagined.

Could she be planning to overthrow Father? If so, what would that mean for the rebellion? For our fight?

"We need to watch out for her," I said.

"We do. Tomorrow I'll assign a team to watch her. We need to understand her agenda."

"You caught me by surprise, Father. I thought we'd moved on from this. Mom told me you understood about my feelings for Gabrielle."

He leaned forward and intertwined his hands. "I understand them. I know what it is to be in love. I just thought Grace was a better match for you."

I opened my hands in protest. "But you don't even know Gabrielle."

"How can I trust someone I don't even know? Women can be manipulative. I need to meet her before I accept her."

I trusted Matt was preparing her to deal with my father. He was paranoid as hell even though he hid it behind his strong countenance.

"You'll love her. She's devoted to our cause."

He frowned. "What was her last name again?"

"Jones. She was raised by her mother, who died from cancer five years ago. Gaby turned eighteen that same year."

We'd prepared for this scenario. It was part of her file. The data was already in the system. He could check, and it would be there.

Father shifted in his chair. "What type of cancer?"

This woman had existed. Her baby had died in childbirth, but Nina took care of it. Since that happened during the war and some records got lost during that time, she created a whole persona, and Gabrielle was born.

"Pancreatic."

Father humphed. "All the advances and we still can't figure cancer out. At least life expectancy has improved, but now that will all change. We won't have to worry about it soon."

But at what expense?

My grandmother died from cancer at an early age. I never met her.

Father grew up without a mother, and he took after grandpa, who was as twisted and hungry for power as Father was today.

I was too young to remember, but Mom told me that after losing most of our homeland to sea level rise and extreme temperatures, Father decided to join the wars on this continent and create his own government with the help of the elite families of our country.

He defeated his enemies with the best weaponry and mercenary army money could buy, taking most of the eastern coast. By oppressing the population of the conquered regions and imposing his regime, he secured his position and the allegiance of the elites.

When we were teenagers, Matt found a journal in his father's office and showed it to me. After the war ended, his father and mine assigned a fund to medical research. At first, most of it was to battle cancer and other incurable diseases. Then they started working on genes, creating the Genetic Enhancement and Population Control Program, taking control over the procreation rights of the citizens to use them as lab rats.

And now he was playing God.

It seemed he got tired of fighting the diseases and decided to annihilate them by creating a superior human. One who didn't have to worry about sickness or weakness of any kind.

I wondered if he'd ever stop or if he'd keep looking for ways to cheat death.

"When did she graduate from the facilities? How did she end up at the clinic?" Father asked.

"Two years ago, she worked as a secretary in a medical facility. Matt went to get some medical equipment and met her. He brought her in right after that. We needed someone to take care of the clinic when we were off on our missions, and she was willing to help."

"And why wasn't I told about her?" His tone was rigid. He didn't like being kept in the dark.

"I didn't think it was important. As for Matt, you know how he is."

"Yeah. He's always resented me for the divorce. I've never understood why. It wasn't my fault they separated. I just told Frank his wife had some radical ideas that were dangerous. That as minister of health, he had to control her. It's not my fault he couldn't do it."

I bit back an insult and said what he wanted to hear, "I understand, but I don't think he does."

Father was such a self-centered man that he couldn't even grasp the idea of being guilty of tearing Matt's family apart.

He threatened to take Frank's position away if he didn't control his wife. When Lisa said she would stick to her ideals, Frank had no other choice but to leave her. Matt lost his family because of my father.

Father shrugged. "At least he still visits and has seen the righteousness of our way. He's a good man." He stood. "If you love Gabrielle, I'm willing to give her a chance. We'll see what she can offer. The soldiers will keep an eye out for her. I'm sure she'll be with us soon."

I relaxed. If I could get my father to like her, we stood a chance against him.

Chapter 15

Abi

January 3, 2214

The year had passed and gone with no time to celebrate. No time to relax.

A constant dread filled the bunker, and every single soldier was on high alert, training nonstop from dawn till dusk.

Command was as active as always, with Mark giving out the assignments for the day and runners coming and going.

Tammy crossed another name off her list. "Almost done. Twenty more to go and the interviews are over." She looked at Nina. "What's my next assignment?"

"We'll move you to the computer room. I need help with the databases. Would that work for you?" Nina took the list.

Tammy bit her lip. "Sure, I can help, but I don't know much about computers."

"We'll train you. We need as many hands as possible on this." Nina went to her desk and dove into her world.

I'd been helping Tammy all morning, but what I truly searched for was a way to talk to Abraham. I needed to tell him about Jacob before I left. I almost asked Matt to help me, but I decided this was something I needed to do by myself.

Abraham stood. "Well, ladies, I'm off. Anyone want to accompany an old man for lunch?"

This was my chance. "I think I'll accept that offer." I glanced at Tammy. "See you later. My stomach has been growling for the last thirty minutes."

"I noticed." She laughed. "Thanks for the help!"

Tammy and I talked a lot lately. For the last couple of days, I'd been playing Cupid between Maria and her. Tammy said this was her moment to do something big for the rebellion and she wanted Maria to be more understanding.

Both were right, so they were working on their schedules to make some time for each other.

"Ready when you are, Mr. Jackson."

He gave me a beautiful smile. An image of Jacob popped into my mind.

He bowed comically. "Glad for the company, Ms. Davis."

We walked side by side to the dining hall and got our food, then he followed me to a table in the back.

"So how's the training going? I've seen many new cadets lately," he said.

"It's going great. I'm feeling hopeful that this could go our way."

"I hope so too." He looked down. "I wish Jacob was here to see this. I'm still waiting for him to appear at any moment. Did I tell you about him?"

If I needed more proof, here it was. His name made a dent in my soul. I swallowed the lump in my throat. "No."

A soft smile covered his face. "He escaped a couple of years ago to join the rebellion. When I found his note, I looked for him but wasn't lucky. Nevertheless, I kept hoping I would find him. One day, I grew tired of teaching the NWG bullshit and decided to take my chances. It was a narrow escape, but I did it, and here I am. I keep hoping to one day find him roaming the halls. He's a real fighter and has an amazing soul."

How could I keep this man in the dark for so long? Waiting for his son. Believing he was alive somewhere.

My fears ended up hurting people and holding me back. I couldn't go on like this. I couldn't let my anxiety control me.

The heaviness in my chest was unbearable as I controlled my tears from spilling. I swallowed hard. It was now or never.

"Mr. Jackson?" The crack in my voice was impossible to hide.

"Yes?"

"I need to tell you something, but it can't be here. Is there anywhere more private?"

Abraham gazed at me. "Sure. We can go to the school room. The children are away, so it should give us enough privacy." His eyes searched mine. "Is everything all right?"

I nodded. My throat burned so badly I couldn't speak.

We finished our lunch and went next door. The room was the same as before, minus the children. He left the door ajar and stood by the teacher's desk. The classroom behind it was closed.

He sat and gestured for me to do the same. "I'm all ears. Whatever you need to get off your chest will not leave this room."

I missed having a father. Abraham's gentle smile as he waited for me to talk reminded me of mine.

My father was a great listener, always ready to hear me and help me get through my menial problems as a child. I touched his watch and could almost hear his voice. "Remember, Abi, even when the world is dark, a single spark can start a fire, and nothing can stop it once it begins to burn."

I'd always remember those words because they were his last words to me before he was murdered.

My heart swelled, and my father's words gave me the courage to talk.

I looked at Abraham. "I've been keeping something from you. It's about Jacob."

"You...know him?" His fingers twitched as he leaned an inch forward. "Is he okay?"

I intertwined my hands in my lap and gazed down, unable to meet his stare. "I'll never find enough words to describe what I felt for Jacob. He saved me in so many ways. He was everything to me, and I loved him."

He stood and furrowed his brow. "Saved. Loved. I don't understand."

I glanced up and met his eyes. "He wanted to save our friend, and he was caught." My voice broke. "He was murdered trying to save us."

And there it was.

I waited for any reaction, but he just stood there. His eyes glazed over, and tears started spilling out. He closed them, then collapsed onto the chair. His shoulders curled over his chest, and he covered his face with his hands. His body trembled.

Minutes passed. Abraham's painful sobs shattered my soul.

As much as I tried, I couldn't breathe. Everything blurred.

Not now. Be strong.

I closed my eyes and counted to ten, and the air started to come in.

"Mr. Jackson." I sobbed. "I'm so sorry."

He exhaled hard and swallowed, his Adam's apple bobbing. "I sensed something was wrong. I searched for so long and then arrived here. So many young people, but none were him. I hoped that maybe I was mistaken. That he was safe, and we'd meet someday."

He took a picture out of his pocket and passed it to me. "That's the last picture we took together. I always carry it with me."

Jacob stood next to his father, not so different from when I met him. It was a selfie taken by Abraham, whose left arm was perched over Jacob's shoulder. In the background stood a mahogany bookshelf filled with old books. Jacob's dark skin gleamed against the light of an oil lamp that glowed behind them. His glasses didn't hide the intensity of his dark irises. He held a book to his chest.

His father stood maybe an inch taller than him, smiling. His right arm stretched as he took the picture.

I could almost savor the moment, the intimacy of a peaceful night at home.

The tears flowed freely down my face as I touched his image. "He missed you and always talked about you. I'm sorry I didn't tell you once I realized you were his father. I was a coward."

Abraham took the photo back and shook his head. "You were just scared." He looked at the picture, and a tear dripped from his cheek. "How did it happen? When?"

The memories from that night were a stab in my chest. "It happened two years ago. We lived in an abandoned subway tunnel. A small patrol found our group. They were beating our friend, and he tried to fight them." I covered my face and took another deep breath. I'd never forget his eyes before he died as they urged me silently to stay hidden. They reflected his fear, the moment he knew he'd die then and there.

"An officer overpowered him and shot him." I took out Jacob's trench knife. "This is yours." I slid it toward him. It was rightfully his after all.

"I wondered where this had gone." He took it, and a sob left him as he stroked his finger over it. "Did he die quickly?"

I nodded.

"And your friend, did she make it?"

I shook my head, touching Bonnie's thread band.

"It must have been hard, going through that. I'm glad he saved you." He paused. "How long were you two together?"

"Four months, three as a couple." A small smile left me. Jacob made me so happy.

He offered the dagger back. "Take it. It's yours now. I know he would've wanted you to have it."

I pressed a hand against my heart. "Are you sure?"

He nodded.

I covered the hilt with my hand and sheathed it. The tension ebbed away as if Jacob was right here with me.

"Thank you for telling me." His tone was soft.

My chin trembled. "I don't deserve your gratitude."

He tilted his head. "You're just a girl, and you've suffered so much. Who am I to judge you?"

How could this man forgive me just like that? No matter what I'd been through, nothing excused my behavior.

I was always like this. Staying behind the lines, waiting for someone to save me, avoiding uncomfortable situations.

I couldn't continue being this way. This man was hurt. And I was doing the same with Sarah and Jimmy. I needed to make amends. I had to face my fears.

"Abi, you could've stayed quiet, but you pushed forward and came to me. You gave me closure. Now I know. Now we fight for him and all they've taken from us."

Abraham was right. Our fight was just starting.

I pushed my shoulders back. My pain receded as determination filled my soul.

There was so much we wanted to share that we stayed there for hours, reminiscing about Jacob.

Once outside, Abraham extended his hand to me. "If you need anything, let me know."

I hugged him. At first, he hesitated, but then he hugged me back.

He ruffled my hair. "Take care. I'll see you around."

I went to the infirmary to tell Matt. He was having coffee with Aoki. They both turned toward me.

I stayed by the door. "Hi. Am I interrupting?"

"No way. Come in." Aoki put a chair for me between them, then went to a counter and took out a mug. He served me some coffee from a tumbler. "So what gives?"

I blew air over the coffee. It was steaming hot. "I just talked to Mr. Jackson."

Matt scooted forward. "You told him?"

Aoki looked between us. "Told him what?"

I faced Aoki, who sat to my left. "Mr. Jackson is Jacob's father."

Aoki widened his eyes. "Your Jacob?"

I'd told him about Jacob one time when he came over to draw some sutras. He'd listened and comforted me that day. It was just after coming back from our failed escape attempt.

"Yes."

"And how did it go?" Matt searched my eyes.

"It went well, but I waited too long to tell him." I sipped my coffee, allowing the dark roast to warm up my body. "I need help."

It was the first time I accepted that I needed some kind of help to deal with whatever was inside me. While I chatted with Abraham, he told me how important talking about our problems was. Maybe therapy was what I needed.

Matt took my hand. "I'm glad you got it off your chest. And that you're finally open to getting help. I know you've always dealt with things on your own, but we all need a helping hand sometimes. How was he?"

"It was hard. He suspected it but was still hopeful. He thanked me for giving him closure."

"How long did you wait to tell him?" Aoki's voice was stern.

"Aoki," Matt said.

Aoki's eyes narrowed. "Tell me, Abi. How long did you wait?"

I'd never seen him like this. His muscles bunched up beneath his sleeves, and his eyes were dead set on me.

"A month." My voice quivered.

"You should have told him sooner. Not knowing kills you little by little." His gentle gaze was full of pain. "You can get trapped in a never-ending loop." His voice trembled, and he pressed his lips together.

I reached toward him. "Aoki, are you—?"

He stood before I could reach him. "I need to get the prepping for dinner done. Carol's waiting for me." He walked to the counter and rinsed his mug in the sink.

I glanced at Matt, and he shook his head.

Aoki gave Matt a peck on the lips, then passed by me without a second glance and left.

"What was that all about?" I asked as soon as the door shut behind him.

Matt closed his hands around his mug and took a huge swig. "I don't think it's my right to tell you. Talk to him. He loves you."

I looked at Aoki's now vacant chair. "I've never seen him this mad before."

Matt rested his elbows on his knees. "It's complicated."

I slumped forward. Suddenly, the room was too big for us.

"I'm glad you talked to Mr. Jackson. You gave him peace," Matt said after a moment.

"That's what he said." I sighed. "Why does this keep happening to good people? How long will we have to take it until we're finally free from all this?"

He covered his brow with his free hand. His golden curls curtained over his face. "I wish I could tell you, Abi. I just choose to cling to hope and keep fighting."

And there it was, like a dim light barely shining at the end of a never-ending tunnel. As if you were submerged in the sea, swimming up but never able to reach the surface, slowly drowning.

Hope was a feeble thing. It could easily slip between our fingers as we fought to grab onto it.

Would we ever have our city back, or would we forever be trapped in their grip?

My mind wandered to the memorial center and all the candles lit there. Then to the ones that were not there and those who still suffered without a way to escape.

How could one hope after so much darkness?

I entered the kitchen just before dinner and bumped into Carol.

"Hey!" She hugged me. "I haven't seen you in a while. How are you doing?"

Between training and the strategy meetings, I hadn't visited.

"I'm good. How are you holding up?" I was certain she was in a bad place after Diane left with the other children more than a month ago.

She shrugged and lowered her gaze. "As best as I can. I miss her so much. We both do." She took a deep breath, then rolled her shoulders back. "It's hard, but Diane's safe, and that's all that matters. Steven and his wife are good friends. She's staying with them."

Many children were left without their parents, but Connor made sure to assign a team to care for them. They'd be all right.

I touched her arm. "If you need to talk, I'm here."

She nodded. "Thank you."

"Well, I have to go. Need to do some stuff before dinner." She reached the door and waved back. "See you later."

My lips were still drawn in a smile when Aoki came into view.

"Abi?" He sighed heavily. "What are you doing here?"

"Can we talk?"

He dried his hands with a towel and looked around. Some soldiers were having snacks at a table in the front corner of the mess hall. Training was harsh and long, and we needed our sustenance. I assumed they were waiting for dinnertime.

"Okay." He moved to a table and gestured for me to sit.

Once down, I searched for the right words to broach the subject. Aoki was important to me, and whatever was happening, I wanted to help. Each of us had our own demons. I just never expected Aoki's gentle soul to have them also.

"You want to know what that was all about in the infirmary." There was a hint of sadness in his voice.

"I was a coward for not telling Mr. Jackson sooner. I'm sorry if I hurt you in any way. You're my friend. I want to fix this." Knowing he was mad drilled at my heart.

He took my hands. "There's nothing to fix. I love you, and I'm sorry for scaring you. There's a lot you don't know about me. I would've told you before, but I keep everything buried deep. Today, when you told us about Mr. Jackson, everything came back to the surface."

His gaze was downcast. "Mom and Dad were the ones who helped us escape. When I graduated from the facilities, I was assigned to work in the kitchens inside the government center. My living space was to the east near the walls. I couldn't swallow working for the elites, so the idea of escape was on my mind. When I went to say my goodbyes, Mark was waiting for me with a rucksack slung over his back. He was sixteen at the time."

Aoki rested his elbows on the table. "They'd heard about the rebel group that hid in the forest and said that if there was the slightest chance we could find them, they'd do whatever was in their power to help. They were planning to sacrifice themselves so we could escape. I tried to convince them to come with us, but I couldn't sway them. The patrols were difficult to avoid, especially if we were four."

He took a deep, shuddering breath. "That night my parents went opposite us toward a patrol. They started running as soon as the patrol spotted them. That's when all hell broke loose, and Mark and I ran the other way. The cracking sound of bullets filled the night's silence. We ran for hours and hid in the forest. Our parents were lost, and we didn't even know what became of them. The next day, as we walked north, runners caught us. After passing the security protocol, they took us in."

I held back my tears and covered his hands. "God, Aoki. I'm so sorry."

Aoki looked at our joined hands. "You're the only person who knows about this other than Davon, Matt, and Mark."

"Do you know what happened to your parents?"

He nodded and clenched his fists beneath my hands. Tears dropped on top of them.

"Six years passed without me knowing if they escaped, were arrested, or were killed on the spot. With each passing day, my soul broke no matter how much Matt tried to help. Then Davon came with the news about Sarah, but he found something else. Their names were listed in a logbook of one of the facilities where they keep unruly citizens. They're inside Electi, working to death for the elites, and we can't do anything about it."

My heart caught in my throat as I thought about Davon going in to save Deb while Aoki's parents lived in misery.

"There must be a way. We'll get them out."

He used the towel to dry his face and sat back. "We all have someone we lost. At least I know they're alive."

Was there nothing we could do? There had to be a way.

"But, Aoki..."

"It's all right, Abi. I've made my peace with it. Once this is all over, I hope we can be together again, but I won't dwell on it. We need to keep moving forward for all the citizens who are suffering out there."

He stood, and I followed. "Don't worry about me, and focus on the mission. You're leaving soon." He embraced me. "Sorry for scaring you. You have no idea how much you mean to me."

I hugged him back, hoping to ease his suffering, putting all my love into it. "I love you, Aoki. I'll get them back for you. I promise."

He held me tighter, and it was as if my soul recharged with a newfound purpose.

I'd never hold back again. I would fight for my family until the end.

Chapter 16

Abi

January 6, 2214

I yawned. Soft jazz music played from my music box, or MP3 as Matt called it. I had taken a liking to the double bass. Almost like a heartbeat, its warm tone wrapped around me and filled my space. Its rhythmic thumping told a story.

Connor helped me set it up. I also started taking some natural pills Matt recommended so I could sleep better, and they worked.

I stood in front of my mirror, naked. My scars stared back at me, reminding me of the constant threat that lay ahead. I touched my right thigh. It ached sometimes. The pink skin was uneven from when Matt stitched me. I occasionally limped after training, but I hid it as best I could.

The mark on my left breast looked pinkish and raised, an eternal reminder of that horrible day. I brushed the thin line where a bullet grazed me that night some NWG soldiers ambushed us at the dead drop. Then there was my face and the scar that stretched from my right cheek to my chin.

I'd carry them with pride like Matt told me and remind myself that we were alive and still fighting.

It seemed like ages since I joined the rebellion, but it had only been a few months. My body was a half-written book from a story that would soon reach its climax. How many more pages would my foes write before we took it all back?

Soon I'd be back out there on the battlefield. But this time it was a hushed one, as we readied for our first strike. The silence before the war cry.

After donning my training gear, I pulled my hair up in a high ponytail. My highlighted curls cascaded down to my ears. They reminded me of Deb just before she sent me away.

I reached the mess hall and grabbed buttered toast and coffee, enough to survive resistance training with Maria. Truthfully, I couldn't believe I did half the shit she put me through.

"Morning. Can I sit with you?"

I stiffened at Jimmy's melodic voice, one that once eased and comforted me but now reminded me of so much pain.

I breathed hard. I needed to fix this. I couldn't go without having my best friend back. Without forgiving him.

I looked up.

His blue eyes lacked their usual luster.

"Sure." I slid the food tray a bit to the side.

Jimmy sat beside me, bacon all over his tray with toast and orange juice. He didn't like coffee but was crazy about bacon.

"The meeting is today, right? Are you going?" he asked.

Last Thursday, I drank some beers with the guys, Jimmy included. Small talk was not my forte, but at least we could maintain a conversation.

"Yes, I have training with Maria, but we'll be there."

Today was my last strategy meeting. Matt and I were leaving next week.

David and Jimmy didn't know about it yet, and, from my experience, they'd surely object.

Even though Jimmy told me he'd help me, I was sure he'd complain about me leaving so soon.

As for David, he'd become one of my best friends, but he was over-protective at times. We'd grown close and talked daily. We had a lot in common. He was set on making me the best sniper on his team. He told me I reminded him of his cousin, one he lost contact with a long time ago during the first years of the regime. They were close, but when his parents were forced to move to the northern slums, they never saw each other again.

"What time is the meeting?" Jimmy asked.

"Around ten." I was almost finished with breakfast. "You'll join us, right?"

He looked at his watch. "Sure. I have therapy at eight, but I'll make it in time." He took a bite of his bacon and moaned.

I chuckled, then covered my mouth. How long had it been since I last laughed with him?

His eyes glistened as he watched me.

"What?"

He smiled and shook his head. "I didn't think I'd ever hear you laugh again. At least not in my presence."

I sighed. "Me neither. Small steps, right?"

He nodded. "Small steps."

I tapped my plate with my fork. "Jimmy?"

He sipped his orange juice. "Yes?"

This was not who we were. It was as if a frigid abyss separated us, trapping us in a state of inertia. As if we couldn't move forward. It was driving me nuts. "Can we talk?"

He jerked his face toward me, eyes wide. "Here or somewhere more private?"

I shrugged.

He put the glass on the table, then nodded.

We finished in silence, and I followed Jimmy through hall D and out into the forest.

Two months ago, we came to this same spot together. I sat. A chilling wind moved through the woods, and the snow collected by the pine trees fell. The vast forest extended with no end in sight, and the snowcapped mountains gave a majestic feel to the horizon.

With my heart in my throat, I leaned forward. "We can't go on like this. I feel...empty."

Jimmy's crunching footsteps stopped behind me. He covered my neck with a scarf, then sat by my side. "You don't have to forgive me. In truth, I don't deserve it."

I gazed at him as he looked at the horizon. His sandy-blond hair was ruffled by the wind, and his eyes shared the same hue as the sky. He was such a beautiful person inside and out. How he lost control that night was a mystery to me. But he had. It happened.

It seemed impossible to push away everything that had transpired that night. I'd never forget the terror of not knowing if I'd lost Davon. The anxiety that took over me. The long weeks afterward when I didn't know whether Davon made it or not. It almost broke me.

Then there was Jimmy and the monster he let out that night. The hatred I witnessed when he pushed me away and shot Davon. I remembered his bulging eyes when I shot him and the pain when Davon asked me to take Jimmy back. The moment I shut the world out and followed that order because Jimmy's life was in my hands.

I couldn't go on like this. These feelings were like venom, eating me from the inside. I needed to forgive him.

"I don't think I can ever forget what you did, but I want to forgive you. I need you in my life." I touched my temple and looked at the ground.

Jimmy shifted beside me, and when he sniffed, I caught a glimpse of a tear running down his chin. "I'm not worthy of you."

My heart ached for him. He looked so fragile. "Don't say that, Jimmy. You made a mistake. A terrible one. But I believe you when you say you're sorry. I've known you forever. You're good inside."

I leaned against him. "I don't like my world without you. It's too dark. Too lonely."

The warmth of his arm as he hugged me to him was like traveling back to our youth. To those days we'd find a way to meet even though it was forbidden. To the long nights when he'd hold me as I cried my eyes out after my parents' deaths.

"Thank you, Abi. Thank you. I missed you so much." He kissed my temple.

We stayed there until it was time for his therapy session.

Matt left a note this morning about needing to talk to me, so I tagged along to the infirmary.

Lately, he'd been teaching me how it all worked inside Electi, how the government functioned, and what encompassed the New World Government's territory.

With control over most of the eastern coast, they had a lot of power, but the NWG wasn't the only government in control of this continent.

There were at least three major governments to the west and one to the north. Matt didn't know much about them, but at least two had allied themselves with the NWG. Nevertheless, they all wanted one thing—to gain complete control over the continent.

In short, the war wasn't over, and they kept fighting for power.

Promissa was the NWG's largest city and the seat of the government, but there were other cities. A man higher in rank than General Lavigne ruled one of them. His name was Thorne Steele, the general of the army.

A madman. One who stopped at nothing in war and who worked hand in hand with Jordan Niles from the city of Halcyon.

Matt briefed me about President Orville, the leader of the New World Government. A wealthy and sophisticated man who acted as the public figure in command of the entire area. He was a widower and lived in Electi with his only daughter, Grace. He dealt with bureaucracy and public affairs, whereas Jordan Niles was the mastermind behind the elite oligarchy.

Davon had once had a relationship with Grace, one his father had always wanted. Matt said it was after Elaine died and Connor sent him to Electi. He called that time the dark years, saying Davon was another man. A womanizer. One who didn't care for anything or anyone.

My skin burned when I thought about him that way. To picture him being intimate with other women, then pushing them away. Everything ended with Katherine, the last woman he was with before he met me.

Warmth filled me at the man he'd become. The one I fell in love with.

A group of cadets passed us as we entered hall F.

"Come on. General Diaz will give us hell if we're late," one said.

Training was harsh and merciless but necessary. In the real world, no one would stop to give you time to recover, so we trained for endurance, strength, and agility.

Matt was finishing up with a patient when we entered the infirmary. "Hey, guys!"

"Jimmy said he had therapies, so I thought I'd drop by before training." I cocked an eyebrow. "You wanted to talk?"

"All set," Matt said to the patient, then walked toward us. "Yes, it's about the mission."

I opened my eyes wide and angled my head slightly toward Jimmy.

Matt shrugged. "It's all right. I was going to tell him anyway at the strategy meeting."

I held my breath, waiting for Jimmy's reaction.

"What's happening?" Jimmy darted his eyes between us.

"Abi and I are going out next week. Into Electi."

Jimmy's legs wavered, but he recovered. "So soon?"

I knew it.

"I'm more than ready." I crossed my arms.

Jimmy held his hands up. "Don't get me wrong. I'm okay with it. It's just..." He shook his head. "Forget it. Whatever you need, count on me."

"Thank you." I crossed the room and leaned on a countertop, facing Matt. "What did you want to talk about before the meeting?"

He took out three chairs. "Please sit."

I sat beside Jimmy.

Matt opened his lab coat and sat in front of us. "It's about our cover. Our stories need to be straight."

I looked at my watch. Still on time.

"We need to fabricate a story that will explain my injury. Connor suggested we say the insurgent group you infiltrated discovered you and that when I went to help you escape, they shot me."

I bent forward. "If we're going with that, I need to know how I got caught."

Matt leaned over the left armrest, resting his jaw on his fist. "We'll say someone found you writing a coded letter while the group moved east."

I dipped my chin. "And how do we explain the surgery? They might find out if they check."

"We'll tell them you helped me treat the wound, which still needs time to heal. This is why you should learn how to suture and clean wounds. At least the essentials. Rachel will help you. After all, you worked for us at the clinic. It's part of your cover."

I shook my head. "Matt, you know I'm terrified of all of this." I motioned around me. "Are you sure it's needed?"

I rubbed my hands over my cargo pants. God, I was sweating like crazy.

Matt sighed and rubbed his brow. "Abi, I've told you before, Jordan Niles is a calculating man. He's not easy to fool. He knows how to read people, and he'll be watching you. You need to be ready."

I wanted to run and hide. What was I getting myself into?

"There's something else. Jordan will want my arm checked, but if they find the implants from the operation, they'll suspect something doesn't fit. For that, we need to bring Mom in. Connor already approved. She's always been on Promissa's side, and I'm sure she'll prove loyal to us and help us from within."

I clasped my sapphire necklace. "Do you think we can deceive him?"

He furrowed his brow and pressed his lips together. "I don't know. In terms of the injury, I'm sure he'll trust Mom. No matter their differences, she's always been ethical in her profession. As for you, he's very suspicious of new people. I'm sure Davon has already started paving your way, but even then, Jordan may ask you to prove your loyalty to him. If we get him to trust you, we're hoping he'll let you in."

My heart raced to the point of pain.

A chill ran through me, and I doubled over. Was I about to faint?

"Abi?" Jimmy bowed toward me. "Are you okay?"

I slowed my breathing. I couldn't falter, not when I was so close to getting there. "Yeah. I just need some water."

Jimmy retrieved some water for me from the kitchenette. "Here."

I took it.

He eyed Matt. "Are you sure you can keep her safe out there?"

I stood. "Jimmy?"

He held an arm out to hold me back.

Matt darted his gaze between us. "We'll protect her with our lives. We won't let anyone hurt her."

I humphed.

Jimmy put his arm down.

I stood between them. "I can take care of myself."

Jimmy took my hands in his. "I know. And I'm sorry. I don't doubt your strength. But you still don't understand how they work. Not truly. We've seen enough to make your skin crawl. Stick to Matt and Davon. Follow their orders to the point. Stay focused, and don't let your hatred tempt you into stirring off track. Can you do that?"

I bit my lip, and my voice dropped to a murmur. "I can."

Maria crouched next to me. "Come on! Ten more push-ups. And stop whining."

I'd been working out since 8:00 a.m. The circuit consisted of a weight-lifting exercise, a body weight movement, a core exercise, and a short cardio interval. This was my last round, with a minute in low plank and thirty seconds of mountain climbers to go.

I completed my last push-up and sat on the mat, massaging my shoulders. My thighs hurt, and my core couldn't take it any longer.

Maria stood. "Come on! We're almost done for the day."

I glanced up. "Don't you care that I'm dying here?"

She put her hand on her hip. "No. Actually, I don't, and no one out there will."

My body trembled, but I got in a low plank position.

Lately, Maria was ruthless in her training, especially since Connor said we'd move out into Electi soon. And I got it—she wanted me to be ready. Consistency was key, and it was already paying off.

Every passing day, my body hurt less, and my muscle mass had grown since I arrived here. I could lift more and exercise for longer periods of time. At least tomorrow was my rest day, one thing to look forward to.

I was about to start the mountain climbers when the door to the training room slammed open. I sat up, and Maria straightened.

Matt's face was pale, his eyes bigger than I'd ever seen them. He darted them around the room until he found us.

"What happened?" Maria's voice boomed throughout the room.

Everyone stopped what they were doing.

Matt ran to us and grabbed Maria's arm in a tense hold. "It's the energy bunker. It was attacked!"

My heart hammered against my chest. I stood and dried my sweat with my towel.

Maria covered his hand. "Tell me everything. What do you need?"

"As many soldiers as you can spare. We're moving half our forces to the farming and engineering bunker." He let go of her arm.

Maria turned to the cadets. "Soldiers! Get your gear ready, and wait for orders. This is not a drill."

Everyone dispersed.

I moved to his side. "Is everyone all right?"

Matt pressed his lips together. "It's best if we move to command. Connor's waiting."

A heaviness weighed across my breast. How many had we lost?

We followed him. Once we entered, the alarms started, one long siren followed by two short bursts. I'd been learning them, and this one meant to get ready. A high alert for soldiers. Civilians were to go to their rooms and wait for further orders.

Once in Connor's office, I recognized someone standing next to the desk. "Yuxuan?"

Major General Yuxuan Li turned toward me.

I stepped back.

His uniform was bathed in blood, and gashes ran across his arms and face. Blood coated his long black hair. He held the hilt of his *jian*, a Chinese double-edged sword. It showed signs of battle.

He bowed slightly. "Abigail."

Bile rose to my throat.

Behind him stood a PRF soldier. She was also drenched in blood, gauze wrapped around her left arm.

What the hell happened out there?

The room was packed. Jimmy sat in one chair and Councilmember Faez in the other. I'd only seen him once when Davon and I visited the bunkers.

Faez took off his glasses and squeezed his eyes, then put them on again. His dark eyes were red rimmed, and his brown hair was ruffled.

I stood between Matt and Maria at the back of the office. Both breathed hard, their state no different than mine.

"Where's Sarah?" I whispered to Matt.

He shrugged.

I hadn't seen her in a while. Where could she be? And why wasn't she here?

I had to talk to her. I couldn't put it off any longer.

Nina stood next to Connor behind the desk, showing something to him on her tablet.

"Everything's set, then?" Connor asked.

She straightened. "Yes, sir."

"Thank you." Connor sat. "I gathered you here because the energy bunker was attacked. It had been evacuated as a precaution since our dead drop was compromised. Nevertheless, a skeleton crew was still inside, working on the last details."

Yuxuan moved to Connor's side. "I was assigned to the energy bunker a week ago to aid in its evacuation and defense. Just before dawn, General Lavigne and a group of about a hundred NWG soldiers swarmed the area. Even though land mines were set around the perimeter, they only took care of about a third of them. Our soldiers defended the zone as best they could, but they were overpowered." He gripped the desk, head down. "They all died."

My limbs trembled. This was war. It had come to us at last.

Matt inched closer, enough that his arm grazed mine. A sense of calm flowed from him like a stream, and I breathed.

Connor motioned toward Yuxuan. "I can take it from here if you want."

Yuxuan shook his head. "We got most people out through the emergency exits. When the entrance of the bunker was blasted away, myself and four others were waiting inside. We didn't stand a chance against so many, but the others needed time to get as far away as possible. So we fought."

I swallowed hard. It was a nightmare. Five people against so many. Was this how it would be for us out there? Did we really stand a chance?

"During the fight, three of our group died. When only Corporal Mathews and I were left, we led the NWG soldiers down a hall. We set a bomb there to ensure no one followed in case of an assault. We escaped through the same exit the citizens had used. Once outside, Corporal Mathews pushed the trigger. He's sure the blast took care of the soldiers who were behind us."

I blinked. He? So Corporal Mathews was a man.

"We ran south for five miles, then west for three more. Once we were sure no one had followed us, we came here," Corporal Mathews said in a deep voice.

Yuxuan hunched over. "Fourteen of our people died today. They fought till the very end. One of them was Councilmember DeLuca. She died defending the bunker with us."

Jimmy rose. "In the name of our captain, who can't be here due to the emergency, I want to thank you for what you did out there. We just got communication from farming. The people you helped made it—all twenty-three of them. Still, even one death is too much."

Yuxuan closed his eyes for a moment. "All of them died honorably. They will not be forgotten."

Connor nodded. "They will be missed."

I clenched my fists. How many more would we lose to this war?

Jimmy slumped onto his chair, and I walked toward him. I put my hand on his shoulder. He covered it with his own and squeezed it.

After a short pause, Connor sighed. "Councilmember Faez arrived yesterday to talk to Nina about the energy system and to ensure all the data was moved flawlessly to our main database. Last night, they finished downloading the false data onto the energy bunker database. Nina can explain better."

Nina tapped on the tablet and showed us a map. "If they follow the data we left, it'll take them on a wild goose chase all over the eastern area of the forest and away from us. But the NWG has their own tech team, and they will eventually discover it's a false trail. We're still hopeful this will give us some time."

"Will there be retaliation for the lives lost?"

We all turned toward Faez. His hands were locked into fists.

He narrowed his eyes at Connor. "Or will you do nothing?"

Connor stiffened. "Major General Li, Corporal Mathews, thank you for everything. Nina will take you to the infirmary to be checked."

Both soldiers followed Nina out.

Connor sat back. "This was a huge loss for the PRF, and I assure you we're working on a strategy. We understand all you've lost and—"

I jumped back as Faez stood and slammed both fists on the desk, sending a loud thud throughout the room.

"That was my home! DeLuca was my family, and all those people lost today had families too." Tears sprang from Faez's eyes. "Tell me you have a plan!"

Connor took a deep breath. "Faez, please trust me on this."

Faez scowled. "How, Connor? First you lose Deborah, then Davon. He's out there feeding them intel as far as we know. The attack today will be the first of many. I'm sure he already gave them all they needed."

My blood boiled at the accusation. If they only knew the risks Davon was taking to help us.

Connor gestured for Faez to sit.

Faez did, his expression hard.

"Councilmember Faez, I'm putting a lot at risk here. I need you to promise that what I'm about to disclose will not leave this room," Connor said.

Faez flinched back. He fixed his gaze on Connor. "I made an oath to the People's Revolutionary Front, one I would never break."

Connor interlaced his fingers on his desk. "Then you need to know that Davon is on our side. He's not a traitor. His arrest and escape were a deception to get the real one—a spy that is hiding among us."

I bit my lip. Would the council accept Davon's innocence, or would they all turn their backs on him like many did?

I took a step back and bumped into Matt. He rested his hand on my lower back. "Calm down. I'm right here."

The tension in the room was palpable as we all stood still, eyes locked on our general of the army.

Faez froze, then glanced around the room. "But...why hasn't the council been informed of this?"

"We don't know who the spy is, and we couldn't risk it. At this moment, Davon is focused on finding out who they are and us on trapping them as soon as they slip up. He alerted us of the possible attack on the energy bunker. That's the true reason for the evacuation. We received his letter a week ago."

Faez blinked. "We need to inform the others. We should've made this decision together, as it was meant to be. That's what we agreed on when we started this community."

Connor leaned back in his chair. "You're right. That's why I'm holding a council meeting in a week. As for the people, I vote to let them continue assuming Davon is the traitor. It's our best option if we want the spy to gain confidence and make their move, but I hope Davon uncovers them before this happens."

"Let's hope your plan works." Faez rose. "Tomorrow I leave for farming. I need to be with my people."

"Take Corporal Mathews back with you. He'll ensure you make it safely." Connor held out his hand.

Faez took it.

"This will not stay unpunished. We'll take back what's ours no matter what," Connor said.

After Faez closed the door behind him, Maria moved forward. "This isn't good, Connor. How much time do you think we have until they realize the intel is fake?"

Connor took out his journal and started writing. "We don't know. Maybe a month or two." He tapped the pen against the page. "I trust Davon knows what he's doing. Once Matt and Abi are inside, we can start taking on allies. Our spies in Promissa are working without pause to find the rebel factions that are hiding within the city. You and David will continue training our soldiers, and Yuxuan, Katherine, and Mathews will take over the training in the rest of the bunkers."

He wrote something down, then looked at Jimmy. "How is the preparation of the caves going?"

"The runners already moved the generators over and started preparing the common dormitories and kitchen area. Mark got some engineers to help us. They're designing plans to use the stream for potable water and showering purposes. They're also creating a restroom area."

Connor stood, clasped his hands behind his back, and paced. "Will they be ready on time?"

Jimmy scraped a hand through his hair. "We're working as fast as possible."

Connor placed his fist on the desk. "Work faster. What happened today could happen again. We need to have a backup plan, somewhere to go in case of another attack."

Jimmy rose. "I'll leave now to get the message out. It'll be done." He gave me a reassuring nod, then left.

My tension ebbed a bit. I could almost hear his words: "Everything will be all right."

Matt, Maria, and I were the only ones left.

"Maria, are the soldiers ready? Do we have enough weapons?" Connor asked.

Maria nodded. "They're ready and anxious to get out there. As for the weapons, we're expecting a shipment from the import bunker. It should be here tomorrow."

"Good." Connor looked at Matt and me. "As for you two, be ready to leave in two days. We're running out of time."

Matt squeezed my hand.

War had just begun.

January 8, 2214

"How are you feeling about today?" David stretched his legs on the forest floor.

We'd decided to have breakfast outside. Tonight Matt and I would leave Janus Peak to take on our mission, and I wanted to have a moment alone with my friend.

"Good. Worried. Terrified." I glanced at him.

He sighed. "If it makes you feel better, I feel the same way."

I frowned in confusion. "About what?"

"About you going into Electi."

I sighed. "David..."

He laid his arms back and looked up at the sky. "I've told you how I feel about it. I know you need to go and that there's nothing I can say to convince you otherwise. But I worry."

When the light struck his eyes, his golden irises glittered.

I mirrored him. "And what about you? I worry about you too, you know. What will you do without me?"

"I'll have to find a way to survive." David chuckled.

We were joking, but I didn't know what I'd do if anything happened to him.

I gazed at the sky. It seemed endless. "I'll be careful out there. I promise."

I hoped that was a promise I could keep.

"I will miss you, Abigail Davis." He tilted his face my way.

His bronzed skin, like mine, seemed radiant under the sun. His warm smile eased my turbulent thoughts, and I smiled back.

"And I will miss you, David Martinez."

Matt and I agreed to pack together to make sure we had everything we needed. Two heads were better than one.

"Are you sure you have everything you need?" Aoki asked Matt as he went over his list.

"I think so."

Connor and Maria had already briefed us, and we'd said our goodbyes.

"Be safe out there, and bring your sister back. I love you." Connor's words gave me strength. There was no doubt in them. No hesitation.

I was already done and was drawing shakyos on the table. Shirokuro rested over half of my work, asking for attention. Everything went silent, and I turned my head.

Aoki hugged Matt from behind. Matt rested his head on Aoki's shoulder as Aoki peppered kisses on his nape. It was a beautiful moment. A private one.

When would they see each other again? A shiver ran through my body as I remembered the attack on the energy bunker. What if the same happened here? Would our loved ones be safe?

I shook my head and refocused on what had to be done. I couldn't live my life based on what could happen. I needed to act and do whatever was needed to move the mission forward. They'd be safe.

I stood. "I'm going to try to find Sarah. I haven't said my goodbyes."

My therapist told me I needed to talk to her. To make my peace with all that happened. This was my last chance to fix it.

Aoki came to me and hugged me.

I embraced him back. "I'll miss you so much. Please be safe."

After a moment, he took a step back and held me at arm's length. "We'll be okay. You take care out there. Do what you must, and come back safe." He kissed my temple.

"Will do." I clasped Matt's shoulder. "Come to Davon's when you're ready to leave."

His glassy gaze held mine before he nodded.

I stepped into the hall and found Jimmy, his hand primed to knock on my door. "Jimmy?"

He smiled. "Hi. I wanted to say goodbye." He approached me. "Good luck on your mission." He took my hands, his eyes downcast. "Please be careful out there, and don't worry about us."

Leaving my family behind under such a threat broke me even though I was thrilled to be back with Davon and to save Deb.

I took a step forward and hugged him tightly. He held me to his chest, and I breathed in his earthy aroma. I was so small in his arms, and I let myself bask in his embrace.

He cupped my face, then kissed my cheek. His tears mixed with mine. "Don't let your guard down out there. Come back to us."

I rested my hands on his chest. "I wish I'd forgiven you sooner. Now our time is up." I touched the cane he always carried. "I'm sorry for shooting you. I never wanted to hurt you."

He shook his head. "Don't apologize. I'm the one who's humbled by your forgiveness. I never thought we'd break through this."

I smiled. "You're my friend. I'm glad to have you back."

He curled his lip up and then put some space between us. "Tell Davon that if anything happens to you, he'll have to deal with me."

I chuckled. "You'll never change."

He shrugged. "It's my job to worry about you. I'll see you again soon."

I nodded. "Be safe."

I'd looked for Sarah everywhere since yesterday. Where was she hiding? It seemed like I was always one step behind. Was she avoiding me on purpose?

I decided to look outside, as it was the only place I hadn't checked. As I reached hall B, Tammy came in from the forest.

"Hey, Tammy!" We met halfway through, just past her apartment. "Have you seen Sarah?"

She smiled. "Yeah, I was just with her." She slid her hands into her pockets. "She's seemed pretty bummed lately, and when I saw her go out, I decided to follow. I asked her about it, but she said she's fine."

I exhaled hard. "I've been looking for her since yesterday."

Tammy tilted her head. "You're leaving for import today, right?"

Everyone thought we were going to import to change places with Yuxuan. He'd be taking our spot here in Janus Peak, and Katherine would stay to train the soldiers with Corporal Mathews, who'd just come in from the farming bunker.

More people volunteered daily to fight, and our army grew by the day. Still, we needed more.

I fidgeted with Mom's bracelet. "Yeah, that's why I was looking for her. I wanted to say goodbye."

"And how about saying goodbye to your friend?" She smiled.

"Come here." I hugged her tight. Her sweet scent wafted through me. "I'll miss you. Be careful, okay?"

She stepped back and grasped my hand. "I can't believe we're on the verge of war. What if we lose all this?" Her blue eyes glistened with unshed tears.

I held her hand. "We have to trust we'll make it. Promise me that if anything happens, you'll follow Maria. She'll keep you safe."

"I have a badass girlfriend, don't I?" She chuckled. "How long will you be out there?"

I shrugged. "I'm not sure. Connor didn't say."

I had no idea what to expect out there or how long our mission would take. Hell, we didn't know if we'd make it out once inside. For all we knew, Jordan could be waiting to strike.

I pushed those thoughts away.

She pocketed her hands and shifted in place. "I hope it's not too long." She cocked her head toward the end of the hall. "Now, go to your sister. She needs you."

"We'll see each other again soon." I prayed my words were true.

"I'm sure we will." She hugged me again and went into her apartment.

I exited the bunker. "Sarah?"

She sat on the ground, facing the city. "You're leaving tonight." She didn't glance back.

I headed toward her. "I am."

She patted the space to her right.

I sat.

She hugged her knees. "I thought you didn't want to see me anymore."

I winced. God. This was my sister. She'd suffered so much loss, and I made her think she'd lost me too.

I turned to her. "You'll always be my sister. I'm so sorry. I should have come to you sooner."

Her emerald eyes were hollow. Her face was gaunt.

I touched her shoulder. "Sarah, are you feeling okay?"

I saw her a couple of days ago when passing through the common area. What had happened to her since?

She shook her head. "I'm sorry about everything. I hoped you could understand, but I know you won't. No one would."

Was she even listening to me? What was she talking about?

I bent slightly, trying to catch her gaze, but she kept focused on the horizon. On Promissa.

"What do you mean?" I asked.

"Nothing. It's just..." Her hands trembled, but she held them together. "Know that I love you no matter what happens. You're my sister, and I'll do anything to protect you."

I clasped her ice-cold hands. "No matter what happened between us, you're my family. Nothing and no one will change that. Ever."

She looked at me, her eyes glassy and red. "Please be careful. And remember, I'll go to any lengths to keep you safe."

She kept repeating herself and talking in riddles. I wondered if all that had happened triggered some of her trauma. Our parents' death. Carlos's murder. Charlie's disappearance. Deb's imprisonment. She'd been through so much.

I failed as a sister. I should have noticed before tonight.

I hugged her. Her sobs broke me, and I gripped her tighter. "Everything will be all right. I'll come back to you soon."

She grabbed my shoulders. Her intense gaze pierced through me, her pupils unusually large. Her eyes were almost wild. "Promise me you'll run.

Run if you see any danger. Run if they find you out. Forget about me. Don't try to be a hero."

Whatever this was, she was consumed by fear.

I held her face and shook my head. "Deb will be back soon, and we'll go through this together. Whatever happens, I won't rest until we're all safe and back where we belong."

I straightened. "I won't run from them. Not again. Not ever."

She wrapped her arms around me. "I love you. I always will."

"Me too."

We stayed like that for a few minutes.

Sarah looked at her watch. "You should go. It's getting late."

I nodded. "I'll walk you to your apartment."

We hugged again after she opened her door.

She cupped my cheek. "You'll always be my baby sister. And I love you. Never forget." She entered and closed the door behind her.

This wasn't right. It was too final. To leave her like this broke my heart.

I went back to Davon's apartment and got everything ready. I was just finishing putting my boots on when Matt came in with his backpack in tow, using his shirt to dry his tears.

I glimpsed Aoki in the hall just as he closed their door. His face was wet with tears, his skin pale.

I hugged Matt.

"Thank you." He breathed into my neck. "It never gets easier."

"We'll make it back."

He stepped away. "I know."

Matt put his pack down and went to the bar.

I got my weapons and put them on the bed, then closed Davon's chest. "Matt?"

He gulped down a shot of whiskey. "Yes?"

"I'm worried about Sarah. I don't know. She was saying weird stuff. It was almost as if..." Did she believe something bad would happen? Did she know something we didn't? "I think with all that's happened she's reverted to her old trauma."

Matt put the glass down and leaned against the bar. "I noticed something last week. She kept pacing in command and asking if they'd found anything. I told Connor about it. He's going to talk to her and already told the therapists to work with her. He fears the same."

I took a deep breath and hoped she'd get the help she needed. I'd never forgive myself for pushing her away.

I just had to trust Connor could help her. He was family.

I sheathed my pocket khukuri and my trench knife in Jacob's leather belt, then put my gun into my holster. I hauled on my hiking backpack, and Matt helped me adjust it. It was huge and held most of my belongings.

I looked at the sketch Sarah made of the three of us. I brought it to Davon's after I came back.

Would we ever be together again?

I swallowed my tears. "Do you think she'll be okay?"

Matt glanced at the paper, then at me. "She'll be okay, and soon the three of you will be together again." His voice was firm, and I believed him.

I nodded, then put my glasses on. "Then let's go."

We walked down our hall. Today I'd leave the bunker using the same door as when I arrived. Most people had already turned in when we left.

Matt stepped out first and helped me up.

A fierce breeze met us as soon as we walked through the hatch. Despite my hoodie, the cold seeped into my bones.

"Remember the plan. Just go with the story. I'm sure Jordan is already looking for us. If you get nervous, breathe like Aoki taught you. Don't let them see you break because that would make them suspect you. You belong with us. From now on, you may as well be an elite."

His words shook me to the core. An elite.

My stomach clenched. How long had I dreamed of having my vengeance for all they'd taken? Now I'd be one of them.

We walked in silence. The snow crunched beneath our feet.

After an hour, we took a break and sat by a maple tree.

"What will you do once we get to Electi?" I asked Matt.

He popped a peanut into his mouth. "Visit Mom. It's been a while since I've seen her."

I took a gulp of water. "What about your father?"

He shrugged.

Maybe I was pushing the limit, but I wanted to know why. I knew about the divorce, about what Jordan did to them. I understood what his father worked on, but still...I would do anything to have mine back.

"What happened between you two?"

He rested his back against the tree. "After the divorce, we just grew apart."

I crossed my legs beneath me. "Was he a good father?"

He smiled wistfully. "The best. And a good husband. Mom and Dad are very open in terms of relationships, so they had an open marriage. I've always envied their love. Their trust and devotion were unparalleled. I'd never seen a couple so dedicated to each other. I'm sure he still loves her, and she feels the same way too. She's told me."

He sipped some water. "In our home, no politics were spoken. And even though we had our differences, Dad never asked us to change. We had a happy home. When Jordan destroyed that, when he took away my family...I just wish things could be different."

Davon's father wrecked a beautiful family. It only made me hate him more. To lose it all must have been hard. "I'm so sorry, Matt."

"Don't be. Dad did all he could, but Jordan wouldn't give in. I just wish there was some way we could fix it." Matt stood. "Let's go."

We fell into a good pace as the night deepened. The silence was eerie except for the rustle of branches and the occasional hoot of an owl. After a few more stops and a whole lot of walking, we finally arrived at checkpoint four.

"Arms up," someone yelled up front.

Matt already had his arms raised, but I stood frozen.

"I said arms up!"

Matt elbowed me.

I was about to put my arms up when a shot rang out.

Matt tackled me to the ground and shielded me with his body.

Even though it was cold, beads of sweat ran down my face as Matt glanced wildly around us. His breathing, like mine, was shallow and fast.

I shivered.

This was all wrong. Were they arresting us?

The shouts were much closer than before.

I tried to breathe, but the pressure in my chest was too intense.

Matt said something to me, but I couldn't hear him. His urgent gaze was the last thing I saw before my world went black.

Bright lights were all over me, a mask pressed over my nose and mouth. I tried to get it off, but someone stopped me.

"Breathe."

"Matt?" I searched for his mellow voice.

"Gaby?"

I strained my eyes at the name, which still sounded so foreign to me.

Then I found him sitting to my left. His green eyes were huge, and he held both my hands. "Thank God you're all right. We made it."

We made it?

I looked around. I was inside a vehicle—an NWG ambulance if I was to guess by all the medical equipment around me.

A middle-aged soldier sat to my right, his focus set on a file. His white uniform carried the coiled silver snake symbol of the NWG on its shoulders.

I shuddered. We were already inside. But why was I in an ambulance?

I returned my gaze to Matt.

"You had a panic attack, but you're safe now." He brushed a loose strand of my curly blond hair behind my ear. "You can relax now. We're safe."

I focused on Matt and took a calming breath. I had to control my rising pulse.

"Dr. Anderson, we need to start the interrogation," the soldier said.

Matt squeezed my hands, then took the mask off and helped me sit up.

"Dr. Anderson, please." The man signaled for Matt to leave.

Matt nodded. "I'll be outside."

The soldier strapped sensors to my fingers and chest. "You will answer yes or no. Is your name Gabrielle Jones?"

A lie detector test, as Matt had predicted.

My insides recoiled. I couldn't fail now.

"Yes," I answered in my most calm and clear voice.

My pulse was still a bit high, but it could be explained by the panic attack. Nevertheless, I had to breathe slowly to take it down a notch. Gabrielle Jones should feel safe at this point.

"Are you twenty-one?" He sounded almost like a robot.

"No. I'm twenty-three."

"Answer with a yes or no." His voice was stern.

Shit. "No."

The soldier watched the monitor beside him and wrote something down.

He was trying to trick me. It was normal to do this. A way to find out if the person was lying or not.

I'd trained for this. Matt was the one to carry out my interrogations at the peak. The key was to believe your lies and answer as firmly as you could.

"Are you a Promissa citizen?"

That one was easy. "Yes."

"Do you work at Dr. Anderson's community clinic?"

"Yes."

"Are you in a relationship with Minister Davon Niles?"

I pictured Davon's smile, his dark eyes focused on me. I'd see him soon. "Yes."

"Are you part of a rebel group?"

I took a relaxing breath. "No."

"Have you in any way engaged in rebel activity?"

This was a tricky one. "Yes."

"When partaking in these rebel activities, were you doing it by conviction?"

"No." My stomach flipped as I answered, but my pulse was stable.

The soldier shifted in his seat. "Were you undercover at the time?"

"Yes."

"Did they find out you were an undercover agent?"

"Yes."

"Did Dr. Anderson aid in your escape?"

I looked outside. Matt chatted with another soldier. He winked at me. I could do this.

"Yes."

"Did anyone follow you?"

I shook my head. It couldn't be perfect. Matt said it was normal for anyone to be nervous during these tests. If I was too calm, they'd suspect me. "I don't think so."

"Yes or no, Miss Jones."

"No."

"Are you here to help the NWG?"

Concentrate, Abi. "Yes."

"Are you in any way tied to the rebel group?"

"No." My pulse rose.

The soldier jotted down something.

"Do you sympathize in any way with the insurgents?"

"No."

His brow furrowed. "Do you share any ideals with the insurgents?"

"Yes."

We'd decided that if by any chance my pulse spiked during a question, I'd answer it truthfully and then fix it.

My logic on this one was that Gabrielle Jones was a Promissa citizen after all, and even if she worked for the NWG, she still empathized with the citizens' suffering.

"Do you plan on acting on these shared ideals?"

I looked into the soldier's light-brown eyes. "No."

"Do you plan to harm Minister Jordan Niles or his family?"

I kept my breathing under check. "No."

The soldier closed his notebook. "That will do for now." He exited the ambulance and said something to Matt.

Matt rushed in. "I'm sorry I had to leave, but it's standard procedure. Are you better?"

I nodded.

"The shot was an accident. A newbie. First day out. It seemed he was nervous, and when you didn't put your arms up, he shot, thinking we were rebels."

"God, I thought..."

Matt angled his body, blocking the guards outside from view, then put a finger over his mouth.

Someone could be listening.

I blinked twice.

"What happens now?" My heart was bursting out of my chest. Did I pass the test?

Matt sat back. "They're comparing your answers with mine. It should only take a few minutes."

Matt held my hand while we waited. He squeezed it as the soldier who interrogated me came back into the ambulance.

"I'm sorry about the soldier who shot at you, Miss Jones. He's been reprimanded. I wanted to welcome you personally. We're glad you made it."

He stepped off and closed the back doors.

I darted my eyes to Matt.

He smiled. "Now we go home."

Home. Into Electi.

I relaxed for a moment before I went rigid.

We made it. Now it all began.

Chapter 18

Davon

January 9, 2214

Her blood-curdling scream was deafening as I pulled another nail off. I sneered, but inside I was dying.

During the past two weeks, I'd beaten Deb to a pulp. Her left eye was swollen. Her nose was broken.

My father had doctors visit her regularly, and he gave her days to recover between sessions. She was fed and allowed regular baths. He said it was a mercy, but for her it must be worse than torture because as soon as she regained her strength, she was brought back to me to start it all again.

The logic behind all this was sick. It was only a matter of time until she lost the baby.

I told Father we couldn't keep this up, but he insisted she was strong and that the doctors said her womb was healthy.

I was sure she knew. Sometimes she looked at her stomach and set her pleading eyes on me.

She was protecting the child and was fighting for him.

My father still watched from the other side of the mirror, so I had to keep going.

Forgive me.

The light thud of the nail as it hit the metal tray sounded more like a boom as the room fell silent.

"Still nothing to say? How much are you willing to sacrifice for them? Who are you protecting? Where is your secret base?"

Deb's sobs were quiet as she straightened and breathed deeply. Her resolve was unbreakable.

She was sweating a lot, and a torrent of tears marked her face. Her body quaked. Her eyes were downcast, and her jaw clenched. She'd never talk.

"I can keep this going. I have nowhere else to be. It's your choice."

There was no one inside the room but Deb and me, so I crouched in front of her, angling my body to conceal us.

I squeezed her hand.

Her eyes flicked to mine for an instant, and she jerked her fingers a bit. She teared up, and it broke me.

I picked up a plastic bag from the table, then stepped behind her, facing the mirror. "How about saving your breath?"

Maybe if she fell unconscious, I could give her a reprieve. I covered her face.

She thrashed violently, and I took the bag off.

She gasped.

"Are you ready to talk?"

She shook her head.

"Then let's give it another try." I held the bag against her face.

Her movements slowed, and she slumped.

I removed the bag and touched her neck.

Her pulse quickened under my finger.

I exhaled. It was enough for one day.

This was the second time she'd pretended to be unconscious.

My father stepped in. "What the hell was that? I told you not to kill her."

I smiled. "She's fine. Just resting for a bit. I'll see her again in a few days." I looked at the officers. "Take her away."

The guards lifted her, and we left the room.

Father and I walked back to my office. I took a deep breath. After yesterday's council meeting, being in his presence was even more suffocating than before.

Three days ago, Lavigne and his troops took over the energy bunker. He came in yesterday to inform the council. The number of casualties was low compared to the people who lived inside that bunker, but still...so many had died.

Tomorrow Dr. Singh wanted me to inspect the bodies and sign for their release.

I shuddered at the thought of how many familiar faces now lay dead in that cold room.

I reigned over my impulses. Everything in me wanted to run back to Janus Peak. To be with my family during these hard times.

I closed my eyes and focused my thoughts on Deb. I had to get her out.

Father grabbed my shoulder as we reached my office. "Are you good?"

I glanced at him.

His eyebrows drew closer as he held my stare.

I shook my head. "It's nothing. Just a headache."

"Do you need to see a doctor? You've been off lately. Do you want to talk?"

God, I needed to be careful. Father knew something was up.

"Nah. It's nothing. I'm just worried about Gabrielle. I hope she's safe." I wasn't lying. I hadn't received news about their arrival, but with every day that passed, it became harder not to think the worst.

What if something happened to them? Could Connor have sent them to defend the bunker?

No, he wouldn't do that.

I needed to calm down. This was not like me. I never lost control.

Abi and Matt were okay, and soon I'd see them.

He patted my shoulder. "Don't you worry. We'll bring her back in no time. I have my best people looking for her."

Father insisted on sending more people out to look for her after our conversation in the library. I'd finally accepted his help, knowing they were coming back soon. They should have a plan already.

"I hope you're right." I turned the doorknob, ready to get into my office and away from him.

"Son?"

I turned. "Yes?"

"I'm leaving in a couple of hours and will be away for the next two weeks. There's a meeting in Halcyon. General Steele and the rest of the NWG leaders will be there, so I'll leave you to handle Miss Davis. Be careful. She's a wild beast."

A jolt ran through my body, and I suppressed a smile. This was the best news I'd received in a long time.

I just needed to get word out to Connor and complete the extraction within the next two weeks. We had one chance.

I shook Dad's hand firmly. "Don't *you* worry. Have a good trip."

He pulled me into a hug. "I'm proud of you, son."

An urge to push him away took over me, but I closed my eyes and hugged him back. "Thanks for giving me this chance. I won't let you down."

He stepped away. "We're going to make everything right, as it should be."

His footsteps echoed as he left the building.

I entered my office. With my back resting against the door, I took three long breaths. I hated his mind games. His fucking bullshit.

I'll get the plan ready tonight. It's now or never.

The ride into Electi seemed to take hours, my mind boggled by all that had happened during the last couple of months. Thinking that soon Deb would be safe was a relief, but it didn't stop the darkness from seeping in.

What if something goes wrong?

The lights were already out in Promissa. Empty land lay between the two cities. In the distance, the lights from the district seemed like a halo. My fingers twitched with contained rage against the armrest of my seat. Where was the justice in this?

The train halted. The station was empty except for the maintenance workers and the soldiers standing guard.

Bayat and O'Hare walked behind me for the two blocks to my apartment building. This was one of the things I hated about being back in Electi—the constant need to have bodyguards with me. But I'd changed the rules.

The prison and my apartment were off-limits. They only followed me whenever I went into Promissa and back. Inside Electi, I roamed alone.

My father wasn't happy about it, but it was my choice. He'd given me the power to do so.

We shared the elevator with a drunk couple. Once they left, I placed my key next to the PH button and pressed it.

The ring of the elevator announced our arrival. Bayat and O'Hare went ahead. They pulled their guns out and aimed toward the wall next to the elevator shaft. I was about to close the elevator door, as was expected in this type of situation, when my whole body froze.

"Wait. She's with me!" Matt's voice sounded urgent.

I glanced into the hall. Her highlighted curls dropped to her shoulders. Her honey-green eyes glistened behind her glasses as she darted them toward me, then back at the gun's barrel.

Matt stood beside her, both hands up.

"Stop!" I yelled.

"Are you sure, Minister Niles?" Bayat maintained her aim.

"They're safe. You know Minister Anderson's son, and this is my girlfriend, Gabrielle." The name sounded foreign coming from my lips.

Both lowered their guns and bowed toward Abi.

"We're sorry." Bayat holstered her gun.

Abi straightened from where she was perched against the wall. "It's no problem."

Both bodyguards turned to me.

"Should we expect her to accompany you from now on?" O'Hare asked.

"Yes." I suppressed my urge to crush Abi against me, but I needed to deal with these two first.

"Should we ask for extra bodyguards for her?" Bayat asked.

"No, you two will do fine."

"Okay, then we'll leave for today." Bayat entered the elevator, followed by O'Hare.

Once the elevator door closed, in one long stride I reached her, took off her glasses, and pulled her in.

Her gasp as I kissed her head and doubled over her was music to my ears.

She's real. She made it.

She wrapped her arms around me.

Her flowery scent traveled through me like a balm, easing all the anxiety from the last two months. She was here at last.

I cupped her face.

Her lips parted, and I closed the gap. The kiss was hard, full of need. With our bodies pressed against each other, our tongues clashed, and she grabbed my neck to deepen it.

Her sweet taste was addictive, and I couldn't get enough. I'd missed her so much.

We broke the kiss and touched our brows together, panting as someone cleared their throat, bringing us back to the present.

Matt had a naughty smirk on his face and his hand over his eyes when we both looked sideways. "If you're done with her greeting, how about a 'Hello, Matt. Thanks for bringing her back to me. I'm so glad to see you, my best friend and the most amazing human I've ever met.'" His green eyes peeked from behind his fingers.

I chuckled and drew him into an embrace, careful with his arm. "I can't believe you made it." The lump in my throat was close to bursting. "God, I'm glad you're here."

Matt hugged me back. "I know. Same here." He jerked his thumb toward the elevator. "Will those two be a problem?"

"Nah. I can manage them. They only answer to me." I grasped Abi's hand. "Let's get inside."

We entered, and Matt and I sat on my black sectional sofa.

Abi left to take a bath.

I cocked my head toward the bathroom. "Is she all right?"

"As right as can be." He looked down at his hands. "Look, Davon, a lot happened in these past two months. You should know Abi's anxiety has skyrocketed since the night of your escape."

This was what I'd feared since that day. Two months, and I wasn't there for her.

Matt took a deep breath. "Promise you'll not freak out."

"I'm freaked out." I grunted.

Matt raised his eyebrows. "You see what I'm saying. Please calm down, and hear me out."

The pressure in my chest was overwhelming. Something happened, and I needed to know. "Calm down? I haven't seen you in two months, and you confirmed my fear that Abi's been suffering out there alone. Now you're telling me not to freak out. So cut the bullshit, and tell me what happened."

Matt jerked back. "She wasn't alone. We've all suffered. You have no idea how it's been out there."

I rubbed my brow. "I'm sorry. I didn't mean it that way." My hands shook, so I tightened my fists on my lap.

Matt covered my hand. "Sorry. I'm just so fucking tired."

"I know."

We all were.

"Okay, here goes. When we arrived, a soldier got nervous and accidentally shot at us. I tried to calm her down, but she had a panic attack and passed out."

My heart stammered. "They shot at you?"

"As I said, it was an accident. A rookie thought we were rebels."

"Fuck!" I raked my hair back.

Matt put his hand on my shoulder. "Listen to me. She's dealing with it, and she's much better now, but you know how stubborn she can be. I wanted you to know."

This whole situation was impossible. What would happen when she asked about Deb? Because she would and she deserved the truth.

"Is she taking any meds?" I asked.

Matt nodded. "She's been taking sleeping pills, and Aoki and I have taught her some methods to deal with an attack. David has also helped her a lot."

"David?" Was he back at the base?

"He came back after your escape, and they've become good friends. He's also been training her with the sniper, and she's quite good."

The memory of David crouched by the bed of his dead parents flashed in front of my eyes. He'd suffered so much and never talked about it. Just like Abi. "It's good that they're friends. I think they can help each other a lot."

"Me too." Matt stretched his arms up. "I'm parched."

I stood. "Want a beer?"

"Sure."

I went to the kitchen and came back with two beers.

"Did you tell them we were coming in from the forest?" Matt asked after having a taste of his lager.

I took a swig, and it soothed some of the tension. "Not exactly, but I did tell them Gabrielle was undercover with a group of insurgents. Father was looking for her. Other than the asshole that shot at you, how did it go?"

"As well as it could. We came in through checkpoint four. They gave us both a polygraph test."

I narrowed my eyes. "But she just had a panic attack."

What the hell were they thinking?

He sighed. "I told them about it, but they said they'd take it into consideration when they studied the responses. I was crazy with worry and scared shitless after her interrogation, but she did a great job."

I itched to comfort her. She must have been so scared. "So I take it everything went well?"

Matt nodded. "They took us into Electi right away." He drank some beer and chuckled. "She didn't even let me stop by my apartment. She wanted to come straight to you, so we waited."

"How long did you wait?" I asked.

"Around two hours. I tried to convince her to rest in my apartment, but she wouldn't move." He rested his elbows on his knees. "I'm glad we made it."

"Me too."

I went into the kitchen and prepared a tray of cheese and crackers. I put them on the coffee table in front of Matt.

When Abi turned off the shower, I decided to brew some coffee.

Her arms encircled my waist as I foamed the milk. "Hey, you." Her soft voice was music to my ears.

I turned and drew her to me.

She crushed her body against mine and pulled my neck down to her. Her soft lips met mine in a gentle kiss.

She pulled back and breathed in. "You made coffee?"

She was fucking adorable.

"I wouldn't dream of welcoming my girl without a coffee in hand."

She played with my hair, which was much longer than when I left, before brushing her thumb down my stubble. "I can't believe I'm here. That I'm touching you."

I leaned into her touch, then took her hand and kissed her palm. "I'm here." I moved it to my chest. "This is real."

Her eyes glazed.

I hugged her. "Don't cry. We're together. Everything will be okay." I cupped her face. "Go to Matt. I'll get this ready and bring it to you."

She nodded.

She went to the table, took a couple of crackers, and slumped next to Matt.

"Does your thigh hurt?" Matt whispered.

"A little, but it's normal. I'm only tired."

Matt grasped her hand. "It was a long day."

As usual, she didn't want anyone to be concerned. I was at ease knowing that she had someone to talk to. It was evident they'd grown even closer these last couple of months.

As I approached them, I unbuttoned the top of my white silk shirt, then sat next to her and stroked my fingers over her hands before placing the mug between them.

She sighed. "Thanks."

My heart melted when she breathed in the aroma and closed her eyes. I put my arm around her.

She took a sip and settled back into me.

I squeezed her shoulder. "I'm sorry about the energy bunker. I saw the number of casualties. You received my letter in time, then?"

Matt stood and started pacing. "We evacuated everyone and moved the data to our central system. The generators were taken to the farming bunker, and the people moved to the other bunkers until the caves are ready."

I stiffened. "You're thinking of moving to the caves?"

Abi put her hand on my thigh. "After we lost the bunker, things went crazy. Mark has the runners working on getting the caves ready in case of an attack. We sent soldiers all throughout the system, and they're ready to defend if needed."

Something didn't add up. "What happened to Jimmy? Connor said he was okay."

"He's all right, but Connor demoted him after what happened." Matt popped a chunk of cheese into his mouth. "Mark's the new captain of the runners."

Abi put her mug down. "Jimmy's part of the strategy team, though, and he's been working nonstop with Mark on the assignment." Abi lowered her gaze. "He needs a cane and is recovering slowly."

I wondered if they were on speaking terms or just worked together. I'd already come to grips with what transpired and partly understood his actions. He never trusted me and blamed me as soon as suspicions arose.

But what about Abi? I'd ask her later.

I looked at Matt. "I need to go to the prison tomorrow. We don't have to worry about my father, as he left earlier today for Halcyon."

Matt widened his eyes. "General Steele?"

I nodded. "And all the leaders of the NWG."

Matt bowed his head. "This might work in our favor. How long will he be out there?"

I smiled. "Two weeks."

Matt grinned. "We'll get her out."

"We will."

"Davon," Abi said, "how's my sister?"

My stomach turned inside out. I expected her to ask about Deb, but there was so much she didn't know. I pondered about telling her about the pregnancy, but now that Matt had told me about her anxiety, I couldn't just blurt it out. I needed to plan it out. To prepare her.

"I should leave." Matt finished his beer and threw it in the recycling bin. "I'll see you tomorrow."

After he left, a couple of minutes passed in silence.

"Davon?"

I hunched forward. "Deb's strong. She's holding up."

Abi squeezed my upper arm. "Don't lie to me. You promised you'd be honest."

I swallowed hard as I recalled Deb's bloody fingers. Her broken nose. How could we come back from that?

I closed my eyes. "She's messed up." My voice cracked. "Father hasn't left my side."

The room went still. When I turned to her, tears streamed down her face.

I drew her toward me. "I'm so sorry, love. I understand if you can't forgive me. You know I hate this. She's my friend. I don't know if she'll ever forgive me. I sure as hell will never forgive myself. That's why we have to get her out before my father returns."

"There's nothing to forgive. We knew what we were getting into when we started this mission. Connor too. It just hurts." She sobbed into my chest.

We stayed like that until she fell asleep.

Chapter 19

Davon

January 10, 2214

Warmth spread over my neck and down my chest. I opened my eyes. Abi was naked, slithering down my body.

"Abi?" I rasped.

She kissed my chest. Her golden strands gleamed as the first rays of sunlight met them. "I've missed you."

I trailed my hands down her hair and traced my thumb over her mouth. She parted her lips, taking it in. The warmth of her mouth and the way she kissed it turned my blood to fire.

She trailed her way down my abdomen, driving me crazy with her scorching kisses. Her curls brushed over my thighs, and she wrapped her lips around me.

I closed my fists on the sheets. *So fucking good.*

Her eyes locked on me, and she took me deeper into her mouth.

I couldn't control the jerk of my body at her touch. "You're so beautiful."

Her eyes glinted, and her rhythm intensified.

I caressed her hair and lifted my hips, wanting more. Her exquisite torture had me gasping for air.

I glanced down at her lovely eyes. I was on the verge of losing myself. "Please, love. I want you."

With one last stroke, she moved up and straddled me, then slowly settled lower and took me in.

We made love, taking our time to worship each other. We let ourselves go in a beautiful bliss as we climaxed together, bursting into a million pieces. It was all encompassing. Earth shattering.

She slumped over me and kissed me deeply. "I love you, Davon."

I tucked her wild curls behind her ears and cupped her face. "And I love you. You're my everything." I kissed her brow and hugged her to me.

We basked in each other till our bodies relaxed.

I brushed my lips against hers. "I'll prepare breakfast. You rest."

She moaned, half asleep already.

The black silk sheets tangled beneath her waist. Her leg bent as if I lay next to her. She looked like an angel.

Yesterday I would have never imagined waking up with her so soon.

I put some jazz on, remembering how she loved it, and made scrambled eggs with sausage, toast, and bacon. As the coffee aroma filled the room, she stirred.

I went to the bed and kissed her cheek. "Breakfast is ready."

She offered me a sweet smile, then opened her eyes. "It smells heavenly."

I chuckled. "I'll wait for you in the kitchen."

After giving me a peck on the lips, she rushed into the bathroom. "I'm staying in today, right?"

"You are. Matt's coming over for lunch, and then I'll leave for the prison. I won't take long. Matt said he'd prepare dinner."

"Okay. I'll be out in a minute."

Ten minutes later, our breakfast was set at my enormous dining table, and we sat together, looking at the city.

Abi couldn't stop staring at the district. "It's surreal. Look at them. Shopping, having breakfast at those restaurants. Is that a pool?"

"That's the public pool." I took a piece of bacon.

Being in Electi and witnessing elites take pleasure in everything that was denied to her must be painful.

She glanced around. "And look at this place. God, it's more than four times the size of our apartments at the bunker."

I lowered my head. *This is awful.*

She covered my hand. "I'm sorry. It's not your fault. I shouldn't have said that."

I shook my head. "You should. You have the right to be raging mad at all this. Your people suffer as we enjoy our luxuries without a care in the world."

She squeezed my hand. "But you care."

I sighed. She was too good for me.

Abi and I talked for about an hour, making plans for the week. The first thing on the agenda was to plan the extraction. Second was to introduce Gabrielle to my mother. Once she won her over, winning my dad would be a piece of cake.

We worked out in my home gym. Since my shoulder didn't hurt much, last week I asked my therapists to remove the cryotherapy chamber and take it to the Promissa Medical Facility. They shouldn't be denied the advances we had in Electi.

In its place, I created a weight-lifting area and installed a boxing bag. I also had space for training exercises.

Abi showed me some of the techniques Maria had taught her.

We sparred for about an hour. She'd gotten good at fighting and was careful to never hit my shoulder.

I showed her ways to attack using her khukuri and trench knife. She needed to hone her skills a bit, but with training, she'd be a force to be reckoned with. Her height gave her an advantage in terms of dodging attacks, and she was agile and fast as hell.

After a hot shower, we called Matt. He and I needed to decide on a strategy to get Deb out.

He arrived, and we sat to brainstorm. There was a lot to plan, but I had no doubt we could do this. Deb would be free soon.

"There's salmon!" Abi yelled from the kitchen while Matt and I checked the prison blueprints.

"That'll work. Put it on the counter. I'll be right there to start prepping for dinner," Matt said.

"So what do you think? Will it be believable, or will my father suspect?" I asked Matt after explaining my plan.

"I think it'll work, but she'll have to hurt you, really hurt you for it to be convincing. Abi won't like it," Matt whispered.

I glanced at the kitchen. Abi hummed while arranging everything Matt needed for dinner on the countertop.

"She'll understand. She always does," I said.

Matt pinched his throat as he looked at the blueprints, marking Deb's escape route.

"Matt?"

He looked up.

"You know I'll make it. Deb will know how to do it without causing grave damage."

He slumped. "I'm worried about her mental state. Torture victims are known to be unstable."

I understood the risks, but I'd take them. I had to free her.

Abi sat at the table in front of us. "What are you whispering about?"

"Deb's extraction," Matt said.

She frowned. "And who's getting hurt?"

"I am," I said.

She lifted an eyebrow.

I took a deep breath. "Deb must take me hostage. She'll grab one of my knives from the interrogation room and make me take her out of the building. No one will dare go against her if I'm in danger. Before she escapes, she'll have to stab me."

Abi leaned forward. "But can't she just graze you? There's no need to hurt you more than necessary."

I took the hand she placed on the table. "You have no idea what I've done to her."

She squeezed back. "You said she was in bad shape. Do you think she's ready for this?"

I sighed. "I hope so. Even though Father is away, his lackeys in the prison will inform him if I'm not doing his bidding. I need to keep visiting her, but I'm giving her a couple of days before the extraction so she can get strong enough. Since he always gives her time to recover after hard sessions, it won't be suspicious."

Abi cocked her head. "Your father's showing mercy? Why would he do that?"

Because she's pregnant with my brother.

God, I wanted to tell her but not now. She'd just arrived. It could break her.

"It's not mercy. He loves mind games. He gives them hope for a couple of days, and then he crushes them." *I'm worthless.* I hated lying to her. "We need my father and the security team to believe the escape is real, and for that, she must hurt me. For real. Because as Father sees it, she hates my guts. It needs to look like she tried to kill me. If not, he'll never believe it."

She closed her eyes for a moment. When she opened them, she nodded. "I understand. And will both of you be all right?"

"We'll make it. I trained Deb. She knows what she's doing."

She sighed. "Okay, so we need to get her on board and get a letter to Muñoz with the date and time for the extraction."

I smiled. Abi had changed. There was a fire in her that wasn't there before.

Matt took out the calendar. "How about Monday? It's the seventeenth, and Jordan won't be back till the twenty-second."

"That would work. If something goes wrong, we might have another chance before he comes back," I said.

Abi studied the calendar. "That only gives us a week."

I tightened my jaw. "Then let's get to work."

The pungent smell of formalin swarmed my senses, and Dr. Singh extended his hand.

I grabbed it. "Good afternoon. I'm here to inspect the bodies and sign the paperwork."

"Perfect. Follow me, please." He turned. "I'll show you the bodies and then get the paperwork. It's in my office."

I followed him to the wall full of metal storage units.

"Fourteen died. We seem to have the leader of the group. Her uniform was black, different from the gray one the rest of the rebels wore. Want to check the body?"

DeLuca.

"Sure." I swallowed shakily as he slid it out and pulled the sheet down.

She didn't deserve this. No one did. Her face was half gone. A bullet had hit the left side of it. Her jaw rested at an unnatural angle, and part of her skull was cracked. My stomach churned, but I covered her head and stepped back.

"What will happen to the bodies?" I winced at a gurney with a naked body on the other side of the room, his chest full of bullet holes.

"Usually, the bodies are cremated and their ashes buried in a location north of here. For this group, Minister Niles asked for something else. He wants to put them in gibbets around the perimeter of Promissa."

Bile rose to my mouth. They were to be displayed as a warning to all who dared oppose my father.

Dr. Singh entered his office and emerged a minute later with some papers. "Your father stated that, as minister of security and sedition control, you are now responsible for everything that happens within the prison as well as with the rebels. If you agree with your father's proposal for the bodies, please sign here." He pointed to a line in the bottom-right corner.

I gripped the pen and swallowed my pain. I had no choice.

"Sure. They should know what happens to those who oppose us." I signed.

All these people who trusted me, and I signed a consent form to never let them rest. To display them as if they were nothing but trash, taking away their dignity. It was as if I had signed my own damnation.

"Thank you, Minister Niles." Dr. Singh took back the papers.

"I'm leaving, then." I needed to get away from all this before I lost it. I wanted to scream and destroy everything in my path.

"Have a great afternoon," he said as I left the room.

Time seemed to slow as I made my way out, needing Abi more than ever.

The aroma of home-cooked salmon hit me as I entered the penthouse. Soft rock played in the surround system of the apartment.

Abi giggled. It had been a while since I'd heard her laugh, and it filled me with ease.

I glanced to the right toward the kitchen. Matt wore my "Rock On" apron, opening the stove to check on the salmon.

I took my coat off and loosened my tie, unfastening the first two buttons of my pink shirt.

Matt, ever cautious, must have sensed someone had entered because as soon as he closed the oven door, he turned to me and went into a fighting stance.

I widened my eyes and put a finger to my lips.

Matt relaxed and nodded.

Abi's back was to us, thankfully. She moved her hips to the song.

I walked toward her. The music was so loud that she still hadn't noticed I had arrived. I caught her from behind, and she jumped, released a loud screech, and spun around, knife in hand.

I put my hands up while Matt laughed his ass off. "You could've said she had a knife on her!"

"But where's the fun in that?" Matt smirked.

She glared at me. "What's your problem, approaching people who are armed from behind?"

Her words took me back to when I surprised her in the shooting room back in Janus Peak. It seemed so long ago.

"I'm sorry. Now, could you put the knife down so I can hold you?"

Her eyes gleamed as she set the knife on the cutting board, and I stepped into her space, capturing her between me and the counter. Her body melted against mine as I held her.

This was just what I needed.

She cupped my cheek. "What happened?"

I shook my head. "I don't want to talk about it. Do you need any help?"

She nodded and made some space for me beside her. "How about you peel the potatoes and I cut them? I'm making sautéed potatoes. Aoki taught me the recipe two weeks ago, and I've been dying to try it out."

"Sure." I took the peeler and started working.

We moved around the kitchen in harmony, laughing at Matt's antics and Abi's moves.

For a moment, everything seemed so natural. Like nothing could ever disturb our peace.

A while later we sat at the table.

The rich flavor of the salmon was incredible, but Abi's face as she took her first bite was more exquisite. We talked about menial stuff during dinner, but after we finished, I knew the conversation I was avoiding had to happen.

Matt served red wine, and we sat on the couch.

"What happened at the prison?" Abi asked.

She sat to my left, while Matt slouched in the corner on my right.

I swirled my wine. "As Connor should've told you, I'm now minister of security and sedition control. Everything that relates to rebels and prisoners falls under my authority. Today I needed to come in and sign some papers. When I went to the morgue, the doctor showed me DeLuca's body."

Matt flinched. "Did you see anyone else?"

"Just one more—a male soldier full of bullet wounds. DeLuca was almost unrecognizable. What happened out there was a massacre."

Abi shifted next to me. "I figured as much. Yuxuan and Mathews looked like hell. Their uniforms were covered in blood."

I tensed. "Yuxuan was out there?"

She nodded. "He barely escaped with Mathews. Thanks to them, twenty-three people made it out. DeLuca and two others died while giving them time to escape."

"God." I put the glass on the coffee table and leaned forward, covering my brow. If Yuxuan had died... "I should have stopped it."

Matt touched my back. "There's nothing you could've done. Your father ordered it."

My body trembled, the blood rushing through my system with uncontrolled rage. I was losing it. I gripped my hair and screamed. I was fucking useless.

"Davon?" Abi's soft voice cracked through the pounding in my ears. She crouched in front of me. She caressed my hair, then massaged my neck. "We're here. You're not alone anymore."

She took me into her arms, and I cried. I was powerless. Our world was crumbling in front of us, and I couldn't do shit about it.

Matt threw his arm around us, and I stayed there. Cocooned. Safe. With my family.

Chapter 20

Abi

January 13, 2214

*D**eb,*

Today is Thursday. On Monday, we'll get you out. I'll come for you at night after giving you a day to rest. I'll make sure we're alone inside the room. Before I restrain you to the chair, attack me, then take one of my knives.

I've included a map of the way you'll take to escape. I'll have a key card in my back pocket. Take it, and once you're at the door, stab me. It must look like you wanted to kill me. Once you're outside, run for the forest. A team will be there to get you out.

Memorize this, then get rid of it. Leave nothing behind.

I hope you'll someday forgive me for all I've done to you. I wish you the best.

—D

I clutched the letter Muñoz would give Deb tomorrow.

In the past four days, we'd reached out to Connor via Muñoz and received confirmation that a team from the peak would be there on Monday.

I tried to keep to a normal routine, but I wasn't sleeping enough, and no matter how much I wanted to believe everything would work out, many negative scenarios swarmed my thoughts.

Would Deb make it out? Was she in her right mind after all Davon had done to her?

My stomach churned. What exactly had he done? How much had he hurt her?

Every time I imagined the things he'd done to her, my throat closed up, and I had to remind myself that he had no choice.

Davon is a good man, I repeated as my brain again pushed forward an image of Deb suffering, hurting, and alone. I wiped my tears away.

Davon left every day at six in the evening, and once in the prison, he followed the same routine: take Deb into the interrogation room, torture her, and stay in his office till ten. This way the informants would notify his father of his new nightly routine, and when the escape happened, they wouldn't find it strange that he was there.

Every night he arrived after midnight and took a long bath. He acted like he was okay, but sometimes I'd hear him sob over the sound of the shower. Then as he slid his body next to mine, he'd hold me tight and whisper in my ear that he was sorry.

When we were together, he seemed happy. But his eyes spoke volumes, and the shadows beneath them talked of his sorrow.

I couldn't imagine the weight of all this on him nor fathom the emotional state of my sister at what her best friend was doing to her.

My mind was a mess of emotions. The man I loved was the "villain" in all this and my sister the victim. How could I choose between them? How could I push my feelings away and concentrate on the mission?

My heart ached for them both and for all they'd lose.

I closed my eyes.

In four days, Deb would be free. I should've felt somewhat relieved, but the weight of time kept pushing me down.

Our mission was the stepping stone for the revolution to progress, so we focused on its success. We tried to take time off to enjoy each other's company, but the responsibility on our shoulders was too much.

Today he'd take me to meet his mother, and while I visited, he'd leave the letter for Muñoz to deliver. He wanted me to write Deb a message since I wasn't going to see her for a while. We planned to go back to the bunker in a few months, but nothing was certain.

I took the pen while Davon prepared the coffee.

Hey, sis,

I made it. I found Matt and Davon, and they took me to your home. It's incredible, and the people there are amazing. What you all accomplished is surreal.

I'm in Electi with Davon and Matt. Connor sent us on a mission to get you out, but it's much more complicated than that. He'll explain later.

I'm so sorry for all you're going through. I would give everything to be with you, to help you deal with it all, but I won't be able to go back with you after your escape. We need to stay and complete our mission.

This may come as a shock, but Davon and I are together. He's good to me. I know it's not my place, but please know he has no choice with what he's doing to you and is drowning in sorrow with every passing day.

I miss you so much it hurts. Please be safe.

Love,

Abi

I folded the letter and gave it to Davon, who sat next to me, drinking coffee.

We still hadn't had breakfast, as was our routine. Morning coffee, then breakfast, and after that, we sat and watched the sunrise together.

He tilted his head and caught my chin gently, wiping a rogue tear with his thumb. "You're crying."

I shook my head and sipped my coffee. "I'm all right."

He took the mug from me and put it on the table, then grabbed my hands so I'd face him.

He caressed my cheek. "You're not. Please talk to me."

I inhaled and closed my eyes. "It's too painful, Davon. I...I can't stop thinking about Deb all alone in there and what you're doing to her day by day."

When I opened my eyes, his pained stare met mine.

I brushed his jaw. "I know you suffer too. I hear you at night and see it in your eyes. Can't you do anything to alleviate her suffering?"

He blinked. "I try, but he has eyes everywhere. It's like he never left. Watching her suffer at my hands is killing me. Sometimes when I'm with her, I have to detach myself from my actions. It's like I'm watching myself do all those terrible things." He looked down at our clasped hands. "It makes me sick, and I know I'll never be able to make amends for it."

When he looked up, tears freely rolled down his cheeks, and his eyes appeared haunted. "I can't take it anymore. I feel so lost. I just want this to be over. I need to get her out."

My heart was about to burst out of my chest for him. What would have happened if I hadn't come to him? Would I have lost him?

I pulled him to me and hugged him as tightly as I could. "We'll pull through this." I breathed in his musky aroma and buried my face in his neck. The roughness of his stubble let me know this was real. That we were together. That I'd made it. "I love you."

He kissed my neck. "I love you too. I..." He sobbed. "I was so alone, and I didn't know if I'd ever see you again. I still can't believe you're here."

I closed my eyes. "Me either."

He cupped my face and kissed me. A soft, lingering kiss. His love filled me to the core, and I knew we'd make it together.

"I'll get the breakfast, and we can watch the sunrise after." He went into the kitchen and brought back toast and strawberry jelly.

After breakfast, we sat on a love seat to watch the sunrise. It was our moment.

I rested my back against his chest.

Just as the sun rose on the horizon, he said, "I'm sorry I made you stay."

His words stabbed my heart. It hurt so much when he asked me to stay, and even though I understood, it still hurt.

"You don't have to apologize. You made the right call as our general. Jimmy made it thanks to you," I said almost robotically, as if I had practiced it before.

He held me tighter. "Abi, my choice was for you. You would've never forgiven yourself if Jimmy died."

I turned in his arms. "And what about you? What if you didn't make it? Did you ever stop to think how I'd feel if you died?" I was almost yelling, so I took a deep breath to calm my restless heart. "It was an impossible choice, so I took it as an order from my general. It was the only way I could leave you behind."

I'd never spoken about this reality even to myself. But it was the truth. That morning, when he told me to stay, I couldn't choose. I was dying inside. Then I remembered his words: "You'll obey my commands. Understood?" And I did. I obeyed and took Jimmy back.

Davon's muscles bunched around me. "God, I just…"

"Let's not talk about it. It's in the past, and nothing good will come out of torturing ourselves about how we would've done it differently. We're together now. That's enough."

We held each other in silence, watching a new day begin.

A black electric sedan waited for us in front of the lobby.

O'Hare bowed before opening the car door for me. "Hey, I'm sorry about the other night."

When he straightened, his smile was contagious, and I couldn't help but give one back. "It's no problem. I understand."

"Whatever you need, call us. Our contact information is saved on your phone," Bayat said from the driver's seat.

Davon gave me a cell phone yesterday, and I was still trying to figure out how it worked.

I nodded and went in. It was an elegant sedan with black leather seats. There was a minibar that opened in front of us and a darkened glass partition between the front and back seats that provided us with privacy.

"So this is what freedom feels like." I glanced at Davon.

He sat beside me with his chin propped in his hand as he watched the city pass by us. He looked sophisticated in his charcoal suit. An elite through and through.

I'd never seen this side of him before, and his beauty took my breath away. With his hair styled in a half bun, I couldn't help myself as I caught one loose strand and tucked it behind his ear.

He turned to me. His eyes were soft as he took my hand. He entwined his fingers with mine and squeezed.

I moved closer to him as a stunning lake came into view. Gazebos and parks surrounded it. Children played, and couples strolled around it.

Why couldn't we have the same? Why did they take all this away from us?

Davon stroked the back of my neck languidly, relieving some of my pent-up stress. I closed my eyes and moved my head in a circle.

"Lake Egregie," Davon said.

To our left, we passed mansion after mansion. Their size and the backdrop of the forest and the mountains with the lake in front made them seem unattainable.

Who the hell lives here?

In all my life, I'd never seen something so lavish.

Back in Promissa, we lived day by day, not knowing what tomorrow would bring. Everything was monitored and controlled. Adults were only allowed to go to work. Youngsters were homeschooled and only learned what the government approved. The food each family received depended on their job, and water and electricity were restricted.

If only the Promissa citizens could see this.

I gritted my teeth until my jaw hurt. This was wrong.

Davon pointed toward a white mansion with marble balustrades and columns. "That's my childhood home."

I gasped. It looked magnificent.

The car circled around the entrance, and Bayat opened the door for us.

Davon stepped out, readjusted his suit, and buttoned it. He offered me his hand. I emerged from the car and took it all in.

The cool wind ruffled my hair, and I had to hold it back to see what lay in front of me.

A butler opened the doors to let us in. "Mr. Niles. Miss...?"

"Jones," Davon said.

He bowed slightly. "Welcome."

He took our coats once inside. My mouth hung open.

A grand staircase with dark railings curved up to the second floor on both sides of the central area. White and cream tones dominated the room, and a large crystal chandelier hung from the center, illuminating it with a warm glow. The ceiling's intricate moldings added to the elegance of the room.

We followed the butler into a sitting room to the left. The floor was of white marble, the opposite of Davon's penthouse's black marble floor. Arches supported by columns divided the space.

The butler stayed behind as we entered. "Please make yourself comfortable. Mrs. Niles will be with you shortly."

Two art pieces adorned the walls. One was a painting of this house depicted as the background of Lake Egregie. The other was a family portrait. Davon's mom held him as a child while his father had an arm around her back, the other helping to hold Davon.

His mom had long dark hair and high cheekbones. Her light-brown eyes gleamed.

As for his father, it was like looking at a mirror image of his son. They were almost identical except Jordan was clean-shaven and his hair was shorter than Davon's, reaching his ears. He was a handsome man, and his smile was captivating. Even in a painting, there was an intense aura around him. This man radiated power and respect.

He reminded me of the first time I set eyes on Davon and the chill that ran through me as he stared at me that night. He carried his father's commanding strength, emanating control and authority. A dominance that could make people fall to their knees. That's how strong it was.

Two large cream Victorian sofas were positioned in the center of the room, red cushions resting upon them. Green plants were placed around, giving it a natural feel. We sat on a settee to the right, and a maid brought two glasses of lemonade. She set them on the rounded glass table in front of us. Its base was carved with antique floral designs and painted in a golden hue.

I'd never been in a more luxurious space before. Even though it was so elegant and entrancing, I couldn't help but get sick at its opulence.

A pounding headache began to set in. How could they live like this while others were stuck in poverty? How could they enjoy these riches, knowing the families of Promissa were denied so much?

I glanced again at the painting to my right. It was beautiful. Davon only knew this world as he grew up. This was his home. Some of my tension ebbed away as I imagined him as a teenager, sitting here with his mom and dad, being a family.

Davon put his hand on my thigh, touching my skin beneath the skirt of the navy-blue sundress he'd bought for me especially for today. I felt kind of exposed with its spaghetti straps and plunging neckline, but Davon assured me his mother wore this kind of dress at home and I would fit right in. The hemline was shorter at the front, exposing my legs, and longer at the back. A white floral design with leaves adorned the lower half of the flowy skirt.

"Are you okay?" He handed me one of the glasses.

I took it. "Your home is..."

He dropped his chin. "It's too much. Wasteful. Offensive." The shame in his comments was tangible.

I covered his hand with mine. "It's true that it feels like an irony in comparison to what the people face outside, but I want to believe this home was built with love."

He widened his eyes. "Love? Maybe once upon a time, but now it's gone." He shook his head. "Now I only see shadows. A façade that hides so much pain and violence." He looked at the family painting. "Mom doesn't know."

I squeezed his hand, getting his attention back to me. "What doesn't she know?"

His dark gaze captured mine, and I could almost see those terrible memories running through it. "About the atrocities my father did to me. About the shadows that blacken those long-gone happy memories she treasures."

"Why didn't you tell her?" I didn't have my mother and would have done anything to have her back. The love of a mother was immeasurable. If he had told her, I was sure she wouldn't have permitted his father to continue hurting him.

He shrugged. "She's a kind soul, and she loves Father. I couldn't do it to her. I couldn't bear to destroy what she cherished most—our family."

Footsteps approached from the foyer.

Davon stood and offered me his hand to help me up. "She's here."

The woman who entered the sitting room embodied grace and beauty. She walked straight but with a soft gait that carried strength and elegance. When she saw Davon, her face brightened, and her white teeth flashed a beautiful smile.

Davon's eyes sparkled like a child's, and we stepped forward in unison. He let go of me for a second to hug her.

My heart swelled at the devotion in her eyes before she closed them, embracing him back.

He let go and gestured toward me. "Mom, this is Gabrielle." He motioned toward her. "Gaby, this is Rebecca."

In one stride, she came into my space and hugged me tight. "God, I was so worried about you. It's great to finally meet you."

I stood frozen, and ever so slowly, I curled my arms around her. Her warmth glided through me and reminded me of my mother. I swallowed to contain my tears.

She took a step back and cupped my face. She glanced at Davon. "She's beautiful." She stroked my scar. "Who did this to you?"

A flash of fear ran through me, and words wouldn't form.

Davon put his arm around my waist and held me close. "The rebels. She was found out during an undercover mission and beaten. But she's all right."

She laid a hand over her heart. "God, what a terrible ordeal. Davon told us Matt was the one who helped you escape?"

I leaned into Davon. "Yes. I can't believe I'm finally here. Davon didn't do this place justice."

She raised an eyebrow. "You mean Electi? Is this your first time here?"

I nodded. "It is. I never imagined a place like this could exist. We live with so little out there." I let my eyes drift away from hers and took in my surroundings. This was part of the plan.

Davon wanted his mother to open her eyes to the reality of the world outside Electi. He wanted Rebecca to make up her own mind and see his father for whom he really was.

"Are you talking about Promissa?"

I sighed. "You have so much. To be able to roam around the city, to have a drink with friends, to dance to music."

Rebecca shifted back a step. Her brow wrinkled. "I don't get it. I know Promissa is an industrial city and work is the priority, but it surely can't be that bad."

I furrowed my brow. "Have you ever visited?"

"Just the government center. I've never really been anywhere else. But I thought..." She touched her wedding band and darted her eyes between us. "Is it really that bad?"

"I'm just glad Davon brought me here." I bit my lip.

Davon gripped my chin and kissed me softly. "Let's not talk about this, love. We need to turn the page and enjoy this new chapter of our lives."

Even though it was an act we'd practiced, his kiss gave me comfort, and his words carried some truth. We'd take on this mission and finish it together.

Rebecca took a seat in front of us, and we sat back, sipping our lemonades.

"I'm sorry my husband isn't here. He was so anxious to meet you."

"And I him." I glanced toward Davon. "Davon talks a lot about his father."

She curved her mouth in a soft smile. "I'm glad. You see, there was a time they didn't see eye to eye. I'm relieved they finally made peace with each other." She sipped her drink. "So how long have you been together?"

Davon leaned forward. "Almost a year. We met two years ago when Matt brought her into the clinic as an assistant."

"Wow, a year is a long time. Did you live together out there or just once you arrived here in Electi?"

Davon rolled his eyes. "Mom!"

I chuckled.

She gave us an apologetic smile. "Sorry. I didn't mean to pry. I was just curious."

"We lived together for a month before we got separated," Davon said.

No need to lie on that one.

I squeezed his thigh, and he covered my hand with his.

"It must have been hard," his mother said. "I can't imagine being away from Jordan. I mean, he travels but never for so long. You were two months without knowing each other's whereabouts, right?"

Davon nodded. "But that's all over now."

"Hopefully," I said.

"What do you mean?" Rebecca asked.

"You see, many don't understand the NWG ideals. The need for the regime. And they are fed up and ready to fight back." I fidgeted with my glass. "I kind of understand them, living like that for so long."

I met Davon's eyes. "But when I met Davon, I knew people in Electi were good and only did what was needed to prosper. Working toward the common good. The NWG protects us and gives us what we need. And if we work hard for it, we can reach a better way of life as a united nation."

My throat burned from the lies I said, my mouth from blurting out all the bullshit the NWG had instilled since my childhood. A crawling sensation ran through me, but Davon squeezed my hand to keep me focused.

Rebecca leaned forward and clasped her hands together. "Davon, does your father know about this?"

"I'm sure he suspects it. It's one of the reasons I brought Gabrielle in. I'm sure she can aid our cause."

Rebecca sat back and crossed her legs. "I'll talk to him about it when he comes back."

And there it was, exactly what Davon wanted—for his mom to take our side and convince her husband to trust us.

Now the ball was in my court, and once Jordan arrived, I'd have to earn his trust.

My leg started shaking, and Davon grasped my knee. I breathed slowly, counting in my head like Aoki taught me.

"That would be perfect." Davon kissed my cheek, then whispered in my ear, "Breathe. I'll be back soon. I love you."

He stood. "Mom, can I leave Gaby here for a couple of hours? I need to take care of something at work."

"Sure. It'll give us some time to get to know each other." Rebecca rose and hugged him.

He glanced at me. "I'll be back after lunch."

He nodded to his mother and left.

January 13, 2214

Our drive to the station was uneventful, and I got on the train to make my way into Promissa.

When I looked at the bar, I almost stepped out of my train car and into the next one, where my bodyguards were.

What was he doing here?

My schedule was set so I wouldn't meet with other members of the council.

I took a deep breath and sat next to him.

The bartender set a coaster for me. "Minister Niles, the usual?"

I nodded.

Setting the glass on top, he dropped two whiskey stones inside and poured the eighteen-year-old scotch whiskey I preferred.

I swirled my drink and turned sideways. "Cheers."

Frank Anderson and I had grown apart over the years, but he understood hierarchy and knew well to never step out of line when related to the Niles family.

His bright-green eyes settled on me, and a small shiver ran down my spine at the resemblance to his son.

He tucked a brown curl that had escaped his ponytail behind his ear and centered his gaze on me. He clinked his glass against mine. "Cheers."

Hopefully, he wouldn't bother me.

Today Muñoz would take the letter to Deb. Even though I was sure it would go off without a hitch, I worried if Deb was in her right mind and would understand what she needed to do to escape.

When Father left, I took it easier on her, trying to ease her suffering now that I didn't have his constant presence behind me. But then I received his phone call.

The prison had cameras inside the interrogation room and in the common areas. I had access to them and should have known he had access too. I was sure he had informants inside, which only meant he still had trust issues.

He'd been watching, and he was curious as to why I took it easy with her. I told him I worried about my brother and that I needed to find a way to make her talk without the beatings.

That's when he gave the order to use waterboarding. He was growing impatient.

I cracked my neck from side to side.

Two nights ago, Deb fell unconscious after what I hoped was the first and last session of waterboarding. The sensation of drowning it gave the victim made most people talk but not her.

I nearly blew my cover when she wouldn't wake, shaking her with all my might, tears about to flood out of my eyes. But then she coughed, and I almost hugged her. No torturer wanted their victim dead before getting the intel, but what happened that night bordered on despair, and I couldn't show that.

Deb was like a sister to me, and with every day that passed, I saw less and less of her old self. I needed to get her out.

The doctors assured me she was still pregnant and the baby was healthy. I hadn't told Abi or Matt about the pregnancy. Maybe it was better to get

Deb out first and then tell them. Abi was drowning in misery because of
Deb's situation, and I didn't want to add to her suffering.

I'd attach a letter addressed to Deb and Connor to the key card the day
of her escape. They needed to know. Then I'd tell Abi and Matt.

"How's Matt doing? I heard he arrived." Frank's question hung in the
air for a moment as I came back from my drifting thoughts.

I almost forgot he sat next to me.

I took a drink. "He's good."

Matt would reach out to his father in his own time.

"Why didn't he come earlier? What was he doing in Promissa?" Frank's
gaze was focused on the windows that showed the valley that separated
Promissa and Electi with the backdrop of the forest.

I shrugged. "Running his clinic as usual. I've told him about the dangers
of sympathizing with the city folk, but he's too much like his mother."

"Ah. Lisa." His eyes gleamed.

He'd always worshipped Lisa. She was his everything. There was no
doubt about it. You only needed to observe them at their home or at all
the social events they frequented to see it.

The separation affected all of them, especially Matt. He suspected his
parents were still in love, as they frequently visited each other.

He finished his drink in one gulp and tapped the glass on the bar.

The bartender refilled it with gin.

We stayed silent as the train arrived at the government center's station.

"Davon?" Frank said as I reached the exit door.

I looked back, one foot already on the steps. "Yes?"

A flash of pain passed through his features. "If you see him, tell him to
come to me if possible."

He stood from the barstool, leaving his drink untouched. As he approached me, his usual alluring and suave countenance was replaced by a haunted expression. "Tell him...I miss him."

Then, as if I'd only imagined it, he pushed his shoulders back, righted his cufflinks, and tapped my shoulder. "Have a good day, Minister Niles."

I stepped off the platform and walked to where my sedan was parked. Before entering, I glanced back.

Frank continued toward the government center and didn't look back.

I frowned. What was that all about?

Frank was never as up front with me as he was today.

My first council meeting came to mind, and I remembered the short glance that passed between Lavigne and Frank. Could he...?

"Minister Niles?" O'Hare called from the car.

I shook my head and climbed into the sedan, heading to the prison.

After entering my office, I put the letter inside the bureau and started to work.

Tomorrow I'd send for the doctor to check on Deb and use Sunday night as an excuse to let her rest. She needed her strength for Monday.

It took about an hour for me to finish a report about the energy bunker takeover. Lavigne wrote it, but I had to ensure everything was detailed and had to put it on file for Father.

Apex Genome Project. I held the file, and my insides turned. It had been sitting in the bureau since my dad last touched it.

I flexed my fingers and rested back in my chair. I couldn't put it off any longer. I needed to understand what we were dealing with.

The lights from the city shone brightly as the train made its way into Electi. Examining the file took longer than I imagined, and I took it home to study it further. It was way worse than I thought.

Lately, I'd opted to walk back home from the station. It allowed me time to process my workday. I stopped and looked up at my apartment. The lights were on, but they blocked anyone from seeing through.

Earlier, I sent a driver to pick up Abi and take her home.

I sighed. At least she was safe for now.

I shivered under my coat and walked two blocks to my building. Matt stood outside, vaping.

"Go home. I can manage from here," I told O'Hare and Bayat.

Bayat was about to protest when O'Hare touched her arm. His attention was on the lobby.

"Sure, call us if you need anything," he said.

I walked toward Matt. "What the hell, man?" I took his vape and put it in my pants. "It's been years."

He pinched his lips together and pocketed his hands.

I grabbed his shoulder. "What's the matter?"

He exhaled and sat on a bench.

I followed.

He rubbed the back of his neck. "It's Dad."

I widened my eyes. "Wait. Weren't you supposed to see Lisa today?"

Matt nodded. "I went to her house in the afternoon. We had lunch, and she listened to everything I said. She's scared, but she's with us." He chuckled. "She was relieved you were just acting. Her exact words were 'I never wanted to beat up Davon as much as that day in the hospital.'"

"I'm glad she knows." *First Lavigne, now Lisa. Maybe we can do this.*

"Dad arrived when I was about to leave. He wanted to talk to me."

"I saw him this morning on my way to Promissa. He asked about you."

Matt shifted toward me, his brow furrowed.

I put my hands up. "I didn't tell him you were going to your mom's house."

He sighed. "It was just bad timing. I overstayed. The thing is Mom insisted we sit in her study and talk."

I thought back to Frank's words earlier today. "He seemed changed this morning, a different person."

Matt laughed inwardly. "Yeah. That's what I thought too. And I think he has good intentions in his own way." He folded his hands over his lap. "He wants me to move permanently into Electi and work with him on some projects."

An empty feeling grew in the pit of my stomach. "What projects?"

Matt set his eyes on me. "The Elysium and the Apex Genome Project."

I froze. Frank had his own agenda. But how much did he tell Matt?

Matt grabbed my arm. "You knew about it! Didn't you?"

He should've heard it from me first.

I jerked away and rose. "I was going to tell you but..."

Matt stood. "But what?"

I raked my hair back, taking off the band holding it. "I don't know how to tell Abi."

He tilted his head. "I don't understand. Everyone must know. Just tell her."

I put my hands in my pockets and looked down. "It's not that simple."

Father's words echoed around me: "Deborah Davis is carrying your baby brother."

Matt gripped my shoulder. "Tell me. What is it?"

"Father told me about it three weeks ago, but I wanted to wait till Deb was out to tell you guys." I took a deep breath. "Deb's pregnant with my brother."

Matt's nostrils flared, and his stare turned sinister. "I'm fucking killing him."

I knew exactly how he felt. "Take a number."

"How far along is she?"

"Two months, three tops."

Matt exhaled hard. "There's still some time. Does she know?"

"I think so. Father hasn't told her, but I've seen her look at her womb." I sat on the bench and slumped over my leather briefcase.

Matt crouched on the ground. "Davon, we need to tell Abi. She has to know."

I gave him a vague nod. It was time Abi found out how deranged my father really was.

Chapter 22

Abi

January 13, 2214

My phone rang. I pressed the green phone image on the screen. "Hello?"

"Hi! It's Rebecca. I'm calling to check if you made it home safely."

Davon's mother sounded gleeful. We'd spent the day together, just talking and getting to know each other. She was a wonderful woman and loved her son to the moon and back.

"I did. Thanks for everything today."

"Of course, dear. Tell Davon about your idea for an under-the-stars garden party. We're going to have so much fun! I can't wait to introduce you to all my friends, especially Lisa. I haven't seen her in forever."

Part of our plan was to have a garden party the night of the extraction. Girls only. I needed an alibi. Now we only needed to create one for Matt.

"Sure. I'll tell him once he gets home."

Rebecca paused. "He hasn't come home yet?"

I glanced at my watch—eleven already. "No, but he's been like this lately."

Rebecca grunted. "It must be because Jordan is away. He's always working, but at least now I have you. Well, I guess till Jordan arrives since you'll probably work for him also."

"Right. But I'll still visit." No lie in my statement. What was not to like about Rebecca Niles? Well, maybe the fact that she was crazy in love with a psychopath. But that was not her fault because from what Matt told me, he had a way with people. If I could just make her see the truth about him.

"Great. Well, call me whenever you want. We can have lunch together. Or go shopping." She sounded happy.

"That sounds great. We'll talk later, then. Good night."

"Good night. And tell that son of mine to stop working so hard."

I chuckled. "I will."

The call was over before I could press the red dot on the screen.

The door rattled, and Davon came in, followed by Matt. Both had grim expressions.

Davon threw something in the trash can and put his briefcase on the coffee table in front of the sofa. He drifted his gaze across the room until he saw me on the opposite side and froze.

My heart raced. *What the hell is happening?*

Without giving me a moment to question him, he took four long strides toward me and held me to his chest, pressing his body against mine. He gripped my nape and kissed me, then touched his brow to mine. "How was your day?"

"All right, I guess. What's going on?" I searched his eyes for an idea of what was happening.

He straightened and trailed his hands down my arms. "I'll explain."

He took my hand and led me toward Matt. He was already sitting on the sectional sofa but didn't meet my eyes.

If Matt couldn't look at me straight, something was definitely wrong.

Was it about Deb? This was just like when I arrived at Janus Peak and discovered Deb had been taken.

My stomach roiled.

I took the couch, and Davon sat on the coffee table, facing me.

I clasped my wrist and gripped Mom's golden heart.

Davon took my hands in his. He brushed his thumb over my fingers. "Remember what I found two years ago?"

I thought back to our conversation at the base. "About the facilities holding Promissa citizens?"

He nodded. "Yes, and about how elites used surrogate mothers to have their children."

A dropping sensation took over me. Where was he going with this?

I focused on him. "What's happening?"

He looked at our joined hands. "Abi, the government is editing the genes in Promissa citizens' gametes held in the Reproductive and Genetic Investigation Center in Electi. They're creating enhanced humans to work and fight for them."

I gripped his hands. "What?"

My chest tightened at his revelation. What the fuck were they playing at?

He kept my gaze. "They're also modifying elite gamete genes to create people far superior in intelligence, health, and strength to rule over that workforce. To oppress the citizens even further. Their main goal is to eliminate the remaining Promissa citizens once they have enough of these improved specimens."

I tugged back, but Davon held me firm. "Eliminate, as in kill? But that would be genocide."

"Yes, mass murder by the same government that promised to protect the city." Matt's fevered stare made me shudder.

I sat forward. "But they just started, so we still have years before this happens, right?"

They were playing God, but they were still babies.

Davon shook his head. "They started this project ten years ago here in Promissa but more than twenty years ago in the rest of the NWG region."

Time stopped around me. Promissa was the last area invaded by the NWG, but they had control over most of the eastern coast territory for over twenty years. If what Davon said was true, they had an army ready to attack when needed.

A chill ran through me, and the hair lifted all over my arms and nape.

Davon leaned closer. "I know this is hard to swallow, but you need to know because Deb is part of this program."

I jerked back. "Deb? What do you mean she's part of the program?"

Davon stared down.

What the hell was he implying?

I gritted my teeth and lifted his chin. "Tell me. What do you mean?"

"Deb's pregnant."

My whole world stopped. Everything turned for an instant, and I doubled over. Deb was pregnant?

Davon pulled me to him.

"What? But..." My entire body trembled, but Davon held me tight.

"She's carrying my parents' baby. My brother. I'm so sorry, sweetheart."

It was like a punch to my gut, and I struggled to breathe. My chest pressed hard against my heart, and my vision blurred. What could possibly be worse than this?

I plunged into a void.

I opened my eyes to the strong scent of alcohol and someone patting my cheeks.

"Abi?" I followed Davon's soothing voice.

He massaged my temples.

I was resting on his lap.

Matt stood from where he crouched beside me and put away a handkerchief.

"God." I held my brow, trying to subdue a pounding headache. "What happened?" I sat upright. "Deb!"

Davon grabbed my wrist, but I wrenched it free and left the sofa.

I held on to Matt as everything spun around and around.

"Breathe for me." Matt gripped my shoulders.

Davon stood beside me.

"Give us some space, Davon," Matt said.

"I...can't..." The air wouldn't enter my body.

Matt leaned over so his eyes were level with mine. "I'm right here. Everything will be all right. But you need to breathe."

I listened to his voice. I could hear Davon pacing beside us, but I focused on Matt's breathing.

My chest relaxed, and I calmed down.

"Are you better now?" he asked.

I nodded.

Matt let me go and stepped back so Davon could take his place.

He hugged me. "I'm so sorry."

I was numb. His words replayed in my mind. "Deb's pregnant?"

"Yes." His voice was low and raspy.

"With your brother?" I stayed still, waiting for his answer.

He glanced down. "Yes."

No, it couldn't be. Maybe he got it wrong. "Are you sure?"

"Father told me a while ago."

A while ago?

With a scowl, I pushed him away, but he had a strong grip on me. "Let me go."

He lied to me. He knew, and he lied to my face. "I said let me go!" I shoved him hard, and this time he did.

He scrubbed a hand over his face. "I'm sorry. I..."

I flinched. "You've been torturing her even knowing this." A rogue tear escaped my eye. "How could you?"

"Please, Abi. Let me explain."

His eyes carried so much pain. He took a step toward me and held my hand. "I tried to reason with Father, but he's out of his mind. He said if she lost the baby, he'd just put her through the procedure again." He slumped over me, his head on my shoulder. "I'm losing her, Abi. I see less of her every day. It's like she's a shadow of what she once was, and it's all my fault."

All those nights when he sobbed silently. Now I understood.

He trembled in my arms. "I know what I've done is unforgivable." He took a shuddering breath. "Please don't leave me."

A deep pain grew in my soul at his words. Like me, a fear of being alone was embedded deep within him. His past haunted him, and he was reliving his worst nightmares, and right then and there I realized I couldn't hold him accountable for what he'd done. He was following orders.

I had to be strong.

I caressed his long dark waves and held him close. "I won't leave you, love. I'm right here."

I don't know how much time passed.

Like the day we first met, we sat silently, eating nuts and dried fruit.

Davon was next to me, his arm across my back.

I leaned on his shoulder, and Matt sat in front.

"Does she know?" I asked, breaking the silence.

Davon kissed my head and squeezed my shoulder. "I think so."

"That's what you believe, but we need to make sure she knows before she leaves," Matt said.

Davon heaved a sigh. "I know. I'm going to attach a note to the key card she'll use to escape. I want her to be with Connor when she finds out. I don't think her knowing right now is a good idea."

With all that he'd done to her, she could have a mental breakdown with this news.

"I agree with Davon. Telling her now would endanger the mission," I said, even though it hurt to keep this from her.

Matt drummed his fingers on the table. "Okay, we'll do that, and if she wants to get an abortion, Dr. Lewis or the nurses can help her."

"I don't think she'll do it." I'd respect her decision even though I knew deep inside that this baby could bring them a lot of pain, especially her.

Matt leaned over the table. "Why wouldn't she?"

My heart broke into pieces for her and Connor. "Because both Connor and Deb have always dreamed of having children and they know it's impossible with how things are now. Also, I don't think she could do it. It's just not her."

Matt pushed himself back and frowned. "You don't know that. This is Jordan Niles's son after all. She might change her mind."

Widening my eyes, I shook my head. How could he say that in front of Davon?

I rubbed Davon's thigh. "He didn't mean that."

Matt stiffened.

"He's telling the truth. I'm as rotten as my father deep down," Davon choked out.

Matt reached over. "Davon, I..."

Davon shoved his chair back. "I'm going to take a shower."

I watched Matt as Davon's footsteps receded into our room. "What the hell's wrong with you?"

Matt raked his blond curls back. "Fuck. I didn't think. I'm such an asshole."

"You are." I put my elbows on the table and gripped my head. "This is all fucked up."

My stomach heaved. Could this be any worse?

Not only was my sister being tortured and now pregnant, but Davon was close to a crisis, with no choice but to be the villain in all this. With the NWG having an army at their beck and call, it was difficult to imagine a positive outcome.

I crossed my arms. "He doesn't need us to lose our shit."

"You're right." Matt massaged his temples. "It's been a long day. I met with Dad earlier, and he wants me to work on this project." He dropped his hands on the table and clenched them so hard that his biceps bulged and his veins swelled across his arms. "This whole situation changes everything."

I covered his fists. "I know. But we have to be strong." I pictured Deb, Connor, Sarah, David, Aoki, Jimmy, and all the others. "We must work together. We can still fight."

"But they have an army." Matt sank forward.

I remembered Paul's cries as they took him. Jacob and Bonnie as they died. Richard's body lying on the floor. I made a vow, and I wasn't about to back down now. "We have much more to fight for. I know what it's like to lose all hope, to have no strength left to move forward. But we're not there yet. We can do this. We're already so close. We can't abandon our people while we still have a chance."

So what if they had an army on the eastern coast? We were hundreds of miles away. If we did this right and they didn't see it coming, we could win Promissa back. After that, we would deal with the rest.

Matt nodded, then searched my eyes. "I'm sorry I lost it."

"We all did." I squeezed his hands. "There's nothing to be sorry about."

Matt left for his apartment, promising he'd talk to Davon later.

I turned the lights off and waited for Davon in bed.

When he finished, he didn't say a thing and just lay in bed, his back to me.

I cradled him in my arms. "I love you. Everything will be okay."

He turned and held me, then kissed my head. "I love you, darling."

January 16, 2214

"Hey, babe. I prepared some pancakes. They're a bit burned, but I think they turned out fine," I told Davon.

He wore only black sweatpants and no shirt.

I licked my lips. How did I get so lucky?

He offered me a devilish smile and put his hair up in a bun before coming into the kitchen and hugging me from behind. His warm breath on my back reminded me of our lovemaking this morning.

Goosebumps ran down my arms and neck as he licked my flesh with his velvety tongue.

"I bet they taste as sweet as you."

His words sent fire to my core as I recalled his skilled mouth.

I twisted my face to the side, caught him by the neck, and kissed him.

He stroked my cheek down to my neck. "You're so beautiful."

I leaned into him, and he stepped back.

"But I fear if I don't get you a cup of coffee soon, I'll get in trouble."

I hit his chest. "Hey! I'm not that addicted."

I was.

He raised both eyebrows. "Whatever you say."

He prepared our coffee while I arranged the table.

Three days had passed since he told me about Deb.

Matt and Davon were back to normal. Yesterday they took me to the district with Rebecca to buy a dress for the garden party and then went to have some drinks in a bar while we shopped.

Four bodyguards watched over us, two in the front and two following behind, not counting the others who hid around the district. This was my first time in a public space, and I was in the company of one of the most important women in Electi. Today all the tabloids would have a picture of me and a big headline that would probably read, "Mystery Woman Out with Rebecca Niles."

It was of great importance that I became known by Electi's citizens before Davon's father arrived. Davon still didn't trust that his father accepted me fully and feared I could be in danger.

Knowing I'd be face-to-face with him in a week or so made me want to run and hide. But I had to keep up my persona and be the woman he expected me to be. So I swallowed hard and kept my chin up.

Rebecca paid with a card in every shop. I asked her about it, and she told me their system was based on credits, depending on your position. Elites administered everything, and all the other jobs were done by Promissa citizens. I wondered which of them were abused and lived in those facilities and which were the "lucky ones" who got to work inside Electi but lived in Promissa.

That made me remember my aunt and uncle. I was out of words when Davon told me to watch out for Aunt Annie since she was the one who took care of him when he arrived. I kept my eyes open, but she worked as a private nurse, and we hoped she was assigned to another family already. As for my uncle, I prayed he was sent far from here. If one of them recognized me, it would all be over.

We met back at the central fountain. It was like nothing I'd ever seen.

A memory of Jacob, Bonnie, and me sharing a canteen came to my mind. The sandy feeling in my mouth as days passed with only drops of water to drink. The dryness of my throat when I spoke. The weakness and the pain. All that suffering, and here they had this.

My hands twitched, and I stood on edge.

Davon peeked from the other side, just behind the water curtain that fell from the ceiling and into a reflective pool. He shared a pained glance with me before shaking his head and pocketing his hands.

Matt walked toward us and took two of Rebecca's bags.

Davon grabbed mine and whispered, "I know it's a lot, but bear with me."

I nodded and held his hand.

"Hey." Davon offered me a mug. "Are you okay?"

I sighed, coming back to the present. "Sure."

I looked out. The district was peaceful. Some people were arriving, mostly workers.

Today was the calm before the storm as we prepared to rescue Deb at last. Muñoz had slipped the letter into her cell. Now we could only wait.

We solved Matt's alibi dilemma. He'd go out for drinks with his father.

As for me, the garden party would be a success, according to Rebecca, but I wondered how I would survive it, knowing Davon and Deb would be in peril.

Davon had stayed at home for the last couple of days. The doctor who checked Deb apparently called Jordan to tell him she should rest, and he'd told Davon to take a few days off.

It was a welcome reprieve. If the wait was eating me slowly, I wondered how she was holding up.

"Are you going to see Deb today?" I asked.

He poured honey over his pancakes. "I'm going to work to check if there's any letter from Connor. Then I'll visit Deb at her cell, but I won't take her into the interrogation room. Not until tomorrow. That's what I said in the letter."

Being alone in that cell would play with her mind, and even with her following the instructions to the point, we worried if she'd remember what to do.

"Right. I forgot. At what time will the rescue happen?"

"About 10:00 p.m. I'm leaving you at Mom's and then taking the train to Promissa. Matt will take Lisa to the party and then meet his father at a private club near his place." Davon moaned as he tasted his pancakes. "These are delicious."

I smiled. "Thanks. This coffee is pretty amazing too."

He kissed my cheek. "Nothing can ever go wrong when it's coffee and you."

We were indulging in our breakfast when my phone rang. I lifted it. Rebecca.

"Hello."

"Oh, hi, my dear. Can you talk? I know how young couples are, and if you need your privacy, I can always call later."

My face warmed at her statement.

Davon lifted the corner of his mouth as he pointed to the red mug I was drinking from and then to my face.

I rolled my eyes. "No, it's all right."

"Perfect. I was wondering if you could come today and help me decorate the garden. I can get someone to do it, but it's more fun if we do it ourselves."

Rebecca was a free soul, and no one would imagine from the way she acted that she was such an important person. She liked to do things on her own and live life to the fullest.

"Sure. Sounds cool. When do you need me there?"

"Come for lunch."

I looked at Davon. "I'm sorry, Rebecca. We have plans for lunch, but I can get there right after."

Matt had arranged lunch with his mother. He wanted her to meet me now that she was on our side.

"Oh, that's too bad. Then we'll go into the garden conservatory directly. That's where we'll have the party."

"A conservatory?"

What the hell was she talking about?

I glanced at Davon, but he was focused on eating.

"Don't you have conservatories over there?" Her voice sounded perplexed.

Of course not, I thought to say. "I've never heard of one."

"Really? Well, no worries. You'll love it. It's one of my favorite places, after the library, of course."

They had a freaking library?

"You have a library?" I tried to keep my voice neutral, but I must have sounded like an ignorant child.

She paused. "Today I'll give you a tour."

I dipped my chin and played with my pancakes. There was so much I didn't know. "You don't have to."

She must think I'm clueless.

"Of course I must, dear. Oh, and tell that son of mine to come by too. He can help."

"I'll ask him, but he has work today."

Davon mouthed, "Tell her I can't."

I put her on speaker.

"On a Sunday? No, no, no. That won't work. Tell him if he's not here, his mother will be heartbroken. Also, we need someone tall to hang the string lights I bought."

Davon sank back into his chair.

I chuckled. "I'm sure he won't let us down. Take care, Rebecca. See you later."

"See you."

I pressed the red dot and hung up.

Davon sighed. "Is she for real?"

I looked at him out of the corner of my eye. I knew he had a lot on his plate between today and tomorrow, but this was his mother. "Yeah, but you can come later. She wants to decorate the area for the party tomorrow. You heard her—we're too short to hang the lights she bought."

"Okay, I'll arrive before dusk to help you. I'll call Matt. I'm sure he can get you there after our lunch with Lisa."

I took a bite from my pancakes. They were not half bad.

I knocked on Matt's door and smiled at his camera.

Davon was getting ready and would come for lunch before leaving for work.

"Come in!" he said through the intercom.

The intercom buzzed, and I pushed the oak double doors open.

The moment I crossed the threshold, my day became brighter. This place gave me the same vibes as his apartment back at the peak, and I could almost feel Aoki's influence in its décor. Everything was white, even the floor, with a few dark wood pieces of furniture that gave it an elegant atmosphere.

His place took up half of the twenty-ninth floor and had the same layout as Davon's except for the gym area and the size of each space.

A luxurious white leather sofa and love seat sat to the left, with soft-cream marble counters in the kitchen area to the right. There was a closed door to the right opposite me, which led to the bedroom, and a dining table and resting area up front. The glass walls overlooked the city except for the one side that connected to the next apartment.

"I'm coming. Give me a minute." Matt's voice filtered out of his room.

I sat on the sofa and waited.

The bedroom door swung open, and Matt came out, tucking a burgundy shirt inside his blue denim jeans.

"Sorry. I'm having trouble sleeping and woke up late." He brushed his hair with his fingers, trying to control his golden curls.

I stood. "Are you all right?"

He waved dismissively. "This always happens when I'm on a mission. Seven years of marriage will do that to you. I just miss Aoki."

I grimaced, unable to think of what to say. While I rejoiced in Davon's arms, poor Matt had to endure the time without his husband.

"I'm sorry."

"Don't be." He opened his mouth, then closed it and shook his head.

"What is it?" I went to his side.

His eyes were glazed. "I'm scared for Aoki. What if an attack like the energy bunker happens at Janus Peak? I can't bear to lose him."

I held him as he sobbed. I couldn't fight the burning in my throat. We could lose so much.

Matt put some music on, and we moved into the kitchen.

Time seemed to fly when I was with him.

Davon arrived, and Matt buzzed him in.

He entered. "Hey, guys!"

Lunch was almost ready—roast chicken and potatoes.

Davon put a wine bottle inside the fridge and leaned on the countertop, wearing a royal-blue dress shirt and black slacks. He had his hair loose and looked sexy as hell.

I stood on my tiptoes to kiss him. "We're almost done."

Matt took the chicken out of the oven. "Mom should be here soon."

"God, that smells heavenly." I stretched over Davon, his arms around my waist from behind.

The intercom rang.

I tensed.

Davon kissed my nape. "Don't be nervous. Lisa's just like my mother. You'll love her."

Matt passed us on his way to open the door. "And the best thing is we can call you Abi and we don't have to act like evil bastards around her."

I raised an eyebrow. He had a point.

We followed him to the door.

Matt opened it. "Hi, Mom."

"Hey, honey." A beautiful blond woman came inside, her hair tied back in a long ponytail. She hugged Matt, then kissed his cheek. "I missed you." She smiled wide.

Matt rolled his eyes but couldn't hide his smile. "Mom, we saw each other three days ago."

Lisa shrugged and looked up at Davon, then at me. "You must be Abigail." She took my hands. "Matt told me a lot about you."

I darted my gaze toward Matt.

He winked and shrugged.

I shook my head. "Nice to meet you, Miss Johnson."

"Please call me Lisa." She shifted her gaze to Davon.

Davon stepped to my side. "Lisa?"

Lisa took her purse and hit Davon on his side. Twice. "Don't Lisa me, Davon. You scared the shit out of me." She brought her thumb and index finger close together. "I was this close to beating some sense into you at the hospital. The only thing that stopped me was your injury."

Davon grimaced and curled his shoulders forward. "I'm sorry. I didn't know Matt would bring you in."

"You're forgiven but only because Matt told me you found someone at last." She shifted her gaze between us. "You make a cute couple."

Warmth spread through my face, and Davon chuckled, putting his arm around me and pulling me close.

"Wait till you see Matt and Aoki together. They make such a handsome couple," I said.

The room went silent.

Lisa widened her eyes and turned to Matt. "Aoki?"

"We should sit." Matt glanced at us. "Bring the wine."

"It appears Matt hasn't told her about his husband," Davon said once we were out of earshot.

I cringed. *Me and my big mouth.*

We went to the kitchen, and while Davon uncorked the wine, I retrieved four wine glasses. When we approached the sofa, they were deep in conversation.

"He's a chef. We married almost eight years ago." Matt took his wedding band out of his pocket and put it on.

I hadn't realized he wasn't wearing it. Both of their rings had the infinity symbol engraved around them, but the colors were reversed. Matt's ring was silver with golden carvings and Aoki's gold with silver etchings.

"You're married!" Lisa threw herself at Matt.

Matt chuckled.

"Why didn't you tell me before?"

He shrugged. "I didn't want to throw more your way. Thought it was enough with me being a rebel."

She pouted comically. "I'm so happy for you but so sad I missed it. When this is all over, you're going to have to get married again so I can be there with your father."

Matt tilted his head but stayed silent.

So it was true. Matt's parents still loved each other. But what did she mean after all this was over? Wasn't Frank one of the bad guys? Or was I getting it wrong?

I peeked at Davon, and he had the same perplexed expression I was sure I had.

Lisa grabbed Matt's hand to study the ring. "It's beautiful! Do you have any pictures of him?"

They still hadn't noticed us standing in front of the coffee table.

"I'm sorry. I couldn't risk anyone seeing it and asking questions, so I left it at home." Matt's expression turned sour.

Lisa covered his hand. "It's okay, honey. It must be hard being away from him."

Matt lowered his head. "It is."

Davon took the moment to announce our presence. "How about a toast?"

I put the glasses on the table.

Matt turned to us with teary eyes and nodded.

I sat beside him. "Sorry I blurted it out like that. I didn't know."

He patted my knee. "No worries. I planned to tell her during dinner. That's why I had the ring in my pocket."

Davon passed everyone a glass and raised his. "For Lisa, for love, and for family. May this be the first of many memories together."

We all drank.

The lunch was uneventful. Lisa asked about the mission, and Davon gave her the details. We all had somewhere to be, so we drank our last glass of wine.

"About tomorrow. Are you sure you'll be all right?" she asked Davon.

Davon answered, but their voices seemed distant.

I watched them in conversation and put up a false front, pretending everything was okay. The turmoil inside me was enough to drive anyone mad, but I'd grown accustomed to it. Ever since the day Deb told me to escape, I'd always lived in this constant state of anxiety. I could manage it, but today...

I thought about Deb finally being free, and it offered me some solace. But after so long, I wouldn't be able to see her. To even glimpse her. I missed her and wanted to be with her when she went home. To help her through the pregnancy and through all the trauma. I wanted to hug her tight and be a family again. But that had to wait, as we still had a long way to go.

To top it all off, we were sure Davon would be hurt during the escape. And what worried me most was what was going on in my sister's head. The mind was a powerful thing, and it sometimes surpassed logic.

So many things could go wrong.

"Abi?" Davon's voice broke through my dark thoughts and brought me back.

I shook my head slightly and blinked back my tears. "I'm sorry. What is it?"

I glanced around the table. All eyes were on me.

"Are you okay?" Davon stroked the back of my neck, massaging softly.

"Sure. Why?"

He came closer. "Lisa was talking to you, but you seemed far away."

I met Lisa's honey-brown eyes. "Sorry. What was it you wanted to talk about?"

"I just wanted to remind you that we need to act as if we haven't met for tomorrow's garden party." Lisa drew her eyebrows together. "Are you sure you're all right?"

I glanced at my watch. I needed to get out for a moment and breathe. "Yeah, it's just that Rebecca is waiting for me."

I looked at Matt. "I need to freshen up. When you're ready to go, fetch me. I'll wait upstairs."

I stretched my hand toward Lisa. She took it.

"It was great meeting you. And I'm sorry. I'm just tired," I lied.

Davon stood and helped me up. "I'll go with you. Thanks for lunch, Matt."

Matt winked. "Next time we'll meet at your place."

"Sounds good." Davon reached for Lisa's hand. "Thanks for joining us, Lisa. You have no idea what it means for the rebellion."

Lisa rose. "Come here."

Davon hugged her.

"I know there's a lot I still need to understand, but know you can count on me," she said.

She stepped back and took my hand. "Matt has my number. If you need anything, call."

I nodded.

After a few more goodbyes, we left and climbed the stairs to Davon's in silence.

Once inside, I walked to the side of the apartment that faced the district and touched the glass. I closed my eyes. "Everything will be okay. All is good. I'm strong."

Aoki taught me that when I was feeling down, I should say positive thoughts out loud. He said that it helped one keep a right mind and attract good things.

Davon's arms wrapped around me. "And you are loved."

I slumped into his chest. "Why is it so hard?"

He put his chin on top of my head. "Talk to me, love."

I took a deep breath. "Will I ever get to see her again? Will you be all right?"

Davon turned me to face him. He lifted my chin gently. "Of course you will. We will make it back, Abi. I promised you'd see her again, and you will."

I tried to keep my emotions under control, but when he looked at me, everything I had bottled up came out. "What if they kill her during the escape? What if we're discovered and can never go back? What if the spy finds our location and we lose everything before ever getting back? What if you die?" A torrent of tears slid down my face, and I struggled to breathe.

Davon hugged me to his chest. "Breathe with me."

I followed his breaths like I'd done many times before. The air filled my lungs, and I let it out with him. We breathed as one.

He cupped my face. "There's no way to know for sure what will happen tomorrow, but I promised once, and I'll do it again. Nothing and no one will stop me from getting back to you." He kissed my forehead. "You're everything to me. Please trust me. I will get Deb out and return to you. I promise."

Half an hour later, Matt and I arrived at Davon's childhood home.

I opened my door. "Aren't you coming?"

Matt gripped the steering wheel. "Tell Rebecca I'm sorry. I need to take care of some things."

I furrowed my brow. "I thought we had everything set."

He looked at his hands. "We do. This is something else." He shook his head and smiled at me. "Just go in, and have fun. And thank you. Mom loved you."

I dipped my chin. "Even after the way I behaved?"

"You didn't do anything wrong. We're all under a lot of pressure." He grabbed my hand and kissed it. "Now get in there, and have some fun."

My heart settled down a bit, and I left the car.

He drove away.

Rebecca came out of the house, looking casual in a black top and red leggings. "Was that Matt?"

"Yes. He had to leave in a hurry."

She crossed her arms. "He could've at least said hi. That only takes a minute." She paused. "And Davon?"

"He'll be here later."

"Perfect." She took my hand. "Come in. I'll give you a tour."

The house was enormous, with six guest rooms and two master bedrooms. One was Jordan and Rebecca's and one was Davon's. A beautiful family picture was all that identified it as Davon's room. I picked it up.

Rebecca was by my side in a flash. "Oh, I love this picture. Matt took it on Davon's fifteenth birthday. He didn't want a grand party, just a family day by the lake. He was so happy."

Davon already looked tall for his age, his face clean-shaven and his hair long. His father had an arm around him while Rebecca kissed his cheek. A genuine smile filled his face as he looked at a birthday cake on the table.

A strange pressure built inside me. There was so much love in this picture.

I put it down and walked to the window. The view of the forest gave me solace. I wondered how much longer we would be able to call the forest our home.

Rebecca showed me the library next. It was impressive. I'd never seen so many books. The warm light of candlesticks dispersed across the room and gave it an antique feeling. All the bookshelves were made of mahogany, with a set of two cream armchairs and one love seat in a corner. It was an elegant setting.

She showed me the gym, which was equipped with everything you could imagine, and the entertainment room, which looked like the pictures of old cinemas that Abraham had showed us in his lectures.

Housekeepers roamed around the house with their heads down, and not one dared talk to us.

"Come on, Gaby. Time to decorate." Rebecca's beaming smile reminded me of my mother's.

God, I missed her.

I followed Rebecca out and came to a stop. My arms hung at my sides as Rebecca continued up front.

Behind a hedge stood a lone figure. He was moving plants from a cart to the terrain. His big brown eyes found mine.

I covered my mouth. His jaw was still set at a wrong angle. My vision fogged, and time slowed as a flashback of that day came to me.

His pleading words as the guard beat him almost to death. The reek of urine mixed with blood. The promise I'd made...

He raked his black hair back and blocked the sun from his eyes. Recognition flashed across his face.

I took a step forward. He was about ten feet away. "Paul?"

He blinked, and a sob escaped him. He attempted to tell me something, but no words came out.

Rebecca was far enough away, so I risked my cover.

"Are you okay?"

He shook his head.

"I'll get you out of here. I promise."

Tears rolled down his cheeks. It broke my heart.

His eyes widened.

Rebecca walked toward me. "Hey, so you've met one of our gardeners. He can't talk. No one knows his true name or how he was injured, but he's a good worker."

"Does he live here?"

She explained that the cooks, the butler, and two maids lived in a section of the house in the basement.

Her eyes darted between us. "No. He's part of a new initiative Jordan created to offer residence to less advantaged Promissa citizens. They live on the periphery of Electi."

My blood boiled at the lies Jordan told her. "That's weird. I came in that way and didn't see anything like that. Have you visited?"

She furrowed her brow and looked at Paul. "I haven't."

I shrugged. "Maybe you can ask Minister Niles to take you there."

She nodded. "Yeah, maybe I will. I'm sure he'll take me. We've fought so much over the issue of Promissa, and at last he did something to start the change. He's a good man, and I'm sure he does it for the good of all."

Or the good of just a few.

"Come. Let's go to the conservatory." She took my hand.

I risked one last glance back at Paul and mouthed, "I'll get you out."

He smiled.

January 16, 2214

*D*avon,

> *Connor is on his way to the extraction area with a team of runners and a squad. They'll be there until dawn on January 18 as agreed in your last communication. If nothing happens by that time, they'll abort the mission and await further instructions.*

—Jimmy

P.S. I have no words to apologize for what happened. I now see the error in my actions. Please take care of Abi.

Abi said Jimmy was sorry, but to hear it from him was something I didn't expect. I'd already forgiven his actions. After all, many hated me, as was expected. Now more than ever.

I ran the letter through the shredder before heading to see Deb.

The guards saluted me as I entered her floor and approached the cell.

I opened the metal window. "Good afternoon, Miss Davis. It's been a while. I hope you got a small reprieve and are ready for all the fun we're having tomorrow night."

She was there in a second and spit in my face. "Why don't you just kill me and get it over with? I'll never say anything."

I sneered. "But where's the fun in that? No, I'll enjoy hearing you scream until you can't take it anymore. I'll watch you lose yourself until you have no choice but to tell us everything. Everyone breaks at some point."

She bared her teeth at me and took a step back. "You'll never break me."
Then she blinked both eyes slowly.

I blinked back.

She was ready. Everything was set.

"Mom, where do you want the lights?" I asked.

Abi glanced toward me. She was helping Mom arrange flowers in crystal
vases for each table. White and yellow roses meant purity and friendship,
as Mom explained.

"Everywhere! I bought enough to hang all around the conservatory. I
want it to look like a fairy tale."

I pinched my brow. I hated parties. That was the one thing I didn't like
about Mom, her obsession with throwing the best events even if it was for
no more than ten people.

This would take some time.

I hung the lights from a corner hook. Seven more to go.

The glass panels offered an unobstructed view of the garden. The gray
skies only heightened the sense of impending doom.

I gazed at the horizon. The forest was so close, and its snow-covered
summits relieved the pressure in my chest. I missed being outside and in
nature.

After an hour or so, dusk began to set in, and we turned on the lights.

"Oh." Mom clapped. "It looks wonderful!"

My arm hung around Abi's shoulder as Mom did a 360-degree turn,
inspecting the space.

Abi leaned into me, and I got a sense that something was wrong. I'd ask her later.

"Will you stay for dinner?" Mom asked.

"Sure." I took Abi's hand and followed Mom inside.

We went into the dining room. Our antique cream dining table resembled the one in the sitting room.

The maids served penne primavera pasta with shrimp and mushrooms bathed in white wine sauce. It was exquisite.

I looked at Abi. Her eyes widened at all the food set on the table.

I couldn't imagine what she felt, knowing we had enough to feed all of Promissa without the need to ration food and water. There were no lights out in Electi, no prohibition of internet or leisure activities. We had cars, for God's sake. And credits.

The lie fed to Promissa citizens was enough to cause an uprising. If we showed them how things were inside Electi, maybe they'd take up arms and fight with us.

I'd run it by Connor. We needed to get our hands on the feed from the cameras inside the district and find a way to hack into their broadcasting system. Just a few glimpses of how elites lived would be enough to push them.

When we finished, Mom insisted we stay in one of the guest rooms.

"Mom, I'm sorry. We prefer to go home. Gaby has all her things there," I said after Abi gave my hand a squeeze.

Something was up.

"I understand." She took our hands. "Thanks for coming. It's been a long time since I had the pleasure of spending an afternoon with family and hanging out."

She stepped back. "You remind me of us when we started going out."

I cringed.

Abi touched my hip, settling my raging mind. To compare us to Father and her seemed like an offense.

"When should I come tomorrow?" Abi asked.

Mom smiled. "Six would be great."

I took Abi's hand. "Perfect. I'll make sure she's here on time."

When we opened the door to the penthouse, I stopped in my tracks and pushed Abi behind me.

Someone was here.

"Wait here," I whispered.

She nodded.

Matt sat at our dining table, and the scent of steak permeated the room.

He had keys to my apartment, so seeing him here wasn't a surprise. What came as a shock was his coming in unannounced.

My breath hitched at the number of files that covered my table.

I glanced back and gestured for Abi to come in.

"Matt?" I walked toward him. "What are you doing here?"

Red-rimmed eyes focused on us. "Oh. Sorry." He started piling up the papers. "You need to see this."

What could he have found?

I glanced at the files and scowled. "I don't understand."

My pulse spiked. Pictures of embryos, from the first stages to being a complete organism, stared back at me. They were held inside pods filled with liquid. Some were disfigured, others missing some limbs, but most looked just like babies. Some were much bigger than what you would see after complete gestation.

"I decided to work with Father for the time being," he said. "I need to figure out how they're doing this and how to fix it."

"Matt, this is..." I couldn't find the words. I swallowed hard.

Matt frowned. "Unethical? Something that goes against all that I am?" He shook his head. "We all need to make sacrifices. This is mine. And what I found today, what he wants me to oversee and work on goes above all I could've imagined."

Abi sat and lifted a picture from the table. "What the hell is this?"

Her hand trembled as I took it from her. A child, maybe two years old, sat on a gurney. A description was written below the picture:

Experiment forty-three

Biological age: eleven months

Physiological age: two years

Matt grabbed the picture from me and tapped it. "This here is what I wanted to show you. They're growing embryos using biotechnological chambers where they are nurtured and developed outside the human body. Scientists manipulate nutrients, hormones, and genetic factors to accelerate growth."

The room was too hot. Sweat beads rolled down my temple, and I wiped them away.

How was this even possible?

A human factory built within Electi.

"By their engineering for specific genes, these children are reaching physical and mental maturity in half the time that normal children would. Which means in eight years, the child in this picture will be a twenty-year-old adult."

What the fuck was the NWG doing? A chill traveled across my body.

"How is this even possible?" I put my palms on the table and breathed hard. Dozens of children stared back at me. Instead of names, they had numbers.

An oppressive force crushed my chest, and it was hard to breathe.

Abi covered one of my hands.

I entwined my fingers through hers.

Her eyes were glassy, her eyebrows squished together. "Matt, what does this all mean?"

"Dad has a team of top scientists working on this. Splicing genes and reactivating latent DNA promote rapid development. They plan to use it to advance both genome projects. They manipulate genes to promote physical strength, improve health, and increase intelligence. The Elysium Project employs the first two to build a formidable army and workforce. The Apex Project creates a human with all these characteristics, a weapon more dangerous than any other. By adding these genes that accelerate development and growth, the subjects will be ready in half the time that it would take naturally."

All the hairs on my skin rose in unison. This was far more dangerous than we imagined.

Matt looked through the files. "It still hasn't been perfected, as you can see." He showed us the pictures of the disfigured embryos and some tables titled "Cognitive Behavior Anomalies."

"Some embryos are discarded if they show mutations. Children who show signs of behavioral concerns are studied further to analyze where the manipulation went wrong."

"Lab rats," Abi said. "All the gametes that have been taken from us were never to control the overpopulation problem. They took them to experiment. To use or discard as needed." Her voice was stern, her expression pinched.

Matt nodded and opened another file. He put it in the center of the table. "This is the Prometheus Project. It was created to progress both the Elysium and Apex Genome Projects. The lab started growing these embryos three years ago in artificial wombs, both here and in Halcyon. A month ago, they started experimenting on humans. They believe a real womb might accelerate their development and lessen the embryos' stress levels."

I narrowed my eyes. "What are they doing to them?"

"They're implanting the embryos that are bioengineered to grow faster inside a human womb, but there's no way of knowing if they will endanger their host. The scientists don't know if the human body will adapt to their rapid growth. Also, the pregnancies last about four to six months. It's unnatural, so the babies must be surgically removed from the womb."

Abi browsed file after file, darting her eyes across pages and pages of data. "Which humans did they use?"

Matt tilted his head toward her, sharing her pained look. "They impregnated ten women already. All prisoners."

Abi clenched her fists on the file she held. "Her name is listed here." Her lips quivered. She stood and pushed the paper toward Matt, pointing at it. "Her name is listed here!"

I glanced at it and grimaced. "No. It can't be." I trailed my finger across her name. "Subject 10: Deborah Davis."

I gripped the table with all my strength. "Fuck!" I punched it.

Dad was playing a dangerous game, and my friend was at risk.

Matt rubbed the back of his neck. "I'm sorry. Dad told me about the Prometheus Project when he offered me the job. But I wanted to be sure what it entailed before I told you. I just found out about Deb this afternoon and rushed back. She's in real danger."

"What kind of danger are we talking about?" Abi asked.

Matt sighed. "These embryos require more than a normal one would because of their growth. I would expect the mother to be malnourished and exhausted. The placenta may not be able to keep up with the embryo's needs and, because of the embryo's size, the increased pressure in the uterus could cause placental detachment. Preeclampsia might also be an issue as well as gestational diabetes. Natural abortion or premature labor is possible if the body is unable to support the embryo."

Abi leaned forward. "Do you think Dr. Lewis will be able to help her?"

Matt gripped her hands. "I'm sure of it."

She slumped on the chair. "I never imagined they could go this far."

I paced. Not only were they experimenting on citizens and putting their lives in danger, but they did it with only two things in mind: power and control.

"We need to stop this as soon as possible." I bent over the files and grabbed a picture of a child. "These are innocent people we're talking about. If we get Promissa back and take over Electi, we can help them. But what about those in Halcyon?"

Abi took a deep breath. "One step at a time. We must move forward with our plans. If we do this right, we can save these people and end the experiments, both here and in Halcyon."

Matt and I watched her. She acted like a leader, her calm poise mirroring Connor's.

"First, we reclaim Promissa, followed by the New World Government Center and Electi. Once we've finished here, we'll move on to the rest of the system."

After recovering from the shock of this crazy son-of-a-bitch experiment my father was overseeing, we decided to send the files to Connor via a drive placed inside the note I'd attach to the key card.

An hour later, Matt took the files and his food to go. He was exhausted.

We sat together to eat the steak and fries he prepared for us.

"Davon, I forgot to tell you something." She stopped eating. "I found Paul."

Paul? The one they beat and took away?

I dropped my fork. "How? Where?"

"He works in the gardens at your house. He's..." She grimaced. "He's deformed. When they beat him, they broke his jaw. I think they never set it right."

Fucking monsters.

I tightened my fists. "Did you talk to him? Was Mom around?"

Abi nodded. "She was a safe distance away, so I took a minute to talk to him, but he could only gesture. I asked him if he was okay, and he shook his head. Then your mom came."

She looked down. "Your mom believes your father created an initiative to help Promissa citizens and give them a safe place inside Electi. She believes he's working to unite both cities and that the workers are doing great. But Paul is suffering. I promised I'd help him."

I pinched my brow. How could Mom believe all the bullshit Dad said? "We'll get him out. Did she see you with him?"

"Yes."

"Did she suspect?"

She shook her head. "I don't think so. But I do think your father's going to have a tough time when he comes back."

I narrowed my eyes. "Why?"

She smirked. "Because I told her I'd never seen those living spaces and that she should ask him to take her there."

I sneered. "Do you have any idea how much I love you?" I grasped her hand and kissed her palm. "You're a fucking genius."

She squeezed my hand. "Do you think it's possible to get him out?"

"We'll get him out."

"But what about the officers? Every night they come to take him back. Your mom said that's how it worked."

Nothing would stop me from saving Abi's friend. "I'll handle it."

She moved to my lap. "Thank you for doing this." She brushed my stubble and pulled me to her in a swift kiss. "I love you."

"I love you too." I kissed her deeply.

I vowed to help her fulfill her promise, and I would. Then we'd get our vengeance.

Chapter 25

Davon

January 17, 2214

Lake Egregie was bathed in a warm glow. The sun kissed the horizon, shadowing the outline of the majestic city of Electi. Everything was quiet. All was calm.

Abi and I sat in the back of the sedan in silence.

She clutched the sapphire pendant I gave her on her birthday. She faced the lake away from me.

I placed my elbow against the window and peered out, biting my thumb as the sun continued on its way. Soon the night would come to cloak our world in darkness.

The weight of what lay ahead threatened to crush me when O'Hare pulled into my parents' driveway.

I unbuckled my seatbelt and turned to Abi. She hugged me. Her sweet scent washed over me.

I wrapped my arms around her. Her dark and blond strands slid between my fingers. "You'll receive news once everything's done. I'll send an SOS from my cell phone as soon as Deb's a safe distance away."

"God, I don't know how I'll be able to do this," she mumbled against my chest.

Every time we said goodbye, a heavy feeling took over me. It was hard to think of a positive outcome when so much could go wrong.

I kissed her temple. "Trust me, Abi. After tonight, Deb will be safe."

I reached for Abi's glasses on the back of the center console and put them on her. "You look sexy with these on."

I gave her the most mischievous smile I could manage. She did look sexy as hell.

She slapped my shoulder.

"Oh, that hurts." I flinched mockingly.

She lifted an eyebrow. "That's not your injured shoulder, so stop whining."

I chuckled.

She pulled her glasses up. Her hazel eyes held me captive for a moment. She stroked my left cheek.

Warmth ran through my body, and I closed my eyes.

Her silky lips brushed mine in a soft kiss, and the love contained within me threatened to burst.

She grabbed my collar and deepened the kiss before peppering kisses down my neck. "I'll be waiting for you," she whispered close to my ear and gave me one last squeeze before letting go.

She fixed her glasses and exited the car, closing the door behind her.

Mom waited for her by the front door.

I opened the window and waved. "I'll pick her up later. Have fun!"

"Sure, son. Love you!" She waved back.

As soon as O'Hare turned the car on, the gears in my brain started turning. Tonight our leader, my friend, would finally be safe.

I sent O'Hare and Bayat away. They'd pick me up when I called them. Deb and Connor's letter was neatly tucked inside my back pocket, with a flash drive taped to it. I tied it to the key card to make sure she picked it up.

Two officers brought Deb in. She struggled, growled, and escaped their grip, coming straight at me. They seized her. Her strong gaze and slight nod soothed my worries.

This will work.

"Tsk, tsk." I gripped her chin. "You really think you can harm me? I can't wait to get my hands on you. You'll soon understand who's in charge."

I knew exactly how it sounded, and even though bile rose up my throat at the thought, I needed the guards to think the worst.

One of the guards opened the door to the interrogation room.

I grabbed Deb's shackled hands and pulled her flush against me, then breathed her in. "Give me the keys to her cuffs, and keep guard outside. It's time for me to have some fun with this one."

One reached for his belt and took the key off a pouch. He passed it to me and sneered.

The other watched me. "But, sir?"

I put the key in my pocket. "Guard the door." My tone was stern. Final.

He nodded and stepped next to the other guard.

They both turned away.

I entered the room and pushed her against the closed door. "Welcome back, my dear. I've missed our time together."

The cameras and audio remained active, but no one would watch the live video until Deb was out.

I hacked the security system, added a loop recording, and changed the settings to delay the actual footage by ten minutes. After the time was up, the video would appear as if it filmed live, with no time shift.

It was a trick I learned from Nina.

"What was it you said yesterday about never talking?" I stepped between her legs, then closed my hand around her neck and squeezed.

She gasped.

I slid my other hand up her thigh, then kissed her roughly.

It was a sick practice my father had taught me. Make them believe something horrible would happen so they'd talk. When he ordered the waterboarding, this was another method he recommended.

My stomach roiled, but I needed the cameras to get this. I needed my father to see it whenever he accessed the system.

Her eyes widened, and she struggled against me, but I kept at it until she bit me.

I wiped the blood from my lip. "Let's see if after tonight you think the same."

In what seemed like a second, Deb slammed her head against my chin. She kicked me in the groin with such force that I doubled over in pain.

I trained her right.

She rushed to the table where I kept my tools.

I tried to stand, but she put her shackled hands around me and pressed a knife against the left side of my neck, pointing toward my artery.

Deb was smaller than me, but I knew the moment the blade nicked my skin that I couldn't struggle. I'd taught her myself how to get a larger opponent under control.

"You'll never get your filthy hands on me again," she said against my ear. "Don't try anything, or this knife might just slip." She pressed harder, cutting my skin.

I winced.

"Now, open the handcuffs."

My hands trembled as I searched for the keyholes and freed her hands.

Without letting go of the knife, she snatched the key and the shackles and restrained my hands behind my back.

She pulled me up and opened the door, using me as her shield.

Both officers had their guns out in an instant.

"You!" she said to one of them. "Put your gun down, and kick it away. You, give me your gun. Hammer facing me."

They glanced at me.

She cut a line from my upper jaw to my chin.

The gash burned like hell, and blood dripped down my neck.

The stinging pain blurred my vision. Was this truly an act?

"Next time you look his way for instructions, he dies. I'm in charge now."

Their eyes widened.

"Do as she says!" I yelled.

They complied.

Deb held the blade against my neck and aimed the gun toward the guards. "Handcuff yourselves to each other."

Once they did, she motioned to the interrogation room. "Get inside, and shackle your feet to the chair."

They stood beside the chair where I had tortured her countless times. One of the guards swallowed hard. The other stood motionless.

She scowled. "Do it."

They obeyed.

Once they were secure, she stepped out of the room, pulling me with her, and closed the door.

She sheathed the knife and pushed the pistol against my temple. "Get me out of here, and don't try to play me." She forced me toward the stairs that led down.

When she opened the door, the two soldiers on guard turned and put their hands over their guns.

She snarled. "Unless you want his brains blown out, I recommend you put your hands up."

They hesitated for a second.

"Do it," I said.

She took their guns. "Handcuff yourselves to the door."

They did as ordered, and once she checked they were secure, we moved down the hall.

We were halfway through when the door to the morgue opened and Dr. Singh came out.

I froze.

He went for the alarm system.

Fuck!

Deb aimed her pistol at him and took the shot.

Dr. Singh went down.

My ears rang. I bent over.

She pulled me up and shoved me toward the exit. "Open the door!"

I hesitated, still immersed in my role.

She pressed the gun against my head. "I said open the fucking door."

"You need the key card. It's in my back pocket."

She grabbed it, then gasped. She'd taken the note.

Deb swiped the key card, but nothing happened.

She pushed the gun against my temple. "What's wrong?"

"It needs to scan my face and fingerprint."

She opened one cuff, keeping the pistol firmly against my nape, then restrained my hands together in front.

I put my finger on the glass, and she pushed my face toward the biometric face scanner.

The door opened.

She shoved me against the wall, my face scrunched against it. "Now, how about we put this knife where it belongs?"

She plunged the blade into the lower right side of my abdomen. "Die, you fuck." She yanked it out and stabbed me a second time, then twisted the knife. "Die like the pig you are."

When she pulled it out again, I screamed and hobbled about, turning my back toward the wall. I hunched over and pressed my linked hands over the wound.

Fuck, it hurts like hell.

There was too much blood.

I looked up.

She was trembling, holding the bloody knife in one hand, the gun in the other. Her eyes bulged, and she grimaced. Then her gaze met mine, and a tear slipped out.

A deafening sound filled the hallway. The alarms went off.

We both looked back. Dr. Singh had his hand over the alarm.

Deb glanced at me, then rushed out.

The search lights moved around her. Rapid blasts rang out in the once quiet night.

Run! I screamed inside.

She kept running and disappeared inside the forest.

Officers followed her in.

My heart thundered.

Distant shots echoed from the woods.

I closed my eyes.

Please let her be safe.

"Hold on, Minister Niles." Dr. Singh held me.

His voice sounded far away as I drifted in and out of consciousness.

"Stay awake."

I tried, but everything turned black.

Chapter 26

Davon

January 18, 2214

I opened my eyes to the beep of a heart rate monitor. In contrast to when I woke up after Jimmy's shot, the room was dark. I glanced outside. The sun rose on the horizon.

I narrowed my eyes. *Where am I? Did Deb make it?*

I vaguely remembered her disappearing into the forest, a group of soldiers trailing behind.

Someone moaned to my left, and I shifted. I recoiled as a sharp pain shot down my right side. I looked for the cause of the ache. Gauzes covered my abdomen.

Deb did a number on me. I tried to convince myself that her actions were necessary, but a twinge of doubt entered my mind.

Was she aiming to kill me? If she was, I couldn't blame her.

A pang hit my chest. Would things between us ever be the same?

I pushed the thought away and searched for the source of the moan.

Abi slept in the reclining chair next to me.

Another ache radiated from my side, and I grunted.

"Davon?" Abi sat up. Her hand covered mine in the dark.

I squeezed it.

She stared down at me. "You're awake!"

She gently caressed the side of my face, and I leaned into her touch.

The orange hue on the horizon caught her eyes. Their honey green gleamed in the gloom.

"God, I thought I'd lost you. You almost died on the way here."

Died? A shiver ran down my body. What the hell happened?

Her hot tears soaked my left hand as she brought it to her mouth and kissed it repeatedly.

"I'm okay. In pain but okay," I said. "Tell me. What happened?"

She moved my hand over her chest. Her heart pounded so hard I could feel it. "The prisoner escaped."

Deb's safe. She made it.

I wanted to hug Abi. The plan worked. I closed my eyes for a moment in thanks.

She squeezed my hand. "Dr. Singh saved you. Even though he was shot, he stayed with you until the ambulance arrived. After his surgery, I went to see him. The shot broke his hip bone, but he's recovering. He told me she had a gun to your head and then stabbed you. We're lucky he sounded the alarm in time, or she would've killed you."

We're being watched.

"That bitch." I shook my head. "Sorry, Gaby. It's just...I can't believe she escaped under my watch. How much damage did she do to me?"

"One stab punctured your appendix. The other one damaged a kidney. Lisa said you got here just in time. Much longer and your blood would have been unsalvageable. The sepsis almost killed you." Abi trembled. Her voice sounded lost.

"And the kidney?" Fatigue was gaining on me fast.

She poured water into a glass and held it to my mouth. "Here, drink some."

I sipped, relieving the dryness of my mouth and throat.

She brushed my hair back. "The damage to your kidney was superficial, and there was no need for surgery. It will heal on its own."

I exhaled.

The day broke, and light filled the room.

I glanced out. "Where are we?"

"We're in the Promissa Medical Facility."

I jerked toward her.

"Your mother wanted to get Nurse Davis for you, but Lisa convinced her I could take care of you, given my training."

Thank God. But what the hell was she saying about her training?

I must have reacted in some way because she gently rubbed the inside of my hand and shook her head lightly. She'd explain later.

"Rebecca wanted to come, but your dad called her and told her to wait for him in Electi. He's on his way there as we speak."

Dad's coming? I thought he'd stay in Halcyon.

I touched the obsidian ring my parents gave me with my thumb. Did he really care that much?

Lisa walked in. "You're awake." She stopped by my right side. "How are you feeling?"

Where to start?

"Everything hurts, and it's difficult to breathe."

"The surgeon on call removed your appendix, which burst when you were stabbed. The sepsis had already spread, and they're treating you with antibiotics." She came closer. "I took over your case, and we're moving you to the Electi Medical Center. There we'll keep you under observation and on antibiotics for ten days. We need to watch out for post-sepsis syndrome. The exhaustion, fatigue, and overall pain you're feeling are some of the symptoms, but they should go away as you heal."

She looked at Abi. "He'll be all right."

"Thanks, Lisa," Abi said. "Do you know when we're leaving?"

"Jordan sent an ambulance to move you to the train station. It should be here soon. The train's medical car is ready to transport you." She brushed my arm. "I'm glad you made it."

When we were alone again, I stroked Abi's hair. "Come here."

She complied.

I pulled her in and kissed her.

A sense of calm rushed over me. A million colors swirled through my mind at the touch of her lips. And for a moment, it was only us. Any discomfort, any pain, any doubt about our mission—all dissipated, for nothing could rival this. Whatever fear I had was replaced by hope.

Deb was safe and Abi in my arms. That's all that mattered.

Chapter 27

Abi

January 18, 2214

Davon's sleeping form seemed so peaceful.

I intertwined my fingers on my lap and closed my eyes. The pounding of my heart threatened to break my chest apart.

Last night, we were having drinks in the garden when Lisa's cell phone rang. Her wide eyes and sudden stiffness confirmed this was it.

Lisa explained what happened, and we were about to ride off in Rebecca's car when Jordan called. He was on his way and told Rebecca that, for her safety, she should stay and wait for him. Then he talked to Lisa and ordered her to take over Davon's case and save him.

Lisa dragged me into the car.

The ride was quiet. It took less than ten minutes, as the driver raced through Electi.

Once on the train, we sat face-to-face.

Lisa kept looking at her watch and out the window.

We had about fifteen minutes until we reached Promissa.

"Lisa, how bad is it?"

She took my hands. "He was gravely wounded. The doctors in Promissa are doing their best." She dropped her chin. "He's in surgery."

My heart threatened to leave my body.

She fidgeted with her phone and averted her gaze.

I grabbed her shoulder and shook her. "Lisa, please. Will he make it?"

She pocketed her phone and covered her brow with both hands. She reminded me of Matt when he was uncomfortable about something.

"He was unconscious when he got to the hospital. They did abdominal scans and blood work. He has sepsis." Her grim expression only fueled my fear.

I studied her eyes. "Sepsis?"

"The knife punctured his appendix. This caused an infection that spread throughout his abdominal cavity. In the time it took to get him from the prison to the hospital, the infection entered his bloodstream."

I furrowed my eyebrows. "What does that mean?"

She squeezed my hands. "His blood is poisoned."

I froze. "Poisoned?"

Lisa nodded. "Right now, he's in the medical team's hands. Once they remove his appendix and any infected tissue, he'll have to go on heavy antibiotics and into observation."

My whole body trembled. "Is it dangerous?"

"Very. Once the surgery is over, we'll have a better idea of his condition. But right now, it's difficult to know."

I clasped my necklace and took three deep, slow breaths.

"Can't this train move any faster?" My leg was restless as we crossed the wall into Promissa.

She covered my knee with her hand. "He won't die on my watch. I won't let him."

My thoughts came to a complete stop when the doorknob rattled.

There was only one person who was coming today, and I shivered at the thought of meeting him in the flesh.

I turned toward the sound.

The atmosphere shifted, almost electrified by his commanding presence. Shoulders squared, chest forward, his stance echoed authority. His penetrating gaze swept across the room and sharpened as it found me.

I stood. "Mr. Niles?"

He shook my hand. "You must be Gabrielle. Lisa told me you were here. Pleased to meet you."

He was handsome, with a smile that for sure devastated anyone he directed it toward.

When Matt cautioned me about him, he wasn't lying.

Up close, he was the spitting image of his son. His peppered short hair and shaved face were the only differences between them. Same height, same body type. It was like seeing Davon twenty years from now.

I had to shake off whatever empathy their likeness had evoked. This man had made my life a living hell. Davon's as well. All of Promissa was in shambles because of him and his tyranny.

I suppressed my violent thoughts and forced a smile. "A pleasure to meet you, sir."

I glanced toward the door. Where was Rebecca?

He looked in the same direction. "Rebecca will be here in a moment. And please call me Jordan."

"Pleased to meet you, Jordan."

He smiled. "Much better." He moved to the opposite side of the bed. "Lisa tells me the operation went well."

I gazed at Davon and exhaled. "It did. He was awake when we got here, but they had to put him under heavy medication. The transfer was hard for him."

Davon flinched and winced all the way to Electi. His wrinkled eyes and the strong hold he had on me reflected his pain.

Jordan dipped his chin, then studied Davon. He gripped the metal handrail of the hospital bed. When he met my eyes again, it was like glancing into a storm.

This was the real Jordan Niles. The man behind that smooth façade.

"It had to be done. The technology and equipment in Promissa don't compare to here." He watched me closely.

He knew how disproportionate the difference was between what was available to the Promissa citizens when compared to Electi.

My jaw hurt.

How could he be so blatant about it? Was he trying to provoke me?

"Davon and Matt told me about how advanced your medical facilities were." I took Davon's hand. "When I came with Lisa into Promissa, I was worried. I'm glad we're back here."

Jordan lifted an eyebrow and nodded, then brushed Davon's hair back. "I hate that this keeps happening to him. It's like they're trying to get back at me by harming him." He closed his eyes. A single tear slid down his cheek.

A stinging pain gripped my chest, and a lump formed in my throat. His gesture broke through his thick shell, revealing his actual feelings. This man loved his son.

I forced those thoughts away and remembered Matt's words.

Jordan wouldn't sway me. He loved his son—that was a fact. But he was a twisted man.

After a moment, he breathed in and straightened. "I'm sorry. It's just..." He shook his head, then pressed his lips together. "If it's war they want, it's war they'll get."

The hairs rose on my arms and across the nape of my neck.

He looked at me, a stare devoid of love but full of raging hate. The darkness in his eyes captured me, and I could palpate the wrath hidden behind his irises. His desire to kill. "Will you help me avenge him? Will you help me destroy them?"

I let all my anger toward him and all the pain he'd caused me flow freely through me. I fisted my hands next to my body. "I'll do whatever is asked. They'll pay for what they've done to Davon and what they plan to do to our country." Jordan was the cause of all of Davon's pain. All our suffering. He planned to annihilate us, but he was in for a surprise. He'd suffer for his sins, and in the end, he'd see all he'd built crumble down.

"I like you." He sneered. "I wondered countless times why Davon would fall for someone from Promissa. There's something about you I can't quite pinpoint. A fire burning deep within. I see it as clear as day. You hate them as much as we do."

Someone from Promissa...

I clenched my teeth. I was about to lose it.

The door swung open, and in came Rebecca with a paper bag. Her eyes darted around the room until they settled on Davon. She set the bag on the table at the end of Davon's bed and rushed to him.

Jordan stepped aside, giving her space.

She glanced at me while holding Davon's hand. "How's he doing?"

"They gave him something for the pain. He's been asleep for an hour now."

She turned to Jordan. "Who did this to him? Why does this keep happening?"

Jordan put an arm around her and hugged her. "A rebel did this. These people... They're the ones we've been fighting against. We can't let them roam free. They need to be stopped."

My blood boiled beneath my skin. He twisted everything to make elites the victims in all this, while we'd been trampled upon for more than ten years.

Her eyes were glassy. Lost. "But why? I thought all would be better now that everything is starting to balance out. I..." She shook her head and furrowed her brow. "Davon and Gaby told me about them, but I thought that since we were helping the citizens, they'd step back. Why are they fighting if we're helping them?"

I wanted to shake her, to make her see. How blind could she be?

Jordan opened and closed his mouth. For a mere second, he was out of words. "Trust me, love. I'm as confused as you are. These rebels are trying to sway the people of Promissa against us after all we've done for them. They won't rest until they destroy all we've built. They're not only our enemies but Promissa's as well."

At least he got something right. We'd never rest until we got our freedom back.

"Maybe there's a way to fix this. Have you sat with them? Have you talked it out?" Rebecca asked.

"That's what Davon was trying to do with this one, and look what she did."

Fucker.

"But it doesn't make sense." She looked at me, then at Davon's sleeping form. "There must be another way. I don't think anyone wants another war."

There was something up with Rebecca. Something about that look she gave us.

Jordan caressed her cheek. "You're too good, love. We're trying the best we can to control this so we all can be safe, but if worse comes to worst, we *will* retaliate." He went in for a kiss.

Rebecca angled her body away from the kiss. It was almost imperceptible, but she did, and it landed on the corner of her mouth.

Jordan frowned.

I widened my eyes for a second. Davon told me his parents were madly in love with each other and very expressive. But this...

Jordan pulled her close and took her free hand, holding it over his heart. "Please trust me on this." With his other hand, he stroked her cheek. "I love you. I just want to protect my family."

She watched him closely.

For a moment, I was sure she'd step away from him.

She shook her head, then leaned into him. "I'm sorry. It's just...too much."

He rubbed her back gently. "I know, but we will push through this."

Oh, God. He was back at it. How could he spit out so many lies?

The air was too thick inside the room. Even with Rebecca there, I was suffocating. I turned to leave.

"Don't go." Jordan's voice was demanding.

I stopped and turned sideways. "I really should."

"You're now part of the family." Rebecca took a coffee out of the paper bag she'd brought and offered it to me. "I brought this for you."

A warm sensation swept across my body. "Thank you."

I glanced at Jordan. He observed our exchange with a hint of a smile.

A dropping sensation rushed over me. Even though Davon had suffered at his father's hands, my stomach roiled at the realization of what he'd lose. His family.

Jordan decided to use this time to get to know me, and I lost track of how much time passed.

He asked about my time at the facilities, my family, and how I met Matt and Davon. Questions he already knew the answers to. I suspected he was trying to read me.

Even Rebecca asked him to stop after a while.

My stomach growled just before Matt opened the door, followed by whom I presumed was his father.

Matt hugged me. "I'm sorry I'm late. I came as fast as I could. Mom explained what happened." He murmured in my ear, "I'm so sorry I wasn't here."

I wept as he rubbed my back, then let go of all my sorrow in his embrace.

He patted my back. "There, there. It's all right. Mom says he's stable."

I nodded. "I know, but...we almost lost him."

He gave me one last squeeze and grabbed my shoulders. "But we didn't. There's no way in hell he'll give up. Not when he has so much to fight for. Mom and I will make sure he makes it. We're in this together."

My heart faltered at his statement, and even in this moment when everything seemed so dark, I understood what he implied. Now everything we'd planned would come to be. Now our true mission began.

Matt wiped my tears away and turned. "Rebecca. Jordan." He went to them.

"Enchanté." Minister Anderson took my hand and kissed the top. He looked just like Matt but with long brown hair. It fell over his emerald eyes as he studied me. He was an attractive man, like his son. "You must be Gabrielle. Matt told me a lot about you. It's a pleasure to finally meet you."

I bowed slightly. "Minister Anderson. The pleasure is mine."

"Please call me Frank. Here." He put a bag in my hands. "Matt thought you hadn't eaten, so we stopped by the cafeteria and got you lunch."

Whatever it was, it smelled glorious. "Thank you."

"You're most welcome, my dear." He leaned forward. "Now I'm going to take them away for a bit so you can breathe." He winked at me.

Matt told me about him and his charm. Now I knew who Matt had taken his jovial and quirky attitude from.

The fact this was the man in charge of the genome project still escaped me. He didn't seem like a bad guy. But maybe he was like Jordan and knew how to hide his true self.

Frank took Rebecca and Jordan to lunch, and, finally, we had some time to breathe.

"What happened? Mom told me about his present state, but she failed to explain what happened at the prison," Matt said once the door closed.

"He was interrogating a rebel. I don't know the details, but she took Davon hostage. Dr. Singh was about to pull the alarm when she shot him. Then she stabbed Davon. If it wasn't for Dr. Singh recovering enough to sound the alarm and go to him, he might have died by her hand."

He held his hands over his eyes, then raked his hair back. "We need to find out where they're hiding. We were so close this last time."

I tightened my fists. "Davon's father asked me to help him find them. But now that I blew my cover, I don't know how I can help."

Matt went to the bedside and looked at Davon. "You told me they have spies inside the city. Maybe there's a way we can help find them and get the intel we need."

I nodded and turned to Davon. "I'm sure there is."

Jordan would watch this video feed for sure. Hinting at the idea could make him put us on an assignment to do this.

I smiled inside at Matt's calculating mind. This was a game, and we needed to play it to our advantage.

A while later, Matt left to get me some stuff from home. There was no way I was leaving Davon's side.

It was late afternoon when Davon finally stirred.

He looked at his parents. "Mom? Dad?" He turned his head to me.

I took his hand and smiled, trying to convey everything was all right.

"Son, how are you feeling?" Jordan asked.

He blinked. "Better now. How long did I sleep?"

"Gabrielle says you've been asleep since you got here so between six to seven hours," Rebecca said.

Davon tried to sit up but flinched.

"Should I call the nurse?" Rebecca asked.

He shook his head. "No, don't worry."

Nevertheless, I wanted to check everything was all right. Rachel gave me a crash course in taking care of wounds and giving medical care to patients during those last days at the peak.

"Let me check," I said.

Davon stared at me with parted lips.

Right. I still hadn't told him about my training. "I just want to make sure it's not infected."

He nodded, and I lifted the sheet. The gauzes were clean. His abdomen looked swollen and bruised, but all was normal given everything happened less than twenty-four hours ago.

"All is good," I told Rebecca. "It's normal for him to feel discomfort for a couple of days. Lisa said that because of the sepsis, he'll take a bit longer to feel like his usual self."

"Davon told me you took care of your mother when you were young. I'm sorry about what she went through," Jordan said.

I widened my eyes. Was that sympathy? I didn't know he was capable of it.

"My mother died of cancer also. A lot of our genetic research is devoted to searching for better treatment and hopefully the eradication of cancer for future generations," he said.

I smiled. "That would be an incredible breakthrough."

The advancement in medical research was one of the most important accomplishments of modern civilization. For centuries, scientists had been trying to find a cure for cancer. To think its eradication could one day be a reality was mind-blowing. But I couldn't put aside that he'd created the Elysium and Apex Project, followed by the Prometheus Project.

Davon cleared his throat and looked at his father. "How long have you been here?"

"Since this morning," Jordan said. "We've had plenty of time to get to know Gabrielle. She's a real treasure."

For a split second, my whole body tensed. Was he for real?

Davon gripped my hand hard.

I covered his. "Your parents are amazing. They've been keeping me company."

He relaxed his hold.

I strolled to the window to give them some privacy. After some time, the rosy hue of dusk faded, and the stars made their appearance.

I sighed. I missed those times Davon and I would stare at the horizon from the mountains.

I turned toward the room.

"Honey, are you sure you're all right?" Rebecca asked.

Davon brushed her cheek. "I'm okay."

Jordan put an arm around her. "We should go, love. I'm sure Davon wants some alone time with Gabrielle, and I'm exhausted from my trip."

Rebecca sighed. "Okay." She kissed Davon's brow. "You follow the doctor's orders."

Davon smiled. "Sure, Mom. Love you."

She left the room.

Jordan gripped Davon's shoulder. "I looked at the surveillance videos on my way here. We'll get her for this."

My breath faltered. He'd seen everything. Davon told me his control was absolute. That he watched all, knew all. We needed to be cautious.

Davon nodded. "I can't believe this happened on my watch. I should've been more careful."

Jordan shook his head. "You didn't do anything wrong, son. She's a feisty little thing, and we didn't give her enough credit. We'll get her back. I'm not letting go of her that easily." He patted Davon's shoulder. "I'll see you later."

I swallowed hard at his implication. Deb was his property. His toy.

I glared at his back as he reached the door.

You'll pay for everything, you monster.

January 18, 2214

As soon as the door closed behind Father, the knot in my stomach relaxed.

When I saw him in the room, a familiar chill ran through me.

She met him while I slept.

I should've been the one to introduce her to him. I should've been there to lighten the blow. I never expected him to come in person until his trip was over.

Why did Lisa have to give me those drugs?

When I woke and talked to my parents, Abi squeezed my hand almost to the point of pain while keeping her face in a neutral expression. Her pulse showed her true feelings, as it beat hard against my fingers.

Her hatred for him and the anguish she'd experienced because of his rule struck me deeply. It pressed from within, its massive weight crushing me inside.

I wanted to ask her so many things, but the room wasn't safe. We'd have to be careful.

Abi stroked my arm.

"I'm sorry for all this." I covered her hand.

She trembled. "You don't need to apologize for anything. You couldn't have known it would happen."

She brought my hand to her lips and kissed it. "You're here. That's all that matters. I'm glad everyone involved is safe now. You just worry about getting better."

I ran my fingers through her soft curls.

She leaned into my touch and closed her eyes, taking a deep, cleansing breath.

God, I love her.

I pulled her down until her lips touched mine.

Her sweet taste and soft lips overwhelmed my senses. The need to hold her, to make everything right, consumed my thoughts. She'd be safe, whatever it took.

I brushed my thumb over her scar, then captured her gaze. "We'll win this, and then all this will be a thing of the past."

She hugged me.

Matt entered the room. "You're awake!"

He rushed to my side and gripped the bed railing. Eyebrows furrowed, he assessed me. "You scared the shit out of us!"

I chuckled. "Next time, I'll tell the prisoner to be careful not to stab me in a vital organ."

Matt raised an eyebrow. "Maybe you should have."

We'd told Deb to hurt me, to appear as if she wanted to kill me. She did her job only too well. She knew where to strike, as we trained to take enemies alive, but the stab she gave me was one to kill. Maybe it was a mistake. A miscalculation. But something told me it wasn't.

Did she really try to kill me? Was she still in her right mind?

Torture changed people, and they were never the same. I replayed last night's events again and again to make sense of it all, and one thing was for sure—there was darkness in Deb's eyes during the escape.

I recalled the force behind the blow. The way she stabbed me a second time, then twisted the knife made it all too clear.

I went too far, and deep within, she saw me as her enemy. When she held the bloody knife and darted her eyes to mine, she flinched back. That rogue tear that escaped her eye was the one sign of how all this had damaged her. How confused she was.

How could she trust me after all this? How could she see me as her friend again?

Matt cleared his throat. "Well, I'm glad you made it through the night. You're safe now." He took my medical record from the end of the bed. "Are you in a lot of pain?"

"No. I'm tired, and the area is sore, but other than that, I feel better than before."

I wasn't lying. My body was heavy, and if I moved, the area of the surgery hurt, but it didn't compare to last night.

He wrote something down. "I'm changing your pain medication for one that will make you less sleepy. You'll take it orally. That way you can go back to your usual routine soon. We need to keep you here under observation for the time being. A week or so until we're sure your blood is clean."

Thank God he was changing the meds. I hated not having control of my senses, and I needed to be alert now more than ever.

He took away a bag attached to my IV, changed another that I presumed held the antibiotics, then checked my wound. "This looks great." He looked at Abi. "You can take it off tomorrow morning after he wakes. Clean it if there's any discharge, and let me know if there's any sign of infection."

Abi nodded.

Matt put my record back. "I need to check on Dr. Singh. I'll come by tomorrow." He clasped my shoulder and smiled. "I leave you in good hands. Food should be here shortly. Eat and then try to rest. It will speed your recovery."

His gaze drifted to Abi. "You should try to sleep too. Mom told me you didn't sleep at all last night."

I stared at her. "What?"

Abi glared at Matt.

He shrugged. "Sorry, Gaby, but I can't have you falling ill because of exhaustion. And now Davon will make sure you rest."

Abi rolled her eyes. "I'll try."

"You will," I said.

Matt grinned as he left the room. "Good night."

January 25, 2214

"At last. Home." I sighed as Abi closed the door behind me and put my stuff on top of the kitchen counter.

We'd sent Matt to check the apartment for bugs. It was clear.

She hugged me, careful not to overdo it. "I missed talking to you. For real."

"Me too, Abi. I missed saying your name."

She went on her tiptoes and kissed my neck, nibbled my earlobe, and pulled me down in a passionate kiss.

I let myself go in her embrace and started lifting her shirt.

I missed her touch.

She grabbed my hand. "One more week. Matt said it was safe to be together in one more week."

I opened my eyes wide. "You asked him?"

She put her hands on her hips. "Of course I did. I don't want to risk hurting you. He was glad I asked. Said your wound is almost healed. His exact words were 'Take a week off from going crazy on each other just to be sure.'"

Damn Matt and his big mouth.

She stroked my stubble. "Don't look so gloomy. It's only for a week. And you're not the only one suffering here." She grinned.

It was undeniably true. We couldn't keep our hands off each other after she returned. When everything appeared to be bleak and hopeless, we basked in each other's touch, seeking the calm we could only offer one another. With how messed up everything was, we didn't have anything to rely on except our love. Hell, we had no idea what tomorrow would bring.

"Okay, love. What's your plan?" I asked.

"How about we have some coffee and talk? I feel like we haven't done so in forever."

"Sounds good. I'll wait for you by the sofa."

Fatigue had been constant lately, but Matt said it would eventually disappear. I was to go on daily walks and start exercising progressively but with care.

She hummed as she made the coffee and set two mugs on the coffee table, then sat beside me.

It was a dark roast. My father gave it to us today. He explained it came from the Fringe Council, one of the NWG allied governments.

This continent, even after the war, was rich in resources, but the produce of each region was different, so a trade system existed between the nations in power.

I'd recently gone through my father's archives and found out about how the continent worked. The NWG ruled most of the east, with two allied governments working with them. The Fringe Council controlled most of the south, and the Midland Nexus governed the central part of the continent. They traded with us, and their regimes were similar to my father's.

Father said he wouldn't attack them, but I didn't believe that. He was just setting up everything for the next opportunity. Maybe first he'd try to make a treaty to do it pacifically. Maybe he just wanted them for their armies. But one thing was for sure—his thirst for power would eventually win over, and he *would* attack. I had no doubt.

Yet there were two countries with control of the whole western area of the continent, Rock Haven and Solara Citadel. They stood against my father and his allies. They'd been silent for decades, but who knew until when?

There was Empire City to the north, where we sent those who didn't want to stay in Promissa but didn't want to fight either. Those who wanted a new beginning. I hadn't found a file about the city, so it was a mystery whether they were allies or enemies.

Abi passed me my mug. "This will have to do until you're officially discharged." She raised hers. "To us and our mission."

"To Promissa and its freedom."

The clank of our mugs marked our compromise.

We both drank and leaned back.

"Will you tell me what happened that night?" Abi asked.

"Where to start?" I pushed my thoughts back to that night and held my lower right side as I remembered the knife piercing through. "Everything was going according to plan until Dr. Singh appeared. I didn't account for his presence that late. I should've."

Abi placed her elbows on her knees. "And what about Deb? I know she made it, but was she okay? Do you know if she got hurt?"

I sighed. "Last I saw her, she ran into the forest. There was a shootout. After that, I passed out."

She put the mug down and covered her face with her hands. "In the letter we sent with Muñoz, I wrote that we were together. She knew you were on a mission, but she almost killed you. Why would she do that?"

I stroked her back. "Abi, I did horrible things to her. I think she's not clear if I'm friend or foe." I pulled her against me. "If she's lost and confused, it's all my fault."

She turned toward me. "It's not, Davon. None of this is your fault. It's the circumstances, ones your father created. It has nothing to do with you."

This again. First Matt, now Abi.

I embraced her and kissed her brow.

No matter how many times they said the words, nothing would convince me it wasn't on me also. Nothing would ever erase the things I'd done for my father.

It was easy to say I didn't have a choice, but I'd had countless opportunities to end the problem. No one said it, but I knew it was on everyone's mind.

I could have just sacrificed my freedom and gotten rid of the root of the problem. Connor never asked about it, and neither did the other councilmembers. It would've been easy. But they knew that deep down I couldn't kill him. No matter how many times I'd tried to deny it, I loved my father and had never stopped hoping for his redemption.

But now that I understood his agenda, that all changed. It was hard to conceive there could be any salvation for him. And if he ever dared to harm Mom, Abi, or any of my friends, I knew I'd do it. I'd take his life without pause.

Silence occupied the room for a moment.

"When do you think we'll know if she's okay?" Abi asked.

"Hopefully, soon. I'll take another week and then go back to work. I invited Lavigne over so he could meet you and he and I could work on a game plan. He's been searching the files for a list of the active spies but still hasn't found anything."

She straightened. "Maybe I can help with that."

I furrowed my brow. "What do you mean?"

She took my hands. "I mean...it was part of the plan from the start. Your father already hinted at the idea of me helping him avenge your attack. It's a matter of convincing him I'm trustworthy. Matt and I talked about it when we were out to lunch last week. We tried to find another option but came up with only one." She looked down at our joined hands, fidgeting with my obsidian ring.

What atrocity would we have to commit to gain my father's trust?

I lifted her chin so her eyes were level with mine. "What is it, love? Tell me."

She swallowed hard. "I need to rat someone out. Maybe more. Preferably a spy working in the city. Matt or you need to tell Jordan about my skills with computers. Once I get this intel for him, he'll hopefully trust me and let me work from inside the system." She let go of my hand and raked her hair back, clutching her curls with her eyes downcast. "The thing is we both know who he'll send in to get the information once the rebels are in custody."

I shivered at the thought. "Me."

She nodded. "I just need some time. I learned some stuff from Nina and Tammy. I can easily convince your father that I know what I'm doing. I'll already know the names of the spies and where they're infiltrated. He just needs to think I found them."

I breathed slowly. It was a sound plan. But the burden we'd have to bear was great.

My father wouldn't have mercy on these spies. And whether we got the intel from them or not, the outcome would be the same: death.

How many more would I have to hurt? How much longer could I take this? It was so dark inside me. Every life I took was buried in my soul, reminding me how I'd never be able to vindicate myself.

Who would I have to kill this time?

As always, I reached deep and closed the door to that void, then looked outside and caught her eyes. She kept me grounded. "It's a good plan. I'll contact Connor and get you the information you need. Let's hope Father falls for it."

"There was something else I wanted to ask you. It's about Paul."

With everything that happened, I almost forgot about my promise. But a couple of days ago, while watching her play with Bonnie's thread bracelet, I remembered our conversation. "I thought about it while in the hospital. What do you think about talking to Lisa about him? She has a good home, and I'm sure she can get him a job and a room in it. At least he'll be out of the hellhole he's living in right now."

Abi sat sideways and crossed her legs. She took my hand and gave me a huge smile. "That would be great. Lisa's an angel." She kissed the top of my hand. "Thanks for doing this. It means the world to me."

I nodded. "It's the least I can do. I vowed to help avenge your friends, and I keep my promises."

"What about Aoki?"

Aoki?

I tilted my head. "What about him?"

She shifted in place. "Do you think his parents are still there?"

So he finally told someone else about it. Aoki was so private and always calm. No one would imagine what he went through to get out of Promissa.

"Did he...?" I paused. "When did he tell you?"

"A few weeks ago. There's a lot you still don't know about what happened after you left."

She'd told me about a lot of stuff that transpired in those two months, but from what she said, there was much more.

"Will you tell me? I want to know it all."

She gave me a gentle smile and picked up her mug, then we sat back and talked.

Chapter 29

Abi

January 25, 2214

An hour later, we'd covered all that happened in the two months he was away. Davon was especially taken aback by Abraham's story.

He had his head on my lap and held my hands over his chest. He drew circles with his fingertips over them. "Jacob must have been a great guy. I only met Mr. Jackson once or twice, but having him as a father must have been an honor."

I interlocked my fingers with Davon's. "He would've made a great leader. We were planning on getting here by ourselves, but then everything happened, and, well, I was lost." Sometimes I forgot the numbness that always came with that night's memory. That moment when the world shifted around me and I couldn't keep up. When I became lost in my own misery.

He brought our hands over his heart. "But now you're here. He'd be very proud of you right now. We fight for them, for the ones we've lost, so that no one else has to endure what they did."

Davon's words reached deep within me. There was not one day when their faces didn't flash through my mind. Mom and Dad. Bonnie and Jacob.

He tucked a stray hair behind my ear. "So you're a nurse now?"

I huffed and rolled my eyes. "I don't want to talk about it. Rachel's three-day crash course was exhausting. I barely slept a few hours every night. Maria and her merciless training kept the patients coming in. It was crazy." I shook my head and grimaced.

"I can imagine." He chuckled.

I yawned.

He squeezed my hand. "How about dinner? What do you have in mind?"

"How about some toast? Or we can have cheese and crackers."

"Sure, I'll help you."

I helped him up.

We prepared the tray and moved to the table. He sat across from me.

"I've been meaning to ask you." I drank some water to wash down the crackers. "What do you think about the strategy we've built with our group?"

Davon was our general, and his approval of our plan was important. He'd know if it would work.

Connor had approved, but he gave us specific orders to talk to Davon. He knew more about Electi than all of us combined. If there was a flaw in the plan, he'd notice.

Davon held a cracker between his fingers. He motioned for me to give him a moment and then swallowed. He cleared his throat. "There are a few things that need to be tweaked, but overall, it's a good plan."

I looked out the window. Everyone continued with their day while we sat here discussing the fate of our people. "The sniper team that Mark and David trained is amazing, and Maria, Katherine, and Yuxuan are giving their all in training the military. Jimmy is working on finding possible routes in and out of Promissa. Your maps have helped a lot."

Davon cracked his knuckles. "I'll look into it. Have you heard back from the rebel factions in Promissa?"

I nodded. "Matt went to his clinic last week. He received intel that our spies made contact with the leader of these factions. They asked to meet a high-ranked officer. Matt volunteered."

Davon put a palm on the table. "Wait. He's going to meet them?"

I shrugged. "There's no one else. And he's our lieutenant general."

He leaned back and rested his elbow on the armrest, stroking his chin. "What about my father's spies?"

I intertwined my fingers on the table. "We have it covered. Everyone knows Matt still visits his clinic. In fact, it was one of the conditions he set to work with his father. The leader will come in as a patient. No one will know." I pushed away the nagging sensation that kept creeping into my mind. What if they refused to fight with us?

He exhaled. "I hope it works. We need these people on our side. If not, we won't be enough."

That was our major setback in all this—to have the numbers to fight against the monster that was the NWG army. And we were only talking about Promissa and Electi.

I lowered my head and covered it with my linked hands. "You know, even if we get Promissa back and take down your father, we haven't accounted for the rest of the NWG territory. I said we'd deal with it later, but what if they bring the rest of their militia from Halcyon?" A heavy weight pressed upon me. If they came, could we still hope for a victory?

He shook his head. "I don't think that's going to happen. Something's brewing at Halcyon that has Father on edge."

I stared into his eyes. "What are you implying?"

Davon rubbed his brow. "That Father's hiding something big. The only thing that would make Steele call him would be a threat."

The tension in my body ebbed a little. "That would work in our favor."

If General Steele was preoccupied with his own threat, Jordan would be alone with no backup. It could be our best opportunity to take over.

Davon nodded. "We need to figure out what's going on out there. Because if what I suspect is correct, we must strike soon while they're preoccupied with that threat."

January 26, 2214

"Lavigne should be here in an hour or so!" Davon yelled from the bathroom.

"Are you sure he's not being followed?" Matt asked from the kitchen.

We were getting dinner ready.

Davon came out, a towel around his waist. "Doesn't matter. He and I work hand in hand, so it will seem like since I can't go to work, he's here to talk some things out."

He closed the bedroom door, and the glass walls obscured. I was still shocked by this kind of technology, but every day something new surprised me.

At last, I was going to meet the general of the NWG army in Electi. I gripped the counter and closed my eyes.

Matt took my side. "Are you all right?"

I nodded.

He raised an eyebrow but kept chopping onions while I rinsed some peppers in the sink.

Davon and Matt both considered Lavigne to be a good guy, but I couldn't move past the image I had of him in the forest.

The man was scary. Almost like Jordan.

I couldn't believe he was Carol's father. When Davon told us about it, we were shocked.

Davon opened the bedroom door. He brushed his hair, then put on a black V-neck shirt. His gray sweatpants hung loose on his hips. Very casual for meeting a general.

He sat on a barstool and patted the one next to him. "Come here."

I dried my hands on my apron over my black jeans, careful not to wet my button-down olive-green shirt.

He tucked a loose strand behind my ear. "You need to relax, love. Peter's a nice guy. He's like a father to me."

I brushed my hair back and fixed my high ponytail. "You do understand I know your actual father. I hope he doesn't compare to him."

He smiled. "Not even a bit. I mean a real father. He helped me through a rough spot. Trust me."

I sighed. "Okay."

Matt pushed two glasses toward us and filled one with an amber liquid I was familiar with. "Here, drink some. Whiskey has a way to warm the heart."

I gulped it down.

"Easy there." Davon laughed quietly while he sipped his water.

By our second drink, Lavigne knocked on the door.

Davon drew him into a hug as soon as he stepped inside.

The guy laughed, actually laughed, and his smile was contagious. He was definitely Carol's father—there was no doubt. He shared her dark hair and the same shade of blue in her eyes.

He ruffled Matt's hair. "I'm so glad to see you, boy. It's been forever."

Lavigne patted Davon's shoulder. "I'm glad to see you're alive. That was quite a scare."

He glanced my way and walked toward me.

I took a step back.

He stopped. "I'm sorry. You must be Abigail?" He stretched his hand toward me.

I looked at Davon. He nodded.

I took it. "Pleased to meet you, General Lavigne. You can call me Abi."

Lavigne's eyes brightened. "It's Peter. No need for formalities. I'm glad to finally meet you. Davon has told me a lot about you."

I darted my eyes toward Davon and smiled. "I hope it's all good."

Peter's other hand covered our clasped ones. The warmth that radiated from him settled my raging nerves.

"It's all good." He let go of my hand. "Davon tells me you're going to be working on finding this spy who's threatening the PRF. I'm here to show you what I've found."

"Let's go to the table and talk. Dinner will be ready in about half an hour," Matt said.

"Perfect. Smells divine. Is that one of your husband's recipes? Davon tells me you married a chef." Peter put his briefcase on the table.

Matt blushed. "Yes, it's one of his recipes. I prepared Japanese chicken curry. It's my favorite. I've only cooked it once before." He shrugged. "Aoki loves it."

"I'm glad you found happiness." He looked at Davon. "You too."

We sat and waited for his laptop to upload. "I prepared this computer with all the programs needed to access the files you're looking for. The IT guy you recommended helped me get it done. He's a genius."

Davon chuckled. "That's Joe for you. He learned from the best. Nina taught him everything he knows."

"Who's Nina?" Peter asked.

"Our head of operations," Davon said. "She's odd but brilliant."

I chuckled at this. She was a piece of work. All brain and attitude. I liked her.

"I hope I meet her someday." He typed something on his computer. "Now to what we're here for. I think your plan is good, but someone needs to convince your father that Abi—I mean Gabrielle—knows a way to find these rebel spies hidden within the system. Joe and I will save the intel you need on a fake database that we'll say Gaby decrypted. She'll find the first spy, and once they're apprehended, she'll find the other one a week or two later. Hopefully, your father will be thrilled by her skills."

He glanced at me across the table. "Then you go to work. You need to tell Jordan there's not much you can do from the outside and that you think you'll have a better chance of catching more rebels if you have access to the government database system. Based on his desperation to be done with this threat, we're trusting he'll put you to work."

This was a lot to take in.

I hid my hands below the table and pressed my thigh down to stop my leg from shaking.

"Once inside, it will take some time to break through the firewalls, but Joe assured me you'll be able to hack through the system with the program he downloaded. You only need to connect it while you work, and it will autonomously take care of everything."

I unclasped the top button of my blouse. Why was it so hot all of a sudden?

Davon rubbed my thigh, then came close. "Everything will be okay. You can do this."

The air cooled around me, and I breathed in Davon's musky aroma, taking comfort in his proximity.

"If they check the computer, will they be able to find this program?" Matt's elbow rested on the table, and he supported his brow with two fingers.

Peter shook his head. "Negative. Joe says it's untraceable."

"Okay." Matt relaxed back and nodded toward me. "Abi's safety is what matters most. If you can attest to that, we can proceed with the plan."

I went to Peter and stood beside him. The screen showed codes I didn't understand. "So all I need to do is be there, and the computer will take care of the rest?"

Fuck. This looked complicated. If it wasn't for Matt's reassuring gaze, I would already be out the door.

Peter tilted his head toward me. "Yes and no. I'll show you the basics in the next two weeks. I'll work from my office and connect remotely to this computer daily. Once a week, we'll meet here in person. Joe planted a firewall that should hold until I'm done training you and we erase any evidence of our contact."

"Okay." I only knew basic stuff, but at least I knew something. "When do we start?"

Peter curved his lips up. "After dinner."

I gripped the back of his chair. "Sounds like a plan."

Our mission was finally starting. I just needed to make sure I wasn't caught.

When I looked at the three men sitting at the table, my hammering heart relaxed. I would succeed.

Chapter 30

Abi

February 1, 2214

Today was Davon's first day of work, and he was running late. He'd woken early to remind me a week had passed. And what a way to remind me.

We had a fun morning all right.

I had no plans of leaving our bed, too exhausted to move.

The sun shone through the window, hitting his chiseled chest. The satin black sheets covered only his lower half.

I lay on my side and trailed my fingers over the contour of his tattoo. He jerked a little and moaned in his sleep. I never tired of watching him. This man who almost died getting my sister out. This man who got my friend into a safe place and out of the "prison" that held him captive.

I settled into the crook of his arm and placed my palm on his chest.

His warmth encircled me as he pulled me tight against him. "Everything okay?" He kissed the top of my head, languidly stroking my back.

I sighed at his soft caress. "Just thinking how lucky I am to have you."

He chuckled.

The rumble of his chest did things to me.

"You're blind. It's me who's lucky."

I hit his chest playfully. "Don't say that."

He shifted until our eyes were level. "You're everything to me, Abigail Davis, and I'll never tire of saying I don't deserve you." He moved closer until his lips met mine.

The touch was soft and slow at first. Then, as our bodies pressed against each other, it became urgent. Raw. Our bodies entwined, and I lost myself in him. In his love.

Half an hour later, we forced ourselves out of bed and ate a late breakfast.

"I need to go, love. I have a council meeting." He gave me a peck on the lips.

"Wait." I stood from the dining table and fixed his crooked burgundy tie. I brushed my hands down his gray suit. "Now you look your part."

He lifted an eyebrow.

"What? It looks good on you. There's no denying it."

He humphed. "You know I hate it."

"Yeah. But it doesn't mean I have to." I slapped his butt. "Now go and do your spying stuff."

He smiled. "Same to you. Be careful today. Okay?"

I nodded and followed him to the door. "I will."

"When is your meeting with Father?" He waited by the door while I picked up my glasses and purse from the coffee table.

Matt and I would spend the morning together and then head to Jordan's house.

We decided Matt would be the one to recommend me for the job. That way, if Jordan inquired about my abilities, Davon would confirm them. We didn't want to appear as if he was just trying to find a job for his girlfriend.

"Rebecca asked Matt and me to come over for lunch. Jordan agreed to meet us afterward in his study." I rolled my neck and fluffed my curls, then strode toward Davon.

I was wired up inside. Today we'd throw the bait in the hopes of catching and reeling Jordan in. We needed this plan to work.

Davon put an arm around my waist and pulled me close. "Okay. Remember the plan."

"Don't worry. Matt and I have it covered," I said into his chest.

He hugged me. "I love you."

"Me too."

I was wired up inside. Today we'd throw the bait in the hopes of catching and reeling Jordan in. We needed this plan to work.

"Gaby!" Rebecca almost tumbled over me when I exited the car. "I'm so glad you came."

Matt stepped out.

She hugged him. "You too, Matt. The only one missing is Davon. I can't believe he has already returned to work. He's just like his father."

I cringed inside at the thought. Davon was nothing like him.

"Miss Jones," O'Hare said. "We'll pick you up at five."

He waved at me from inside the sedan.

Bayat remained with Davon, but he insisted that O'Hare stayed with us in Electi.

"Okay." I waved goodbye.

I'd begun to see what Davon told me about. His two bodyguards were not bad people, and O'Hare was totally infatuated with Miss Bayat. Too bad she didn't care for his advances. Still, I rooted for him.

Rebecca patted Matt's shoulder. "Go right in. There are some refreshments in the sitting room. I need to talk to Gaby."

I raised an eyebrow, wondering what she wanted to talk about, then noticed the garden was taken care of. She must've found someone else to take Paul's job.

"Sure, Rebecca. Thanks." Matt entered the house.

Rebecca stood beside me. "Are you looking for Paul?"

I froze. I widened my eyes as I glanced at her.

She looked around, then grabbed my arm. "Come."

She pulled me to a bench in a remote spot in the garden. "I know you must be wondering how I know his name and how I know you've met him before."

My whole body trembled. Was our operation done for? Was I uncovered?

She held my hand. "I won't tell Jordan about it if that's what you fear."

I jerked toward her. "I don't know what you're talking about."

I needed to fix this. How much did Paul say?

She took a deep breath and looked toward the small flowers that carpeted the ground. Their vibrant colors stood out against the gloomy gray sky, and their sweet perfume contrasted with the bitter sensation in my mouth.

Her gaze was distant. "I asked Jordan for this garden when we moved here. It was such a beautiful place. So new." She looked down at our hands. "We lost a big part of our country to climate change, and our resources were dwindling, so he came here in search of a better place. Once the war was over, he brought us in. I couldn't believe we'd get to live in such a pristine place."

"Rebecca, where are you going with this?"

Fuck, fuck, fuck.

This was all messed up.

"I knew Jordan had taken over the area, but I thought you—the people who originally lived here—had come to some agreement with the New

World Government. That we were looking to someday live as equals." She closed her eyes. "The day you met Paul in this garden, I saw you from a distance. You were talking to him, and I somehow knew you'd met him before. That afternoon, after you left with Davon, I gave him a notebook and asked him his name." She gazed at me with pained eyes. "I asked him how he was, and he wouldn't answer. I told him your name and that you were with my son. That he could trust me."

Her eyes glazed over as she stared at the horizon. "He told me how he got caught by soldiers, and his face was disfigured during the beating. He didn't say how he met you, but he did explain about the facilities where they took him."

I squeezed her hand, no longer able to contain my true feelings.

I couldn't talk. My chest constricted at her words, at the memory of that day.

"On our way into Promissa the morning after Davon's attack, I asked Jordan about his *initiative* and told him I wanted to visit where these people lived. He said I shouldn't worry about stuff like that." Her hand shook. "When I insisted and confronted him about wanting to know what was happening out there, his whole demeanor changed into one that was dark, oppressive. He was no longer the sweet and caring man I married. He ordered me to stop nosing around and to be grateful for what we had and all he'd done. Then, as if nothing had happened, the man I adore came back and apologized, saying he only wanted what was best for me."

A lone tear spilled down my cheek, then another. "Rebecca, I..."

She patted my thigh. "Don't, Gaby. I don't want you to say anything, and I'm not going to ask, but there's something that tells me you and Davon know so much more. I see him, and I know there's something going on, and it's not what it appears. I love Jordan. I love him with all my heart, but it hurts to know he's been lying to me. I know I haven't been progressive in understanding. Life just seemed so happy. So easy. But now that I know, I can no longer ignore it. How can I?"

She stood and paced around the garden. "When Lisa came this week, saying she needed more hands to care for her estate, she asked specifically for my gardener. I asked her who sent her. She hesitated but told me it was Davon. She confirmed what I suspected—that you both are involved in something far bigger than I understand."

I rubbed my eyes and stared at the ground. "I don't know what to tell you."

"Just be safe. Know I'd never do anything to harm my son. Whatever is happening, I trust you both."

I rose. "But maybe you should—"

Rebecca held up a hand. "I won't leave his side. I need to find out how deep his lies go. Even as brokenhearted as I am for not knowing the true face of the man I'm deeply in love with, I will stay. For you."

Was she with us? Would she feel the same way when we came to take Jordan down?

I wanted to say that she should leave Jordan and go with Lisa. But would I do that in her place?

If I ever found out Davon had been lying to me all his life, I'd be destroyed from the inside.

What if Jordan harmed her?

"Rebecca, please." I covered my mouth and sobbed.

She hugged me like a mother would her child. "Everything will be all right. For now, let's keep this between us."

We walked back to the house.

When we entered, we met Matt in the foyer.

"Mom told me she came by the other day."

Rebecca darted her eyes to me, then to Matt. "Yeah, she told me she needed more hands for her house. My gardener left with her."

"He should already be making himself at home." Matt looked at me. "You see, Gaby, Mom has this rule. Every one of her employees has room and board secured. They become part of the family."

Rebecca sighed. "That's so good of her. She doesn't like Jordan's initiative and prefers to take matters into her own hands. That's why Jordan doesn't get along with her."

"Who do I not get along with?" Jordan wrapped his arms around Rebecca and kissed her nape.

She leaned into him. "Hi, love. It's nothing. I was talking about Lisa."

"I just don't like her ideas." He glanced at Matt. "Since you started working with Frank, have you finally accepted that what we're fighting for far surpasses your mother's ideals?"

Matt's smile was tight. "It definitely has sparked my interest."

Jordan nodded. "I'm glad we have you on board. At last, our sons are taking on what we've built."

Rebecca rolled her eyes and stepped out of her husband's embrace, then led us into the dining room. "Lunch should be ready. Afterward, you can all go ahead and talk business."

I followed her.

Matt stayed two steps behind, talking with Jordan.

Rebecca put her arm through mine. "Jordan is kind of taken with you." She winked. "He says you'll be working for him. Just know, he lives for work."

"After working with Matt and Davon, I'm kind of used to it."

She nodded. "As long as you're okay with it. But don't forget about me and the girls. We really enjoyed the other night except for how it ended. Will you make time for us if I plan to get together again?"

I squeezed her arm. "Of course."

The girls were women in high government positions, some of the coun-cilmembers' wives, and women who supported the NWG projects. Part of my mission was to infiltrate the social groups in Electi and find possible candidates to aid us from within.

What I found at the garden party was that most lived happily with their comforts but were ignorant of what happened outside their walls. They kept asking me about Promissa. Some didn't even know we didn't have schools.

That's what affected them the most. They couldn't understand why the young people were forbidden a good education. Why would the NWG do something like that to a future generation?

Lisa decided to help me since I'd be occupied with finding the spy. She made a list of possible allies to our cause and took over the responsibility of bringing them to our side. Being an elite gave her an advantage. Maybe she saw something in Rebecca to risk telling her about Davon's petition.

Jordan took the head of the table, with Rebecca to his right. Matt and I sat on the left.

"It's a pity Davon can't be with us today. I tried to convince him after the council meeting to come for lunch, but he said he had work piled up," Jordan said as we started lunch.

"Yeah, he was anxious to get back to it," I said.

He nodded. "So, Matt, how's work going?"

Matt straightened. "Everything's good. One step at a time. Research is something Dad and I are very passionate about."

Jordan furrowed his brow. "Frank tells me you're still visiting your clinic in Promissa."

Matt raised his glass toward a maid, who filled it with wine. "That's my baby. I'm not going to leave it yet, but I plan to eventually. It's just I've kind of grown attached to my patients."

Jordan grunted. "You know we can't have that. I understand if you like your practice as a doctor, but to treat Promissa citizens privately is a waste of resources. They do have their own medical facility."

Rebecca dropped her fork.

We all turned to her at the clatter.

"Oh. Sorry." She picked it up.

I clasped mine tightly.

A waste of time because they planned to get rid of us all. This man was pure evil, masked as our savior.

"I understand." Matt took a sip of his wine, and his Adam's apple bobbed heavily as he swallowed. "I'll think about it, but for now, I'm keeping my practice. At least once a week."

Jordan shrugged. "Whatever. I'm sure in no time you'll see my point."

Lunch was over, and after saying our goodbyes to Rebecca, we entered the study. When I glanced about, I could imagine Davon basking in this warm and antique ambience. As he'd said, they shared the same taste in décor.

A katana was on display, one Davon said was his father's most prized possession. It looked magnificent.

A large desk sat at the end of the study, with a glass panel that offered a pristine view of the forest behind it. It gave the space a fresh feeling. The desk matched the dark wooden paneling on the walls. Built-in bookshelves surrounded us, filled with either books or weapons.

We settled on one of the two black leather settees.

"Do you drink, Gabrielle?" Jordan asked from the bar.

It was opposite a fireplace, which gave the room a cozy atmosphere.

"Sure," I said.

"Matt?" Jordan asked.

"I'm okay." He gave me a quick glance.

My heart was about to burst out of my chest, but Matt's presence grounded me.

It's showtime.

"Let's cut to the chase." Jordan took the settee in front of us after passing me my drink. He sank back into the seat, legs crossed. "Gabrielle, you've traveled with them. What can you tell me about the rebels?"

I blew out a breath. *Here goes nothing.*

"The group is called the People's Revolutionary Front. I was with a faction that guarded the perimeter of the forest. I tried to find out more about their way of life and where they were hiding, but no one knew. Just the higher-ups." I took a sip of my whiskey and let its warmth sink down.

My hands started sweating.

Jordan watched me, his attention fully on me.

He leaned forward and spread his legs, then put his elbows over his knees, holding his glass with both hands. "Did you at least get the name of their leader?"

I smoothed my pants, trying to cover my restless leg.

Come on, Matt. Just say it.

"Deborah Davis," Matt said.

A vein throbbed in Jordan's brow, and his arms bunched up as he gripped his drink. "You're telling me we had their leader in our grasp, and we let her slip right through our fingers?" He slammed his drink on the table with such force that we both jumped in place. He glared at Matt. "Fuck! Why didn't you tell me before?"

"Minister Niles?" I used a soft tone.

He breathed deeply, his demeanor calming. "Yes?"

Was this the same man who went crazy on Matt a moment ago?

I wanted to run and hide from him. There was a dark air about Jordan that could swallow you whole if you let it. One moment he was violent and the next composed. There was no middle and no way to know how he would react.

You can do this.

I put my drink next to his and mirrored him. "Davon never shares what happens inside the prison, so I didn't know about her until the attack. And still, it was just two days ago that he confided to me her name. That's when we asked for this meeting."

Jordan raked his hair back, a gesture Davon sometimes did when he was anxious. "Sorry about that. It's just..." He breathed out. "I knew she was part of the rebellion, had suspected it since she disappeared after helping her sister escape three years ago. When she came back to get her older sister out, I knew she was one of them. But their leader?" He squished his eyebrows. "That I didn't expect."

I stilled as he mentioned my escape. What would happen if he connected the dots and found out who I truly was? I shivered.

Jordan rose. "We need to get her back alive. She took something from me."

My pulse rose. *His son.*

My heart could probably carve a hole through my chest by the way it pounded.

Calm down, Abi.

He frowned. "I have someone already inside. They've been there for more than a year now but have been radio silent since. I had to send in another one to check what was happening, and again, it's been six months and nothing. We need to find a way to get that location."

There's more than one.

My heart lurched as I turned toward Matt. His gaze stayed with Jordan, but a bead of sweat dripped from his brow.

Matt tucked a stray curl behind his ear, wiping the sweat discreetly. "That's why we came. Gaby found out rebel spies are inside the city, even in the government. If we get a hold of them, they might know more."

Jordan moved behind his settee and put his palms over its back, his stance calm.

Matt studied him. "You knew about this?"

"I know everything that happens inside what's mine." He clenched his hands over the settee. "The problem is finding out who they are. We've found some, but it's been a couple of years since the last one. Everyone checks. There's not even a hint of foul play, but we know they're inside."

"I can find them," I said.

Jordan gave me a quizzical look. "What do you mean?"

I took my drink and settled back. "During my two months out there, I befriended an IT girl. I asked her about her work, and after I swore secrecy, she told me she created new personas for the spies within the city. They use the names of real people who lived in Promissa during the wars. She said it's perfect because all Promissa records from the last ten to twenty years were destroyed during the wars, so no one knows if these people escaped or died."

My stomach turned, and nausea hit me. This was risky, but it was the only way to get Jordan to trust us—to give him real information.

Davon should be sending the letter explaining our plan to Connor right about now. He didn't ask his permission, just told him to let us know two names. Two rebels willing to sacrifice themselves for the cause.

I closed my eyes briefly. I'd never be able to erase these two souls from my mind, whoever they were, because as it was, I put a death sentence on them.

I hoped they didn't die by Davon's hand before I found the spy. We counted on the program retrieving the lists before that happened.

I fiddled with Mom's silver bracelet before getting back on point. "If I can access the city's database from a safe location, I'm sure I can find these people."

He tilted his head. "And what makes you think you can do this when my whole team hasn't been able to?"

The harshness in his words made my stomach recoil, but I kept strong. "Because I became her apprentice and she showed me how they did it. And because I stole one of their computers and yesterday broke through its firewall."

The dark voids of Jordan's eyes caught me for a moment before the corner of his lip lifted into a sneer. "I like where this is going. Tell me more."

Half an hour later, after much explaining and convincing, Jordan said he'd think about it and let me know. We said our goodbyes, and O'Hare was already there to pick us up.

"Now we wait." Matt slumped into his seat, letting his head fall back. He closed his eyes. "That was exhausting."

I settled sideways. "Do you think it'll work?"

He opened one eye to look at me. "I think so. Like father, like son."

I slapped his thigh.

"Hey!" He looked at me with a pained gaze. "I just mean he's taken with you. In other words, your father-in-law seems happy to have you in the family."

I raised an eyebrow. "I don't know how to take that."

He patted my knee. "It's a good thing. You were brilliant in there."

Ten minutes later, I waved goodbye to O'Hare and followed Matt. We decided to have some drinks with Frank in the district. He'd been bugging Matt about going out so he could get to know me better.

We entered Darkest Red. The bar was as expected, dark with dimmed red lights all around it. The furniture carried the same colors, giving it a modern and sensual vibe. Jazz played in the background as we passed a group of people in a booth to our left. Other tables were filled with couples, while a few drowned their sorrows alone.

Frank sat at the bar with a brunette to his right. She stroked his thigh sultrily, and he did the same to her. Her black minidress bunched up, close to revealing a bit too much. At the same time, Frank kissed the neck of a guy sitting to his left. The man wore a black shirt with gray slacks. His eyes closed as he angled his head to kiss Frank on the lips.

Matt cleared his throat when we stepped closer. "Dad."

Frank turned. "Oh, you're here! Give me a second."

Both his companions fidgeted with their drinks.

Frank whispered something in the man's ear. Even in the dim light, I could see the man flush.

Then he moved to the woman, muttered something in private, and kissed her softly, squeezing her thigh. She giggled.

He stepped away from the bar and went with us into a booth cornered in the back.

Matt sat beside him, and I faced them both.

The waiter came. "Anything to drink?"

Frank winked at him. "The usual."

He smiled nervously. "Of course, sir."

The waiter turned to me.

"Whiskey for me," I said.

Matt nodded. "Make it two."

My phone beeped.

"Are you at the bar?"

I smiled and texted back.

"We just got here."

"I'm on my way. Just got off the train. —D"

"Was that Davon?" Frank asked.

"Yeah." I pocketed my phone. "He should be here any minute."

Frank rested back. "I'm glad you took the time to come. It can't be work all the time."

Matt chuckled and glanced at the bar. "I see that."

Frank put an arm behind Matt. "Come on, son. Don't be so judgy. Just because you choose not to participate in such activities doesn't mean I have to behave like a rock. I have needs."

"I know, Dad. I've never judged you," Matt said.

Frank smiled sweetly. "I know." He turned his attention to me. "So, Gaby, how are you liking Electi?"

I swallowed all the raging words I wanted to yell at all the elites who chose to live this way at the expense of others and gave him one of my best smiles. "It's wonderful."

"I'm glad Matt brought you in. You shouldn't be out there. You belong here with us."

I knew he meant well, but when did they begin to decide who belonged where and why?

The door opened, and the last rays of the sun altered the ambience for a second. I turned my head, and my heart eased into a mellow rhythm.

Davon was here.

A waitress took his jacket, and he told her something.

She pointed toward us, and he made his way to our table. He shook hands with Frank and Matt, then sat beside me, kissed my cheek, and put an arm around me.

"Glad you could come. Are you feeling better?" Frank asked.

Davon traced circles along my back with his finger. "Just a bit tired, but I needed this. It's been a while."

The waiter brought our drinks, then put a glass of whiskey in front of Davon. "Minister Niles, compliments of the bar."

He nodded. "Thank you."

Everyone knew who he was. I guess it came with being the son of the most powerful man in the NWG.

Three months ago, he was just one of us. A general but with no special treatment. To see him with this much power just for being Jordan Niles's son was surreal.

Matt picked up his glass. "To a new beginning. May we all work together to make this country one to be proud of. May we reap what we sow and reach what we all wish for."

The meaning of his words etched deeply into my soul.

His gaze locked with mine. "Cheers."

We all clinked our glasses and took a swig.

February 1, 2214

I wasn't lying when I said I needed this. The rich taste of the whiskey warmed my chilled soul. I just wanted to forget about my fucked-up day.

If the prison was secure before, now it was impenetrable, with the highest security system my dad could spare. Of course, I had approved of all the changes, being the one who was attacked. More soldiers were stationed around the jail's perimeter, and security was enhanced inside the halls.

Muñoz was cleared and could move in and out of the premises, so the comms were still up.

As soon as I opened the secret compartment in my bureau, the day became fucked up.

With Deb back, everyone was happy, and hopes were up. Connor needed everyone to continue believing that I was the traitor, so he told everyone he and his team had set up an operation to take her out. They believed him.

The situation inside our system was deteriorating. The problem now was that NWG soldiers were situated in and near the energy bunker, and people were getting angsty after the attack, pushing Connor to the limit. To make it worse, two runners were found dead five miles away from Janus Peak.

To this he added the pressure from the council, whose members already knew about our mission and wanted results.

There was also Deb's pregnancy and mental state, plus the threat of having a spy lurking around the peak.

I wanted to forget about everything for a minute and drink. The whole thing was a fucking disaster, and we were stuck on this side.

"Davon?" Frank waved a hand in front of me.

I chuckled. "Sorry. My day was hectic."

Abi caressed my right thigh. I held her closer.

Frank sipped his drink. "I'm curious. Now that Gabrielle is here, how is Grace taking it?"

Abi's hand stilled.

I turned to find her eyes wide and set on Matt's father.

Fuck. I should've told her. With everything that happened, I forgot about Grace.

It wasn't Frank's fault.

Frank darted his eyes between Abi and me and jerked back. "Oh. I'm sorry. With all the attention the tabloids gave it, I thought Gabrielle knew."

I raised my hand to stop him. "Don't worry." I clasped Abi's hand. "We'll be back in a moment."

I rose from the booth, taking Abi with me, then signaled a waitress. "Do you have a room available?"

She nodded. "Follow me."

She opened a curtain, and we went into one of the VIP rooms in the back. It had a large sofa and a bar.

This place assured privacy to its members and everything they needed to have a good time.

I hugged her once we were inside. "She's nothing to me."

She pushed me away.

My chest hurt at her rejection.

"Matt told me about what you had with Grace, but what did Frank mean about how she'd take it? Did something happen between you two these past months?" Her lips trembled, but she kept her gaze fixed on me. She was hurting.

"No. She wanted to, but I rejected her." I reached for her.

She stepped away. "What did Frank mean about the tabloids?"

God. How do I put this?

I rubbed my brow. "At the New Year's celebration, I asked her to dance so I could end things in a cordial manner, but she decided to make a display. In the photos, we look like a couple."

She scowled. "In what way?"

"She kissed my neck and whispered in my ear. But they got it all wrong. I told her it was over, and she threatened me. She was mad that I refused her."

How could I make Abi see there was no one else but her?

Abi squinted.

"Ask Father. He can attest to what happened that night," I said.

She sank onto the sofa. "How come I found out about it from Frank?"

Because I'm an idiot.

I held her hand. "With everything that's going on, I forgot. I put her in the back of my mind when you arrived. You and the mission were my priority. But I should've told you. She's dangerous."

She looked up. "How dangerous?"

"She threatened to ruin my life, and I found out through Father that she's sleeping with General Steele. I don't know what her plan is." I sat next to her and covered her hand. "I'm sorry you had to find out this way. You're the only one for me, Abi. I'm not that man anymore."

Her big eyes settled on mine.

I'd never seen her look more beautiful than at this moment. I covered her nape and pulled her to me. Our lips met in a loving caress. My chest swelled as she pulled me by the hip and deepened the kiss.

"You're mine." She leaned her brow against mine.

I brushed her lips. "Only yours."

A while later, we came back to the table.

Frank smiled mischievously. "Everything good in paradise?"

Matt elbowed him but couldn't hide his smirk.

God, these two were one and the same when it came to being annoying. Abi sat.

I scooted in beside her. "Everything's perfect."

"I'm sorry. I thought you knew," Frank told Abi. "But just so you know, that woman is a snake. Everyone knows Davon ended things. It's the tabloids that like to gossip."

Abi nodded. "Thanks. Davon explained."

Time to change the subject. "How was lunch?" I asked Matt.

Their meeting's success was crucial to our plan.

Matt smiled. "Everything went better than expected. I'm feeling good about our possibilities."

My headache receded a little. Now I only needed to wait till Father contacted me.

"What are you two talking about?" Frank asked as he finished his gin and tonic.

Abi leaned toward him. "We had a meeting with Jordan today. We threw some ideas in to deal with our present situation. He liked them."

"That's good," Frank said.

"Yeah. We're hoping we can use them to deal with the rebel problem," I added.

The waiter brought us another round.

Frank raised his glass. "Cheers to being rid of these rebels and moving our program forward."

Matt dropped his glass on the table, and half his drink spilled.

"Everything okay?" Frank asked.

Abi took some napkins and helped Matt clean the table, not without slipping her hand over his and giving it a squeeze.

Matt straightened. "Yeah, sorry about that."

Frank sighed. "No worries." He took a swig of his drink. "As I was saying, we'd do much better without them. Right, son?"

Matt nodded. "Definitely."

Frank gave Abi one of his charming smiles. "I'm glad to have you with us. You're one of us now, and soon you'll never have to worry about these rebels again. You'll be surprised by the plans we have for them." He looked straight at me. "Right, Davon?"

Abi fisted her hand on my thigh, and I interlaced my fingers through hers.

Keeping calm during these conversations took a lot from me. I couldn't imagine how it was for Abi.

I raised my glass and smirked. "You're right. They'll never see it coming."

Half an hour later, I squeezed myself out of the booth. "If you'll excuse us."

Abi was right behind me.

"Leaving already?" Frank stood.

"Yeah, I'm kind of tired," I said.

Abi took my hand. "Me too. Might as well get some rest."

Frank winked. "We're all adults here. You don't need to make an excuse to leave."

I smiled. "Thanks, Frank."

"Can we talk in private for a second?" he asked.

"Sure." I glanced at Abi and Matt. "I'll be right back."

He gripped my shoulder once we were out of earshot. "I don't know if you talked to him or not, but thank you for bringing Matt in. I never imagined he'd say yes to working with me."

I shook my head. "I didn't do anything. He'd made up his mind before coming to me."

"Still, if you weren't back in Electi, I'm sure the chance wouldn't have come up. So thank you." He smiled.

I grabbed his other shoulder. "No problem."

With that, we walked back to the booth.

Frank kissed Abi's hand. "Always a pleasure to see you, Gabrielle."

She offered him a tight smile.

I clasped Matt's arm. "See you later?"

"Sure." He hugged Abi goodbye. "See you."

We'd meet at Matt's in an hour or so. There was a lot to talk about.

Before the second knock, Matt opened the door to his apartment.

I followed Abi in.

Classic rock played in the background. A dartboard stood opposite his coffee table, which had two empty beer bottles on top.

Before I could say a thing, Matt started venting. "I'm going crazy working in that lab. All your father asks for, Dad makes it a reality. He's a fucking genius."

Matt had it hard, and I didn't blame him. Throughout our lives, we lived in the shadows of the two most powerful men in the country. And making peace with that fact was hard.

"Give it here." I stretched my hand, and he passed me a dart.

I threw it. I wasn't as good as him, but I hit close to the bullseye. "Whatever you're going through, know I get you."

Matt took the dart off the board. "I know. It shouldn't affect me this much, but it does." He took a shot, hitting the bullseye. Since he started therapy at the hospital, his shoulder had improved a lot.

"After Dad's toast, I thought about Aoki and all our people. And I almost lost it." He retrieved the dart.

He glanced at Abi, who sat behind us, fidgeting with her nails. An obvious attempt to appear unbothered.

I clasped his shoulder. "We're all dealing with a lot, but we'll make it through. As for the peak, I need to talk to you both. There are new developments, and we're going to need to step up our game."

Both Abi's and Matt's attention turned to me. I sat on the love seat, and they shared the sofa.

"Before you say anything, I have something important to tell you both," Abi said just as I took Connor's letter out of my slacks.

I furrowed my brow. "What is it?"

"It's your mom."

My heart skipped a beat. "What about her?"

She bit her lip. "She knows about Paul."

Matt widened his eyes. "But how?"

This could mean the end of everything. Unless…

Abi clasped her hands together. "She saw us talking that day and asked him in writing. Paul didn't say anything about me, but he did tell her about the reality back at the facilities and how he was taken. Your mother suspects we're here for our own agenda. She knows you're hiding something."

"Is she telling Father?" My voice was no more than a whisper.

It was as if the world was held in a standstill and the three of us were the only ones left.

"She confronted Jordan. She's heartbroken."

I clenched my fists, crumpling the letter. "Did he do something to her?" I would kill him if he touched her.

Abi crouched in front of me. "He only told her to stop asking. He didn't harm her."

I closed my eyes. *Thank God.*

I remembered my father's short temper. "She should leave him."

Abi took the letter and put it on the table, then gripped my hands. "She's staying with him. She said she'd do it for us."

I flinched back. "For us?"

"She said she'd never ask what our true purpose for coming to Electi was but that she trusted us."

I frowned. "I don't understand. Does that mean she'll help us?"

Was she on our side?

Abi stared at our joined hands. "I guess." She shrugged. "I'm not sure, but I think so. She told me Jordan was no longer the man she thought he was, not after he'd lied to her all along."

"God. I wanted Mom to know, but I never expected her to find out on her own." I let go of Abi and doubled over.

Mom was in danger. If Father found out what she knew and saw her as an obstacle to his plans, there was no telling what he might do.

Someone grabbed my shoulder. "We'll make sure she's safe. Your father loves her. I doubt he'd ever harm her." Matt's voice broke through my dark thoughts.

I nodded and took a moment to compose myself.

"You're right. We need to trust she'll be okay. Father adores her." I squeezed Matt's hand and grabbed Abi's. "Thank you both."

They nodded and went back to the sofa.

"At least now she knows. It's better this way." I grabbed the letter.

Anything was better than not knowing the true face of Jordan Niles.

"Now about this." I held the letter up. "You can read it later if you want, but I'll narrow it down to the most important and urgent issues."

They both leaned forward, giving me their full attention.

"First, Deb arrived at the peak with the team. She's safe."

Abi exhaled hard and covered her brow, murmuring something.

"Connor and Deb read the note."

Abi looked up. "What about the baby?"

"They decided to keep it." I paused.

Having this baby could lead to so many problems. I could only hope they'd be able to push through them.

"They'll raise him as their own. For now, they're keeping it a secret. Connor fears people might rush into war if they know what's really happening out here."

Abi nodded. "I think it's the right decision."

Matt sat back and crossed his arms. "He shouldn't keep this from the citizens. They should know what's going on."

"And they will," I said. "Give him some time."

Matt huffed.

The empty feeling in the pit of my stomach grew. Now for the hard part. "About Deb. I don't plan to keep anything from you, so I'll just say it. She's not well. I mean, physically she is. Dr. Lewis said the pregnancy is going well. But emotionally..." I looked down. "She's having problems reasoning if I'm good or bad. She's been having nightmares and doesn't remember what she did to me. Connor found out about the severity of the attack on me via Muñoz."

She'd never be able to see me in the same light again. I'd lost her, a part of me that I'd never be able to get back. My sister.

Abi's anguished expression broke me. "Is she getting help?"

"Sarah and a group of therapists are trying their best, but..." I raked my hair back.

Abi gripped my left knee. "The important thing is that she made it and she's getting help. We'll talk to her when we get back. I'm sure we can get through this. She just needs time."

I covered her hand and squeezed hard.

I put the letter back on the table, then bent forward and intertwined my hands.

"What else happened?" Matt looked at me. "What's got you on edge?"

I stared back. "Two runners were killed five miles east of command."

"Fuck!" Matt shifted forward. "Are they planning a diversion?"

I nodded. "Yuxuan mobilized a group of soldiers east. They'll go on their own to the north and do a series of attacks, mostly bombings, to get their attention away from the west."

Matt lifted an eyebrow. "There's more, right?"

I sighed. "There's always more. Connor needs us to hurry. The council knows about our mission and is pressing him for results, more so after the energy bunker loss, but he's giving us time. David is running the strategy meetings with Maria. They're almost ready. The children and families were moved between the caves and the farming bunker, and the rest of the bunkers will be used as military facilities. The only missing piece is finding the spy."

"We've got that covered," Abi said. "But there's something you should know."

"What?" I asked.

"There's more than one spy. Jordan told us that six months ago, he sent another one in."

I covered my brow. "I suspected as much, but I dared to hope." I exhaled hard. "I'll let Connor know. But about the meeting, what did Father say about you working with him?"

Abi shifted toward Matt. "Your dad liked our idea and said he'd think about it. Matt said he kind of likes me, so it should work."

I grunted. "I don't like it."

"What? That he likes Abi? But that was the plan from the start," Matt said.

I understood the need to get Father to like her and bring her in, but I wished for the opposite—to get her as far away from him as possible.

"I know, but I don't trust him."

I searched Abi's eyes. She seemed unfazed, in her element.

I grimaced. "Just be careful, okay? Let's hope we can find the spies soon."

We must get back home and get everything set. Their genome projects, the rising army, and the threat from Halcyon could gang up on us, and then it'd be too late.

"We need to step up our game and tread carefully so the NWG never suspects, because if they do, they'll call for backup, and we'll be fucked," I said.

Abi was on her feet in a second. "Let's not dwell on the negative and focus on getting things done. Right now, we only have each other. We'll follow the game plan, do our jobs, and when we're ready, go back there." She moved away from us. "I'll prepare dinner."

She went to the kitchen, leaving us with our mouths open.

"Who is this woman, and what did you do to my girlfriend?" I asked Matt.

"Something changed that night." Matt looked at me. "The night you left her. We dealt with a lot of stuff before she was better. But after that, she became stronger. Do you see it?"

There was a spark in her. A strength far greater than what I'd seen before. It pulled me in. I nodded. "I do."

February 8, 2214

A week later, Father invited me home, most likely to talk about Abi.

He was on his phone when I entered his study.

"Grace, we've been through this already. I'm not pushing Davon to marry you. He already made up his mind, and you need to move forward." Father's tone was serious.

I made to leave, but he signaled for me to sit. I opened my suit and sat on the settee to the left.

"Your father understands. Stop using him to try to convince me on this matter." He rolled his eyes. "Do whatever you want. You're acting like a brat, and I won't tolerate it. Either you stop insisting, or I'm taking you off the team."

I stiffened for a second, then settled back.

Team? What the hell was he talking about?

He drummed his fingers on the desk and raised his eyebrows. "Okay. Much better. We'll talk later." He hung up.

"Grace?" I asked.

"Yes, it's been a while since she whined about what you did. I've told her again and again that nothing will come of it. I hope she got it now. She seemed calm by the end of the call."

I furrowed my brow. "And since when do you talk to her?"

His features tightened. "And since when do I need to explain my affairs? Be careful how you speak to me, son. We're working together, but know your place."

We were supposed to be equals if he wished for us to work together. I was not backing down now. This was a game for him, and if it was power and control he wanted to see, I'd show him.

"If you want me to take after you, I need to know this stuff. I can't work with you if you won't trust me." I stood and started closing my jacket, my eyes set on him.

He searched my eyes for a moment before his lips curved up. "I thought you'd shrivel and run at my words, but I see I was wrong." He took the papers from his desk and organized them into a pile, then went to the bar and served two glasses of whiskey.

"Sit. There's much to talk about."

After clinking his glass with mine, he loosened his tie and sat opposite me. "What I'm about to tell you doesn't leave this room."

My heart pumped fast, but each beat weighed heavily on me. "You know I'd never betray you. Your words are unnecessary."

He smiled, and it was a smile that brought back memories from those dark years. The same one he had whenever I won a fight in the training grounds or whenever I got someone to talk during one of my sessions. He was proud.

I wanted to rip that smile off his face. To punch him so hard that no one would recognize him once I was done.

Fucking lunatic.

"We're watching out for our enemies to the north."

To the north? But who was...? I held my glass tightly. Could he be talking about Empire City?

"We have grounds to believe they've been thwarting our trade with other countries. General Steele and a group of carefully chosen citizens are investigating this threat, and I appointed Grace as chief of this operation. Her father insisted on her taking a role in the government, what with his present health condition."

Was President Orville stepping down?

I shivered at the thought of Grace overseeing such an operation. Had she truly grown to that point?

I wanted to learn more about the threat to the north, but first...

"Health condition?" I asked.

Father took a swig of his drink. "President Orville had a stroke just after the new year. His condition worsens by the day. He understands he needs to step down in a couple of years if this continues, and he wants Grace to take his place."

My pulse rose. This was news to me.

From what I'd seen, she was still as spoiled as ever. Was this all part of her plan?

Father didn't even mention this at the council meeting last week. Was he scared someone might try to usurp the government? Or that they'd take his place?

In a large gulp, he finished his drink. "Obviously, Grace doesn't have complaints about taking over." He walked to the bar. "I fear she may have something to do with the president's deteriorating condition. I've sent the best nurses and doctors to treat him, but he keeps getting worse. The nurses say that she sometimes sends them away for long periods of time, saying she wants to take care of him herself."

I pressed my lips together. If this was true, she was more dangerous than I ever thought possible.

Father came back with the bottle of whiskey.

I held my glass up, and he poured more into it, then filled his own and sat.

I cocked my head. "Do you think her capable?"

Father chuckled sarcastically. "I do. I even hinted to Orville about it, but he refuses to believe her capable of such a thing. That's why I sent her away."

I leaned forward. "Aren't you worried about her taking over the presidency? She might be planning to take you down."

He shrugged, but for a moment, worry flashed through his eyes. "I'm being careful. I have a lot of dirt on her. She won't be able to take our place. If she does, she'll end up with nothing. That woman... I'm glad you cut ties with her. She's a snake."

He was the second person to reference Grace in that way. What the hell did she do?

"What kind of dirt do you have on her, other than thinking she's trying to kill her father?"

"Well, to start, she's been sharing the beds of many government officials for years."

All those glimpses at the New Year's party. The ogling eyes from the men. It all made sense now.

I raised my eyebrows. "But why?"

My father sighed, then shook his head. "My best guess is she's ensuring that no one stands in her path. For the last year, she's been very active in Halcyon's politics. She managed to convince her father to hide it from me."

I jerked forward. Orville did something behind my father's back? This was unprecedented.

Father raised his hands. "I already talked to him. He knows he shouldn't go against me. After all, I'm the one who runs the show. He promised to follow the protocol, but I'm keeping a close watch on Grace."

"What kind of decisions did she make?" I asked, my drink forgotten.

"She implemented a stricter code inside the facilities and started the citizens' disposal."

"Disposal?" Bile rose to my throat. Was he implying what I thought he was?

Father relaxed and crossed his legs. "Operations at Halcyon are much further along than at Promissa. The elimination of the citizens was scheduled to begin in two years, but she started without my consent."

Maintaining a straight face proved impossible, but I did as best as I could. I drank and consciously stopped my limbs from trembling. Inside, my blood boiled at his revelation.

It was real. The extermination of the citizens had already started, and Grace was up for it.

"This isn't news to you. I'm sure you already know about our plans. Frank told me Matt took some files from the lab last month."

If he knew about Matt taking the files, what else could he know? Was he keeping an eye on Lavigne? Could he already know about us?

Nothing escaped my father, but when I searched his eyes, there was nothing off. And something told me he wouldn't trust me with this intel if he didn't have complete trust in me.

I raised an eyebrow. "Matt told me about it. But the Prometheus Project is just starting. I didn't know you were that ahead in Halcyon."

He grinned. "Our advanced army is ready over there, and it's true that we're just starting the human trials, but I wanted to wait and make sure everything ran smoothly before going ahead with the Purge Directive."

A purge? God.

I nodded. "What exactly did she do?"

He glared at his drink. "She ordered the nurses to inject a lethal solution to about twenty patients that were over seventy. She thought it was a waste of resources to keep this population at the Halcyon Medical Center. It's true, but my orders were clear. Two more years, and then we could start. I reprimanded her, and she promised to keep to the original plan."

A lump in my throat grew for those elderly citizens. I had so many questions, but I couldn't let my façade drop. This new persona, the unscrupulous and obedient son of Jordan Niles, loved violence and hated the rebels.

"You're right. We can't let her make the decisions. But who will keep her in her place while you're here?"

"General Steele. Since they're so close, I figured he was the best bet to keep her in her place."

"Do you trust him?" I asked, thinking maybe Grace and he were in the same boat. What if they planned it together?

He sneered. "You don't know him. He will keep her under control."

I sipped my drink. "What's this about the north? Which enemy has their eyes on you now?"

Over the years, we'd had many threats. We'd been able to maintain our territories and signed many peace agreements over the years, especially knowing some countries had better armies than ours. With a good trading treaty, most problems were washed away, and many things were forgiven.

"Empire City."

The city where I'd sent the Promissa citizens who wanted to flee not only the NWG but also us.

"I don't know much about them," I said.

"It's the capital of the Liberty Enclave. They control the north, most of the sea, and, what's worse, they have a great army. They're the last vestiges of the government that once ruled over this country. The government that turned to ashes a long time ago by decades and decades of wars. Or so we thought."

I leaned forward, almost at the edge of the settee. "Wait. You didn't know about this city?"

Dad laughed. "Of course I knew about it. I just thought we'd destroyed that country completely. I didn't know they were one and the same." His expression darkened. "Our trades began to disappear on their routes. Our allies accused us of not fulfilling the treaties. Threats were made, and we started investigating. That's when we found their emblem—a rising sun behind a great city. It was hidden on the train freight that carried our products, painted over the roads our transport took. No one knew who was behind it or who the symbol belonged to until a month ago when a letter arrived."

"What did it say?" The hair on the back of my neck rose.

My father gazed north through the window behind his desk. His eyes were as dark as the night. "It said to be prepared. That they'd come for us and take back their country."

February 22, 2214

Two weeks had passed since my meeting with Father. He asked me later about Abi's skills, and after a long talk, he approved of her plan.

After our meeting, I decided to learn more about Empire City. The Liberty Enclave was ruled by a council chosen by their citizens, just like that of the People's Revolutionary Front.

Their goal was to take their country back. From what little I found, the country that existed before the wars was democratic. The people had a say in everything that happened inside their country, just like in Promissa before the NWG took over.

The country fought for decades, but after their central government was destroyed, the large cities branched off on their own, creating their own government. Promissa was one of these places.

I wondered if they'd help us get our city back or if they were just like the NWG, looking to invade and take everything.

Were our people safe up there? Would they fight with us if we asked?

I sat with Abi and Matt to talk about the meeting. I told them about Grace and what she did in Halcyon. At first, Abi trembled, and Matt held her, thinking she was having a panic attack, but she escaped his hold and gripped the table.

She snarled. "I will fucking kill her."

If she didn't hate Grace before, she hated her now.

After she calmed down, I explained about the threat from Empire City. We all believed this new development could be good for us. Two enemies united against another.

A week ago, I sent a letter to Connor and explained what happened in Halcyon, the new threat from the Liberty Enclave, and about there being two spies.

We received a reply yesterday.

Davon,

Thanks for the intel.

Another spy. That complicates things. But we'll keep doing what we're doing and hope to find something soon.

As for the Liberty Enclave, that's some good news. Whatever threatens the NWG helps us. I'll send an envoy to Empire City. If they're planning to fight the NWG, we need to know their plan. We'll offer an alliance and see where that goes.

Yuxuan and his soldiers made it safely, and their mission is going as planned.

Deb still isn't talking much, just as I explained in the last letter. Aoki tried to convince her you were good, but she won't listen and will only talk to Sarah and Tammy. She's trying to make peace with you and Abi being together. Sarah has tried to explain that she felt the same way before but that you were good. She appears unconvinced, always asking why Abi hasn't come home yet. I've tried to reason with her, but I don't want to push it. The pregnancy has her on edge. It's too much to take. I want to give her time. I hope you understand.

As for your mission, two of our spies volunteered. I've included their names and where to find them. Know that they understand what the mission entails and that the council won't hold anything against you if worse comes to worst. We pray that we all can find peace after such a hard decision.

—Connor

I closed my eyes. I'd never make peace with killing a fellow rebel, and with the pressure Father had lately, I knew the possibilities were high that he'd order the kill.

"Thomas Phillips and Joanne Gray," I said as I discussed the letter with Abi.

She repeated their names a couple of times. "Do they know?"

"They do. Both were briefed on our mission and volunteered. They're two veteran spies and have been with us from the beginning. Thomas lost his family during the wars. We found him while searching for the bunkers. He works at the train." I passed her his file.

She eyed it. "And Joanne?"

"She works inside the food development facility. She's the one who gave us the intel on the Promissa rebel factions. Having noticed their ongoing food drives to the slums, she investigated and found one of the members worked in her same facility. She's the one who made contact. She's fully devoted to our cause. They both are."

The day was gray. I hadn't seen the sun in all of February. I dragged the spoon across my plate. The oatmeal tasted bland today, mirroring our mood.

After Dad gave Abi the go, she started working from home with Lavigne. In two weeks, she'd learned as much as she could, but now it was time to reveal the name of the first rebel spy to my father. Then after a few weeks, we'd reveal the second.

"What else did Connor say?" Abi asked.

"Just as Lavigne informed us yesterday, Yuxuan and his team made it, and the NWG soldiers followed them. For now, our people are safe."

Abi sighed. "That's a relief." She fiddled with her food. "And Deb?"

I dropped my spoon. "Not good. She's been holed up. She's worried that you're with me and wants you back."

Abi stopped eating. "Do you think she'll change her mind about you?"

I shook my head. "I don't know. Everyone has tried, but she won't listen. And I get it. I do."

I held the back of my neck with both hands and breathed deeply. How would I face them after all this? I broke her.

"Is she talking to anyone?" Abi asked.

"Sarah and Tammy mostly. They were very close before she went off to free Sarah. She sometimes talks to Aoki, but she's been keeping her distance. Connor doesn't want to push her." I pushed my plate away.

Abi looked out toward the forest. "I wish I could be there with her. Maybe she'd listen to me." After a pause, she stood and took her plate. "Are you done?"

I slid my discarded oatmeal toward her. "Not hungry."

She picked it up and went to the kitchen. She came back with more coffee, then pulled out her phone.

"Are you texting him?" I asked.

In the two weeks she'd been working for Father, he'd given her his personal number.

I bit the inside of my cheek. The idea of him being this close to Abi sickened me.

"Yeah." She showed me the screen, which had three dots displayed on the text box. "He's already texting back."

My fingers twitched, and my pulse quickened. I should've been glad everything was working out, but something deep inside me had me on edge.

Her hand covered mine. "Davon?"

"What?" My tone was dry.

She pulled her hand away.

I grabbed it. "I'm sorry. It's just…"

"You're doing it again, you know." She scowled and tried to pull free.

I held on to her. "I don't understand."

"You're being overprotective. When I agreed to come with you, I told you I was coming to work. That I wanted to be part of the mission. You're treating me like a fragile girl who suffered too much trauma and can't handle things on her own."

The sting of her words hurt me deeply. "Abi, you've got it all wrong."

She crossed her arms and slouched back, taking her eyes off me.

I sat beside her, trying to catch her gaze. "Love, please look at me."

She did. Her eyes were wet with unshed tears. "You don't believe I can do this. Do you?"

I touched her cheek and passed a finger over her scar, the one she suffered that night at the cave.

She closed her eyes for the briefest moment.

"It's the complete opposite. I know you're more than capable, and you're doing an amazing job. But your closeness to Father drives me crazy.

I worry he's playing a game with us. What if he already knows and is having his fun before he arrests us?"

These past few weeks, this was my constant fear. He'd taken her in, but what if it was another of his vile games? What if one day she never came home?

She narrowed her eyes. "You don't know that. We need to have faith and keep at it until we find what we're looking for."

"But what if the spy already told him about us? What if he arrests you?"

"Davon." She caressed my chin and the sensitive flesh under the scar Deb gave me. "No one knows I'm out here."

Maybe I was being paranoid? But I'd keep my eyes open, nevertheless. You could never be too careful with my father.

I leaned into her hand. "Maybe I am being paranoid, but please understand—he's ruthless."

Her phone beeped, and after she read the message, she put it away and came closer. She stroked my hair back. "Do you want to come with me today? Your dad just asked me to go to his office at the government center."

I shook my head. "Matt and I will take the train with you. He has his meeting today with the leader of the rebel faction, and I must be ready for Father's order once you give him the name of the spy. I'm sure he'll arrest Phillips immediately. I'll take O'Hare with me, and Bayat will go with you. You should do this alone."

She smiled. "Thank you. Your trust means a lot to me. And don't worry. I'll be careful." She stood. "I need to get ready."

She wore her pink pj's and fluffy-eared slippers. Fucking adorable.

Mom got them for her as a gift just because. They were very close to each other already, more so after Mom found out about Paul. They talked all the time, and it warmed my heart. If only things were different...

I hoped in the end we could save those we loved because as it was, my heart was already tearing into pieces at the prospect of losing Mom.

Chapter 32

Abi

February 22, 2214

This wasn't my first visit to the government center, but it was the first time I witnessed it as Jordan Niles's seat of power. Instead of being the place of freedom and prosperity that I once knew, it now stood as an omen of oppression to Promissa and the dominion and control of the New World Government.

My body went numb as I glanced about. Why couldn't we live in harmony?

In one of Abraham's lectures, he showed us accounts of Promissa before the New World Government invaded us. We had our own army, which dwelled on the periphery of the city. Wars were always a threat, but there were times of peace as well.

When I was about five, maybe six, it was one of those times, and Dad took us to see the city center. I remember the building was magnificent but not as big as today. Or as unreachable. It was open to all, and citizens could express their opinions on recent developments, with the government representatives to defend their rights.

Promissa was a city of prosperity. Once a bastion of the old government, we became independent and created our own. It was alive, with new technologies blooming daily, skyscrapers and lights everywhere. Just like in Electi, some people worked, while others enjoyed a day out.

People were happy, and education was key to the city's stability.

There were laws that allowed for population control without jeopardizing the citizens' freedom. Everyone had free access to birth control. Two children were allowed per household. Once they were born, their parents would undergo sterilization, with the option of freezing their gametes in case of death or the inability to reproduce naturally.

Promissa generated clean energy harvesting technologies, and huge laboratories worked on advancing science to create safe resources to feed the people and keep the city running without the worry of contaminating or endangering the environment.

How did it all come to this? Whatever we had before was now lost to the greed of the elite.

I took a deep, cleansing breath and moved forward, each step heavier than the last.

Bayat followed behind as I walked through security. A soldier pointed me in the right direction, and I entered the elevator, arms at my sides. Bayat turned a key to access the twentieth floor.

The whole city of Promissa could be seen from here. My heart ached as the mountains came into view. My family. I'd been away for a month and a half, and I missed them dearly.

The elevator's ping announced our arrival, and I followed Bayat down the hall.

A secretary showed me into a lavish office. White walls and furniture made it look modern and minimalist to the extreme. A small bar sat on the left and a sitting space in the center. At the end, centralized as if to symbolize power, sat Jordan behind a white desk with a crystal top. Behind him, a glass panel gave a complete view of Promissa.

He stood and rounded the desk. "Welcome, Gabrielle." He showed me to a seat. "Would you like something to drink? I have juice and coffee."

"Just water. Thank you." I'd never denied a good cup of coffee, but something about sharing one with Jordan hit me wrong.

He set the glass of water on the table and sat in front of me. "How are you doing? Is my son treating you right?"

His smile was breathtaking, like Davon's. Their resemblance was uncanny.

I nodded. "He's very good to me."

"And Electi? How do you like it so far?" He slumped back in his chair and crossed his legs, looking regal.

My pulse quickened. His presence was suffocating.

I wanted to stop the small talk, give him the name, and get on with my mission.

What the hell did I think of Electi? It was a fucking joke.

"It reminds me of Promissa before the..." I choked.

The blood froze in my veins. Fuck. How could I blurt that out?

Jordan watched me and sipped his coffee, his gaze penetrating. Silence took over the room, and we just stared at each other.

I shrank back. Sweat trickled down my back. This was it. He was going to arrest me or worse.

"Do you resent me for what happened to your city?" His tone was deadly calm.

Should I lie now or answer him truthfully? From what Davon and Matt told me and the man I'd come to know, he had a keen eye for lies. And even though we were constantly lying to his face with this mission, in this moment, I was his prey.

"I just..." My voice was thick, as something clawed at my throat. "I just had a flashback from before the wars. When the city was prosperous. My mom would show me around. That's before she got sick." My eyes misted, and I blinked.

"I asked you a question, Gaby. Do you resent me for it?" He studied me. Everything quivered inside me at his piercing stare.

I gripped my sapphire necklace, grounding myself. "I don't. Maybe before I met Davon I did, but he changed everything. When I met him, I had this idea of you being the villain, but both he and Matt gave me a chance to glimpse into your way of life. You couldn't be evil. You couldn't be because Davon was so good. He's an amazing human being. He truly cares, same as Matt. I now see what you want to build."

I was close to bursting into tears.

He leaned forward and placed his mug next to my glass, then clasped his hands together without taking his eyes off me. "Are you scared of me?"

A tear slipped from my eye, then another. My heart was close to breaking out of my chest.

He sat beside me, then took my hands in his. His touch was gentle, fatherly. "You don't need to fear me. I understand how you feel. And I'm glad you finally see what we're trying to do here. It's for the good of the citizens. They must be proud of their role in all this. We'll make a new country, one where the citizens will have the advantage. One no one would dare to attack."

He took a handkerchief from the inside pocket of his suit and dried my tears. "I'm glad my son found you. I want you to see me as family."

His eyes were true. His words were heartfelt. This man was a contradiction. I couldn't believe Davon came to be the man he was. With a father like Jordan, it was easy to lose oneself in his lies.

"So your text this morning said you had some intel for me." He took back his mug and leaned back, facing me.

I drank some water and let it ease my dry throat, then put it back and got my computer. I turned it on and looked for the file I'd created on Thomas.

Jordan came closer to look at the screen. "What are we seeing?"

I peeked at him. He had one eyebrow raised in question, his eyes darting across the codes that filled the screen.

"I found this yesterday." I clicked, and a picture of a man in his forties popped up. He was bald with gentle brown eyes. I cleared my throat. "This is Thomas Phillips. He's a rebel spy who works at the Central Train Station."

Jordan widened his eyes and took the computer to his lap. He looked at me, and his lips twitched. "You did it. I didn't doubt your skills, but this..." He shook his head. "I'm impressed.

All these years, and all we needed was one of their computers. Did it take long to break through their security?"

"It was hard, but I pushed through. If I had access to a more efficient system and a better bandwidth, I might have gotten it faster." I threw the bait.

Hopefully, he'd make up his own mind about it.

Jordan nodded. "I might be able to work with that."

He took out his phone and dialed. "Hey, Davon." After a pause, he looked at me. "Yeah, she's sitting right next to me. Call the Central Train Station at Promissa. There's a man there. Give me a second." Jordan snapped a picture of the screen. "I just sent you a pic."

"Tell them to arrest him. He's a spy. I want you to start with him today. Getting these rebels is a priority. You know what you must do."

I shuddered at his sneer. Malice permeated every word he uttered. It spread over the room like poison.

He hung up and gave the computer back to me. "Can you get me more names?"

I forced myself to sit still and held his stare. I smirked. "I sure can."

After we had lunch, Bayat came to take me back home.

As I left the lobby, I released a pent-up breath.

"Abi?" a man said.

I stopped in my tracks. My heart lurched into my throat. He used my real name.

Bayat brushed her fingers over her gun.

I stood still for a second before I slightly shook my head, hoping to hell he'd get the message. I never thought of him as someone who hated me. He was just absent. Not interested.

And for the love of God, at this moment, I prayed he was a good man and wouldn't rat me out.

I tilted my head. "I think you've mistaken me for someone else."

Uncle Scott took a step forward. His immaculate white uniform showed his rank as lieutenant of the NWG forces. His dark and gentle features reminded me so much of my father. His tender gaze showed me he cared.

He looked at Bayat, then at me, and bowed. "I'm sorry for troubling you. I was mistaken. You remind me of my niece. I haven't seen her in years."

I pushed back my shoulders. "What's your name, soldier?"

He approached me, and Bayat opened her holster.

I grabbed her shoulder. "At ease. Please let me talk to him, I just want to see if I can help him find this person."

He stretched out his hand. "Lieutenant Scott Davis, at your service."

I shook his hand. In all our years of living together, we never held hands. It was surreal. "Gabrielle Jones."

"An elite?"

I smiled. "You could say I'm an adopted elite. I came into the city with my boyfriend. And you?"

"Born and raised in Promissa." There was a glint in his eyes.

Did he suspect I was a spy? And if he did, would he turn me in?

My hands shook, so I pocketed them.

Something inside told me I could trust him, so I went with my instincts. "Do you live here?"

"I used to live in a neighborhood not far from here until three years ago. I moved after a difficult divorce." He pointed back with his thumb. "Now I live in the military housing project west of here."

Divorce? He left Aunt Annie?

The load that pressed me down lightened a bit. If he left her, maybe he was on our side all along. That woman was a vile creature.

"I'm good at finding people. Are you searching for your niece?"

He cocked his head. "I've been looking for her for the past three years." He squeezed his eyes shut. When he opened them, pain etched his features. "I never got to tell her how much I loved her and how proud she made me. Maybe one day she'll know hers was also my fight. Maybe when I meet her again, we will find the peace we longed for."

My eyes watered at his revelation. Our fight.

Could he possibly be an ally to our cause?

I needed to find out. "Do you mind if we share our contact info? Maybe I can help you find her."

"Miss Jones," Bayat said. "With all due respect, I advise against this."

I turned toward her. "And I choose to do so. If I'm capable of helping someone, I'll do whatever I can."

Her eyes flashed for a moment, then she nodded.

I took out my phone. "Mr. Davis?"

He grabbed a notebook from his side pocket.

"Don't you have a cell phone?"

I didn't know if the military that lived in the housing units were given the privilege, but I hoped so.

"No, but I do have a government-assigned email."

I had an email also, but everything was monitored, so we had to be careful.

An IT guy just gave me one so I could enter the web through the government domain. I needed to talk to Lavigne about this and maybe get in touch with Joe. He might be able to help me evade the security.

If what Uncle Scott said was true, he was with us, not against us.

Davon suspected many NWG soldiers opposed the regime. I had seen it with my own eyes when that soldier saved Paul.

If we could get them to leave their ranks and join us, it would be a game changer.

He jotted down his email, taking a bit longer than expected, then broke the page and folded the paper. He gave it to me.

"Thank you for this, Miss Jones. It means a lot to me." His eyes said more than his words.

I nodded and smiled. "I'm glad to be of help."

Bayat and I stepped into the sedan, and I opened the note. *Tell my niece if you find her, there's much to talk about. Lt. Scott Davis.*

My heart swelled. He was with us.

I made my way back to Electi but with renewed hope.

Matt texted me on my way home. He said to come by his apartment for some coffee. My knee was restless as I waited for the train to arrive.

Half an hour later, I reached his apartment.

I knocked on the door, and he opened it. His smile spoke volumes, his eyes glinting with hope.

He pulled me into a hug. "Abi, they're with us."

A spark kindled.

I withdrew and studied him. "For real?"

He chuckled. "For real."

We laughed together at the news. The Promissa rebel faction would fight with us.

"Tell me everything." I sat on his love seat, feet up on his ottoman, drinking a strong coffee. He sure knew how I liked it.

Matt settled next to me, his legs crossed over the sofa. "Their leader is a tall, slim fellow in his thirties. He's a true mastermind with cells all over the city, each with a ranking superior who answers to him."

"That's huge. This means they're not just some rebels causing havoc around the city. They're organized." Adrenaline pumped through me. "And what's their goal, other than to destroy the regime?"

Matt's emerald eyes glowed with excitement. "To revitalize the city. To give hope to those far down the ladder. They live in buildings you'd think are abandoned and meet in the underground to gather for their cause. They steal from the facilities, and even though many have been caught doing so, they keep going. They're fearless."

I remembered my three years outside and how difficult it was to move around without being detected. "But how do they do this with all the patrols swarming those areas?"

Matt sneered. "Oh, that's where he surprised me the most. Soldiers."

My mouth dropped. "What?"

He nodded. "Just what I said. NWG soldiers are covering for them."

I put my coffee down and faced him fully, then grabbed his arm. "How many?"

He jutted his chin. "More than enough."

I jumped in place. "Do you know what this means?"

Matt laughed and pulled me to him. "We have a chance to win this shit!"

We were like children, laughing without a care. We calmed down after a moment.

My heart was still going over a hundred miles an hour. "So it's true."

"What is?"

"I just met my uncle near the government center."

Matt shifted in his seat and leaned closer. "Your uncle? You saw him?"

I took his hands. "Matt, he protected my cover. He hinted at him fighting with me."

He narrowed his gaze. "But he's a lieutenant, right?"

"He is."

"And you're sure he's with us?"

I nodded excitedly. "Positive."

He laughed almost maniacally. "This is very good news indeed."

If we planned it right, we would have a fighting chance. I couldn't wait to tell Davon about it. He was going to pass out after hearing all this.

I thought back to the bunker, and hope blossomed in my soul. We could make it. I imagined David's face when he found out about it through one of Connor's communications. Maria's relentless training as she prepared soldiers to take over the city with renewed courage. Jimmy's gentle smile and Mark's quirky comments as they celebrated with a couple of David's home-brewed beers.

My whole body vibrated with glee. We could win.

March 12, 2214

T his was already my second month in Electi, and the mission was taking a toll on me. I slept less with each passing day, my mind too riled up to rest. Every day we had a new problem to solve, an elite to visit, a spy to activate. The days had gone by so fast.

Lavigne finished my training, and Joe created an end-to-end encrypted email so that only my uncle could read my message. Afterward, it would be deleted automatically. I wrote to him only once, telling him I couldn't find his niece, with an encrypted message hidden within from Davon. It asked for their support when the time came. Nothing accurate in case he got caught or someone in his ranks was a spy.

We got a response almost immediately.

Miss Jones,

Thank you for taking the time to search for my niece. Please let me know if you need help with anything. No matter the time or place.

Lieutenant Davis

Davon's soft caress pulled me out of my thoughts. I missed waking up like this.

"Stop overthinking, baby," Davon whispered in my ear.

My back rested against his chest. He softly brushed my side, slowly moving between my legs.

I gasped.

"Let's forget about everything, at least for now." He moved his fingers languidly toward my core, then pressed them against me.

I opened to him.

His sexy chuckle reverberated down my body. "That's more like it."

A moan escaped me when he softly touched my sensitive spot.

Ever so slowly, he pushed a finger inside of me.

I arched up and angled toward him.

He took my breast into his mouth.

"Davon!" I yelled in ecstasy.

His mouth and hands drowned me in pleasure.

I reached between his legs and stroked him.

His tongue was merciless against my breast as his fingers reached that special place.

My breaths came hard but shallow. It was too much. Too intense. Everything burst inside of me, and stars filled my vision at the force of it. I brought my legs together as he pushed me to the edge of my sanity and everything shattered around me. I screamed his name, and he kissed me, swallowing my words.

"Please." I needed more.

He kissed my neck and nipped at my shoulders, sending ripples of pleasure down my spine. Then he moved against my back, gripped my hips, and slid inside me.

My body responded to his hard thrusts, curving against him, taking him even deeper.

His strong arms held me flush against him, holding me captive as I succumbed to the pleasure only he could give me.

He slid out of me and moved me on top.

I straddled him, clasped his shoulders, and took him in.

He caressed my breast and down to my hip, and we fell into rhythm. It was pure bliss. His dark eyes were on me, pushing me to take control.

I leaned forward to grab the headboard and moved as he took my breasts with his hands, then into his mouth.

He latched onto me, and my pleasure climbed and climbed. He thrust against me once. Twice. His grunt as he pushed up for the third time was raw. Powerful.

I let myself fall with him. My whole body quivered with pleasure as his muscles bunched up beneath me and he pulled me against him as he came undone.

Spent, I lay on top of him, with him still pulsing inside me.

He kissed me deeply, thoroughly. Until the need for air made us stop.

I laughed and cupped his smiling face. "You sure have a way to make me forget about everything."

"Same goes for you." He tucked a loose curl behind my ear. "I love you, baby."

I kissed him softly, then whispered in his ear, "I love you too."

After twenty minutes of gentle caresses and giggles, it was time to face the day, and, unfortunately, it was one we were dreading.

Davon buttoned up his black shirt and pushed it inside his jeans. I fixed my royal-blue sleeveless top over my ripped jeans and pulled on my black leather jacket, one identical to the one Davon had back at the peak.

He got it for me a week ago when I glimpsed it at a storefront.

Davon walked to the door and pulled on his black knee-length overcoat. He looked so hot in it that all I wanted was to take it off him and resume our earlier activities.

He furrowed his brow, then gave me a roguish smile. "I know that expression."

He put his arms around me below my leather jacket, skimming up my shirt.

I pushed against his chest, intending to move him away, but he wouldn't budge.

He took my chin and angled my head toward him, then traced my lips with his until I was the one to pull him by the nape and deepen it.

His musky scent, like leather, mixed with the honeyed taste of his kiss as our tongues met. He moaned into me and pressed me against him.

He kissed my cheek, then the top of my head and took a deep breath. "God, I love you. I wish we could just run away from here and forget about everything."

I leaned against his chest, embracing him below his coat. "But we can't. And we won't."

He humphed.

"We should leave." His words carried a solemn tone.

Neither of us wanted to go to today's meeting.

Davon had carried out his job, torturing Thomas to the brink of death, but he still wouldn't talk. Now it was Joanne's turn. And we already knew she'd die before talking.

O'Hare drove us to Davon's childhood home.

Once inside, the butler led us to Jordan's study.

Jordan sat behind his desk, going through some paperwork. The top buttons of his shirt were loosened and his hair disheveled.

"Father? Is everything okay?" Davon held my hand, brushing his thumb inside my palm.

Jordan's gaze swept over us, and he closed a file. He fixed his shirt and combed his hair back. Stubble covered the lower part of his face, just like Davon's, which was unusual for him.

"Yeah. I'm sorry. I lost track of time." He gestured for us to sit.

Could this be about the threat from the north?

Connor still hadn't heard back from the group that left a month ago. What if something happened? I tried to keep a positive attitude about it, but we didn't really know if the Liberty Enclave would receive us. We only hoped they would.

My mouth went dry. I cleared my throat.

Davon went to the bar and brought me some water, then we sat.

"I hope you're here to give me another name." Jordan rounded the desk and leaned on it, facing us. "Mr. Phillips kept his mouth shut, and we need this intel. It's crucial for us to find this rebel group. We seem to be going in circles."

I drank some water, then opened my computer. "It's difficult with my lack of resources, Jordan, but I found one name. I'm sure I could do better with a faster system. Who knows how many are already inside the government?"

Davon stooped forward. "Father, with access to the government's system, Gaby might be able to uncover more spies. She's been working non-stop at home and only found this one."

He nodded. "Who?"

I walked over to him and showed him the screen. Peppered black hair reached her shoulders. Joanne smiled as she talked to a worker, pointing toward a machine.

I steeled my nerves. "Her name is Joanne Gray. She's part of the administration inside the food storage facility in Promissa."

"Maybe she's the one who has been aiding them." He looked at Davon. "Do you remember the group we talked about a couple of years ago? The one that gave food to the people in the city without our permission."

Davon nodded.

Jordan breathed heavily. "They've continued their activities. We've been searching for someone inside the food facility for some time."

He darted his eyes between us, then murmured something.

I clenched my hands inside my jacket and glanced at Davon.

He shook his head.

I closed the computer. "Sorry, Jordan, I didn't catch that."

"I'll give you access to an office inside the government center. But only two days a week."

I exhaled. "Thank you." I sat by Davon.

Jordan took his seat behind the desk. "Know that you'll be under constant supervision. It's not that I don't trust you. It's protocol."

"I understand," I said.

I hoped to hell Joe's program would run unnoticed because as it was, a minor slip was all Jordan needed. A war raged inside of me between the urge to hole myself up and never come out and the desire to fight against this man and all he represented.

"Now that it's all settled, I need to speak to my son in private. Rebecca should be waiting for you in the library. She wanted to show you some books." He raised one eyebrow. "Romance novels she thought might interest you."

My skin warmed. Rebecca loved romance novels. She'd shown me a few. They were not vanilla.

Jordan's lips curved up. "Well, Gabrielle, I never thought I'd see that color on you."

"I'm..." I stood, and Davon followed suit. "I'll just go."

"Don't be ashamed, dear. Now, go ahead. We'll meet you at lunch," Jordan said.

I moved to the door and opened it.

Davon blocked me from Jordan and caught one of my curls between his fingers. "See you later."

I closed my eyes and leaned into his touch. "See you."

Davon turned away and shut the door behind him.

After lunch, we went home to fix dinner.

In the car, Davon held my hand and squeezed it while looking out into the city. Ever since he came back from the study, he'd been too quiet.

"What happened after I left? I thought you'd be happy now that we have access to the system. We'll surely find the spies."

He played with my fingers. "It's over."

I turned to him. "What?"

What the hell did he mean?

I brought his eyes to mine. "Tell me."

His sure gaze was now lost, his skin pale.

He rubbed his brow furiously, then closed a fist over his chin. "He ordered me to kill Thomas and to do the same to Joanne if she doesn't talk." His eyes were sunken in, filled with unshed tears.

I grabbed him by the nape and brought him to my shoulder.

He sobbed, then put his arms around me and took a deep, shuddering breath. "That's not all."

I jerked back.

He shook his head and grimaced. "He's bringing over part of Halcyon's forces into Promissa. He believes something's brewing, and he won't risk it. He says the Liberty Enclave troops might be planning to attack both Halcyon and Promissa, and he needs to protect both cities."

I struggled to breathe. "Do these troops include the enhanced soldiers?"

He closed his eyes. "They do."

"How many?" My voice was small.

Did I want an answer?

He opened his bloodshot eyes. "At least a thousand."

My heart lurched. One thousand enhanced humans. How could we fight that?

I zoned out. There had to be a way. "We can still do it."

He furrowed his brow. "Abi..."

"We can!"

Davon reached for me. "Abi, be realistic. How can we possibly beat them?"

I shifted, putting some space between us. "Please, Davon. Let's wait for Connor's envoy before giving up. If the Liberty Enclave is willing to join us, we might have a fighting chance. And our scientists can work on better weapons, ones that we could use against them. Matt can find a way to get the files on these soldiers, and we can see what they can do. Learn their weakness."

"Weakness?" Davon sighed. "We're talking about enhanced humans here. Ones that do not fear death. How can we fight against that?"

I put my hands over his heart. "By not fearing death either. By not giving up."

March 15, 2214

"Here we are," Jordan announced as we stepped into the enclosed semi-circular cubicle I'd be working from.

This was my first day at the government center, and he personally gave me a tour of the building.

Every step I took was guarded. Every phrase thoroughly scrutinized. I couldn't make a mistake now, not when we were so close to getting what we wanted.

With only two days a week to connect to the main server, I had to make the most of it and get Joe's program up and running. We needed that list.

I'd never met Joe personally, but we talked through a secure line over the phone. He explained how everything functioned and how the program would stay hidden in the hard drive while I worked on what Lavigne had taught me this last month. The program was disguised as antivirus hardware and was undetectable.

I hoped it worked because at this very moment, they were checking my computer. Jordan had accepted that I worked with my own computer, the one I told him I'd stolen. I convinced him I was decrypting the data they left.

We'd left some encrypted files that, if found, would hint to them as to how I was obtaining my intel, but their decryption would only link to empty records.

I wiped my clammy hands over my black slacks and looked at my watch again. They'd been checking it for an hour.

"They'll be done with your computer in a moment. We just want to make sure it's clean of any viruses or unwanted hackers. I also want to recheck if we can find any way of accessing their system from it." He clasped my shoulder. "Again, it's not that I don't trust you, but my IT team can be more thorough. I hope you understand."

I suppressed a shiver at the contact. After all he'd done, his sole presence induced a panic in me.

Two days ago, Davon suffocated Thomas using a bag, per Jordan's request. Then as if nothing had happened, Jordan invited himself to dinner at our place.

That night goosebumps rose on my skin after Jordan hugged me goodbye. Then I ran to the bathroom and threw up.

Matt and Davon insisted I should take the anxiety meds Matt prescribed at the peak, but I didn't want to. I'd deal with it on my own.

After everyone left, Davon showered for hours and never came to bed. I found him in the morning, watching the sunrise, and sat with him. No words were shared. We just sat there together.

"Gaby? Are you okay?" Jordan stood in front of me. His eyebrows were drawn together.

I blinked. "I am. Sorry. I'm tired. You were saying?"

"I was telling you about the IT team checking the computer."

"Oh. Yes. The more eyes, the better. I hope they can be of help." I crossed my fingers in my mind. "The data is encrypted, but I'm working on it. That's how I found the first two spies, but they're using advanced software. They must have engineers on their side."

Jordan folded his arms across his chest. "I think so too. To hide and be able to maintain a community outside our grid is commendable. I just hope we can get them alive. I bet we can learn from them, maybe even use them to our advantage."

My skin crawled at his comment. Use us? I bet they would. Just like they did to all those poor souls they had trapped in those facilities.

"Chairman Niles, it's clean."

I breathed out as a woman handed my computer to Jordan.

He put it on my desk. "There you go. Will you be starting today?"

I sat and connected my computer. "I will. Thank you."

He smiled and left the cubicle. "Perfect. I'll be in my office if you need anything. I do hope we can find more rebels this way. Maybe even their location. I don't know what's up with my spies, but they're MIA."

I softened my features when all I wanted was to ask him about the spies. "I hope they're okay. The security within the rebel cells is strong."

Jordan dismissed my comment with a wave of his hand. "My spies are the best. I'm sure they're okay."

I nodded. "Let's hope so."

I worked for six hours on what Lavigne had taught me. Just codes and search engines that wouldn't come up with anything. I just needed to appear to be working and let the program run its course.

I went home, and we all had a silent dinner together. After we found out that the Halcyon forces were coming into Promissa and about Davon's having to kill one of our people, a sense of gloom grew within our group. We needed to move forward, but how? How did you find light in all this darkness?

March 26, 2214

Today was Matt's twenty-ninth birthday, and everyone was invited. This was the first time that Jordan, Rebecca, Lisa, and Frank would all come together for dinner.

Someone knocked.

When I opened the door, Matt waited with a beaming smile. He gave me a bowl. "I brought bean salad. Mom and Dad love it." He walked over to the kitchen counter and took three bottles of wine from the bag he held.

"So how does it feel being twenty-nine?" I asked.

Matt smirked. "Amazing. Seven months of being able to rub in Davon's face that I'm older and wiser than him is truly precious."

I giggled.

Davon rolled his eyes and threw a piece of potato at Matt.

Matt barely evaded it. "I rest my case."

Davon chuckled and hugged him. "Happy birthday, man."

Matt patted his shoulder. "Thanks for this. I'm not that excited about your father being part of the guest list, but thanks." He sobered a bit. "It would be perfect if Aoki was here."

This was not the first time they were apart, but the stakes were higher than last time.

"Soon we'll be back, and you'll be able to see him." The truth in Davon's words was palpable.

Matt eyed us. "I'm counting the days. I don't think I can handle working with Dad much longer."

Davon continued cutting the potatoes. "Is the Prometheus Project progressing?"

"Sadly, yes. We already brought in the women from the prison."

I gripped his shoulder. "Did they all make it?"

Matt shook his head. "Only six. The other three died. Two from preeclampsia and one from kidney failure due to malnourishment."

Nausea churned in my gut, and I closed my eyes. "I need a moment."

I ran to the bedroom. *Breathe.*

Just today, I received a letter from Deb. I didn't know why it took her so long to write, but Connor kept asking us to give her time to heal.

I sat on the bed and opened the bedside table. I unfolded the letter.

Abi,

I miss you. I wish I could see you.

I'm sorry I've taken this long to write, but I've been dealing with a lot. I'm trying to make peace with you and Davon being together. My mind is all jumbled, and I've been in therapy since I came back. I can't see Davon, not yet. I'm so sorry. I know he helped me escape and that he was my friend, but it's hard to reconcile that with what happened in that room.

As for the pregnancy, I'm due in a month or so, according to Dr. Lewis. I'm weak but keeping strong. I couldn't get rid of him. He's innocent of whatever that monster has done. I'll make sure this baby knows the truth when he grows up. Connor has accepted him and is helping me with the process.

I'm writing to ask you to please come back. I can't trust your safety with Davon. I need to see you. To have you with me. Sarah also misses you.

Please consider it.

Love always,

Deb

There were smudges across some lines. She had been crying.

I hugged the letter and prayed for her health. I didn't know what I'd do if I lost her.

Davon said Connor told everyone at the PRF about the genome projects the NWG was running. He couldn't hide Deb's pregnancy anymore.

When Connor showed them the files and explained what they did to Deb, they wanted to take revenge. He convinced them we needed more time.

There was a knock.

I looked up to find Davon by the door.

He sat next to me. "Are you better?"

I nodded, unable to form words.

He put an arm around me and pulled me to his shoulder. "She'll be all right. Deb's getting all the help she needs."

"I know. It's just...I miss her so much. She's hurting, and I just want to go over there and be with her." I kissed his hand, taking in the comfort of his scent.

He kissed the top of my head and nestled his chin over it. "We need to believe that soon we'll be with them again. We can't let this darkness pull us in, love."

Matt came in and crouched in front of us. "What Davon says is true. We need to keep strong for our loved ones."

I put the letter away and grabbed his hand. "This is crazy. How can the thirst for power make you do something like this?"

Matt grimaced. "I ask myself the same question every single day. I don't know when my father lost his empathy. His ethics. Sometimes I wonder if he does it out of fear."

The same thought had entered my mind many times. I couldn't see Frank being so evil. We continued meeting for drinks over these past months, and everything in me told me his heart was in the right place. It was as if what he said was the opposite of what he intended.

"I've suspected the same, but I can't be sure," Davon said. "Father has a way of coaxing people to do his bidding."

A soft knock on the front door announced someone's arrival.

Matt stood. "Take your time."

I straightened. "It's okay. I don't want to spoil your birthday. Let's have some fun."

After Davon made sure who was at the door, Matt went to open it.

Frank and Lisa stood on the threshold. Frank snaked his arm around Lisa's waist, holding her flush against him as they walked in.

Lisa glowed in a yellow minidress. Frank wore khaki slacks and a white button-down shirt.

We all eyed them suspiciously, at the closeness between them.

Matt narrowed his eyes. "Mom. Dad. What's this?"

Lisa embraced Matt. "Happy birthday, son. It's been years since we last celebrated your birthday together."

Frank pulled him into a hug. "Five years to be exact."

Matt took a step back and gestured toward them. "What's going on?"

Frank wrapped his arm around Lisa's shoulder. "Son, we decided to get back together. You know we never stopped loving each other. We want to give us another try."

My heart was lit by his words. Was this for real?

"When did this happen?" Matt asked.

Lisa sighed. "It's been happening for a while now, but this year we decided to risk it."

Matt took both their hands. "I understand. But what about Jordan?"

Frank winked. "We're keeping it a secret for now."

Frank turned to Davon. "If you can give us some time, we'll eventually tell them. With all that's happening right now, we don't want your father to know. Can we trust you to keep this secret for us? Lisa assured me we could do so. Lavigne too."

Davon frowned but nodded. "Sure, just make sure you tell them when the time comes. Everyone deserves happiness, and I'm glad for you both."

Lisa's eyes sparkled as Frank sighed. "I told you he'd understand." She squeezed Matt's hand.

Matt grinned. "I'm glad you finally got back together. I always knew you still loved each other. As Davon says, everyone deserves happiness."

"Thanks, Matt." Lisa embraced him.

Frank stayed frozen in place, but Lisa pulled him over.

I opened a bottle of wine and served five glasses. "To love."

"To love," they all said.

We sat on the sectional sofa, waiting for Jordan and Rebecca. They were bringing the cake, so it took longer for them to arrive.

Davon's phone vibrated. "They're coming up. Mom needs help with the cake."

He went to the hall and waited for them.

Frank and Lisa put some distance between them.

"Thanks, Davon. You're a lifesaver." Rebecca's melodic voice rang through the hall before she entered the apartment.

Davon carried in a huge cream-colored cake adorned with black borders and white candy pearls on top.

Rebecca rushed inside, followed by Jordan, who held a bag with both hands.

Lisa embraced Rebecca, and Frank kissed her hand, as was his usual way of saying hello.

Jordan put the bag on the table, then hugged Davon. He came toward me and hugged me too. I gasped silently and clenched my fists by my sides, managing to keep breathing. Davon's presence at my side kept me strong.

Jordan shook Frank's hand and approached Lisa with a tight smile, then shook her hand also.

Davon pulled me to the kitchen.

Rebecca followed behind. "Everything okay?"

I turned. My hands trembled, and she took them in hers.

Davon nodded, then went to check what Jordan had brought.

Rebecca looked toward Jordan, who laughed at something Frank said. She blocked the view. "You need to calm down. He notices everything." She fixed a strand of hair behind my ear. "If he asks, I'll tell him it's woman stuff. He won't insist." She winked.

Davon came to my side, and she held both our hands. "I love you both so much."

He scrunched his forehead. "Mom?"

"I'm all right." She cupped his cheek. "Just happy to be here."

He kissed her hand. "I love you too, Mom."

She nodded.

"Rebecca!" Jordan said. "Come see this."

She stiffened, but she placed a smile on her face and turned. "Coming, love."

I looked up at Davon, whose gaze followed his mom. "Do you think she's all right?"

His Adam's apple bobbed as he stared. "I hope so, for Father's sake."

"Do you need a break?"

He shook his head slightly. "Nah. It's okay. I'll go ahead and set the dining table so we can get on with this."

I gave him a peck on the lips. "I'll go with you."

After an uneventful dinner, we sang "Happy Birthday" and cut the cake. I hadn't had any since the night of my birthday when Richard was murdered, a night I'd never forget. I'd sometimes wake up to the sirens, covered in sweat, crying in Davon's arms.

Rebecca and Jordan gifted Matt a crystal whiskey decanter with two glasses and four granite whiskey stones. It was beautiful.

As for Lisa and Frank, they gave him a silver watch embedded with diamonds in an obsidian panel. It was a piece of art.

Davon and I gave him our gift. His eyes glazed over as he took the silver necklace. It had a yin-yang pendant, with an "M" and an "A" engraved on the back inside of an infinity symbol.

His eyes darted across the room. "Thanks. I'm glad you took a moment to be with me today. I hope we can do this again in the future."

Davon's fingers twitched against my palm, and I clasped them.

I had a hunch this would be the last time we came together as a family, and it broke my heart. Not for Jordan but for Lisa and Frank, who'd become my friends, and for Rebecca, who was like a mother to me.

My hope crumbled in the face of what lay before us—war. How could we protect them when it broke out? How could we be sure they'd survive?

Chapter 34

Davon

April 6, 2214

Red water ran down the white porcelain sink drain as I frantically scrubbed the residue from the last two hours of work. The remnants from what I'd done to Joanne.

Today, I cut off two of her fingers, and after her agonizing screams ended, she talked.

She ratted out the rebel faction, but the names weren't real ones. She just wanted a reprieve.

I went into my office and closed the door behind me, then rubbed my eyes and walked toward the bureau.

Davon,

The spies are acting at last. Our systems have been glitching since yesterday. Please let us know if you've found anything.

Everything's safe. Just a week ago, Nina moved all our data to the import bunker, and another copy was sent to the caves. She thinks it must be someone under her, but they're covering their tracks.

Here's a list of all the people working with Nina right now.

Be careful out there.

—Connor

My hands shook as I read the list. Twenty names were written on the note. The emergency must have allowed new people to work with Nina because most of them had other jobs. I knew all of them, but some caught my attention: Pedro Ibañez, Sarah Davis, Abraham Jackson, Tammy Mc-Greggor, and James Thompson. God, even Jimmy was on this list and Jacob's father. If any of them turned out to be a spy, it would be a stab in the gut.

I took out my phone and texted Lavigne.

"Peter, can we meet for drinks later?"

"Tell me where and when."

"Three at Darkest Red."

"I'll be there."

Lavigne was aiding Abi with the decryption of files, and it was going well. Yesterday, the program finally found a list of what we believed were active spies, but it was encrypted. If he compared Abi's list to Connor's, maybe he'd find the culprit.

I sat in our usual booth. The door opened, and Peter walked in.

"What will you have?" the waiter asked.

"A beer," Peter said.

"Whiskey for me," I said.

The waiter bowed and left us.

I shook his hand. "Thanks for meeting with me. How was your day?"

He took the hidden note and pocketed it. "Good. A troop finally found some of the rebels that we've been chasing for a month."

I gritted my teeth. Were they Yuxuan and his soldiers?

The waiter brought our drinks. "Drinks are on the house. It's a pleasure to serve you."

We both nodded.

"Did they get their leader?" I asked.

"It doesn't seem so. They found six soldiers. Four were killed on sight, and two are on the way in for interrogation. A team is searching for the rest."

Yuxuan was safe, and most of his patrol survived.

I closed my eyes for the lost souls.

I raised my glass. "Cheers to small victories. We'll get them eventually."

Peter clinked his beer against it. "Cheers."

I took a sip of whiskey. "What are you going to do later?"

Peter peeled off the label on his beer bottle. "I think I'll just have this beer and go home. Suzanne and I want to visit our daughter's grave. Today is the seventh anniversary of her death."

I pursed my lips. He was right—Carol had been with us for seven years. I guess they needed to visit the grave for appearances.

Peter told Suzanne about Carol a month ago. She'd been ecstatic and vowed to never tell a soul. She was a good friend of Lisa's and shared her ideals, so Peter told her about our mission, and she was aiding Lisa in recruiting elites to the cause.

"I'm sorry, my friend." I tilted my head and raised my glass again. "To family."

"To family."

We chatted for a moment, and once we finished the drinks, we said our goodbyes.

He'd get back to me if he found something. I hoped soon.

When I finally went home, I found Abi spread across the bed. It was 6:00 p.m.

She must be exhausted.

I took off my shirt and my shoes and lay beside her, holding her tight. I let myself go as her flowery aroma surrounded me. Only with her could my body and mind finally relax.

I opened my eyes to the first glimpses of daylight. Abi slept on my chest. I kissed her temple.

She moaned sleepily, then jerked awake. "Did we sleep through dinner?"

I caressed her side down to her hips. "We did."

She sat up. "Fuck. I was supposed to call Lavigne last night."

I drew circles on her back. "Just send the files over, and take a break. You've been working nonstop."

She glanced back and pouted. "But..."

I gave her a stern glare.

She huffed. "Okay." She yawned heavily.

I wanted to tell her about the spies, but she needed a break. I'd tell her later.

She walked to the bathroom. "I'm taking a shower."

"Can I come too?" I winked at her.

She gave me a once-over. "Sure, but behave."

I didn't.

An hour later, we were eating cereal for breakfast, both too exhausted to deal with cooking.

Abi opened the computer and sent the files to Lavigne.

I tapped the table, getting her attention. "Baby, I need to tell you something."

She closed the computer. "Sure. What is it?"

I rested back on my chair and rubbed my neck. "I received a letter from Connor." There was no easy way to put it. "The spies have emerged. They're messing with the system."

She put her cup down. "Do they know who they are?"

I pushed the cereal away and crossed my arms over the table. "No. Nina's trying, but it's been impossible. Connor sent me a list, and I gave it to Lavigne yesterday. He'll look into it."

"Are they people I know?" Her eyes watered but stayed focused on me.

It pained me to see her like this, but she needed to know. "They are. Many good friends. Jimmy, Sarah, Tammy, and even Abraham. They're all suspects."

"No." She shook her head. "None of them can possibly be it." She covered her face.

I brushed her elbow. "I'm sorry, love."

She took a deep breath. "We need to find out who this person is." She stood. "I should go to the government center."

I grabbed her hand. "You can't. You already used your two days."

She sat, then raked her hair back and gripped it tight. "Ugh. This is so frustrating. We can't just sit here and wait."

"We must. Lavigne has the list. Let's just hope to hell he finds something."

"I had a chat with Dad." Matt opened the bottle of wine.

We just had dinner at our place and now sat at the dining table, awaiting news from Lavigne.

"About what we talked about?" Abi asked.

The Halcyon army had arrived two weeks ago. We asked Matt to find out if they had any weaknesses, but we still didn't have an answer.

Matt served the wine and sat. "First of all, you need to understand what they did to these people. They're not only stronger than us but far surpass us in endurance, cognition, and health. Their bone density is incredible, and they've modified their genes to have faster recovery from injuries as well as a boosted immune response to infections and disease. And the genes associated with pain perception have been altered so they don't feel it."

I scowled. "How are we supposed to defeat them?"

"Good question." Matt pressed his lips together.

Abi swirled her wine. "That last part could give us an advantage. Pain is a protection response. Eventually, even if they don't feel it, injuries will take them down."

"True." I drummed my fingers on the table. "But if they can heal faster, their bodies are more resistant than ours."

Matt sipped his wine. "Both of you are correct, but there's more. I also found out they are boosting their brain to increase focus and decision-making. Psychological conditioning makes them extremely dangerous on the battlefield. They are taught to kill with no empathy. The problem is they sometimes lose control. Some have killed each other during training. Many undergo cognitive behavioral therapy to work on this issue, because as it is, most have a complete disregard for human life."

"That's some fucked-up shit." What the hell had my father created? "Do they have any weakness?"

Matt shrugged. "They're human, just like us." His lips twitched. "Sorry. I wanted to lighten the mood."

I rolled my eyes.

Matt sighed. "But for real. We need to be more aggressive and use heavy and long-range weapons. I wouldn't recommend one-on-one combat. We need a strategy."

I could work with that. "Have you seen them in action?"

Matt nodded. "We watched them train this morning. They use heavy armor, but there are weak points we can attack. The neck and the sides being the most obvious."

Abi leaned forward. "So bullets, arrows, throwing knives, sniper rifles. They can all reach them without getting too close."

My mind went through all I had learned about war strategies. There was a chance if we planned it right. I remembered some of the NWG tactics I'd learned during training. "How about bombs? Not only heavy bombs but gas grenades, maybe even ones carrying a paralyzing agent."

Matt sat back. "That would work. If we stop them for a time, it will give us an advantage. I'm quite sure bombs will take them down, but they brought thousands. Many will push through in battle."

Abi stared at me. Her eyes were huge. "But won't our soldiers be at risk?"

"Not if they're prepared," Matt said. "We need to talk to our engineers and get masks designed to go with our battle gear. They've been working on a better armor for the last year, so at least we have that covered."

I grabbed my wine. Its rich and fruity flavor soothed the sourness in my mouth. "I'll contact Connor ASAP. We need to start working on this, even more now that the spies are starting to stir up trouble."

Abi rolled her shoulders back, cracking her neck from side to side. "This is hoping the NWG hasn't thought about the possibility of being attacked in this way. What if they already have this gear available?"

I massaged her neck. "They may, but we just need to catch them off guard. Maybe they won't expect this kind of attack from us."

Father was full of himself. I was sure he underestimated the rebels, more so after the energy bunker attack.

"There's something else," Matt said, catching us by surprise. "To maintain their strength, health, and endurance, these soldiers are subjected to heavy supplements and 'medications.'" Matt made quotes with his fingers.

I frowned. "What do you mean?"

"Their metabolism is so fast that their bodies demand three to four times the amount of nutrients ours do. To support their heightened activity levels and enhanced recovery, they need a tailored supplement regime."

"What does this mean for us?" I asked.

Matt's eyes gleamed. "That if we could somehow block them from getting these supplements, we may be able to slow them down."

I jerked my head back. "That might work. If we find the location of the labs where they create these supplements, we could target them and cut their supplies. We need to find that intel."

Matt finished his wine and set the glass down. "I'll look into it. I wish there was more I could do."

I covered his hand. "You've done more than enough, brother."

After a few minutes, Abi rose and paced behind me. "Isn't Lavigne supposed to be done by now?"

Lavigne responded to us almost immediately after Abi sent him the files. We were waiting for him to decrypt it and compare it to the names and descriptions that Connor sent in his letter.

"Give him time. You know how hard decrypting the code can be." I took the empty glasses to the kitchen.

A hard knock resounded across the apartment, and we all stood at attention.

Being closer to the kitchen, I walked to the door. I jumped back as another harder knock shook it.

I opened it.

Lavigne wore a hoodie that hid his face. He darted his gaze wildly across the apartment and came inside, eyes bulging. "Good. You're all here. You need to go now. All I could buy you were ten minutes."

Ten minutes? What the hell was he talking about?

I looked at Abi, who stood frozen in place.

Matt rushed toward Peter. "What do you mean?"

Peter took a deep breath. "Go get your things. You need to leave Electi."

We all stared at him, dumbfounded.

"Do it! Now!" His scream woke us.

Abi and I ran to the bedroom, while Matt left for his apartment.

We didn't ask any questions. We didn't even speak. We just followed orders from the man who had become like a father to us out here. The least expected hero of the PRF.

"What's happening?" Abi's eyes were wild as she grabbed what she could and shoved it inside her rucksack.

My pulse thundered in my ears. It was almost deafening. "The only thing I can think of is that Father knows about us." I closed my pack and put my combat boots on.

I was almost done when Abi went to the dining room to get her laptop.

"Leave it!" Peter yelled.

Abi stopped mid-step. "But the files!"

Peter shook his head and passed her a pen drive. "Here's everything we've worked on. It's untraceable. The computer, on the other hand, has a trace on it."

She swayed in place.

I caught her arm. "I don't understand, Peter. Please tell us what happened."

Peter glanced at his watch. "I was decrypting Abi's files and comparing them to the list you gave me when an urgent message arrived through the government portal. I intercepted it before it was thrown into quarantine, which usually takes around fifteen minutes to clear out. The message came from outside our grid. It's from Leslie Gibson. I came as fast as I could."

"Leslie?" Time stood still for a moment before I connected the dots.

"Who's Leslie?" Abi grabbed my shoulders.

She'd changed her appearance, but I knew I'd recognized her from somewhere. The red hair. The glasses. The innocence she portrayed. Her nose that was always buried behind a book.

But those blue eyes. Those blue eyes were the same calculating ones from the day she hijacked the government system.

My nostrils flared, and I tightened my fists at my sides. The pressure crushed against my skull. She was a genius, a mastermind. And she fooled us all.

How could I be so stupid?

I shook my head. "I'm sorry, Abi. I should have known before. And now it's too late."

She grabbed my wrist. "Just tell me."

This would break Abi's heart, especially since they'd grown closer during the time we were apart. Hell, she even designed the PRF symbol.

We only saw Maria's happiness and were blind to it all.

"Tammy. Tammy's a spy," I said at last.

Abi's gaze grew glassy, and for an instant, I thought she'd lose it.

I stepped into her, but she put space between us and rolled her shoulders back. "I'm okay." She looked at Peter. "What did the message say?"

"She identified Davon as general of the People's Revolutionary Front, second in command after General Connor Harris. She also mentioned Matt and you, Abi. She included the coordinates to your main bunker."

A massive weight pressed against my chest to the point of pain. My breath caught, and I widened my eyes. The peak was in danger.

"We need to run!" Abi dashed into the kitchen.

"Fuck!" I bit my lip and rushed after her.

Abi filled our canteens, half the water spilling onto the floor. Her whole body trembled.

I hurried to the security box and took out our weapons. Abi was right behind me. She put the canteen on my pack, then started arranging her weapons on her.

"Are you coming?" I asked Peter.

He shook his head. "I'll go with you until I know you can make it out of the city safely, but I must stay. They should already be looking for me. I took Suzanne to Lisa's place and left my phone there before coming here. They'll cover for me, but I need to be back ASAP to respond to your father and get the troops there. I fear he'll send in the Halcyon troops."

A chill ran down my spine. We'd never get there in time.

Lavigne gripped my arm. "Please protect my daughter and her family. I'd never forgive myself if something happened to them. I already spoke to those under me who are opposed to your father's rule. We'll back you up when the time comes. I just hope what we've done is enough."

I clasped his shoulder. "I will protect Carol and her family. I promise. Thank you. You've done so much for us."

He smiled, then went to Abi, who had just put on her rucksack. "Did you get to the sleeper agents in time?"

She nodded. "I left a time drop where Davon told me."

Peter exhaled hard. "Good. If they act from within and take the minister of transportation hostage, we should be able to get inside Electi's walls when the time comes."

"There may be another way," I said, remembering the tunnels. Ones that, if real, we'd use tonight.

They both turned toward me.

Matt barged in with his rucksack. "Can someone explain what's happening?"

Abi walked to the door. I followed.

"Leave the phones," Peter said.

We threw them at the coffee table.

I ran outside. "Let's go."

Matt grabbed my arm hard. "Tell me!"

I clasped the side of his neck and pulled him to me, our brows almost touching. "They know about us. About everything. Tammy's a spy. She revealed our identities and the peak's location. We need to run."

"Aoki." Matt caught Lavigne's gaze. "Do we still have time?"

Peter shook his head and pressed the elevator call button. "I don't know."

We rushed inside.

Bayat and O'Hare came into the lobby as we stepped out of the elevator.

Matt and I took our guns out in unison and aimed at them.

"Go!" I yelled at Abi and Peter.

Abi hesitated.

I caught her gaze. "I'll be right behind you."

They ran.

Bayat's eyes darted from Abi to me. She nodded and smiled, turning her back to us, gun aimed toward the street.

The sound of sirens blasted in the distance, getting closer with each second that passed.

O'Hare stepped back. "Run!"

My hands shook.

His features softened. "We'll hold them for as long as we can." He took his pistol out and joined Bayat.

I lowered my gun, and Matt followed suit.

Would I ever be able to repay them?

My chest expanded, and I closed my eyes, praying they'd be safe, then ran toward Abi and Peter.

We exited through the back door and dashed into the alley. We didn't look back when the shots erupted and just ran.

We sprinted south of the Central Train Station until we reached the apartment complex I saw on the maps. I stopped at the service entrance. If the passage was still there, it would lead us to the tunnels.

Peter held my arm. "What are you doing?"

"Hopefully, saving our asses." I picked the lock, and the door opened.

He nodded. "Then here's where we part ways." He hugged me. "Take care, son."

I fought back tears. He'd done so much for us. For me.

He clasped my shoulder in a strong grip. "Whatever you find out there, don't give up. That's what he wants. Keep fighting. We'll see each other again on the battlefield."

My throat tightened at his promise, and I gripped his shoulder back. "We will."

He grasped Matt's arm. "Take care out there. And remember, your father will always put you first, no matter what."

Matt furrowed his brow. "I don't understand."

Peter shook his head. "Some things are not what they seem."

Matt raised his eyebrows, and a soft smile filled his face. "Dad?"

Peter smirked. "Frank's a great actor, isn't he? He's always been on your side. He's never stopped fighting for you." He passed Matt a pen drive. "Here's everything you need to know about the projects. Everything you need to take them down. He's trapped, like many of us are, but he's never given up."

Tears ran down Matt's face, and I held my own back.

Frank was always on our side.

Abi wiped her tears as Peter made his way toward her.

He held her hands. "It was a pleasure working with you. You have what it takes to take them down." He pointed his thumb back at both of us.

"And if these two give you any trouble, put them in their place. You can handle anything." He winked before turning and running away.

After a quick breath, we entered the building. Flashlights in hand, we went down one floor.

The room was full of tools and equipment.

I waved my flashlight around. "There should be a door somewhere. It leads to a tunnel system hidden beneath the city that goes all the way into Promissa and out to the forest. I found out about it some weeks ago. Look for a steel door."

We separated and looked around.

"Here!" Abi yelled.

I rushed to her. There was a workbench blocking the door. Matt and I moved it to gain access.

A rusted padlock held it closed. I grabbed a wrench from a toolbox and broke it.

Darkness swallowed us when we entered. It was freezing inside, the air stale. The sound of our hurried footsteps echoed around us and something else. Rats.

Abi ran by my side. Matt guarded behind.

We'd been running for what seemed like an hour when Abi broke the silence. "Do you have any idea where we are now?"

"We should already be beneath Promissa," I said as we crossed a third junction.

I studied the maps carefully last week. I hadn't told Connor about it because I wanted to make sure they still existed. I couldn't risk our soldiers getting trapped.

"What's the plan?" Matt's voice echoed from behind.

My flashlight went off, but I hit it against my palm, and it turned back on. "Once we reach the forest, we run north to the peak."

"Do you think they'll get there before us?" Abi's voice sounded raspy.

"I hope not." I continued running, avoiding the only truth I knew.

They'd reach it before us because, knowing my father, he'd want us to suffer a loss so we'd know what it meant to go against him.

After another hour, we reached a dead end. The tunnel was blocked with debris.

I grunted. "It should have taken us farther out, just inside the forest perimeter."

Matt tried to make way, but it was too much, and we couldn't waste any time.

If I was right, I knew why the tunnel ended here. "Matt?"

Matt continued clearing away rocks, just to find more behind. "We can do this!"

I tapped his back. "We don't have time. Let's go back."

We'd passed a door about five minutes ago. I hoped to hell it was open from the other side.

Matt looked at me, his face ashen. "Okay."

Abi pulled out a rock. "But we can clear this! I'm sure we can."

I grasped her shoulder. "We will eventually. But first, we need to get out of here, or we'll be too late."

She exhaled hard, then slumped and followed me.

After retracing our steps, we reached the door.

I pushed, and on my fourth attempt, the door budged a little.

Matt and Abi stepped in to help, and after a loud crash, the door opened farther.

I peered inside. A steel-wire shelf unit lay on the floor. "There's something blocking the door."

After a minute, we moved it enough for Abi to fit through. She pulled the shelving unit away, and we entered.

The walls were broken, debris everywhere. The place was abandoned.

Six months had passed since we'd been here, but it seemed to be much more.

Abi frowned. "Is this...?"

Matt glanced around. "We're in the western outskirts?"

I nodded. "Back to where it all began. This is why the tunnel collapsed."

"The bombings," Matt said.

I nodded. "The bombings."

Abi moved toward the exit. "Now we find a way into the forest."

After drinking water and eating a protein bar each, we took out our weapons and ventured into the city. Our shadows lurked behind us as we moved from building to building, just like last time. The only difference was we moved the other way—west.

We needed to use the only checkpoint that was never breached, checkpoint one.

The patrols we encountered rushed east.

Why weren't there more soldiers? I darted my eyes around, but all was desolate. Quiet.

My heart thundered. Something was wrong. It didn't make sense.

When we reached checkpoint one, there was no one in sight.

"This doesn't feel right." Matt paced. "The perimeter of the city should be swarming with soldiers. Unless..."

"Unless what?" Abi asked.

"Unless capturing us isn't my father's priority," I said.

My insides twisted as I realized what was happening.

He already sent the army in. Now I was sure of it. I could only pray Connor got everyone out in time.

Abi stood beside me. "What do you mean?"

All their faces flashed through my mind at once. All the people I loved were in danger. I couldn't lose them.

I clasped her hand. "We need to run. We may already be too late."

We rushed into the forest. Into darkness.

April 7, 2214

I t was still dark when a quick succession of gunfire came from the north. The roar of a fight rang in the distance.

The enemy had already invaded our home.

Every nerve in my body fired at once, sending a rush of adrenaline through me. We needed to get there. We had a mile to go by my calculations, so we continued running.

The crunch of the snow and the break of twigs up ahead meant we were getting closer.

"Weapons ready," I whispered as I spied a small NWG patrol about a hundred yards ahead.

We slowly moved past it, keeping a safe distance.

I peered back at Matt. "Scout ahead."

He nodded and disappeared into the forest.

"Stay behind me," I said to Abi.

The sun started making its way up the horizon.

I walked ahead until a rustle of leaves and a loud humph made me turn.

Abi struggled as a soldier grabbed her by the neck and put a gun against her head.

He cocked it. "If you try anything, she dies."

She tried to get him off her, but the guy wouldn't budge.

"Don't fight him," I said.

Abi stopped.

My stomach plummeted at the sheer terror in her eyes.

I dropped my gun, then put my hands up. *Where the hell are you, Matt?*

Another soldier approached. "Well, well, well. Look who we got here. Davon Niles in the flesh." His gaze moved over Abi. He wet his lips. "Oh, and the famous Miss Jones, or should I say Miss Davis?"

I hissed at him.

His eyes were sunken in, his nose crooked. But what I hated most was his fucking sneer.

I wanted to wipe it off his face.

"Oh, did I upset you?" He pouted mockingly. "You know, I was one of the first your father sent off to find you. I wish you could have seen how pissed he was after finding out his own son and his sweet Miss Jones had betrayed him." He tilted his head toward Abi. "Have you ever seen Jordan Niles pissed off? I mean *really* pissed off. I've seen him mad before, but this time it was different. Even your mother couldn't control him." He chuckled.

I clenched my fists and growled. "What did he do to her?"

He shook his head, making a tsk sound. "That's confidential information." He came up to my face.

I bared my teeth at him. If Father touched Mom, if he dared to hurt her, he was dead.

"You seem to be a little confused here. You see, I'm the one in charge here, and your little girlfriend here will be dead in a matter of seconds if you so much as flinch." He gripped my neck and squeezed. "So you'd better behave."

I swallowed hard.

I was fucking killing him.

"I can't wait to see what he has in store for you two." He turned around and rubbed his hands together. "Where's Mr. Anderson? I was hoping to get some one-on-one with him."

My muscles shook with pent-up rage. I wanted to squeeze the life out of him.

I glanced at Abi and noticed her rasping breath.

He cocked his head toward Abi, then raised an eyebrow and smirked. "Well, since he's not around, how about we start with you while your boyfriend watches?"

Her chin trembled.

"What's going on, princess? You want a piece of this?" He gripped his crotch with one hand, then grabbed her right breast with the other and squeezed hard.

Abi jerked, tears smudging the dirt on her face.

I stepped forward, my fingers itching to reach for my chaaklo and open them all up. It would be a painful, slow death.

The soldier at her back kept a strong hold.

A bark of laughter escaped their leader, and he glanced back. "What do you think, boys? Want to have some fun with this one before taking them back?"

Two other men joined him, each with a disturbing smile on their face.

I was about to lose it when Abi held my gaze and slightly shook her head. Then her fevered stare moved to him.

"Cat got your tongue?" He was in her face.

Her unblinking stare sent shivers through my spine. "You don't remember me, but I remember you. You killed an incredible man and raped my friend." Abi snarled as he came closer.

My breath caught in my throat as I realized who this man was.

A bitter taste filled my mouth at the sneer he gave her. This man deserved a painful death, and I'd make sure she was the one to give it to him.

He gripped her hair and yanked back, turning her head up so he could stare down into her eyes. "Why would I remember a thing like that? Do you have any idea how many I've killed? And why would I care for any of the princes and princesses out there? They only exist for my pleasure."

She didn't even flinch as his spit landed on her face. He forced her mouth open and kissed her hard. He winced, then licked the blood smeared over his lower lip. "You'll be sorry soon enough for your bravado."

I jumped as three shots rang through the air. Three bodies fell onto the ground.

Abi scurried over to my side. Her face was coated in blood.

Matt came out from behind a tree, his gun aimed at Jacob's killer.

The man scampered across the forest floor away from Matt. His once white uniform was now covered with the blood of his fellow soldiers. He took his pistol out, but Matt shot his hand, then his right foot.

The gun flew off as he fell and hollered in pain.

"Don't kill him!" I yelled.

Matt frowned but stopped.

Abi walked to the soldier and crouched in front of him. She unsheathed Jacob's trench knife, putting her left-hand fingers through its knuckle-duster grip. "How does it feel?" She cut a deep gash across his cheek.

He held his face. Blood poured through his fingers.

I'd never seen that wild look in her eyes before. It was as if her demons had taken control. Dark. Intense. Merciless.

If I was the one at the end of that blade, I would be shitting my pants.

My pulse quickened, and my chest expanded. She was terrifying, and I couldn't be prouder.

"How does it feel to have your life in someone else's hands?" She slashed his other cheek, then held him by the shoulder. "I watched him die after you shot him. I heard her screams as you and your minions raped her to death." She unsheathed her khukuri and slowly drove it through his stomach.

Her face was mere inches from his. "Their names were Jacob and Bonnie."

His agonizing scream filled the forest as she shoved the khukuri deeper and twisted it. Blood seeped from his mouth.

She smiled. "I hope you rot in hell for all that you did." She yanked the khukuri from his belly, spilling his guts on the forest floor, before slicing his throat so deep that his head dangled for a moment before he collapsed sideways. Dead.

She dropped her khukuri, and her hands shook violently.

I knelt beside her and held her. The warmth of her tears wet my shirt.

I cradled her. "It's okay. It's over."

Matt stared motionless at the gruesome scene but didn't say a word. He took Abi's khukuri and cleaned the blood off it.

Abi was finally breathing calmly when Matt gave it back.

"He deserved worse. This is war, Abi. There will be more. Hold your head high. We're right behind you." Matt helped her up, and I followed.

"We have to move." Matt took the lead.

The whizzing of bullets carried throughout the forest. Hundreds if not thousands of soldiers engaged in combat on one side of the mountain. The gray and white uniforms clashed as the white snow was bathed by the violence of it all.

A loud boom crashed all around us.

"Down!" I covered Abi with my body as the shockwave of the bomb blasted around us and the strength of it pushed me down.

We stood. Dozens of our soldiers' mutilated bodies covered the forest floor.

In the distance, a muffled sound followed by the screams of soldiers caught our attention.

They had reached our field mines.

The NWG forces dispersed as one after another started exploding.

And that's when I saw them.

A company of massive men and women followed behind the NWG soldiers, their dark-gray armored uniforms almost invisible against the forest background.

These soldiers rushed through. The mines detonated beneath their feet, but they kept going. For every one that died, a dozen followed in their place.

My feet faltered. They would annihilate us all. It was a nightmare.

"Watch out!" a soldier yelled.

The buzzing sound of a bazooka echoed behind us. It hit the spot, and dozens of the Halcyon soldiers were blown away by the explosion.

"Come on! I'll take you to command," he said.

I turned as I recognized the voice of my dear friend. "Mark?"

He gestured for us to follow. "Hurry! We don't have much time!"

We ran behind him.

I glanced back as another bomb obliterated more of our forces. The PRF soldiers kept moving forward, holding the Halcyon forces back. But it was in vain, as more enhanced soldiers kept pushing onward, soaking the earth with rebel blood.

A pang hit my chest as I found a face I recognized on the battlefield. His body was impaled on a tree, chest torn open by his enemy's blade.

A shudder swept through me.

The soldier's victorious sneer was replaced by wide eyes as a gush of blood escaped her mouth. A blade protruded from her neck.

"Die, bitch!" Anna screamed as the Halcyon soldier slumped down. Dead.

Anna was drenched in blood as she inspected Pedro's body, then hugged him. Her body shook, but she drew herself up and took a step back. She turned away from him and widened her stance, facing the battlefield. She ran toward it.

My gut clenched as Anna disappeared into the fray. This was what we trained for. Abi's soft tug on my arm brought me back from the battlefield. "We should go."

We ran opposite the battle and around the peak toward hall E's exit.

People were being escorted out of the bunker. Runners directed them north toward safety as our main forces kept coming out and heading toward the fight.

Once we were inside, the alarms blared nonstop, a call to abandon the bunker. The command center was pure chaos.

Matt threw himself at Aoki the moment he saw him helping citizens out. They held on to each other, and we continued forward.

Two soldiers apprehended me.

"Let him go! He's with us," Connor said.

The soldiers hesitated for a moment before they released me. They wouldn't disobey a direct order from their general.

Connor hugged Abi. "Are you okay? You should leave with the citizens. Deb is with them, same as Sarah. Go. You'll be safe there."

She held his arm. "I won't. I promised I wouldn't run. I'm here to fight."

He cupped her cheek. "I don't want to lose you."

"I know. But I need to do this."

Connor nodded.

He clasped my shoulder. "They arrived an hour ago. We've been taking the citizens out, but out there, it's a bloodbath. What happened?"

"It's Tammy." I paused. "She's a spy."

Connor froze. "Tammy?" He darted his eyes around the room, then widened them at me. "Maria! She went to look for her. She hasn't come back."

The blood drained from Abi's face as she dumped her rucksack and rushed out of the room, tripping over soldiers and citizens.

"Abi! Wait!" I did the same and ran after her.

My heart pounded, my legs close to collapsing from hours of running, but I made it to hall B.

Abi stood in the middle of the hall, just a few meters away from Jimmy and Tammy. They were both bleeding profusely. They circled each other, knives aimed toward one another. Jimmy limped but held his ground.

"Jimmy!" Abi screamed.

Jimmy's attention darted to her, and Tammy seized the opportunity to kick his knife to the floor.

She moved behind him, her blade dangerously close to his neck. "If you make a move, I'll kill him."

The hall was empty. No one would help us.

"Kill her! Forget about me, and do it!" Jimmy said.

Abi kept her gun aimed at Tammy. "Why?"

Tammy's lip curled up. "Oh, poor baby. You thought I was your friend?"

Abi's hand trembled, and I could hear her silent sobs. "Let him go!"

Tammy glanced inside her open room. "Now, don't do anything stupid, or my hand may slip."

Jimmy looked inside, and pain etched his face before he jerked it away.

I swallowed hard. What did she do?

She went in, the door hiding her. I saw the pistol before she came out with Jimmy as her shield.

She approached the exit. Halfway there, she kicked Jimmy in the thigh, forcing an anguished scream from him as he collapsed.

She pointed the gun at us and continued walking backward, eyes fixed on Abi. "Every day I thought of a different way to kill you, but I had to keep being pathetic little Tammy."

Abi reached Jimmy and crouched next to him.

I aimed my gun straight at her. "It's over, Leslie."

She laughed, the sound echoing across the empty hall. "And you? Do you think you're better than me? You fucking traitor. Mixing yourself with this trash. You had everything, and you gave it up for them?" She cocked her pistol at Abi. "I'll kill her, you know. Just to see your face when the light leaves her eyes."

"Davon..." Abi's voice shook, her eyes wide as she crawled toward Maria and Tammy's apartment.

Smirking, Tammy watched raptly. "Ah, this will be good."

Jimmy trailed behind Abi. "Don't go in. Please."

Tammy chuckled. "Go right ahead, dear Abi." She didn't stop her path toward the exit.

I walked toward the room, gun aimed at Tammy. Blood drenched the floor. "What the hell did you do?"

Tammy stared at the pool of blood, and for a split second, I thought I saw her chin twitch before she blinked and grinned mockingly. "Needy thing. To believe I could love her." She snickered. "She got what she deserved. She's nothing to me."

She was almost at the exit when I reached the room.

My vision flooded with rage. My insides burned.

Maria lay dead on the floor, her innards spilling from the countless stab wounds on her body. Her eyes were open but cold.

Abi's scream was a deafening boom against the silence that enveloped the abandoned hall. She dashed inside and covered Maria's body as Jimmy went to her and held her close.

Then, in what seemed like less than a second, Abi pushed Jimmy away and rushed into the hall, shooting toward her former friend.

Jimmy followed her out.

Tammy screamed as a bullet caught her shoulder, but she shot back.

The bullets ricocheted against the walls, and I threw myself over Abi, Jimmy right beside us.

Tammy flew up the stairs and opened the hatch.

That's when I saw it strapped to her waist.

My whole body tensed. *No.*

I managed to stand with Abi. Jimmy stumbled back a step or two, pushing us back.

Once outside, Tammy glanced in with a sneer. "Now you get to see your little rebellion die."

She took the pin off a grenade and threw it down the hall.

To be continued...

T hanks for reading *Rule of the Elite,* the second installment of the Promissa trilogy.

Follow Davon and Abi as they fight to free Promissa in *Breaking the Regime.*

Please follow my author pages. Reviews are greatly appreciated.

Goodreads:

https://www.goodreads.com/author/show/49079198.E_R_Phoenix

Amazon:

https://www.amazon.com/author/erphoenix

Acknowledgements

To my husband, David. You urged me to follow my dreams and not worry about anything else. You told me you'd never seen me this happy before and helped me pursue this crazy project. You're my right hand, and have supported me all the way, never letting me go astray and pushing me forward. Throughout all my struggles, you've been my fortress. I'll never be able to thank you enough. You are my inspiration, my strength, my everything.

To David J., Karina, and Mariana, you make me want to create a better world. If there's someone I write for, it's for you. Never stop fighting for what you want and never stop being who you are. You are enough.

To my friend Nathalie, for always being there to support this crazy endeavor of becoming a writer. We met at the perfect moment and now I can't imagine going through this journey without a friend like you. You have an amazing soul and give so much unto others. Please follow your dreams and share them with the world. Thank you for everything you've done for me and for being right by my side throughout my journey!

To all that have at any moment felt lost and confused. To all that have let others tell you how to behave or who to love. Fuck them all! Love who you want, be who you want to be, and stay true to yourself no matter what. At the end, it's your life.

No matter how dark it may get, there's always light at the end.

Embrace those who appreciate you. Fall in love. Be free. Love yourself.

Each of you make the world a better place.

About the author

E. R. Phoenix is a full-time novelist born and raised in Puerto Rico. She's enthusiastic about the environment, freedom, human rights, and societal justice.

Dystopian fiction is her favored reading and writing genre. She combines this with romance, particularly when love appears suddenly in a dangerous setting and is impossible to resist. Her tales are filled with action, danger, suspense, steamy romance, and individuals who would stop at nothing to defend their cause.

She's worked as a middle/high school science teacher and as a personal trainer. When she's not writing, she spends most of her time reading and being with her family. She loves dancing, hiking, watching anime, going to the beach, and playing videogames.

E.R. Phoenix is best known for her Promissa Trilogy books.

She currently lives in Vega Baja, Puerto Rico.

Keep in touch with E.R. Phoenix via the web at:

https://amazon.com/author/erphoenix

https://www.goodreads.com/author/show/49079198.E_R_Phoenix

https://www.facebook.com/erphoenixauthor/

https://www.instagram.com/e.r.phoenix/

https://www.tiktok.com/e.r.phoenix/